A Scent in the Night
ISABELLA MONTWRIGHT

Cerridwen Press

What the critics are saying...

5 Enchantments "Ms. Montwright drew me in and took me by the throat and kept me reading. [...] The ups and downs of this book, the tight suspense, the lush love scenes will keep you reading. This book is great romantic suspense reading. I wouldn't hesitate to read it again, and probably will because I enjoyed it so much. And I look forward to Ms. Montwright's next book." ~ *Enchanting Reviews*

4.5 Stars "Montwright immediately captures the reader's attention with provocative dialogue and vivid descriptions. The suspenseful, well-developed plot will also keep you engaged until the final page." ~ *Romantic Times Reviews*

"*A Scent in the Night* has so many things happening at once. [...] This is not a simple romance that is all roses for our couple, but one filled with angst and the uncertainty of a future. [...] If you like a story that will keep you on the edge of your seat and a passion between two people that can't be contained, *A Scent in the Night* should be on your must read list." ~ *Fallen Angels Reviews*

A Cerridwen Press Publication

www.cerridwenpress.com

A Scent in the Night

ISBN 9781419957963
ALL RIGHTS RESERVED.
A Scent in the Night Copyright © 2007 Isabella Montwright
Edited by Helen Woodall.
Cover art by Syneca.

This book printed in the U.S.A. by Jasmine-Jade Enterprises, LLC.

Electronic book Publication December 2007
Trade paperback Publication August 2008

With the exception of quotes used in reviews, this book may not be reproduced or used in whole or in part by any means existing without written permission from the publisher, Ellora's Cave Publishing Inc., 1056 Home Avenue, Akron, OH 44310-3502.

Warning: The unauthorized reproduction or distribution of this copyrighted work is illegal. Criminal copyright infringement, including infringement without monetary gain, is investigated by the FBI and is punishable by up to 5 years in federal prison and a fine of $250,000.
(http://www.fbi.gov/ipr/)

This book is a work of fiction and any resemblance to persons, living or dead, or places, events or locales is purely coincidental. The characters are productions of the author's imagination and used fictitiously.

Cerridwen Press is an imprint of Ellora's Cave Publishing, Inc.®

A Scent in the Night

Dedication

☙

In Memory of John Higgins.
See you on the next side, Machiavelli.

Trademarks Acknowledgement

☙

The author acknowledges the trademarked status and trademark owners of the following wordmarks mentioned in this work of fiction:

Armani: GA Modefine S.A. Corporation
Barbie: Mattel, Inc.
Bentley: Bentley Motors (1931) Limited Corporation
Beretta: Fabbrica D'armi P. Beretta, S.P.A.
Bronco: Ford Motor Company
GI Joe: Hasbro Industries, Inc
Glenfiddich: William Grant & Sons Limited
Glock: Glock, Inc.
Jacuzzi: Jacuzzi Inc. Corporation
James Bond: Danjaq, LLC LTD LIAB CO
Jeep: DaimlerChrysler
Lamborghini Countach: Same Deutz-Fahr S.p.A
Land Rover: Ford Motor Company
Lexus: Toyota Jidosha Kabushiki Kaisha TA Toyota Motor Corporation
Mercedes Benz: DaimlerChrysler AG Corporation
People Magazine: Time, Inc
Porsche: Dr. Ing. h. c. f. Porsche Aktiengesellschaft Corporation
Smith and Wesson: Smith & Wesson Corp
Versace: Gianni Versace S.P.A. Corporation
Viper: Directed Electronics, Inc.

Prologue

August 2004, Montreal, Quebec, Canada

Kneeling on a small grassy hill, Lorelei stared at the purple and yellow flowers she had placed before the marble headstone.

Nicholas Simon Rochefort
1935–2002

She smiled faintly as she remembered him. Tall and broad-shouldered, he had always been solid and strong, even when he returned from abroad to face a very ill, orphaned young niece. Uncle "Roche" had been her salvation.

She was sure he would have welcomed the two long-stemmed roses she'd added to his favorite irises. The roses were for her parents, whom she'd lost eight years ago.

The early morning breeze ruffled the delicate flower petals. Lorelei looked up at the blue sky, catching the scent of the freshly cut grass on the Mont-Royal.

Two years ago she'd lost the steady rock she had leaned on since being suddenly orphaned as a teenager. Uncle Roche had joined her parents, the beloved parents circumstances hadn't allowed her to bury and guilt hadn't allowed her to properly mourn.

Her mother and father had disappeared quite mysteriously on what was to be a second honeymoon of sorts, leaving her with myriad questions and haunting, devastating regrets. The numbing fear that they met with a violent death had nearly destroyed her.

Uncle Roche had tried to help her recover from her loss, to convince her she was not to blame, to encourage her to go on living a full and happy life. But even he hadn't known her secret guilt. He had been unable to find out what happened to her beloved parents and her obsession to learn the full truth had gone unanswered. Now she mourned and planted flowers at his grave, trying, unsuccessfully, to put closure to her grief.

But her heart remained heavy, her soul burdened with remorse.

Her recently broken engagement to Christian Renaud had caused her pain but her calculating ex-fiancé didn't even come close to hurting her the way losing her parents and her uncle had.

Christian, she understood. He was a greedy, selfish man who was after money and didn't care how he got it. True, she had shared a great deal with him but never her grief. He had not known about her past, nor had he shown any sign that he cared to. And that had suited her just fine. At least she'd thought it did—until he too, left her, taking with him a large chunk of her change. She had been so keen on keeping her heart safe, on keeping her shameful secrets, on retaining a certain amount of emotional distance, that she hadn't read the signs that he was about to help himself to her loot.

As hard as it had been at the time though, she had quickly closed that chapter of her life, knowing her heart had never really been involved in the relationship—and utterly relieved that it hadn't been. She had picked up the broken pieces, thinking surely she must have learned some new lesson from the disaster. Of course, it was hard to say just what that lesson might be.

Lorelei scanned the meticulously groomed landscape, admiring the huge maple that served as her landmark, guiding her through the cemetery's countless lanes to her uncle's grave. She imagined that its branches were somehow protecting her.

From more grief? From herself?

Death was inevitable, she reflected. The only question was the timing.

She had struggled with the mystery of death, railing at the cruel manner in which it had taken her parents, robbing her of any rational certainty about how they passed on. She'd vowed it wouldn't catch her unaware in the same brutal way.

She wouldn't let it. She would decide when to meet it.

She left her uncle's grave, walking in the shadows of a row of weeping willows. The farther she walked, the farther the lane seemed to stretch ahead. Such was le Cimetière du Mont-Royal.

The city of Montreal, with its three million inhabitants, surrounded the mountain on which the cemetery perched, its majestic St. Joseph Oratory almost touching the clouds, paying tribute to those buried under it.

She bent and picked up a daisy that had strayed from a gravesite before continuing along the path. On this, the second anniversary of Uncle Roche's death, as she prepared to leave Quebec for her upcoming trip to the United States, she felt as if another chapter of her life had ended. This time, though, she would write her own conclusion.

Chapter One
୨୦

The ocean was restless. Waves were licking at the sand, scooping away all they could and slapping back what they couldn't, their power like that of the Porsche Lorelei had driven here to Cape Cod earlier that night.

Determination had brought her and determination would help her decide what to do next. She could take the proverbial easy way out, choose her own terms. Or she could ride the tide like the clumps of seaweed that drifted and dunked with the angry waves, some floating, others landing at her bare feet while she ventured on her lonely walk in the night.

Would she finally fulfill her teenage death wish because of money problems? No. Christian wasn't worth it. Besides, she would hurt the people who really did love her. People like Maurice and Annabelle.

Kicking sand from her path, she stopped walking and looked up at the moonlit sky. She knew sheer defiance could last only so long. And she was tired—oh so tired—of fighting. She wanted peace and maybe quiet Hyannis Port, Massachusetts, would give her some. The work she had to do here would be challenging but satisfying. It wouldn't empty her out, leave her frustrated or angry.

The moon was full, illuminating the path left by the gleaming water slapping at her feet. She had very little anger left in her. Very little of anything else either. So she simply continued to walk, enjoying the feel of the warm waves on the summer night.

On her way back to the Siren, the beachfront hotel where she would be staying for the next few days, she spotted a fenced garden surrounded by huge cypress trees, at its center an oval swimming pool. Its underwater lights accented its blue mosaic walls, making the pool look like a piece of sky alive in the ground.

She decided to take a closer look. Pushing open the wooden gate, she climbed a few stone steps. The shimmering water drew her and she spotted a rocking chair and a small table nearly hidden by the trees and tall hedges flanking the fence.

She didn't really know why she chose to linger in this secluded place when she had luggage to unpack, schedules to plan and the car to store somewhere safe. But she wasn't ready to go back to her room and shut herself off from the world. That wouldn't work tonight. She was oddly restless.

So she perched in the rocker and gently rocked to the rhythm of the ocean, imagining herself drifting with the waves. The ocean breeze lulled her after her long, intense drive from Montreal to Cape Cod.

It would have been an even longer drive, Lorelei mused, if she had been a reasonable person driving a reasonable car. But she had not been in a reasonable mood. She had been thinking about Christian.

She had met Christian Renaud shortly after her uncle passed away. He had courted her assiduously but decorously. He had made no intimate demands but had freely declared his undying love for her. Then, soon after their engagement, he had vanished, taking with him her life savings, which she had invested in a joint venture company he had persuaded her to join with him. It hadn't rendered her as heartbroken as people might have thought. She had not loved him. The financial mess he'd created upset her, but as she had learned after losing her parents, things could always be worse.

When she first learned Christian had disappeared, she had felt cheated, betrayed. Yet there had been no "other woman", just a calculated decision on Christian's part. Then her anger had grown, anger that he'd left her helpless. Her efforts to find him, to get her money back, like the police's efforts to track down her parents or their killers, had been fruitless.

That helpless sense that all she could do was wait and wonder was what hurt the most. She had been helpless and unable to find her parents, to rescue them, or to give them a decent burial—anything to fill the void, to salve her grief. To find peace.

Was peace to be found only in dying? She'd wondered about that at nineteen. She still did.

She let out a deep breath and thrust the rocking chair harder.

Through a few wise investments—and more high-stakes risks—Uncle Roche had turned his modest income into a small fortune, enough to buy her the enormously expensive Porsche 959. He had probably known he hadn't long to live, and at the time she'd had no need for another inheritance.

He had known of her love for fast cars and though he'd worried about her safety, he'd hoped the car would help her recover from her grief and from the illness that had almost ended her life. It had been one of his ways of stimulating her interest in living and distracting her from closing in on herself completely. Now that heart-stopping piece of machinery would have to be sold to pay the huge debt Christian had saddled her with.

Too bad she couldn't use her share of the prize money from the culinary competition—assuming, of course, she won—to pay off Marc Delage, the moneylender Christian had insisted she use. Tradition dictated, however, that the winner return the money to the competition's sponsor, Wexford International, to be used in its relief foundation's efforts to feed the world's poor. Still, prize money or no, wouldn't it be wonderful to win the competition? Maurice and Annabelle would be so proud.

She sighed, sleepiness slowly creeping into her limbs. And, finally, having successfully exorcised most of the day's worries, she nodded off.

Chapter Two

Lust in haste, is love in waste.

☙

In the light from the pool he looked like a sun god stepping into a realm of fire. With long golden hair touching his shoulders and with the short white towel wrapped around his waist baring his muscular torso and legs, he walked regally toward the water.

From where Lorelei was sitting, groggily awakening from a trancelike state, he could have been Michelangelo's *David* come to life. With his chiseled profile, long, lean muscles, broad chest and legs that promised strength and speed, he was the work of art she had seen in Florence years ago, when her prurient imagination had all but touched the vivid contours of his form. She had imagined stroking his hairless chest, caressing the thick cords of his neck, closing her hands around his biceps. She had fancied feeling his heartbeat against her breasts, his taut legs bracketing hers, his erection straining toward her, quietly insisting on being let in.

Those fluid movements she had once imagined now seemed magically embodied, literally, in the flesh. Her dream man exuded power in every stride. He was magnificent, she thought. And he was meant to be hers.

He approached the edge of the swimming pool, bent down to touch the water, then turned his attention to the voice calling from behind him. In her dreamy state Lorelei had been seeing only the man. She had not noticed that he had been followed by a woman.

"Galen, darling, come here."

He straightened up and began advancing toward the blonde beauty sprawled on one of the lounge chairs some ten feet away, looking more the predator than the prey of the breathtaking male walking toward her. This was no blushing Venus waiting demurely for her mate. Her legs, straddling the chair, were long, slim and shapely. Her arms were above her head, her hands gripping the back of the chair so that her body arched strategically forward, displaying to wonderful effect her incredibly large bare breasts.

To Lorelei's dismay, the blonde spread her legs wider, more boldly than a cat in heat, revealing the tiny scrap of fabric barely preserving her modesty.

"Come here, soldier and relieve your prisoner from her torment," the woman commanded, all sexy sultriness. She gave her silvery blonde hair a photo-studio toss and shifted her body again, lowering one hand to cup her left breast invitingly.

Curious how the man she'd called Galen would react, Lorelei turned her gaze back to him. Focusing on his face, she noticed its hardness. Even from a distance she could tell he was not relaxed. The muscles in his arms leapt. His hands were closed, almost clenched.

He stopped directly in front of the chair, slowly untied his towel and let it fall to the terrazzo tiles. He paused and turned in Lorelei's direction and she silently gasped at the wonder of his nude body.

For a moment she almost felt his searching gaze travel the distance between them, seeking her out where she hid, immobile in the darkness. For those few seconds she couldn't breathe. The breeze that had gently put her to sleep now felt like an oven as she imagined the feel of this man naked on top of her, his legs bracketing her thighs, the weight of him on her belly, his hands pinning her arms above her head as he penetrated her.

She was stunned at the intensity of her reaction to him. How she had deprived herself over the years, she thought, forgetting that her grueling search for her parents or their killers and the long illness that had ensued were indeed behind her. She had let herself remain untouched, unheld, unkissed, remembering only how she had felt during her seemingly endless hospital stay—worthless, beneath contempt, hideous, her hair greasy and limp, her skin pale and drawn, her eyes dull and devoid of light.

Her high school boyfriend had tried to stay in her life and by her side, to comfort her through her loss and sickness, but she'd had less than nothing to offer him for his efforts. Finally he too, had left—had stopped calling, had stopped caring. But then, she had long since done so herself.

Somewhere along the line she had concluded that she would probably allow a man to hold and kiss and possess her only in her imagination. He would be as proud and strong and confident as David. He would be like the man before her eyes, one who could see her through the darkness and love her despite her past.

But then she had met Christian and she had allowed herself to be swayed toward experiencing life fully. And look where that had led her.

As she watched the stranger, she felt an odd panic building in her gut. Where were all her instincts to protect herself, to flee? She stayed put and watched the man, finding a perverse pleasure in seeing without being seen, in taking what was not knowingly given, in forgetting for once who she was and what she'd experienced—or not experienced—years ago. Tonight she felt herself to be the blonde's equal in beauty and sensuality. The sun god's equal. And so she would stay and feast her eyes and her imagination.

The man had turned to the blonde woman once more. He eased himself down onto the *chaise longue*, straddling it, knee to knee with her. She lifted her mile-long legs and clamped them around his waist while undoing the ties of her string

A Scent in the Night

bikini bottom. When she slid the tiny scrap of fabric from under her buttocks, she took the man's hand and guided it to the neatly trimmed hair at the apex of her thighs.

He looked down at the nest of curls. Then he turned slightly to stare in Lorelei's direction, his eyes seeming to lock on hers. She wasn't dreaming it. Somehow that look of hunger and desire was meant for her and it was preventing him from having sex with the blonde.

The woman wrapped her arms around the man's shoulders, trying to rekindle his interest and Lorelei noticed a huge diamond ring glittering on her left hand. The blonde was married, then. To this god? No. Impossible. More likely she was the spouse of a very rich man who had invested a small fortune in his wife's anatomy to give her the perfect face, waist, hips, buttocks and breasts. But it was the muscular giant with the long blond hair—the woman's pool man, perhaps?— who would be the beneficiary of her husband's largesse tonight.

Yet something had stopped him. With no trace of reluctance he disengaged himself from the blonde, patting her on the cheek as he stood. As an afterthought, it seemed, he bent to kiss one of her breasts, then turned and dived into the pool in one graceful leap.

Clearly perturbed by his indifference, the blonde quietly moaned, then she too, stood up, donned a very short black dress lying on the coffee table beside her and headed toward the house.

Meanwhile the man was swimming his way toward Lorelei.

She remained spellbound in the rocking chair, terrified that he had actually seen her. He surfaced from the water, vaulted gracefully out of the pool and strode into the trees where she sat.

"Have you enjoyed the view, little girl?" he asked in a sarcastic tone, slowly advancing toward her, totally at ease with his nakedness.

Utterly embarrassed but determined not to show it, Lorelei remembered the blonde's calling him a soldier. "Not as much as you enjoyed exhibiting yourself, GI Joe," she answered as derisively as she could.

Galen couldn't see the intruder clearly but her husky mocking, and intriguing perfume made him feel somehow vulgar—and instantly aroused. His reaction to her stunned him. Heat traveled down his spine despite the cool evening breeze on his wet skin. Drawn to her scent he slowly advanced, aware that moments before, from fifty feet away, she was what had distracted him from Vivian's dazzling, if artificially enhanced, body and his intention of servicing it.

The glimpse of the man from far away was nothing compared to him up close. Even in the dark he was glorious— so gloriously male that she wondered how he could be real. Although he was standing just two feet in front of her, dripping wet, his legs braced apart in a threatening stance, his proud sex erect and dangerous-looking, his voice was soft, too soft for a man whose hands were clenched into fists.

"Who are you?" he demanded.

Despite the tremor that ran through her body, Lorelei's legs remained primly crossed, her hands casually resting on the arms of the chair as if she hadn't a care in the world, when in fact she had never in her life felt so suddenly, excruciatingly aware of the sexual feelings ordinary women enjoyed all the time.

"Obviously someone who shouldn't be here," she replied as coolly as she could. She didn't even have time to blink before he leaned over her and grasped a fistful of her hair, tugging her head back against the chair and anchoring it there. His face was but inches from hers, his lips a whisper away from her mouth. His breath was warm, tasting like a heady red

A Scent in the Night

wine. Her heart pounded and she could feel his palm hot against the pulse throbbing in her neck. His thumb stroked her lower lip and she trembled at the sensation.

The woman smelled of spices and musk and something he had long since given up on. Something he no longer deserved. But her scent had somehow brought him home again, set him free again and given him a strange hope that he could be worthy of love again. All in a matter of moments in the night. He could feel his desire for her tightening his loins.

But then with one trembling hand she tugged at his wrist. She was afraid. Afraid of him, he belatedly realized. Even in the dark he noticed her haunted look and wondered what had put it there. When she ceased to struggle, when the fingers on his wrist abruptly went limp, he immediately let go, pulling himself back, horrified that he had caused the flash of fear and, then, that emptiness he saw in her eyes. She fumbled for the room key she had left on the small table beside the rocker. "I'm sorry — I — " she stammered, standing up and nearly losing her balance.

He steadied her by grasping her wrists, her scent again enveloping him like a lusty aphrodisiac. For a moment he didn't give a damn that she was afraid.

"I apologize for startling you," he said as if discussing the weather. "I was simply surprised to come upon a visitor so late at night. May I get you a drink?"

Lorelei felt her skin nearly scorching from his heat. Or was it hers? How she craved to be in this stranger's arms, finally to experience plain and simple lust. It mattered not if he was a god or a pool boy. But then the image of the woman he had been with mere moments before, her restless gyrations and his casual, unromantic response to her sexual aggressiveness, flashed before her eyes. And though that shouldn't have mattered if all she really wanted was to experience plain, simple lust, somehow it did.

She looked up at him, at the hard expression that belied the sincerity of his apologetic words. His eyes were burning her even in the dark and for a terrifying moment she wondered if he might harm her if she refused his invitation. But, no. The blonde was not far away and she would soon be missing him. He stepped back slightly and Lorelei knew he wouldn't force the issue.

Cooler, calmer and somewhat more collected than she had been a few seconds earlier, she ignored his invitation just as she ignored the fact that he was naked and they were alone.

He continued staring at her, his bulk blocking her path of escape. Six-and-a-half feet was a long way up to make eye contact, yet she met him stare for stare, because she dared not look down. Besides, her usual reaction to fear was kicking in. She was getting pissed off.

"Sorry but I'm not a member of the relief crew."

"I beg your pardon?"

Annoyed at herself for trespassing and becoming a voyeur in the first place, she blew out some air before speaking. "Look, coming here was just a momentary lapse…"

He crossed his arms, waiting for her to continue. "Lapse of what?"

"Judgment, of course. And now I'm out of here."

Relieved she'd sounded somewhat normal, she tried to get past him. He caught her by the arms, effectively propelling her right into his bare chest.

"Mind telling me what you were doing here? This is, after all, someone's private property and you are trespassing."

Someone's private property. As in, not his. Had she been right? Was he a pool boy or hired help of some kind, servicing the mistress while the wealthy master was away? "I'm just visiting this area, staying at the hotel down the beach. I came out for a walk and a breath of fresh air and I didn't notice that I'd ventured onto private property. I was tired and I sat down in this rocker and I must have fallen asleep. The next thing I knew, a naked man was standing over me, pulling my hair. You," she pointed out self-righteously, still carefully looking him directly in the eye.

"Bullshit," he answered softly, his eyes now roving downward, over her body, as if undressing her in the darkness.

"Look pool boy, which part of my explanation are you not grasping? Or does it make you feel more of a man to intimidate a woman half your size? Maybe you're overcompensating for not being able to get it up for your employer?" she taunted unthinkingly.

His grip tightened on her arms. "I thought you said you were asleep," he taunted back. "Besides, do I look like the kind of man who can't 'get it up'?" He glanced down meaningfully at his huge erection.

Dying of embarrassment, she couldn't resist nipping his inflated ego in the bud. "No offense but I don't think Adonis has anything to worry about."

"And what makes you think I'd care about the opinion of someone who has to get her kicks by being a voyeur?" he parried. "Alas for you, you obviously don't see very well in the dark. Here, let me give you a better look."

Without a moment's hesitation he dragged her to the edge of the pool, bathing them both in the underwater lights.

The blonde woman was nowhere to be seen. But Lorelei gasped again at his forcefulness and his amazing physique. What had she gotten herself into?

Galen truly saw the intruder then—her unblemished, olive-toned skin, smoky, silver-gray eyes and rich mahogany hair so long and luxuriant any man would love to run his fingers through it, feel it draped over his body. She had an exotic look about her. She also had beautiful shoulders, generous breasts, a trim waist and pleasing hips.

"Now that you can see me properly, would you care to change your opinion? Perhaps you'd even like to join the 'relief crew' after all. I'm not sure I'd allow that, though, now that I've seen you properly. I think I can safely say you're hardly my type of woman."

He wasn't lying. She wasn't his type of woman. At least not lately. Lately the likes of Vivian were more his speed.

This frightened but feisty creature was inspiring visions of hot, unbridled passion, frenetic lovemaking, raw and intense, with one's very soul on the line. Complete domination but also complete surrender. Not simple sex with cynical intentions.

She slapped him — hard.

His head moved slightly from the blow. Stunned, he ground his teeth instead of releasing her. "Lady, you must have a death wish, assaulting a naked, aroused man twice your size. Under different circumstances I might accommodate you," he said grimly. "However, tonight's your lucky night. Go home, little girl, before I change my mind."

As soon as he let go of her arms, Lorelei hurried away without another word. Lorelei couldn't believe she was walking away from her *David*. The man had the body of a god. He had inspired her to lust. He had awakened her from the dead.

So much for a quiet midnight walk to clear her head.

Galen couldn't believe he was letting the enchanting creature leave without even learning her name. The girl brought back ghosts from the past. She had the scent of temptation.

So much for a cool midnight swim to clear his head.

Chapter Three

When you live in the past, you stay in the past.

&

Galen might have let the beautiful intruder walk away, but not for long. As far as he was concerned, they had a score to settle and he had an identity to discover. He picked up the cordless phone on the brass table by the lawn chair and dialed two numbers. "It's me. Come to the pool." And he dropped the set back onto the table.

He waited a few minutes staring into space, waiting for his brother to arrive, his mind somehow drifting from present to past as it was lately doing. When Justin opened the rear door leading from the enormous house to the pool, Galen watched him stride over and for a few seconds, he thought he was seeing someone else. For a heart jolting moment Justin seemed to have Bryan's same tall, muscular build, the same dark hair, the same quick, impatient gestures he had grown accustomed to. Shivers ran up Galen's spine as Justin approached him with Bryan's similar rangy walk.

"What's wrong? You look like you've seen a ghost," Justin said.

For five long years Galen had struggled not to remember Bryan and what they had done to each other. Every once in a while, however, it would all come back to haunt his very soul.

He cleared his throat. "Some woman just walked in on Vivian and me. She probably came in the back gate. Find out—discreetly—who she is. I don't want any complications," he added. "She mentioned she was staying at the hotel but she might have been lying."

Justin grinned at Galen's obvious state of arousal. "Okay, big guy, I'll just follow your...lead."

Exasperated, Galen swore. "Jesus, Justin!"

His brother, however, was already making his way out to the beach.

"Follow her scent," Galen muttered. "I know I couldn't miss it."

Justin headed out the gate concealed behind the tall hedges and leading to the beach, wondering how he would find an unknown woman in such darkness. What had Galen muttered about a scent? He'd probably heard wrongly, he told himself, shaking his head.

Surprisingly though, a few seconds later he noticed a faint perfume in the air. Was this the scent that had set off a man as controlled as his brother? Curious to find the woman who wore it, he quickly headed for the hotel. He only hoped she was really a guest there.

Moments later, at the entrance to the hotel, he spotted her—a woman running for the elevator as its doors were closing. It had to be her. The delicate but delicious scent trailed behind her. He approached Richard Leahy, his cousin Devin's boyfriend, who, fortunately, was working the desk that night. "What's her name?" he asked of the woman.

The young man answered with a smirk. "Like her perfume, huh?"

Even he had noticed. "Never mind her perfume. What's her name and what room is she staying in?" he demanded.

Richard hesitated. He knew the rules. Privacy at the Siren for its guests had to be maintained at all times.

"I own this place, remember?" Justin added impatiently when he realized Richard was hedging. "Richard, I just want to know if she's a journalist. She was over at the house, uninvited, just a few minutes ago."

A Scent in the Night

"Well you should have said so already," Richard answered relieved. "Room two-oh-seven. She left her luggage here. Said she'd send down for it later. She did sign the register, though. Let me see...ah, yes, she signed under the name of Château DesCheneaux. Said her name's Lorelei Dupuis or something. Here, this is her signature." He gestured, handing Justin the register.

When Justin saw the entry, he frowned. "This isn't a signature. It's a scribble," he complained, trying to decipher the writing.

"You really can't make it out," Richard commented as he retrieved the guest book.

"Check the reservation list," Justin said.

"Sure, boss," Richard said, turning to the computer monitor. "Here it is. Lorelei Duplessis. She's Canadian, from Montreal, Quebec," Richard read. "Oh and I think she came in that beautiful Porsche parked outside. If she's with the DesCheneaux group, she's involved in the competition—maybe a cook or something."

Justin frowned. A cook couldn't afford a car like that.

Was she here with someone else? Some questions clearly needed answering and not enough information was available.

Justin pressed Richard for more facts. "I want you to find out exactly who she is, exactly what she's doing here, and whether she came with anyone or alone. And while you're at it, get me her credit and employment info...home address, et cetera. I'll go get the plate number of that car and run it by Doherty. Page me when you have the information and speak to no one about this."

Slightly abashed at having snapped out orders at Richard, he apologized. "Sorry, man. I didn't mean to bark at you that way." What a homophobe he still was, Justin admitted to himself with regret. "How's Devin, by the way?"

Accepting that one of his favorite cousins was gay had been difficult.

Yet Justin had never seen him happier than since he'd hooked up with Richard.

"Your cousin is fine." Richard smiled at Justin's obvious discomfort. "You should drop by for supper one night soon."

"All right, I will. As long as you're doing the cooking."

The two men gave each other parting nods, both of them smiling.

* * * * *

Lorelei stepped into her room and closed the door behind her. She hoped to God she never came face to face with that pool attendant again. How could she have contemplated, albeit only for a moment or two, having sex with him, a total stranger? Yet when he'd touched her—first his hand in her hair, then his thumb on her lower lip, then his powerful fingers wrapping around her arms—she had felt those moments stretching into a lifetime of unbelievable intimacies.

But then she had locked her body the same way she was locking her door, shutting out those feeling of helplessness, of loss of control. Of not being able to set the terms.

Nothing had ever overwhelmed her as much.

"Idiot!" she exclaimed to herself when she remembered that her luggage was still downstairs, her car unstored. She had papers to sign for the hotel, a private indoor parking space to find for the 959 and the kitchens to inspect. She had all but run to her room like a schoolgirl.

Get a grip. You didn't have sex with the guy—not even close, she told herself. Grabbing her purse and keys, she headed back downstairs.

By the time she got there, she was herself again. The lobby, with its plush furniture, smelled fresh and tangy and almost tasted of salt and sea. And the sea always had a soothing effect on her.

"May I help you, ma'am?" the night desk clerk asked.

A Scent in the Night

"Yes, please. I have a room with Château DesCheneaux. My name is Lorelei Duplessis and I believe you have some forms for me to sign for the culinary competition. Also, I left my luggage down here when I arrived. I have to pick that up as well."

The clerk checked his computer. "Party of twelve, right?"

"Yes but not quite yet. Tomorrow the rest of our crew will arrive. It's just me for now." She paused, waiting for him to look up from the monitor. "I also have a favor to ask."

When he did glance up, she smiled and pointed through the huge bay windows to her Porsche. "Could you possibly find me a private garage for my car?"

The clerk arched his eyebrows. "That car is yours?"

She hesitated, knowing that soon she'd have to part with the vintage Porsche if she didn't find another way to pay off her debt. "Yes, it is," she answered.

"Isn't that a—"

"It's a 959 Twin Turbo," she confirmed.

Staring at her and then at the car, the clerk barely paid attention to the phone ringing on his counter. "Is it true that it's faster than the 911?"

"The 959 has four hundred and fifty horsepower, while the 911's yield is at most three hundred."

"What about the new 993 series?" he asked, tearing his gaze away from her car to look at her in wonder.

She nodded. "That's the new one on the German market, with more horsepower. Unfortunately, it doesn't have the air-compression capabilities of the 959, which means that its speed limit of two-sixty is only theoretical."

She paused, gazing out at her pride and joy. "There's nothing theoretical about the two-fifty the 959 is capable of. That power is real."

"Yes but how could one ever really be sure?"

Her lips curved into a mischievous smile. "Oh, now and then one can see the little white hand pass two hundred. Maybe you should answer that," Lorelei suggested.

Irritated at the incessant ring, the clerk transferred the call to the administration office. "So you've raced it?" The clerk sounded shocked.

"Not exactly. I was just in a hurry that day." As she often was when she found a stretch of open, deserted highway. But she didn't share that bit of information with the desk clerk.

The clerk retrieved the forms she had asked for and handed them to her. "Well, what you drive, ma'am, is not a car—it's a work of art. I'm sure Mr. Kennedy won't mind if you park next door, where he keeps his cars." He cleared his computer screen while she signed the papers. "I'll take care of it and I'll also have someone bring your bags to your room." He bent to open a locked drawer, then handed her a key. "This is for the garage. And this is a card for access to the premises."

"Thank you. Before I go, though, I'd like to see the kitchens—if you would be so kind as to direct me..."

After Lorelei introduced herself to the hotel's assistant chef, he agreed to show her the kitchens, although he looked at his watch at least six times during their brief tour, not bothering to conceal his impatience. She began to feel uncomfortable.

"Perhaps I should come back tomorrow when you have more time," she said as they were heading toward the walk-in refrigerator units.

"Perhaps it would be more appropriate if the leader of your team came himself," the man answered in a patronizing tone. "After all, Chef Devereaux and I are making ourselves available to explain to all contestants the inner workings of our kitchens and are graciously agreeing to lend our workplace to total strangers. It would seem fitting that your head chef be the one to visit this arena, rather than sending one of his cooks to do a summary inspection."

She arched her eyebrows at his condescending tone. It wasn't the first time she had been confronted with this stereotypically sexist attitude. "Actually, I am the leader of the Canadian team."

"But you are a wo—"

"Yes, I am and I must say, you have a splendid kitchen. My compliments. I'm sure I'll enjoy cooking here. May I see your storage area? I'd like to be sure it's sufficient for everything my team is bringing tomorrow and everything we've ordered locally."

Little did the man know that upon finishing her bachelor's degree in art history, she had attended two of the best cooking schools in the world. At her uncle's urging and under the tutelage and sponsorship of his old friend, Maurice Leblanc, a well-known chef, she'd spent two years at the Torgiano Scuola di Cucina in the Umbrian mountains of Italy, then continued her studies at the renowned Cordon Bleu culinary school in Paris.

Maurice then hired her fresh from Europe at le Château DesCheneaux, a prestigious Montreal hotel known for its gourmet cuisine and extensive wine cellar. Unlike Maurice, who was DesCheneaux's head chef, Lorelei now specialized in the hotel's exclusive catering services, which gave her freer rein to explore her creativity and combine her knowledge and love of cooking, oenology, botany and art. Despite her relative youth, her skills had made her widely sought-after and they were the reason she, rather than Maurice, was heading up the DesCheneaux team for this enormous catered affair.

Thankfully, she was able to restrict her insecurities to her personal life. Her professional life, while exposing her to a moneyed class she would otherwise prefer to avoid, provided her with both stability and self-assurance. Her colleagues often called her the gentle commander. Some were afraid of her, because the angrier she got, the more silent she became and when her temper did erupt, it could blow with uncommon vengeance.

When Lorelei pushed aside her insecurities, she was in total control of herself and whatever situation she had to face. That self-confidence carried over into her driving and her shooting. Behind the wheel or at target practice she was as disciplined as she was when wielding a meat cleaver, knowing precisely how to accommodate the disadvantages of her petite stature and accompanying lack of upper body strength.

Maurice thought she had developed such inner strength because she'd once had to fight for her survival when she was so very ill. He hoped that one day she would find a man who could take her in his stride and prize her abilities but, he'd told her, he feared that no man would ever be strong enough to handle her.

Uncle Roche had been right to introduce her to Maurice Leblanc. She loved her work. While doing it she didn't feel timid or overwhelmed by self-doubt. And for the first time a Canadian chef had been chosen by l'Institut de l'Hôtellerie as a candidate, accompanied by a team of her choice, to participate in the Sélection Internationale des Gastronomes du Monde, hosted by the Wexford International Beer Company of Ireland, whose owners ranked high among the elite society of Hyannis Port, Massachusetts.

After a collective cocktail party three teams would cater. Each team would then host its own "night of nights", the ultimate soirée, serving seven hundred guests from all over the world.

The International Association of Gastronomy had appointed a panel of seven judges to measure the merits of each team presenting the cocktail party and dinners. The winning group would get the highest award given in the culinary field. Proceeds from the guests' wildly expensive tickets and donations would benefit the Feed the World Foundation, which was funded largely by Wexford International. Though the gesture was not mandatory, the huge winner's purse was customarily donated to the Third World hunger relief organization as well, the victors more than satisfied with the medals that instantly sent their marketability skyrocketing.

Naturally, all her colleagues at DesCheneaux were counting on Lorelei to win for them. Up until now Canadians, not to mention French Canadians, had always been shunned by the international culinary milieu. Considered France's poor relations, they had never been chosen to participate in events such as this one. The hotel considered it a great honor to sponsor Lorelei's team and pay their expenses. Since she would be competing under the DesCheneaux banner she was determined to make them proud.

Though the judges would expect her to offer the finest French-inspired cuisine, instinct had told her to go Italian. Her soirée would feature the best of that beautiful country's regional cooking, the bitter and the sweet.

She glanced at the pastry console the Siren's assistant chef was showing her, then thanked him for his time. Participating in the competition would certainly distract her from her recent hurt and humiliation. On her way out of the kitchens she crossed the lobby and prepared to park her car in the hotel owner's private garage.

The gas gauge signaled she was low on fuel and she decided to drive to an all-night gas station just outside Hyannis Port. Her time with the 959 was growing short and she wanted to take advantage of it as much as she could.

After she took a sharp exit to the highway, her mind kept wandering to her encounter with the blond giant. Would she ever, even under more normal circumstances, go out with a man like that?

Then again, what was normal? Christian Renaud had courted her "normally". But once he convinced her to become the major shareholder in his new company, got said company to borrow money from a private lender and acquaintance of his by the name of Marc Delage and got her to guarantee the loan, he signed himself a check for the loan and disappeared into thin air.

He left her with a huge debt, which she had pledged by signing a lien on the house she'd inherited from her parents. The lender-financier was now demanding payment in full, so she now faced being shafted in full. Even Amanda Fairchild, her best friend and attorney, could not keep the vulture at bay much longer. The time had come for Lorelei to face the music...and pay. She would have to win this competition and parlay the attendant publicity into big contracts—and big bucks—fast. She had no intention of leaving a mass of debts behind her.

As soon as she glided into the gas station, the three night attendants all left their posts and made their way toward her, their tongues fairly hanging out as they gaped at the 959. After all, it was a collector's item and their chances of seeing one firsthand, except, perhaps, in an auto show, were slim to nonexistent.

It gave her pleasure to have the car admired by those who understood the craftsmanship that went into its design and, more importantly, the power under its hood. It gave her particular delight to know as much, if not more, about its inner workings than most expert mechanics did. She knew the six-speed reverse gear box was designed for driving fast on smooth pavement or rough ground. She also knew that the incredible four-wheel drive transmission, unheard of for a sports car of its kind, could bring the 959 to a dead stop on a dime or up to sixty mph within seconds of takeoff. The car wasn't sold in the United States and very few of the two hundred built had ever reached American shores.

Because she was the only woman in the Montreal Auto Club—for that matter, the only one in the world—to own a 959 Twin Turbo Porsche, her fellow members had given her a rather cool reception when she joined the exclusive group. They didn't think a woman deserved to be behind the wheel of such a car, much less challenge the owner of a Lamborghini

Countach. But in mere minutes she had made them all realize that she was an extremely competent driver capable of handling her vehicle's blinding speed.

She had learned early on how to listen to her car—its contented purr, the rumble of its exhaust, the wind over its aerodynamic shape. Maurice had taught her that and more. He came from a family of racing car aficionados as well as chefs.

Lorelei didn't know how the Leblancs came to have this association but she'd long shared both passions—for the culinary arts, man's homage to the importance of nourishment, and for racecars, man's homage to speed and power.

She owed Uncle Roche big-time. After her parents' death and her own near demise, her prize had been this magnificent car, which he'd dubbed Nemesis, after the Greek goddess of retribution. Living well was the best revenge—against death or any other enemy—he'd often joked. Of course, he'd also fretted endlessly for her safety, muttering that the Porsche might prove to be his downfall but he'd hoped owning such an incomparable vehicle would help eliminate her negative thinking. Knowing her fascination with fast cars, he'd hoped she could drive out her problems, crush them under her tires. He had wanted her to begin to heal.

Her uncle had not stopped there, however. He'd also given her his prized gun collection. From it he had hoped she'd learn to aim for a target, to set goals and focus her mind, to keep out whatever might distract her from reaching those goals. It was yet another way of helping her build her confidence, to make sure that when he was gone she would not retreat into the shell she had built around herself when her parents died.

She smiled, remembering Uncle Roche.

To the three young men who'd run to dance attendance on her car, she said politely, "Fill her up, please."

Much as she expected, all three asked in unison if her oil needed to be checked.

Chapter Four

Careful not to be seen, Galen watched the woman from a distance as she pulled into the gas station. She seemed oblivious that someone had followed her, much less that she was driving a very expensive car in the middle of the night alone on an isolated part of the highway. Although the trip was short, she had driven those two miles fast and hard.

When one of the station attendants began almost reverently filling up the Porsche's tank, Galen was tempted to smile as he remembered his own boyhood infatuation with his first sports car. He watched the other two young men admire the ten air vents on the front spoilers, periodically turning equal attention to the lady who had driven the vehicle into their station.

He irritably recalled his own reaction to her at the pool. He had wanted her—badly. He still did.

Holding his gaze on her, he slowly advanced his Jeep to the phone booth beside the automatic car wash and got out as if to make a call, nodding to the attendant filling the tank, who now knew his night crew was no longer alone with a beautiful woman. Galen continued watching the scene with interest.

Once the fuel nozzle was removed and the lid securely locked, Lorelei offered her credit card to the first attendant. The young man looked her straight in the eye for the first time since she'd pulled into the station. "Here you go," she prompted, gesturing for him to take the card. He took it reluctantly, his gaze never leaving hers, his expression unreadable. For some reason she thought of the blond giant, whose eyes had, for an instant, been like those of a predator.

Yet she felt none of the fear this time, none of the yearning for his hunger. Just an awareness that she was a woman.

The attendant smiled, apparently finally finding his voice. "Ma'am, your car is beautiful. But if I had to choose, I'd pick the lady driving it."

"Why, thank you," Lorelei shyly replied.

The young man shook his head and handed the card back to her. "This one's on the house, beautiful lady," he said. "Take care," he added before turning around and slowly making his way back to his counter.

Baffled, Lorelei looked at the other two attendants still standing beside the hood of her car. One of them winked, and the other nodded as they too, calmly walked back to their stations.

"Thank you," she said to the night, since no one was left to listen.

But someone was listening. Galen had experienced firsthand her exotic looks and manner, the intensity in her eyes and that scent that could make any man, young or old, wonder what it would be like to get closer to her. He started the Jeep again and began making plans, preparing to stake his claim. "Aye, all in due time," he murmured in Gaelic.

Eager to feel again the thrill of speed, Lorelei gained the highway seconds later. Her hands were steady despite the queasy feeling she got as the scene by the private pool replayed itself over and over in her mind. As her initial embarrassment receded, she remembered with nervous curiosity the man who had stood in the nude before her. The man who had almost made it feel natural that she would follow him to a bedroom right at that moment—and inevitable that she eventually would.

Control. She needed to maintain her self-control despite the fact that she had desired him, that she had wished for an instant to dash her own defenses and take some pure, simple pleasure without being afraid it was precisely the wrong thing to do.

She accelerated and shifted into sixth gear as she returned to Hyannis Port, trying to banish such bizarre, fanciful imaginings, concentrating on the engine she was pushing hard against the wind.

Hans Besner, Maurice's mechanic, had once helped her devise four different wheel distribution programs, later entered into the car's microprocessor so that she could control traction through sensors installed on the accelerator pedal and the wheels. She had customized the program to respond not only to road conditions but to her moods as well. She had called it a woman's prerogative. Hans had called it insanity. He had claimed she must have a death wish, given her obsession with speed. Lorelei never told him that he wasn't far off the mark.

Still, it was not yet time to fulfill that obsession, not by a long shot. She wouldn't go down now because of financial problems—that would be a cop-out. She would make the decision when everything was settled, when the few loved ones she had left would understand that death was her way of putting closure to her grief, by choosing when and how to die, by making the decision her parents and others like them couldn't. It would be her ultimate revenge on death and it would mean finally liberating herself from all the grief still buried in her heart.

She glanced at the bottom right of the dashboard. It was almost four o'clock in the morning and she was wandering the streets of Cape Cod, thinking and weighing possibilities.

Her most immediate problem was to pay off the debt Christian had saddled her with. When Marc Delage requested the lien on her house to guarantee his loan, the bank was already holding a mortgage on it. Years after her parents' disappearance, when the police had uncovered only evidence of foul play but no M. or Mme. Duplessis, Lorelei had taken out a mortgage to pay for a private investigation firm.

When Christian disappeared with Delage's loan, Lorelei was unable to raise the cash to pay him back. The proceeds of the sale of her house, after the payment to the bank holding the mortgage, would not have been sufficient. Selling her home was therefore not the solution and Delage knew it.

She would have to sell the car.

In fact, Delage had cavalierly suggested that he take the 959, worth over half a million dollars and call the whole deal even. "Over my dead body," she had answered. Lorelei would rather sell it to a stranger and pay back Delage in cash than give the bastard her uncle's precious gift. She had spoken with Douglas Gillen, the dealer who had sold her uncle the Porsche and within hours Gillen had found a buyer. With the money she'd obtain from the sale, she would pay off Delage and lower her mortgage debt. It burned her to give up the car, but she knew she could never afford to buy it back.

She accelerated again, letting the Porsche tear over the asphalt like a bullet.

Her uncle once said he had chosen the car with the color of her eyes in mind. Its exterior and leather upholstery were a rich silver-gray. The wheel mags housing nineteen-inch tires were gold-plated, as were the door handles. The dashboard was mahogany, the steering wheel a match. Her uncle had spared no expense for these three thousand pounds of grace in motion.

"He'll turn over in his grave the day I sell it," she murmured miserably into the night as she made her way back to the hotel.

* * * * *

Galen stood on the terrace of his private suite in the hotel penthouse, looking out over the ocean. He absently watched the horizon, feeling none of the hope that a new day always promised. He hardly even noticed that it would soon be dawn.

He was restless and not even the three straight bourbons he'd downed had done anything to relax him. His calculated affair with Vivian was probably compromised now that someone had seen them together. So was the investigation he and his brother had been feverishly but furtively conducting for the past several years, he thought grimly. Had his wealth shielded him so well over time that he had become careless? But he wasn't careless. He was thorough and focused and determined. If he wasn't, he never would have begun the affair with Vivian Gallagher. Having sex with a woman he had no feelings for, a woman with no scruples, no values but those that came in a fat wallet, revolted him. But it had been his last resort, the only means he hadn't already tried to unmask those who were feeding the war in Northern Ireland, in the so-called name of religion, at his expense.

He had been doing fine until tonight, he thought in disgust. Until he met the stranger with the unforgettable scent. A light breeze stroked his arms, reminding him of the fragrance she wore. The scent of peace, of innocence, of freedom?

But no. The past was slowly creeping back. Again. He could hear Bryan's last laugh echoing in the early morning, could hear Brenna's cry of despair when he told her of her brother's death. His part in it had devastated her, had cost him her love. At one point Galen had contemplated suicide to atone for his sin but he knew that would appease nothing but his conscience. He'd decided he would not take the coward's way out. He would live with what he had done and what it had done to others and attempt to make reparations in whatever ways he could.

But would he ever risk his heart again? Desire another woman so much that he wouldn't care what the consequences would be to him or to her?

He twirled the empty glass in his hand, mentally replaying the scene with the trespasser by the pool. If it were a simple attraction, he could deal with it—eventually it would fade. But this felt different. Very different. He had seen pain and fear in those silver-gray eyes. At first he'd thought it was fear because he had caught her spying on him. But he now sensed it had nothing to do with that. She had not been there to spy. He'd bet on it.

What he had felt in her was the kind of pain that lasted so long, it numbed a person. A pain that slowly ate away at the spirit and buried the soul. He wondered what had caused it, whether like him she herself had done something to create it.

He finished the last drops of his drink and was tempted to toss the empty glass into the angry ocean below, which reflected exactly how he was feeling. Pain like hers led to only one place. And he'd be damned if he'd let her go there, whoever she was and whatever she'd done.

* * * * *

Lorelei returned to her room, pensive and unwilling to give in to sleep that wouldn't be restful anyway in her state of mind. Not even the warm New England furniture promised serenity. Sitting on the four-poster adorned with a pristine white embroidered bedspread, she observed the first glimmer of dawn filtering through the drapes, casting shadows here and there, gently announcing the new day.

She closed her eyes for a moment, wishing her lethargy would pass so that she could unpack her luggage, go over the cooking schedules and evade unwanted dreams.

The next thing she knew, she was lying on the bed, her arms flung high above her head. The stranger from the pool appeared before her again. She could feel his gaze on every part of her body, roving, examining, devouring her. She enclosed him in her arms, her legs, wrapped him in her warmth. He penetrated her and cried her name and his mouth took hers, possessing her just as the rest of his body did.

She woke up in a cold sweat, alone, with the fear of being known that intimately clawing at her. Someone who could possess her that way would eventually know how much grief she still carried. That someone could stop her from fulfilling her plans and then she would continue to suffer and not have her revenge.

She squeezed her eyes shut and felt herself tremble.

Chapter Five

Finer things come to he who waits. (Unknown)

༶

"Have any of the participants arrived yet?" Galen asked his brother early the following morning as they reviewed the work schedule of the extra security guards hired for the event.

"Not officially. I know Donald will be making some pickups at the airport this afternoon, though. I told him to take a minivan instead of a limo. You know how chefs are—they wouldn't part with their cleavers and rolling pins even if God asked them to."

"Remind me to have my head examined the next time I agree that we should personally host a party for seven hundred people. I must have been temporarily insane when I said yes. And it couldn't have happened at a worse time. We're so close to uncovering who's behind using our freighters to smuggle weapons to Ireland, an ATF raid would be hugely inconvenient. Has Michael come up with anything new?"

Justin sat on the edge of the desk and sipped his coffee.

"No but he's getting closer to the *Irish Siren's* crew and keeping an ear out for any info they might have without even realizing it."

Galen leaned back in his chair, tapping a pen on his leg in frustration. "Someone on the inside is screwing us. I hope Michael isn't mixed up in it. He strikes me as a little naïve."

"Come on, Galen, you're talking about Michael Logan. He couldn't afford his father's medical care if it wasn't for us. I'm more worried he'll get carried away and blow his cover. I told him to be very careful and not let anyone suspect his personal connection to us."

"Then let's hope he follows your orders." Reluctantly he straightened and aimed the pen at the wastebasket across the room. "Damn it, we have so little real evidence and we still can't figure out how, with whom, or for whom Gallagher is doing it." He took a pencil from his desk and threw it, this time almost toppling the wastebasket.

"By the way, did Richard ever manage to get any solid information on the senator's past?"

"*Aic.*" Justin replied in their native Irish to mean *nothing*. "Whatever rock that lizard crawled out from under, he and his flunkies have done a damn fine job of burying or whitewashing it. All we learned is that his first wife was from Londonderry and a child from that marriage lived there for a time before fading into complete obscurity. Come to think of it, Londonderry's where Brenna's brother was heading when you…when he died," Justin corrected, carefully avoiding Galen's eyes.

"When I killed him, you mean." Galen rose to stand in front of the huge window behind his desk, his expression grim. Not a day went by without his remembering what had happened five years before.

"You did the only thing you could," Justin interjected, knowing where his brother's thoughts were headed. "He was using Brenna, his own sister, to get to us." He leaned to clasp his older brother's shoulder, remembering the betrayal, knowing how close Galen had come to dying himself. "Damn it, he was trafficking arms with our own trucks, our own ships. He was ready to kill you, kill all of us. Fuck, Galen, stop blaming yourself."

But Galen continued staring outside, still searching for the certainty that would justify his act, certainty he knew had been buried with Bryan Coyle. His next words were not easy. He'd never spoken them to anyone. He faced Justin and knew that even there he would not find the absolution he sought.

"Somehow I've never believed he actually would have killed me. He loved Brenna too much. He knew she'd be devastated if he harmed me. I think I killed him because I lost control of myself. The truth is, part of me couldn't deal with their closeness, the hold he had on her. Deep down maybe I wanted to get rid of him and I was given the perfect excuse. So I killed him, plain and simple and in the process I destroyed her as well."

Only then did Justin realize how deeply troubled Galen still was by his confrontation with Bryan Coyle five years earlier.

"Look, I could tell you that Bryan was up to his neck with gun runners long before you met Brenna. And I could also remind you that, had you spared his life, even assuming he wouldn't kill you then and there, his cronies would have come after us. They would have put bullets in our heads, starting with Mother and they probably would have made us watch the way they did with the Campbells."

Galen continued staring away in silence, unconvinced.

Justin thought carefully. "Tell me something. Did you go into that ship's hold knowing or suspecting you'd find Bryan?"

"You know he was the last person I ever would have suspected."

"Exactly. So when you pulled the trigger, you were acting solely on your survival instinct—an automatic response, no premeditation involved. So how could you believe that you were acting on some deep, dark, secret desire to get him out of the picture?"

"Still..."

"Still what? None of us, including you, even knew that Bryan owned a gun, let alone a state-of-the-art semiautomatic.

Nothing suggested his being even remotely involved in illegal trafficking. So how in hell could you say—"

"I'm not saying anything!" Galen shouted, exasperated. "But I killed someone—do you understand? I killed! Worst of all, I felt no remorse when I pulled the trigger—none whatsoever!"

"So you're saying that makes you guilty of murder?"

Justin stood and paced around the room, getting angrier by the minute. "That means, then, that all the cops who shoot violent criminals commit murder, right? And don't you dare defend that piece of shit to me. Because you know as well as I do that Bryan Coyle was involved in criminal activity. Violent criminal activity. Have no illusions about that!"

Galen glared at him. "What's your point?" He knew that his brother was right but he couldn't bring himself to admit it.

Justin took a deep breath. In a softer tone he continued, "All I know is, it's a miracle his cohorts didn't retaliate after his death."

"That's because of Brenna."

"Maybe, but even so, you've got to let it go. You and I are not responsible for the war. We were just caught in it."

"Like we are now, Justin, like we are now," Galen answered almost to himself.

* * * * *

When she'd finally unpacked, Lorelei took a shower and reviewed her cooking notes by an open window. Seagulls were circling over the shore, some picking up tiny fish from the shallows, some exploring farther waves for breakfast. The sky was cloudy, the air heavy with the scent of rain.

When she opened the balcony door and stepped outside, the swimming pool below came into view, reminding her of the previous night's encounter with the strange, long-haired man. She had no room in her life for a man, not even one to

A Scent in the Night

dream about, she decided. It was even more ridiculous to think that in those few moments when he looked at her, he had somehow miraculously known and understood who she really was. She shook her head and realized it had all been nonsense. The man was most likely just a servant who got caught having a tryst with his older and much richer, married employer. No use losing sleep over it, she concluded. Better call Maurice instead and see how the preparations were going.

Chapter Six

Montreal, Quebec.

Pain makes us more human, more vulnerable,
And therefore more tolerable to others.

༂

As the refrigerated truck backed up into the alley behind le Château DesCheneaux Hôtel, Maurice Leblanc, the chef in charge of its nationally renowned kitchen, was shutting his cell phone, thus ending a mildly reassuring call he had just received from Lorelei. Lorelei, his *petite*, as he affectionately referred to her, was the troubled young woman he had tutored and initiated into the world of haute cuisine and oenology when she completed her university education.

His childhood friend, Nicholas Rochefort, uncle to Lorelei, had taken care of her after the presumed murder of her parents. As an only and cherished child, she was devastated by their disappearance. Maurice often thought that if it hadn't been for "Roche", Lorelei might not have survived the traumatic loss and the illness that had followed it. He shuddered at the thought, for Lorelei had become, over the years, a daughter to him and his wife, Annabelle.

His *petite* had arrived when they were both resigned to being without children upon whom to lavish their love. Lorelei couldn't have been a more perfect "daughter", and with gentle prodding they had gradually erased the stricken look that clouded her silvery eyes whenever she thought no one was looking. Maurice knew—although he wouldn't dare tell his wife—that they hadn't completely wrestled the painful past out of Lorelei, that sometimes he got the impression she was only going through the motions of living, biding her time, waiting. But waiting for what? Sometimes a horrible answer crept into his mind but he couldn't even consider it. As he signaled the driver to stop, Maurice remembered the scene two days before when he watched Lorelei prepare to leave for Cape Cod. He had seen sadness, rather than her customary anticipation, in the way she had looked at her beautiful automobile. He could not help but worry what made his *petite* look so forlorn, as if her heart was being ripped to pieces.

"Must you really go ahead alone, *ma petite*?" Maurice had asked as a concerned father might.

She threw him one of her challenging looks. "*Oui, mon cher*. Before I deliver the car to the buyer, I'm driving her to Hyannis Port for my last..." She paused, then patted the hood of the Porsche. Tears welled up in her eyes. "My last run with her. That way I'll be able to say goodbye to her...and to Uncle Roche."

It was true—although he would admit it only to himself—that he would much prefer that Lorelei drive a sedate, nondescript automobile and not display such fascination for speed. Annabelle would definitely sleep better knowing that their Lorelei wouldn't be racing around in the Nemesis anymore.

Who was he fooling? He'd be even more relieved than his wife. Yet he regretted seeing Lorelei give up something she loved. He knew the attachment she had for the car and the pain this decision was causing her.

"Why don't you keep it, *chérie*?" he had asked her that day.

"If the expenses worry you, Annabelle and I will help you with them. You know we love you like our own *petite fille*."

She answered swiftly, too swiftly for his liking. A rehearsed answer he had thought at the time. "Thank you, Maurice but I must learn to stand on my own two feet. This car has been an emotional crutch for me — *une béquille*, you know? It's time I let go of my security blanket."

He had argued with her. "Fine, so you will sell it. But must you first make a ten-hour trip all by yourself? It's dangerous for a young woman alone. Why can't we at least leave at the same time? We can follow you with the bus and trucks."

"Please, Maurice, I'll be arriving in Hyannis Port long before you." She rubbed his hands, trying to soothe his worried expression. "Besides, I'll have my cell phone, cash and a credit card with me. I'll be fine."

"You should not be on the road so long alone," he'd argued.

"Maurice, stop fretting," Lorelei pleaded. "You are the one who taught me how to really drive the 959. How could you be worried for me? Everything I know, I learned from you."

"Yes but no amount of teaching will help you to avoid the police. The way you drive that *bolide — merde*!"

"That's why I have a cell phone — so I can call you to get me out of jail."

His attempt to keep from grinning had failed miserably. "It is not amusing, what you say, *méchante*! Promise me you will be careful and call me every hour." He looked straight into her eyes. "Also promise me that you will be driving at a reasonable speed."

"What will happen if I don't?" she'd challenged him with a cocky look.

"I'll have to take a hand to your *derrière*, of course."

She had laughed, knowing he could never hurt her. "*Et je t'aime, aussi*, old man." She knew he hated that English expression, even if it came with her love. "See you in Hyannis Port!" She had waved and briskly climbed into her Porsche for her farewell drive.

A Scent in the Night

Today, as Maurice supervised the first carts being wheeled into the refrigerated truck, his plump wife appeared beside him, her long hair, still jet black despite her years, in a bun. She slid an arm around his ample waist and tucked her head under his chin. "*A-t-elle appelé?*" she asked with concern in her voice.

"Yes, she called." He planted a brief kiss on his wife's worried brow. "She'll be fine. She's a strong one."

"*C'est vrai.* Yet ever since she stopped seeing Christian, she has not smiled. I thought that in time she would tell us what happened. Instead she announces she is selling the car, her pride and joy. Why?"

Maurice looked away to avoid showing Annabelle his own worry. "Our stubborn little Lorelei is challenging herself once again. I think she's hurt and doesn't want to depend on anyone but herself to get over her pain."

"She keeps so much inside, that one. Sometimes I am afraid for her."

He turned to face her. "Do you think she would ever..." He trailed off, thinking about Lorelei's behavior over the past few weeks. She had not shed a tear since her breakup with Renaud. But her plans to open her own catering company had suddenly halted. And now she was selling the one thing she cherished almost as much as she had cherished her Uncle Roche.

And she had insisted on traveling alone to Massachusetts—a goodbye drive, she'd called it. His heart suddenly skipped a beat. Could it be that she had decided to end it all?

Non, ça ne se peut pas. "No, it cannot be. She would not harm herself over Renaud, I am sure of it. For her parents she might have but not for that insipid man who could never look me in the eye."

"*C'est vrai.* You are right," Annabelle said.

Putting an arm around her shoulders, he led her toward the door into the loading garage. "Of course I am, *mon amour*. Now let's go inside and see if we can get everybody ready. Maybe we can leave earlier and get to Hyannis Port that much sooner."

"You are just as worried as I am, *chéri*. Admit it."

"I admit nothing. Besides, you worry enough for two people, so why should I bother?"

"You are incorrigible, Maurice but I love you just the same."

He chuckled and laid a gentle kiss on her temple. In an hour he would call the little one again and make sure she was not contemplating anything foolish.

Chapter Seven

Maurice was surveying the hotel reception hall's kitchens when a man wearing a white smock appeared.

"May I help you?" the fellow asked with faint disdain in his voice. "I am James Devereaux, head chef here. And you would be..."

Maurice looked up from the oven he had just opened to inspect. "Maurice Leblanc." Offering his hand to the chef, Maurice identified himself equally stiffly, reflecting ironically that a few centuries before, his Norman forefathers had probably been lords and masters to a Devereaux family or two.

Two trucks and a privately rented bus had arrived at the Siren hotel that morning, carrying nearly half of the DesCheneaux cook staff as well as many of the foodstuffs needed for the lavish culinary competition they fully intended to win.

"*La victoire, mes amis, sera la nôtre.* Victory will be ours, my friends," Maurice had declared in both languages as their driver parked the bus in front of the hotel.

"*Vive le Québec libre!*" one of the cooks had shouted from the back.

A free Quebec was what he was referring to, the same famous four words spoken to the Francophone community of the eastern Canadian province some decades before by Charles DeGaulle, President of France. The bus's occupants had laughed. Even if most remained loyal to the Parti Québecois and its staunch language-rights policies, many no longer really believed that the separation of Québec from Canada would guarantee the respect and survival of the French culture and language.

However, in the United States, in a competition in which who they were and where they came from would be looked at with a magnifying glass, they felt more Canadian, more Québecois, than ever.

"From?" Devereaux continued, his hand limp when Maurice took it.

"DesCheneaux," Maurice answered curtly.

"DesCheneaux?" A mocking smile twitched on Devereaux's lips. "Oh yes, you must be the Canadian group," he said, as if it were a slur.

François and Antoine, two of the twelve people forming the Canadian team took exception to his tone. They both stopped what they were doing and went to stand behind Maurice.

"And you work for?" François asked in turn.

Irritated at his insolence, Devereaux looked over his glasses. He was a tall, wiry man in his late fifties with thinning gray hair, his face wrinkled and his nose aquiline, matching the profile of the American eagle in front of the hotel between the Irish and US flags.

"I am head chef here and, may I add, consultant to the panel of judges."

Oblivious to his name, rank and veiled threat, Antoine retrieved a book from the counter and went to stand in front of the arrogant chef. "If you are a chef of note, then you must know that DesCheneaux is famous for its cuisine and wines."

"I don't doubt for a moment that you are famous in your local Canadian sphere. However, on an international level, I have never heard of DesCheneaux—until today, of course," Devereaux retorted.

"Then, Mr. Devereaux, your education has been lacking," Lorelei said as she approached the small gathering, which quickly parted to let her in. "Doesn't the book *Les Vins et Festins*, which I see Antoine holding, belong to your kitchen?"

With a superior expression Devereaux ignored Lorelei, addressing Maurice instead. "Mr. Leblanc, I demand an apology from your cook, or I will make an official protest to the panel."

"Before any apologies are given, Mr. Devereaux," Lorelei interjected, "and I assure you that they will be before we leave this room, let me remind you of the saying that it is always better to hold one's silence and be thought a fool than to speak and remove all doubt." With the sweetest expression she could muster, Lorelei took the book from Antoine and shoved it against Devereaux's chest. "I am Lorelei Duplessis, the author," she said, offering her hand to shake. "This is my team from DesCheneaux, without whose talents and support I could not have written the book. Which, judging by the fact that you use it, must contribute to your own success as well."

Appearing contrite for the sake of appearance but possibly fuming inside at this public chastising, Devereaux nodded and shook her extended hand. "Since Canada isn't particularly renowned for its culinary art, my mistake was, perhaps, understandable," he offered as way of an apology.

Watching him go red in the face, Lorelei smiled. "Well, Mr. Devereaux, would you excuse us now? We have a lot of work to do and we poor, inexperienced Canadians need all the time we can get."

Devereaux swiftly turned around, muttering under his breath and left.

Maurice and the others applauded Lorelei, then began their work.

* * * * *

The following day, after a last-minute review of the cooking schedule and duty roster, Lorelei was able to tear herself away from the hustle and bustle of the kitchens and go to her room to prepare for the evening ahead. She had carefully retrieved from the trucks all the dried flower arrangements she had prepared in Montreal. She had meticulously supervised the preparation of the *hors d'oeuvres* and the setting of their buffet table.

Chilling the white wines properly had been a challenge, since the Siren's refrigerators lacked individual thermometers and serving wines at the right temperature was key to the success of any reception. Over-chilling could diminish both fragrance and flavor.

When she kicked off her shoes and turned on the water to draw a hot bath, a wave of nausea suddenly came over her. Not for a long time had she suffered such nerves. She rarely worried unless she knew something was going wrong. Don't be so paranoid, she chastised herself. Tonight was just the cocktail party. The "night of nights" might be another story but that wasn't here yet.

After a long soak, Lorelei stepped out of the tub and dried herself. She then made a French twist of her hair, leaving just one lock loose. Her dress was black silk lace set on beige taffeta, giving a see-through impression, its dangerously low back finished with a row of black silk-covered buttons and a small train. It was the most elegant dress she had ever owned, next to the one she was would wear for the formal dinner.

"Time to get this show on the road," she told her reflection. Then she left her room.

Chapter Eight

He and she walked in different directions,
Yet found themselves side by side.

೫೧

Her buffet was divided into three sections, starting with shellfish, then vegetable dishes and finally meats. From steamed clams sprinkled with lemon, Italian parsley and fresh garlic to tiny squid with coriander and olive oil, from marinated octopus to baked mussels drenched with brandy, all were prepared with skill and love.

Lorelei also served cherry tomatoes stuffed with rice and spinach, eggplant croquettes, fried bocconcini, bruschetta with truffles and basil or with olives and oregano. Lastly she was serving fried prosciutto on toasted herbal bread and pancetta with dried marinated tomatoes, roasted peppers and anchovy morsels.

At eight o'clock approximately seven hundred guests were circulating among the buffet tables. Lorelei was flabbergasted to see the number of people surrounding hers.

She had asked Annabelle and her sister-in-law to supervise the service tables but quickly realized she would need at least two more staffers to answer the guests' questions about the food. A passing waiter told her that someone from her crew was looking for her.

She approached the buffet table, trying to catch Annabelle's attention. She had to squeeze between one man who had his back to her and another who was helping himself to some mussels.

The minute she spoke to Annabelle, however, the man to her left slowly turned around.

"Ah, finally, we meet again." A pair of deep black eyes stared into her gray ones, paralyzing her. His lips, not more than three inches away from her own, curved into a smile.

She clumsily stepped back and bumped into Senator Thomas Gallagher, who was reaching for a napkin. She muttered an apology.

"That's quite all right, Miss Duplessis. You're just the person I wanted to see. Have you met our principal sponsors and this year's hosts? Let me do the honors." He gestured toward the two tall men standing beside her. "Lorelei Duplessis, meet Galen Kennedy and his brother, Justin, respectively president and vice-president of Wexford International." He turned to face the Kennedy brothers.

At the sound of that name, that particular name she had only heard once in her life mere hours before, and those eyes she would remember forever, Lorelei was too stunned to react.

"Gentlemen, this is the young woman leading the Canadian group and, may I add to my own delight, who's responsible for preparing this wonderful table of Italian delicacies. Since you're one of the panel judges, Galen, I hope you'll recognize this woman's exceptional talent."

It wasn't enough that she had seen him naked and about to have sex or that she had thoroughly insulted him. The man she'd thought to be a pool attendant was Galen Kennedy of Wexford International, the competition's sponsor and, to top it off, a judge of the culinary contest. A deep sense of irony quickly replaced her shock. Nothing had ever been easy for her. Why should this competition be any different? She swore under her breath in French while the long-haired billionaire stood before her with an unreadable expression.

He was wearing a single-breasted black suit with narrow lapels. Lorelei recognized the cut as Armani. Instead of the traditional white or black shirt he wore a thin silk knit in a shimmering dark gray, exposing the thick cords of his neck. He looked sleek, elegant and devastatingly handsome—with or without clothes. How could she have mistaken him for a pool boy?

His brother was wearing a Versace suit, its charcoal color softening his jet-black hair and strong Irish features. He too, wore his long hair tied back in a leather thong. And he too, Lorelei thought grudgingly, was mouth-wateringly attractive.

Although Galen had been expecting to see the enigmatic visitor to his poolside tonight, he was still having a hard time maintaining his smug expression. Where she had disturbed him before, she now dazzled him. It wasn't just her delicately arranged hair or elegant dress. From her skin emanated that same scent that had drawn him to her a few nights before. He inhaled deeply, relishing it.

But when he flashed a look at his brother, signaling he had recognized her, he noticed that Justin too, was equally absorbed by her. The thought irritated him. So did the lecherous looks Tom Gallagher was casting at her cleavage.

So much for acting nonchalant. It was time to stake his claim. He placed a hand on the small of her back and saw a look of alarm flash in her eyes. "Miss Duplessis and I have already met, Senator. Hello there. Nice to see you again."

He leaned forward and kissed her affectionately on each cheek.

Lorelei wished the flutter in her heart would subside. It would do no good for either of them to acknowledge their first unfortunate meeting or the apparent attraction they had felt for each other. She stepped back, uneasy. "You must be confusing me with someone else, Mr. Kennedy. I don't recall meeting you."

Amused, Galen touched the lock of hair that hung loosely by her cheek. His eyes held hers as they had at the poolside, long enough for her to feel he was literally stripping her of her clothes. "Maybe the words trespassing on private property would ring a bell?"

Her cheeks flushed. Why was he insisting on making public their accidental acquaintance? Did he want to embarrass them both?

She was holding her glass so tightly, she realized it would shatter if she didn't put it down. "Oh, yes, how could I forget?" She looked at the senator apologetically. "It was dark and he wasn't really dressed, so—"

Senator Gallagher almost swallowed a brochette whole, and she hurried to finish her explanation. "You see, Senator, Mr. Kennedy and I inadvertently met the other night when he was swimming in the pool adjacent to the hotel, which I mistook for public property. Our meeting was so brief, it escaped my mind."

"That would certainly explain it," the senator managed to say, his eyes on Galen, his disapproval evident.

"I was swimming with a guest," Galen added cautiously, "when Miss Duplessis arrived. Although I invited her to join us, she declined because she had no bathing suit with her, which was unfortunate, of course."

"Unfortunate that she declined or that she had no swimsuit?" Justin commented with a smile.

"Either way, Justin, I think your brother's guest would have had a few reservations anyway, wouldn't you?" the senator asked Galen in a cryptic tone.

Galen smiled, barely, while Lorelei listened to the veiled tone of disapproval with confusion.

Then Gallagher's expression turned jovial once again.

"Now, now, you shouldn't embarrass the young lady." Turning to Lorelei, he added as conspicuously as possible, "My compliments, my dear. I can't get enough of your delicacies. I mean, of course, those on your table. I hope that once the competition is over, you'll indulge me with your talents again."

Lorelei flushed at his comments, noticing the way the two Kennedy brothers looked at each other, seeming displeased and, oddly, almost suspicious.

At that moment a manicured hand touched the senator's arm and a woman gently pushed herself into the tight circle.

"Darling, won't you introduce me?"

Wiping his lips with a napkin, the senator smiled reluctantly at the woman. "Well, of course. Darling, this is Lorelei Duplessis. She heads the Canadian catering team. Miss Duplessis, this is my wife, Vivian."

When she recognized the woman, Lorelei dropped her glass and everybody stepped back to avoid the splatter and the shattering crystal. All she could picture was Galen Kennedy straddling this blonde on a lounge chair near the pool.

"I'm sorry," she apologized. With shaking hands she bent down to pick up the pieces of glass and nearly bumped into Galen Kennedy's head as he also stooped to help clean up.

"Are you all right?" he asked, concerned. "Why don't you let me do this? The glass is sharp."

"Thanks but I'm okay." Unaware she had already cut herself, Lorelei stood up, only to notice a few seconds later that she had slit one of her fingers. "*Merde!*" she muttered.

"You cut yourself. Let me see." Gently removing what remained of the glass, Galen applied pressure on the bleeding finger. "It's not so bad," he said. Then he put her finger into his mouth, gently sucking the blood away.

Justin gasped as he watched his brother. Then he cleared his throat and put a reassuring hand on Lorelei's elbow.

"Don't mind him, Miss Duplessis. My brother's a fool for damsels in distress. Did you know that saliva, in fact, has special enzymes to disinfect wounds?" Justin rambled on, trying to explain his brother's outrageous behavior.

Galen nodded. "May I get you another drink? White wine, was it?"

"Yes, it was but—"

"It's the least I can do, Miss Duplessis," he insisted.

"And you know what I like, darling," Vivian purred, offering her empty glass to him while glaring at Lorelei.

"Senator Gallagher!" a man interrupted, making his way toward them, inquiring about a golf tournament he and the senator were supposed to attend.

While her husband stepped away to speak to him, Justin offered Vivian some *hors d'oeuvres*.

Galen waited impatiently at the bar. He felt as though the whole world was intruding on him and this woman.

Lorelei Duplessis had obviously recognized Vivian Gallagher, and that was just one of the problems he and Justin now had to face. The other was of a more personal nature. He was uncontrollably attracted to Lorelei, drawn to her without the strength to stop himself. The attraction was so powerful that he couldn't even pretend to be interested in anyone else. Why now, when the timing was so volatile? When Vivian's role might be crucial?

Lorelei's eyes—those cool gray eyes—revealed insight, intelligence and strength, the kind she probably didn't even know she had.

She had prepared her buffet with exceptional taste. The *hors d'oeuvres* were exquisite, even to his sophisticated palate. The floral arrangements and the imaginative presentation of the miniature morsels of food were also most impressive, pretty enough to invite to her table the most skeptical of guests, such as himself.

She knew her wines too. It took guts to serve a French Sauterne, a very sweet white wine he normally disliked, with slices of dry Genoa salamino on an Italian herb bread. The wine usually accompanied a dessert.

A Scent in the Night

She was a paradox, cool and composed yet, he was sure, burning inside. Tonight her eyes betrayed none of the pain she had allowed him to glimpse at the poolside. "I wonder what she hides," he muttered while he made his way back to the group.

"How's your brother, Vivian?" Justin inquired, attempting to distract her until Galen returned.

"As a matter of fact, he just returned from Winnipeg and is glad to be back. The winters in Canada are long and cold, the scenery dismal and the women, apparently, as frigid as the weather." She turned to look at Lorelei disdainfully.

Lorelei couldn't understand the woman's animosity. Didn't she realize what a scandal could erupt if Lorelei revealed her knowledge that the senator's wife was having an affair with Galen Kennedy?

She leveled her gaze on the woman. "Maybe your brother is simply clumsy at sex. Women are rarely actually frigid. That's merely a myth some males use to excuse their own incompetence. Which reminds me of a study I once came across. Did you know that only one out of three American women experiences orgasm with her sex partner? From those figures, you'd almost have to conclude that either two-thirds of American women are 'frigid' or that two-thirds of the men they sleep with are clumsy. So it's likely that even an attractive woman such as you, for example, might feel compelled to fake orgasms, for the sake of not being thought frigid and relieve her libido later by herself, for the sake of getting some satisfaction."

Justin went white and glanced over at Senator Gallagher, who had moved away to speak to the governor of New Hampshire.

When Galen returned, he took one look at Justin's alarmed expression and understood that the situation was getting out of control.

Vivian placed a hand possessively on Galen's arm after he handed her a glass of red wine. "I sympathize with you, Miss Duplessis," she said to Lorelei. "Maybe some women can only attract clumsy men." And she cast a conspicuous smile at Galen, clearly implying that that was not her case.

"Frankly, Mrs. Gallagher, I'd prefer a passionate but clumsy male to an indifferent one," Lorelei retorted.

Galen heard enough to understand what was being discussed as he handed the Canadian chef her drink.

"Gewürztraminer, was it not?"

"How very observant," Lorelei stammered, still angered by Vivian's remarks.

"As I've already demonstrated, Miss Duplessis, I don't miss a thing. Vivian, I think Tom is signaling for you to join him. Justin, will you excuse Miss Duplessis and me for a few minutes? I believe she promised me this dance."

Before she had time to contradict him and disappear into the kitchens from this disaster of a night, he took her glass from her, put it on the buffet table behind him and guided her to the dance floor.

"I didn't promise you any dance," she countered before he placed his hand on the small of her back.

"Shh, this will relax you." The music was slow and soft, and he gently pulled her toward him, closely but not enough to look too intimate.

Lorelei tried to ignore the nerves jumping in her stomach. She hesitated for a moment, then decided to clear the air as diplomatically as she could, even if it killed her. After all, Galen Kennedy was a panel judge and her attitude toward him might jeopardize her team's chances of winning the competition.

"I feel like such a fool for mistaking you for a pool boy," she said. "I apologize."

He leaned back, surprised that she would broach the subject. "That's it? No explanation as to why I looked like a pool boy to you, at midnight and naked on private property?"

He danced her farther away from the senator's group. "I think you mistook me for the help because you're a little on the snobbish side. So why not apologize for that?"

Her eyes lit up with pique. "How arrogant of you. Maybe I made the mistake because you looked so…unrefined?"

He sighed heavily, searching for patience. "Okay, time out. I asked you for a dance, not a duel." He considered his next words, then smiled. "My apologies for sounding arrogant, Miss Duplessis."

She sighed in relief. "And I apologize for calling you coarse. I must admit that you don't sound or act at all the way you did the other night. In a suit you look considerably more…gentlemanly."

His smile was faint, almost sarcastic. "Apology accepted, although it didn't sound very sincere." He tightened his hold on her.

She looked up at him. "Really? Whatever gave you that idea?"

"Well, speaking of unrefined, wouldn't you be offended if I assumed that, being French Canadian and from Quebec, you were the product of unwanted criminals shipped from France to colonize a territory known for its frigid weather and desolation. A place no one in his right mind wanted to colonize, a nation today referred to as France's poor relation? However, since you so graciously apologized, I will not discuss your patriotic shortcomings."

"How magnanimous of you," Lorelei replied tightly. "I guess I asked for that one."

"I guess you did." He leaned closer. "So why don't we quit the small talk and discuss what really happened the other night by the pool?"

"Nothing happened, Mr. Kennedy. We were both under the influence of...of the evening. No harm done."

Lorelei took advantage of his silence to change the subject. "So, judging by your name and the flag in front of the hotel, you would be Irish."

"How good of ye to notice, me dear," he answered with an Irish brogue. "I was born in Ireland and lived there much of my life."

"I see. So what brought you —"

"How long were you there, Lorelei?"

He used her given name so naturally and so intimately that she was momentarily flustered. She moved her head back a little to look up at him. "I was never in Ireland, Mr. Kennedy."

"I meant the other night at the pool."

This lie would require skill. "I don't really remember. I fell asleep shortly after I sat down in the rocking chair. I had just arrived from Montreal and was tired. I guess I woke up when I heard you swimming."

"Do you think you can lure me into your web of fibs — like the Lorelei of the Rhine whose beauty lured sailors into wrecking their ships?" He smiled. "You lie well, Lorelei, but not well enough for me, I fear," he added with a soft burr.

She stopped moving, outraged. "You think I'm lying?"

"You practically described what you saw to the Gallaghers a few minutes ago."

"You must have misunderstood."

He looked annoyed. "Stop lying. It doesn't become you."

"I wasn't lying. I was merely trying to be diplomatic."

He was a little surprised at how adeptly she had made the admission and turned the tables on him once more.

"I don't need your diplomacy. I need your discretion. What went on between Vivian and me is private. You had no business being there." However, he didn't want her to think anything of any significance existed between him and the senator's wife. He felt compelled to elaborate. "Look, I don't think I owe you any explanations but just now Vivian," he whispered, "is a means to an end."

Lorelei put on a sarcastic smile. "And which end would that be, Mr. Kennedy? The one…" Her eyes trailed down his body with no mistake as to where she meant.

Christ, the woman pulled no punches. He knew what he was doing with Vivian was wrong but what choice did he have? Her husband, he strongly suspected, was responsible for destroying lives, hopes, dreams—an entire country, for God's sake! So why should he feel guilty about having sex with another consenting adult, who had no illusions about his feelings for her, if it meant finding some small way to shorten a war?

Blood hummed through his veins. "All your talk of sex is beginning to make me think that perhaps you're either jealous of Vivian, which makes for interesting possibilities, or," his eyes skimmed her cleavage, "you simply need to get laid. Either way, I'd be happy to accommodate you."

She tried without success to dislodge herself from him.

"How vulgar!!"

Ignoring her outrage, he continued calmly. "I can assure you that with me your entire hand wouldn't be sufficient to count how many times you'd clim—"

"Must you be so crude?" she interrupted him, appalled at what he'd nearly said.

"Crude?" he repeated. "I merely picked up your cue from your conversation with Vivian."

His talk of the woman indeed made Lorelei jealous for some obscure reason she'd analyze later. "I draw the line when someone deliberately tries to humiliate me." Her anger mounting, she poked him in the chest, trying to keep her voice low. "However, I understand that you're taking exception to the comments I made about your...masculinity, so to speak. But believe me, I have no interest in it whatsoever."

This was getting them nowhere fast, Galen thought.

Before the week was out he was going to take this little Lorelei's ego down a few notches, enough to hear her scream out his name naked beneath him. For now, though, a more pressing matter needed to be settled to his satisfaction.

He shot her a brief but dangerous look. "As for the part of your earlier conversation I retained the most, Miss Duplessis, it was not about my sexual prowess or lack thereof but, rather, that you almost publicly announced what you had seen." Damned if he didn't wish they were somewhere more private.

"All I did was respond to that woman's unwarranted hostility. And taking into consideration your earlier comments about the circumstances surrounding our first meeting, I was, nevertheless, discreet."

He took a deep breath, because nothing seemed to get through to her. "Look, Vivian Gallagher is using me as much as I am her. I do it because lives are at stake. I wish I could explain but I can't. All I can say is that I don't make a habit of going to such lengths otherwise. In this case I have no choice."

"Are you saying the end justifies the means?"

"In this case, yes," he answered carefully.

"How Machiavellian. Did you know that that kind of thinking has started wars?"

His eyes hardened. "Maybe but that observation sure as hell doesn't apply here. Trust me, it doesn't."

She stared at him with obvious disbelief in her eyes.

"You don't believe me, do you? Fine. But be warned."

Frustration hammered at his temples. "Don't start a 'war' with me, sweetheart, because you won't win. And God help you if you say so much as one word to anyone about what you saw the other night."

Her next words were spoken evenly, despite the inner fury waiting to explode. "You don't have to threaten me, Mr. Kennedy. How arrogant of you once again to think that the entire world and everyone in it revolves around you. Well, I have news for you, sweetheart—it doesn't. You may have no morals but I trust that most of us here do. And we happen to care about this competition, about sharing with others our love for our work and especially about raising money for those who are dying of hunger as we speak. How dare you think my presence here or what I think, say, or do is only about you and the excuses you create in your own mind to justify your behavior? I'll keep silent but only because I will not be responsible for making a mockery and a scandal of this event simply because Mr. Galen Kennedy couldn't keep his perversions in the privacy of his own bedroom!"

The music stopped at the precise moment her sentence did, allowing her to march away from him without a backward glance.

Galen was so stunned by her little tirade, he could have applauded her. He almost felt guilty for threatening her. She was obviously a woman of principle and integrity who would not lower herself to gossip.

She was also as attracted to him as he was to her, he realized with a smile. She had tried her best to hide it, even deny it, but there it was.

His brother tipped his glass to him as Galen returned to the cocktail lounge. Justin's cool gaze spoke plenty. "Smart going, brother."

"What?"

"Let's see." With his free hand Justin ticked off Galen's indiscretions. "Sucking the woman's finger in a roomful of people—in front of Vivian, no less. Having an argument with her on the dance floor. Intimidating her into keeping silent. Have I left out anything? What the hell's gotten into you?"

Galen cast Justin a look. Irritated, he stalked to a chair and sat down. Justin followed but remained standing, waiting for an explanation.

"The bastard knows I'm screwing his wife," Galen said with quiet conviction.

Justin didn't look surprised. "And hitting on the Canadian woman is going to convince him otherwise?"

Galen crossed his arms. "Probably not but it'll give me immense satisfaction to have something Tom wants and will never get."

"Then you're as much a bastard as he is," Justin answered, turning to leave.

Galen snagged his brother's arm before he could walk away. "What was that for? I like the Canadian girl."

"Then why don't you keep yourself safely away from her and let me handle the situation?" he suggested.

"Are you kidding? You're dying to go to bed with her," Galen replied, trying to hide his jealousy, a sensation almost foreign to him where women were concerned.

"And you aren't?"

Galen paused for a few moments, debating whether to tell the truth. "Hell, yes. I'm attracted to her, so much so that I don't know what to do about it."

Clearly surprised that Galen had so readily admitted his feelings, Justin settled beside him in another armchair. He shook his head at a waiter who offered to refresh his drink.

"You can't do anything about it. And you know why."

Galen leaned back. "I don't know what it is about her, but I swear..." He didn't finish his sentence, couldn't, because he would have to reveal a thought, a vague but powerful feeling, he wasn't yet ready to reveal.

"You swear what?" Justin asked. Both brothers sat in silence, watching the crowd thin out. "She reminds you of Brenna, right?" Justin guessed, interrupting Galen's brooding.

"What makes you think that?" he replied, surprised Justin could read him so well.

His brother didn't answer the question. Instead, he swallowed hard and said, "You've already bled too much for her, man. All you're going to do with this Canadian girl is open the wound again, big and wide."

Galen nodded, then stood. "Maybe. But maybe it's time I let all the pus out, once and for all." He clenched his fists in his pockets. "Let me have this one." When Justin just stared at him, he placed a hand on his shoulder. "I ask as your brother and as your friend."

It took only a few seconds for Justin to concede. He loved his older brother and wouldn't deny him. "All right," he answered, standing up as well. "But you owe me. Big-time."

"Don't I know it," Galen acknowledged.

Justin shook his head and steered the conversation toward a lighter tone. "I guess I should wish you luck. From what I just heard and saw, you're going to have a hard time getting any action from the little chef—except maybe a hit over the head with a rolling pin."

Galen laughed and answered in their Irish burr, "O ye of little faith."

"Hey, at least I made you laugh. Now, seriously—"

"Don't—"

"Seriously," Justin reiterated. "Do you think the Canadian woman will talk?"

Galen sighed. "No, I don't think Lorelei Duplessis will say anything. She seems to be much too principled for gossipmongering. Besides, I think she has something else on her mind, even besides winning this competition."

"Like what?" Justin asked, curious.

Galen shook his head in response. "I don't know but I'm sure as hell going to find out."

Tomorrow he would offer an olive branch to the enigmatic Miss Duplessis and apologize. Again, he thought with a trace of a smile.

Lorelei was rinsing her hands in the ladies' washroom when the senator's wife stepped into the adjacent powder room with another woman. "Who's that debutante I saw dancing with Galen Kennedy?" the woman asked Vivian Gallagher.

"She heads the catering team from Montreal. Totally amateurish, if you ask me. She's obviously out of her league," Vivian replied churlishly.

"I guess they decided to let in some Canadians for a change. How amusing," her friend added.

"You make it sound as if they opened the doors to a pack of mongrels," Vivian said with a laugh.

Lorelei paused, furious, as she was reaching for a paper towel.

"You said it, Viv, not me."

Lorelei wasn't going to just stand there and let the women speak about her and her colleagues that way. She strode into the powder room. "Tell me, Mrs. Gallagher, what have you accomplished in life — besides marrying a rich man?"

Vivian turned away from the mirrors and gaped at Lorelei, who suddenly stood before her.

"Obviously not much," Lorelei continued, "so for your sake I hope you have a good pre-nup. Something tells me your husband is probably about as faithful as you are." She nodded goodbye and stalked out of the room, leaving two speechless women in her wake.

"The gall of these people!" Lorelei muttered, running to the kitchens, fuming over Vivian Gallagher and her friend.

Her earlier talk with Galen Kennedy resurfaced and made her even angrier. Maybe she could find something to chop or slice—something that reminded her of one of Mr. Kennedy's more important body parts.

Maurice was fixing coffee when Lorelei all but slammed through the kitchen door. "*Ma petite*, what are you doing here? Is something wrong with our buffet? Is something missing?"

His worried look cooled her off, reminding her that she had more important things to worry about than Hyannis Port snobs. Why get herself all worked up about what some airhead Barbies had to say or about Galen Kennedy's threats?

In a few days she'd be five hundred and thirty miles away from them.

"No, Maurice, everything is delightful. Everyone is enjoying our table the most. Can you believe it?"

"So why are you angry? I've seen that look on you before. You are very, very upset. Who has dared to upset you so?"

She skipped over Galen Kennedy and replied, "Vivian Gallagher, the senator's wife, pretty much said we don't belong here. How dare she, the tramp!"

Maurice gently pried a cleaver away from her and put a finger under her chin. "Since when does the gentle commander cower in front of a woman?"

"Cower? Never. And that's the problem. I gave her back some of what she dealt me." Lorelei was still savoring the expression on Vivian's face when she left the washroom.

"She might retaliate." And ask her lover to intervene? She wondered. "What if I jeopardized our chances of winning this competition?"

"*Mais non, petite*, she is just the vain wife of a man who is not a member of the judging panel. Now, if you had insulted one of the sponsors or judges, then I would say we were in serious trouble." His eyebrows arched slightly at Lorelei's silence. "You did not, did you?"

She gave him a meaningful look. "I did. Boy, did I ever."

Maurice smiled resignedly, recalling Lorelei's rare but fierce tempers. "Which of the two giants?" Even if he rarely stepped out of the kitchens, Maurice was always well informed about his patrons and this competition was proving no exception.

"The blond one."

He smiled. Then frowned. "Did he—how do you say?—come on to you?"

She avoided his gaze. "Why would you think that?"

Maurice frowned again. "What, exactly, did you say to him?" he asked.

Lorelei gave a careless shrug. "I mistook him for a pool boy."

Maurice was obviously confused. "A pool boy? But why would you think he—"

"Maurice, I don't want to talk about it. You know what? I'll think I'll just change clothes and go for a nice drive."

Having made that decision, Lorelei began walking toward the door.

"But it is late, petite. Why don't you go for a swim instead?"

"Swim? At night? Here? *Jamais!*" she exclaimed in French, meaning, never in a thousand years.

Chapter Nine

What we are missing is not necessarily what we need.

☙

The following morning the pool looked so inviting from Lorelei's bedroom window that she decided she'd buy a swimsuit and go down for a swim after she finished her coffee. Her day had not started well but that was no reason to sit around and mope until the kitchens were vacated by one of the other teams. She might as well take advantage of what was left of the morning.

Her earlier call to her best friend and attorney, Amanda Fairchild, had not produced good news. The investigators they had hired to track down Christian and the money he stole from her had met another dead end. So she was back to square one. No last-minute reprieve. She would have to go through with the sale of the 959 after all.

As she finished her coffee, she dragged her thoughts back to the previous night's cocktail party. When she'd arrived on Cape Cod, she had high hopes for the competition. She wanted so much to give Chateau DesCheneaux this victory, to make Maurice proud of her. She wanted to give him and Annabelle something back for their love and undying support, to leave them with good memories and a much improved earning potential. Now, however, she was questioning her chances of winning the competition.

If Galen Kennedy's liaison with Vivian Gallagher became public knowledge before the culinary event ended, she would certainly be blamed. She doubted she was the only one who knew about the affair but she was the one he'd suspect.

With an oath she jerked open the morning paper, hoping that reading about other people's problems would distract her from her own. But what she saw in the society section was a nice big picture of none other than Galen Kennedy.

Afraid the scandal had already erupted, she began reading the article but to her relief nothing was mentioned about his affair with Vivian Gallagher. Instead it said that Kennedy, an accomplished businessman heading one of the largest beer-producing companies in Europe, was hosting the international culinary competition at his Siren hotel to benefit the third world relief organization he and his brother managed and to which they annually donated millions of dollars. The piece added that Galen Kennedy, a Harvard graduate with a master's in world economics, had almost single-handedly revived Ireland's beer industry, which had taken a nosedive some years back with the onslaught of new microbreweries in the West.

So why was this brilliant, worldly businessman having an affair with Vivian "Barbie" Gallagher? From what she had just read, Mrs. Gallagher was his antithesis. Why risk his reputation and the future of his business and favorite charity on a liaison with a woman he didn't appear to have any feelings for?

He had said she was a means to an end. Had Lorelei not been so quick to retort, she might have found out what was behind the affair.

"Politics?" she guessed aloud. Some called it the real art of seduction. And Vivian Gallagher was a senator's wife.

Did Galen Kennedy hope to find some skeleton in Gallagher's closet that would help him unseat the senator, maybe replace him with someone more to his liking? As far as Lorelei was concerned, politics was no art. It was a cynical game played largely by privileged, moneyed men hungry for influence and power.

Having arrived at one of her easier decisions of the day—to take a swim—Lorelei put her hair in a French braid and donned a gold one-piece bathing suit. She tied on a matching wraparound skirt, slipped into a pair of gold sandals and left her room.

From the French doors leading to his suite's balcony, Galen stared down at Lorelei Duplessis as she stepped out into the hotel's pool area, looking for a place to put her towel. Under normal circumstances, the Kennedy family rarely occupied the presidential suite at the hotel. The residence was larger, more comfortable and especially, more private. But running an event such as this required his and Justin's presence on site. Not to mention that there was the added bonus to basically monitor many activities just by looking out from the balcony as he was doing now. So she was going for a swim after all, he thought as he watched Lorelei walking across the terrazzo. She was grace personified, he mused, with legs that went on for miles, smooth, exotic-looking olive skin and generous curves in all the right places to enhance her petite slimness. Lorelei, indeed. She could definitely lure a man to his doom.

She smiled at a young man sprawled on one of the lounge chairs. It bothered him that she did so. She had not yet given him even a semblance of smile. Anger, she had shown him, loneliness, she had hidden. Her pain appeared like a reflection of his own. He kept telling himself to go slowly on this one, that perhaps he was making too much of his reaction to her.

Yet no matter what he told himself, whenever he saw her, he was uncontrollably attracted to her. To his chagrin, he would notice the littlest things about her, such as how she now easily descended the steps into the pool, indifferent to the coolness of the water. How after effortlessly swimming several laps, she picked the farthest edge of the pool to perch on and brood. How she brought her knees up to her chest, nearly burying her face in them as she hugged them to her.

There it was, that silent grief, as if she wanted to cry but couldn't, as if she wanted to shield herself from pain and again was unable to. His heart went out to her. And he decided to join her.

He got into swim trunks and made his way downstairs and outside. There, he dove smoothly into the pool and swam toward the far end, silently surfacing right in front of her.

"Are you okay?" he asked gently.

Startled, she looked up quickly, nearly losing her balance and tumbling into the water. He grasped her legs to steady her.

"Yes, I'm…fine…thank you," she stammered, pulling her legs back up to her chest.

He offered her his right hand. "Hi, I'm Galen Kennedy. Can we start over?"

Lorelei realized she didn't have the will or spare energy to continue dueling either.

He watched her reaction. "I think you're smiling. Does that mean yes?"

She did smile and found it easier than she thought. "I'm Lorelei Duplessis. Pleased to meet you, Mr. Kennedy." And she shook his hand.

Finally, he thought. "You put out an incredible *hors d'oeuvres* table last night. I meant to congratulate you."

"Thank you. But the other participants were just as good," she replied.

He shook his head. It seemed hard for her to accept praise. "They were good but you were better. It's not a sin, you know, to be better."

She looked away, uncertain how to respond. Every time he spoke to her, she had the distinct feeling he was probing her, seeing things nobody else saw.

He wanted to catch a strand of hair that covered her eyes but he kept his hands politely to himself. There would be time for touching, for exploring her textures, for luxuriating in her scent later. He prayed for patience.

"How are the preparations going for your dinner? Are the kitchens up to your standards?" He plucked a ball from the water and threw it back to the group playing with it.

"You have a great kitchen—and I mean that in every sense," she said. "The blackberry muffins they served this morning were amazing. I plan to ask for the recipe, providing it's already copyrighted." She looked at him, smiling.

That was the second smile she'd given him, he noted happily. "Have you met Devereaux yet?"

"Oh, yes," she answered with faint irony in her voice.

Galen leaned back against the side of the pool and closed his eyes to the sun. "He's as tight-assed as they come and proud as a peacock. But he's good at what he does. He was my father's personal chef for as long as I can remember. And I have an ongoing bet with my brother that one day he'll meet his match." He turned his head and smiled. "So what's the scoop? Did you two exchange words—or cross cleavers? And, more important, who won?"

She laughed, this time heartily. "Let's just say that he'll never underestimate a female chef in quite the same way again."

He arched his eyebrows. "Oh? Have I won my bet then?"

She shrugged. "Can't say."

"No fair! I've got a lot of money riding on that wager."

"How could I possibly gossip about him, knowing you're his employer?"

He frowned. "Was he that bad?"

She shrugged. "He committed a *faux pas*—one I think he'll remember for a long time to come."

Galen smiled. He'd get the whole story from one of the snitches in his kitchen. "My money's on you," he said. "So, tell me about yourself. How long have you been with

DesCheneaux?" He knew the answer. He'd committed the entire dossier on her to memory.

"A little over five years."

"And you're already published, right?" he asked.

"Yes, DesCheneaux has a cookbook out, to which I contributed and I have a small volume of my own out too. On catering." She waved away a fly. "The hotel has a wonderful cook staff, thanks to Maurice Leblanc. They all love what they do and they work hard. It's a way of life for them. Writing about some of their best efforts was the least I could do."

She excluded herself from attention, he noticed. "What about you? Do you love what you do?"

"Of course," she replied.

Somehow her automatic response disturbed him, so he probed more deeply. "Is it a way of life for you, as well?"

She looked up at him with a flash of awareness. "Why wouldn't it be?" she asked cautiously.

"Because you look as if you have other things in your life. Other plans," he cautiously advanced.

Her head snapped to attention. "Well, I don't."

"All right," he agreed but he wasn't convinced. It was too soon, however, to confront the matter head-on with her. They had just met and not under the best of circumstances. It was better to wait.

"Well, since we got off to a bad start," he said, "might I invite you to visit my art gallery this morning? I have a fairly good collection of paintings you may enjoy viewing."

Uneasy at his offer to socialize, she decided to decline. "Wouldn't it be considered irregular, if not against the rules, that a panel judge invite a contestant at his home?"

"The gallery at the house is public. Besides most of your colleagues have already seen it. Part of our hospitality policy." Which wasn't exactly true Galen knew. But she had no means to know, so he was free to lie.

"I appreciate the invitation. However I believe it would be best if I came by after the competition."

Her refusals were beginning to annoy him. "Do you think I'm trying to jeopardize your presence at the competition? Is that why you're saying no?"

She suddenly felt foolish for thinking that his offer was a ruse. The truth was she she had this growing and uncontrollable attraction to this man and didn't know if she could deal with it properly. "No, of course not. After all, it's not important who wins but that the competition takes place and, most importantly that the money is raised for the foundation." She knew Galen Kennedy's personal life was not one she approved of, but as for his social ethics, she could not but confirm his ongoing commitment to the famine relief cause.

"If you have a few minutes, why don't you come by now? I'm sure you'll be very busy from this afternoon on."

She hoped she wasn't going to regret accepting. "All right. I'll go change and be there shortly."

"Don't bother. You can come as you are." He smiled and casually vaulted out of the pool.

* * * * *

He took her into an outbuilding, which she recognized almost immediately when they approached the entrance by the beach. This was where they had initially met. When they crossed it, he gestured her toward a rear door, which lead to a large showroom.

"This is beautiful," she exclaimed as they stepped into the softly lit hall and began scrutinizing the various objects on display. "You're a collector?"

"Of sorts," he replied, following her from a distance while he turned on the lights.

Huge sculptured nudes stood in the middle of the room. The walls were adorned with several period paintings as well as more modern murals, most, Lorelei noticed, on the theme of love. She examined each work with interest, noting Galen Kennedy's exceptional taste. Again confusion reigned in her mind, for she never would have pegged him as the romantic type. Not after his unemotional tryst with Vivian Gallagher.

His opportunistic and seemingly casual affair with a woman whose vanity was apparently surpassed only by the superficiality of her personality contrasted starkly with the depth revealed by the works he had collected.

Lorelei noticed a series of paintings of mermaids. One oil that was twice the size of the others captured her attention—a siren. The temptress's eyes were so gray, they were almost silver. Shivers ran down Lorelei's arms. She felt she was staring at herself. She looked up at Galen with a bewildered expression. He nodded in acknowledgment but said nothing.

They entered a second room containing several large paintings. She recognized them immediately. "So you're the private collector who owns these Klimts!" she exclaimed.

Her thesis had dealt with the Vienna Belle Époque, of which Gustav Klimt was an important part. "You must have spent a fortune on them!"

He watched her examine the last of the collection, for some reason feeling apologetic for being wealthy. "An acquaintance of ours was in a tight spot a few years back. He didn't want to borrow money from us, so he sold me some of the paintings he owned."

"Klimt was a very particular painter," she observed.

He surprised her again. "I agree. The nudity in his work is often quite aggressive." He touched the painting they were studying. "But I like his style. Very directed toward the unconscious. A lot like Freud." He paused, gazing at the painting. "Uncovering the secrets of the mind," he murmured.

Then he turned to her, his midnight eyes seeming to swallow her. "I wonder what secrets you have."

She looked at him, speechless, unable to answer.

He turned back to the painting. "Are you surprised I actually know something about art? You wouldn't be the first, so don't feel bad." He gestured her ahead.

"This is our French Quarter, so to speak," he explained as they stepped into a third room. "My mother prefers French impressionists, so we've given her gifts of them over the years. We keep them here so she's forced to come visit every once in a while."

"Nice 'gifts'," Lorelei mused. "Degas, Monet, Boudin," she recited as she passed each work.

At the end of the room Lorelei's gaze fell on a painting of a man and a woman lying naked on the sand, their legs entangled. The man, whose face was buried in the woman's hair, cupped one of her breasts and, with his other hand, her head. Her chin was resting on his shoulder, her eyes were closed and she had a faint smile on her lips—one of bliss.

The painting fascinated Lorelei. She squinted at the painter's signature, trying to read the scribble, then cleared her throat when she noticed Galen watching her.

"I don't recognize the name," she said.

"I bought it from a street vendor in Dublin. Do you like it?"

"It's very good. You did well to place it near the masters."

"Names don't mean anything if a work lacks substance."

What a surprising man he was turning out to be, Lorelei thought, almost with regret.

"So what do you think of it?" he asked.

"The artist captured a very intimate moment, one I almost feel guilty intruding upon."

"But you like it?" he softly repeated.

"I find it...disturbing. This kind of moment should remain private."

"Because it's a painting of two lovers?" He slowly stepped into her line of vision and looked intently into her eyes. "Because it's about surrender—the surrender of self and the merging of two souls?"

His lips were merely inches from her own. She felt her heart beating wildly in her chest. Just when she thought he was going to kiss her, he turned his gaze back toward the picture.

"It reflects a universal feeling," he said. "Perhaps this painting could complement your 'night of nights'."

She stepped away from him, uncertain.

Galen grinned at her reaction. Shy little thing, she was.

"Perhaps. I'll-I'll think about it." She stopped in front of a marble pedestal on which a large, ornate book rested.

"The *Kama Sutra*?"

"Yes."

She knew that the celebrated work consisted of medieval texts on the Hindu philosophy of lovemaking. She also knew that its contents were very explicit.

He noticed her hesitation. "Want to take a look? The miniatures are originals," he pointed out. "As a student of art history, you must be familiar with the work."

She arched her eyebrows. "How did you know my major?"

"Your doss— That is, it was in your *curriculum vitae*," he quickly corrected. "The one you handed in for the press office."

She kept looking at the huge volume on the pedestal but made no move to glance through it. Galen made the decision for her. "Several years ago I acquired the book at an auction. Allow me," he offered, standing behind her to open the book.

On the first page was a miniature engraving of a couple engaged in sex. The woman had her knees drawn up to the curves of her small breasts and her feet were nestled in the man's armpits. A wave of embarrassment swept over Lorelei.

On the right was a text in Hindi she couldn't read.

"The text beside the illustrations explains the various lovemaking techniques and the ways in which a man and a woman can find the deepest pleasure in each particular position." He turned the page for her. "I'll translate for you."

She snapped her head back, surprised. "You read Hindi?"

"Enough to get me through."

"Through what? You have business in India?"

"No, not directly. I learned the language for my university studies. I minored in philosophy. I also figured that to be a good businessman, knowing how to count to ten in a foreign language wasn't enough. You must understand the people you deal with—their politics, their religions, their philosophies."

She shook her head at how badly she had misjudged Galen Kennedy. "My compliments, then. I hear Hindi's a difficult language to learn."

"Thank you." He flipped some pages. "It's unfortunate that Western societies consider the *Kama Sutra* to be strictly erotic material. In fact, the leading philosophers wanted to educate the upper caste in all important disciplines." He paused at one depiction. "The book has more sociopolitical roots than one might think. Here, let's look through a few illustrations."

He pointed at the picture of a naked woman holding her buttocks with her palms, her thighs spread wide. "This position is called The Flower in Bloom. The man caresses the woman's breasts while she offers herself to him...like a flower in bloom."

He turned the page, casually capturing Lorelei's hand in his. "This is Aphrodite's Delight. The man penetrates the woman while she hooks her arms under her knees. As you can see, this position helps the man penetrate her more completely." The skin beneath his palm was so soft, Galen couldn't help but caress it with his thumb, drawing light circles.

He turned the page. Lorelei was struggling to maintain her composure. What would it feel like to have a man inside her, moving to the very gate of her womb? To have this man thrust himself into her slowly, thoroughly, penetrating her as in the illustration?

If she were to allow such a thing to happen, would she lose the last remnant of the fragile control she had on her life? A control she had struggled so hard to achieve? Would she forfeit the right to make her own choices?

"This one is called The Bud." Galen motioned, interrupting her thoughts. "It is yet another version of the woman's surrender. See how she draws her knees to her breasts and waits for him to come to her?"

The image of Lorelei clasping her knees to her breasts came to Galen's mind and his body instantly reacted. He stopped, taking a moment to regain his self-control. Her scent alone could make a eunuch harden.

He continued. "This one is referred to as The Quivering Kiss. The man's fingertips delicately squeeze her clitoris until it begins to swell. Then very, very slowly he kisses it as though he were sucking on her lower lip."

As Lorelei observed the depiction, Galen imagined doing it to her, nipping, biting and suckling until she rose against his mouth and climaxed. He resumed his explanations with only one idea in mind—taking Lorelei Duplessis. And soon.

"Here, as she offers herself to him, he separates the folds and lets his tongue gently probe her, using his lips and chin in a slow circling motion. That's why it's called The Circling

Tongue." He pointed to yet another picture. "This one is called The Lover's Noose. As you can see, the man boxes her thighs within his, his grip so hard, his penetration so complete, it makes the woman cry out from the pleasure."

His lips grazed her ear.

"Stop. I-I've...seen enough," she stammered.

He closed the book, gently turning her around. She might have seen enough but he hadn't. He would have her secrets, and together they would experience something beyond simple primal lust.

Her eyes remained fixed on his chest, so he lifted her chin with one finger. "There's nothing wrong with two people pleasuring each other, sharing their bodies, nurturing their souls." He rubbed her shoulders reassuringly. "There's nothing to be embarrassed about." He lowered his head and brushed his lips against hers—a light, quick kiss that gave her no time to react. Then he drew back a little to study her.

"Your shyness baffles me. You're like a child, yet you're a woman and a very beautiful one. I wonder if you realize just how much power you have."

"I...I have to leave. Thank you for the tour and—"

Without warning his mouth came down again on hers, harder this time, more demanding. He plundered and when she groaned, he swore and plunged his tongue deeper still, feasting, drinking, drowning.

Lorelei responded as if she had been born to it. All traces of guilt vanished as she offered her mouth to him, trying to give him what he was looking for, trying to give herself what she suddenly needed. Then she stiffened, realizing how much she had already given and what it would cost her if she continued. She brought her hands up to push him away.

Galen didn't insist. Instead he touched her lower lip with his thumb. "You can't think this was a mistake. Not after you kissed me back that way."

She couldn't look him in the eye, so she stared at the wall behind him. Why was he making her feel this way? Uncertain, vulnerable, wanting? Galen Kennedy was supposed to be calculating, arrogant, narcissistic. Vivian Gallagher suddenly popped into Lorelei's mind. How many times had he kissed the senator's wife the same way? Worse, how many meaningless affairs had he had over the years? Would she become just another notch on his belt if she allowed herself an intimate relationship with him?

Galen continued holding Lorelei, giving them both time to absorb the emotions their kiss had elicited. As he slid his hand down her left arm, he felt a ring on one of her fingers.

"Is there someone else?" he asked. "Are you married?" The notion of her with another man made him swallow hard.

Angry and scared, she looked away from him. "I have to go."

"Damn it, stop acting like a child and answer me!"

Her eyes narrowed. "No, I'm not married. There isn't anyone else."

"So what's the problem?" he insisted.

"Why can't you understand that I don't want you?"

"Because it's a lie," he countered. "Every time I touch you, you respond to me."

She pursed her lips. Her body might have betrayed her, the sex drive, after all, had no conscience. But he was the wrong person to desire. She had to get away from him before it was too late. "I kissed you back because I was curious. That's all. Now that my curiosity has been satisfied, I have no need for this to go any further."

"Of course. How ignorant of me to think otherwise."

He yanked her toward him until his mouth was glued to hers. He would prove she was lying. He slowly softened his kiss, plying her lips until she started responding, opening herself to him.

As much as she tried, Lorelei couldn't stop him or herself.

But he stepped back from her as abruptly as he had pulled her to him.

Confused, she confronted a dangerous glint in his eyes.

"I don't want to have a meaningless affair!" she cried. She turned to leave but his grip on her arm stopped her.

"You know that's not what it would be."

"It's all it could be."

"Why? Because of Vivian?" The matter with Vivian could be resolved quickly, he thought. He'd find another way to get the evidence he needed against Tom Gallagher.

She shook her head in denial. "There's that, of course."

"And there's something else. What is it?" he asked.

She sighed and faced him with all the resolve she had.

"I don't want to get involved with anyone. I can't."

"Why not?" he asked evenly, frustrated at her evasive answers.

She crossed her arms but said nothing.

"Why not?" he repeated, clasping her arms again, fighting off the urge to shake the answer out of her.

"I have plans, plans that don't include anyone but me."

"Such as?"

"They don't concern you. Look, I appreciate your interest but it's just a momentary physical attraction between us." The truth might hurt his feelings but she wouldn't give him less. "Even if I was to consider an affair, it wouldn't be with someone I don't trust."

His voice became dangerously soft. "What is it about me you don't trust?"

"I know you're having an affair with the senator's wife. How do I know you're not coming on to me just to compromise me into silence?" She waved a hand in the air. "Anyway, you and I come from different worlds. You're rich, politically connected, powerful. I'm not. You can have sex without even caring about the other person. I couldn't."

"Vivian is no longer an issue. I haven't been with her since I met you."

"And that's supposed to reassure me? I saw how you two treated each other. I will not become your next Vivian Gallagher."

She obviously needed meaning in a sexual relationship. She was afraid of him and her lack of trust was natural after what she had seen. He gently squeezed her arms.

"You're an obstinate bit of goods, aren't you? Don't for one minute compare yourself to Vivian. And I know that lovemaking is not just about technique. If you separate sex from love, then, yes, it can be crude. But when a man and a woman feel the need to go beyond words and candlelight dinners, there's nothing more natural and right than physical, intimate pleasure."

She tugged herself away from him and turned to leave.

"Wait. Why don't you borrow the book. You might be surprised at what you'll learn. There's nothing wrong with having needs or with fulfilling them."

After she put a safe distance between them, she turned around. He didn't seem to understand that her reluctance to get involved with him had little to do with sex. "You have no clue what my needs are, so I suspect you're more interested in fulfilling yours. Perhaps your little speech was meant to justify doing just that with your married mistress."

"I told you there was a reason for my being with Vivian, something that's beyond my control at the moment," he bit out.

She retraced her steps. "Let me give you a bit of advice, Kennedy. Vivian Gallagher more than likely cheats on her husband with great regularity, but I doubt she'd go so far as to jeopardize his political career, the career that ensures her financial security and entrée to the upper echelons of society, which she probably values even more than sexual satisfaction."

She advanced a little closer, pointing a finger at him.

"Now, since you're an intelligent man, most likely you've already figured that out yourself. Which means you must know that she'll be of no help to you in whatever scheme you claim justifies your behavior. And that brings me back to the distinct probability that you want to justify the affair to me because in the back of your mind you need to justify it to yourself."

She turned to leave, then stopped. "Although I'd love to see you get a nasty little lesson in the consequences of playing politics in a pool or a bedroom, I have more important things to do than inform the senator or the press about his wife's naughty extracurricular activities. So I give you my word that I'll keep silent but for my own reasons, not for the sake of preserving your undeserving reputations."

He threw her a thunderous glare. "I will eventually prove to you that my attentions to Vivian were necessary."

"You keep missing the point. I don't care if you prove anything. My life will never go in the same direction as yours!"

He walked to her. "Why not?" he demanded as he took her arms again. "Tell me!"

She pushed him away and ran out the door, confused and desperate. The past she had managed to put so neatly aside for the moment was now back in the forefront of her mind, threatening to overtake her again.

Galen stood where she had left him, fists clenched, filled with want, netted with worry. Despite her anger and her hurtful words, he could still see her inner pain and grief. If she could just give him—and herself—one chance, they could probably save each other.

He closed his eyes, an ironic smile on his lips. Damn. Was he falling in love with the little baggage already? Aye, he was afraid he was.

Chapter Ten

Know when to make things happen,

And when to let them happen…

❧

Lorelei ran all the way back to her hotel room—and all the way back to the day she made the decision that she would end her own life. She needed no interference, nothing and no one to stop her from doing what she had chosen to do.

She took a deep breath and forced herself to remember the day the police found her parents' car. It had been splattered with blood and other signs of foul play—the driver's side window broken, one of her mother's shoes on the floor on the passenger's side. But her parents' bodies were never found, nor any forensic evidence that could lead to their abductors.

Still, she knew. She had known all during those horrible months after their disappearance, before the police found the car, what had happened. She'd seen it all in a dream—a dream she'd had the night before her parents left. Three ski-masked, gloved, black-clad men forcing her mother and father out of their car and into a van. Her mother crying out in fear. Her father groaning at his helplessness, a knife at his throat. The last image she'd seen was the now dusty, damaged Lexus abandoned on the shoulder of a deserted country road.

And that, indeed, was where the police had found it.

She had seen it, a day before she had been warned, and not been able to stop it.

All that was left was in an impoundment lot, the only place she could call her parents' grave.

The police had quickly dismissed outright kidnapping as a motive—no ransom demands emerged and the family was hardly wealthy. Their best theories linked the carjackers to an armored-truck robbery, which had taken place in the vicinity. But their search for her parents' bodies had proved fruitless.

Yet her dream still haunted her. She'd had such dreams before that had proved to be prophetic but only a handful of them and her practical-minded parents had never put any stock in them, chalking them up to coincidence, nothing more. Knowing what they'd say, how they'd gently brush her worries aside, she hadn't even bothered to mention that, in her sleep, she'd seen them being abducted and probably murdered. She'd said goodbye to them with hugs and kisses, and she'd kept her anxiety to herself.

When they failed to call that night from their destination, she'd known immediately what had happened. And since that moment she had never stopped blaming herself for their deaths.

Finally she had concluded that the best—the only—way to put closure to her grief and guilt was to plan her own death. And at least that way she wouldn't have to be some modern-day Cassandra, doomed to "see" and predict dire events that no one would believe in or benefit from.

She marched to the bathroom, intending to shower, then face what was left of her future and make it count. For when her affairs were settled, she vowed to face death head-on—nothing and no relationship would stop her. As for this momentary, uncontrollable attraction she felt toward Galen Kennedy...well, if need be she'd face that too. She would stop running from it.

When she flicked the light switch, the bathroom remained dark. As she stepped back into the bedroom, she found a typewritten note by the phone informing her that, due to an electrical problem in her unit, they'd had to shut off the power. They invited her to go down to the front desk so that she would be assigned a new room.

Half an hour later, with a change of clothes and some toiletries for the shower she was planning to take after her swim at the pool, she was escorted to a luxurious presidential suite, compliments of the managing director. He had also added that her luggage would be delivered to her later and the suite would be hers until the competition ended.

But when the bell boy lead her through the brass engraved doors, Lorelei all but gasped at the wall-to-wall Persian carpets, the Carrara marble fireplace in black and pink colored tones and the gold brocade drapes adorning huge bay windows. This was the most beautiful hotel suite she had ever been in. Her eyes continued skimming the large living room, noticing how the tiny drops of crystals from the candelabra shone on the mahogany furniture. Suddenly however her smile all but faded. Several Klimt paintings hung on the wall, and without checking, she was sure they were not reproductions. This suite had Galen Kennedy's name written all over it.

By the time she turned around to tell the bell boy she would not be staying, he had already and discreetly left. So she looked for a phone and called the front desk to tell them she would be returning to her own room. A cold shower sounded better than having to owe the Kennedys any favors. The clerk however was adamant that she stay there at least until the electricians left her room and repaired the wiring. He all but hung the phone up on her. Too tired to argue she tried Annabelle and Maurice's room, but they were nowhere to be found. Resigned and in bad needed of a shower, Lorelei resolutely decided to use the amenities of the luxurious suite after all and then leave.

The bathroom was little short of enormous, with a glorious, blue and gold mosaic pool rather than a tub, equipped with brass fixtures and Jacuzzi jets. Lorelei sat down on the edge and ran her hand along the mosaic designs and pictured herself soaking in perfumed scented water. A bath was beginning to sound much better to her than a shower.

A few minutes later she began running the water, watching the Greek designs of sirens and ancient mariners seem to come to life in the mosaics. She undressed and let her clothes pool at her feet. And somehow, naked in this plush environment, she was aware for the first time in a long time that she was a woman. The depictions of the *Kama Sutra* flooded back into her mind, as did the unprecedented thought that she could be one of those women, attracting a man, driving him to distraction, the ravages of her past and her long illness visible only on the inside.

Before stepping into the water, she tested the temperature with her fingers, for some reason recalling the texture of Galen Kennedy's skin against hers. She knew she would remember him for whatever remained of her life.

The phone unit on the wall suddenly rang and startled her out of her *reverie*. Maurice was on the other end and she deduced they had forwarded her calls to the suite. He told her that he had been informed that the kitchens would not be available that evening for their team to begin preparations and that they had been postponed to the following morning. *Repose toi* he had said and suggested she rest for the day ahead.

Muttering at the inconvenience, she sank nevertheless into the bubbles of the bath gel she had poured in, letting the warm water caress her skin. Then she attempted to turn her thoughts to the dinner her team would present. Focusing on work always gave her peace of mind. There she created, there she shared, there her life seemed to progress.

As she soaped her legs, she heard music begin to play in the next room. She recognized the voice of Loreena McKennitt and a song from *The Book Of Secrets*.

"Who's there?" she called out, alarmed.

Barefoot, in a pair of white jeans and T-shirt, Galen Kennedy appeared in the bathroom doorway, holding a glass of sparkling wine, his face unshaven, his hair disheveled.

Her heart skipped several beats. "What are you doing here?"

Ignoring her question, he looked at his glass, twirling it by the stem. "I tried, Lorelei. God knows I did."

He took a swallow of wine but still wouldn't look at her. "You're much like this wine, you know," he said. "Its bubbles both soothe and stir the senses. You taste it and you want more. You want to satisfy those senses so badly it hurts."

His gaze met hers, intense, dangerous, heated. "I want you," he whispered. "Aye, I do."

In the living room the music was still playing. It was a harem dance — a love song for one, enslavement for the other.

It was hypnotic.

Lorelei saw the ache in Galen's eyes as he clutched the crystal wineglass. She saw his wanting, the self-control he was trying desperately to maintain.

"If you ask me to leave, I will," he said. "But you've got to say it now, because I won't give you another chance."

One day she would look back at what she did then and wonder why it seemed that the moment had come to embrace her future, to run toward it instead of away from it.

She stood up slowly, keeping her hands at her sides, her eyes never leaving his, her chest heaving every time she breathed. Galen watched a droplet of water slowly make its way down her neck to one breast, tripping over the rise, stopping motionless on her nipple as if it were milk ready to be captured and tasted.

"Jesus," was all he could say. She was offering herself to him like Aphrodite and his eyes feasted on her.

With a slight tremor in his hands, he put his glass down on the vanity, then advanced toward her. "Are you sure?" he asked, hesitating by the side of the tub, his voice raw with desire as he tried to grasp that she was actually making the commitment. He waited for a no. It seemed an eternity passed before he realized none would come. As painfully aroused as he was, he still wanted the choice to be hers. "I'll give you everything you need. I'll make you forget the past. But by God, I'll take everything you have."

She wanted to speak but couldn't. She wanted to tell him that she had never done anything like this before, that it wouldn't amount to anything other than this once and that she was afraid. But words failed her. Her mind was filled with only one purpose—to answer the need, their need.

He stepped into the tub fully dressed, determined and delirious with desire. He took her face between his hands, aware that she was trembling. He was a big man, a strong one. Yet he felt weak and humbled as she stood before him, offering the gift of herself.

"You know I can't let you go now." Now or ever, he vowed silently as he brought his lips to hers. He felt their texture, plied them, played with them until she molded them to his, following his rhythm. Slowly kissed her until she stopped trembling, until she gave herself up to him. He breathed his own life into her with an aching moan.

She followed his lead, reassured by his calm ministrations. She realized it was wrong to choose a man who was not of her world, a man with a past she didn't know and a present she couldn't even begin to understand or accept. But she also realized that whatever lay ahead would remain beyond her reach if she didn't face him and whatever there was between them.

He stepped back and removed his T-shirt. She was mesmerized by the breadth of his chest. She had seen it bare once before but this was different. This time it was for her.

His arms went around her while he kissed her neck, his lips and teeth sinking into her flesh. Moments later he brought their foreheads together, his breathing labored.

"Unbutton my jeans," he said in a barely controlled voice.

Once naked, when his skin finally touched hers, he took her mouth again, asking entrance, communing with her body, begging to know what it was that drew him to her, that made him want her—and so desperately wanting her to want him too.

She kissed him, overwhelmed, placing a hand on his chest to feel his heartbeat. It was strong and fast, even faster when she reached down to touch his thigh, caressing his body as he was caressing hers.

"God Almighty, Lorelei, I don't know how long I can hold out." He pulled away, long enough to look at her, to find that her eyes had darkened with her own want and need.

He could see the flow of her emotions, the passion and the courage to acknowledge it.

He knelt down, aiming for the taste of her, that scent that had bewitched him from the first moment he met her. Finally, finally his mouth delved into her.

The Circling Tongue, Lorelei remembered from that afternoon. She stiffened at first, feeling vulnerable and violated. But ultimately she gave in to his need because it was much like her own, to know him, to know pleasure, to think with the body rather than the mind.

She fisted her hands in his long hair, clenching and unclenching her fingers as he suckled her. "Galen," she moaned.

It was the first time she had called him by name. It aroused him, fanned his need. He took it all in, her scent, her taste, her climax. He had imagined it, fantasized about it but never had his thoughts included this desperate desire to possess her—not merely her body but her, the woman whose emotions were kept well beyond anyone's reach. He would make her forget her past, whatever pain it was that haunted her.

And she would make him forget. Make him whole again.

"Take me inside you," he said in a ragged voice, standing up and lifting her out of the water and onto him. Her legs instinctively wrapped around him while her hands buried themselves in his hair. Her mouth fused with his as he leaned her against the tiles, guided his erection to her wide-open entrance and, in one hard thrust, buried himself inside her.

Her cry of pain came at the same instant as his own stunned gasp. Christ Almighty, she was a virgin—or had been until he'd plowed into her.

He went completely still, clamping down hard on his body's instinctive need to keep pumping in and out of her, as he murmured soothing noises and waited for some sign that the pain he'd caused her had eased. He didn't know what shocked him more—that she'd never been with a man or that she'd chosen him to be her first. Regardless, he felt an odd kind of pleasure at being given that which she had given to no one else. Indeed, the mere thought that no other man had been inside her or felt the hot, tight, velvet-slick passage that was quivering around his shaft was nearly enough to make him come then and there.

"I'm sorry," he whispered against her neck. "I didn't mean to hurt you. I didn't know..."

"It's," she sucked in a quick breath, "it's all right."

Yet her silent tears still burned his cheek. "Shh, baby," he said softly. "Let your body get used to mine." Then he kissed her again, sliding his tongue into her mouth, matching the slow rhythm of his cautious, gentle thrusts. She clenched her thighs more tightly around his waist and a minute later he felt her inner muscles clamp around him.

When her hips began moving with his, he lost any semblance of control. Burying his face against her silken skin, he drove into her, pumping again and again, filling her completely, crying out in Gaelic as he spilled himself inside her.

Lorelei felt the heat of Galen's body radiating into her. Blood pounded in her head and deep inside her where she sheathed his hard male flesh. His face was nestled in her neck, his arms, bulging with muscles and unyielding, holding her to him, maintaining the link that now made her part of him. Somehow he had erased the distance, the space, that for so long had separated her from others and from life itself. That dark place that had taken her close to dying.

She felt him shudder and she opened her eyes and touched his cheek. Was that a tear running down his face?

Then she saw his eyes. Minutes before she had seen heat and hunger in them. Hunger for her. Now that heat had seeped away. His eyes were suddenly pools of darkness, drained of hunger, oddly remote, devoid of expression. He was no longer there with her, closer than close but somewhere else, somewhere black and awful and lifeless. Why had he left her? Where had he gone?

"What-what is it?" she whispered.

But he continued staring, as if haunted by a loneliness and anguish much like her own.

Holding Lorelei, touching her, tasting her, penetrating her, Galen had soared to peaks of pleasure unlike any he had experienced. In the aftermath, his unprecedented passion spent, he felt humbled once more, unworthy of such a gift.

And unworthy he was. Bryan Coyle's face abruptly appeared in his mind, his blood spurting out until it turned into a trickle, taking the life right out of him. Bryan, his kin, his brother-in-law, the man he had killed. A part of Galen—and all of Brenna's love for him—had died that day too.

"No!" Lorelei cried out. "No," she repeated more softly when she saw the agony in Galen's eyes. "Just give it up. Give it away. Don't hold on to it." She shook his shoulders and held his face between her hands, looking for some sign of acknowledgment. "Give it to me. Give me your pain!" she cried, more frantic now, nipping his lips, crushing her mouth to his, trying to steal his nightmare away.

Somehow, when Lorelei tightened her legs around him and pressed her breasts against his chest, Galen's ghosts began to fade. He came back to her, to that voice that soothed and stirred him. Hard again, he began moving inside her, until he was grinding himself into her, pressing her to the wall, pounding and pounding until he couldn't tell himself apart from her, until his vision blurred from the burst of light that blinded him when he released himself inside her again.

With his mouth buried in her hair, he inhaled her scent for several long minutes, remembering the only other time he had felt this close to someone, remembering the pain and the torment that had followed.

This time, however, was different.

This time had brought something else.

He stepped out of the tub with Lorelei in his arms and carried her into the bedroom. He lowered her onto the bed, careful not to break their link. He was still inside her and he was afraid.

How many times he had been afraid someone would see how far his guilt and remorse had taken him, how far down they had pulled him, how close the end of his life had come, to a death wish he had never had the courage to act upon. How many nights he had lain sleepless, dreading the next day, dreading facing himself again after killing a man and destroying a second life in the process.

This woman, who still held him, had somehow seen and understood where he had been. This woman still cradled him to her, afraid he would not come back from that dark place. And she had cried for him, begging to take away his pain.

It could mean only one thing. She had been there herself, in that place where slipping into the nothingness from which one was born became preferable to having to feel and fight the sense of deprivation that came from losing pieces of oneself.

And maybe she was still there, waiting.

The nerves in his stomach clenched and a second of panic passed through him. What if she was waiting to...die? Frantically he wondered what in God's name he could do to stop her.

But before he had the chance to ask her, she gently rolled him off her and climbed on top of him. Tears were streaming down her face when she kissed him. When he tasted the warm, salty drops, he couldn't stop his own from flowing.

She looked at him and smiled.

"Sometimes," she began gently, "when you're sad enough and troubled enough that you almost want to die, you're not necessarily looking for the easy way out. Sometimes you're just impossibly weary from fighting the pain, from worrying that you're bringing everyone around down with you and dying seems like the only thing left to do to save your soul and avoid slipping into madness."

Though a novice herself, she wanted to show him how love could heal. Her uncle's love, Maurice's and Annabelle's, had healed her enough to come as far as she had. Her recovery might never be complete but beneath her lay a tortured soul desperate for peace, for whatever would ease the terrible sorrow he seemed to be carrying and she had to try to help him.

Not really knowing how to begin, she instinctively lowered her lips to his nipples, laving them one at a time, circling them with her tongue, then suckling him until he groaned and clenched his hands around the sheets. She lowered her lips to his navel, then lower still, to the most private part of him, her tongue teasing him over and over again until he pulled gently at her hair, motioning her to stop. She responded by taking him into her mouth, tentatively at first, fighting her awkwardness until she drove him totally out of control. For the first time in her life she didn't care where she was going or how it would end. She wanted to love this man and give him all she had. She wanted to know the pleasure of healing.

Galen had never needed anyone the way he needed Lorelei at that moment, when letting go of his self-control was, for once, more important than hanging on to it. "Take me, Lorelei," he groaned. "Take me away with you."

She seemed to understand. She placed her hands on his shoulders, straddling him, sheathing his sex with hers, moving her hips up and down until he quickly reversed their positions, covering her with his body and began making love to her again, this time slowly, not as frantically as before.

His mouth was sensual and soft. Lorelei was hypnotized by his tenderness. She understood that he wanted to give back to her all he had taken so greedily before.

She came again with him, cradled under his chest, her eyes gazing into his, searching for explanations though none were really necessary.

"You were mourning something," she whispered a while later as she lay, sated, in his arms.

Normally he would have balked at such a statement, but with her he felt at peace, able, finally, to begin to talk about it. "I was not mourning something but someone." He paused, searching for the words that had always been so hard to speak. "Long ago I loved a woman much like you. We experienced...an incredible closeness. It's gone now."

He stroked her temple. "She's gone too. But somehow you've brought the feeling back." He kissed her hair and closed his eyes. It was all he would say for now, all he could say.

So, he had been deeply in love once, Lorelei mused. Although she felt an inexplicable wave of jealousy, she also felt relieved. He was not the shallow, superficial man she had thought him to be, or at least he had not always been. Like her, he had once been vulnerable and brought down low, so low he had probably, as she'd guessed, wanted to die. But he had chosen to continue living, perhaps without feeling anything at all.

Sensing he did not want to say more, Lorelei caressed his cheek and kissed it, letting him know she would respect his privacy. For now.

Chapter Eleven

Sex often renders love unnecessary, while love always gives meaning to sex.

೧೮

They fell asleep tangled in each other's limbs, replete from their lovemaking. Some time later Galen awoke, feeling oddly chilly. When he opened his eyes, he realized Lorelei was gone. He sat up, then bolted out of bed, assuring himself he had not dreamed their incredible encounter. He saw light filtering out from beneath the bathroom door and he stalked toward it and turned the knob. The door was locked.

For a gut-wrenching moment he pictured Lorelei lying lifeless in the tub, wrists bloody, sightless eyes staring blindly up at him. He banged on the door, preparing to kick it in.

The door opened and he faced Lorelei, who was clutching a hotel robe around her and frowning.

"What's wrong? Do you need to use the bathroom?" she asked.

He took a deep breath, waiting for his heart to calm down, fighting the urge to shake the life right out of her for scaring him. "Don't you ever lock a door against me—do you understand?"

"No, I don't understand. This is the washroom!" she exclaimed, trying to shut the door on him.

He blocked her with the palm of one hand, trying to banish the horrific image that had flashed into his mind.

"You will trust me to respect your privacy, not force me to," he said. "Now come back to bed." He walked away, staggered at how he had reacted yet unwilling to apologize for his behavior.

She stared at his back, shocked and baffled. "I'm going back to my old room," she declared. She quickly yanked her clothes on, then headed for the door.

For a big man, Galen could sure move fast.

In an instant he was at her side.

"I don't want you to leave," he said softly.

"Too bad, because I am."

He stroked her arm and pushed back a strand of her hair. "Look, I'm sorry I overreacted. I don't know what came over me." He started to unfasten her jeans.

She put her hands on his forearms. "Stop."

"I can't. I want to be inside you. Now." His hands were already pushing her jeans all the way off and he went down on his knees. He looked up into her eyes, silently asking her to trust him.

He would take—she was sure he would—but he also wanted her to give. She closed her eyes in assent. A faint smile touched his lips as he slowly glided his tongue over her, igniting heat in its wake. Lorelei didn't think her legs would hold her up.

"I want us to come together this time," he said, pulling her down to the thick carpet until she was on her hands and knees. When he positioned himself behind her, she let out a soft cry of alarm.

"It won't hurt. You'll just come harder and so will I."

He leaned on her back, caressing her with his left hand. With his right hand under her blouse, he held one of her breasts and began pushing himself inside her. Moments later he plunged in and out in an unyielding rhythm as she held on for dear life. "Come with me, love. Come."

As if her body had a will of its own, at his words she climaxed so hard and so long that she saw stars in front of her eyes. Galen shuddered with her, then collapsed on top of her. This was more than he'd had even with Brenna, he thought. This was inebriation of the body and the soul. His desire to possess Lorelei was so strong, it was almost unquenchable. And he was afraid he would lose her.

* * * * *

Dawn was silently spreading its pale light as Lorelei slowly opened her eyes. She had slept a few hours, she thought. She couldn't remember. But she could smell memories of the previous night, hints of sandalwood, citrus, and pine—of Galen Kennedy and the scent that was so particularly his. However sated she now felt, with the rising sun came cold and cruel apprehension. They had used no birth control. What if she became pregnant?

Galen's arm across her body felt heavy as she came fully awake. How was he going to react to her today, with testosterone no longer ruling his mind? Lorelei slowly moved out from under his biceps, sliding from the king-sized bed.

Once she was in the living room, she began searching for her clothes, trembling. She tried to remember when her period was due. *God, what have I done?* she thought, distraught.

"Are you looking for these?" Galen's voice interrupted her search.

She looked behind her and saw him leaning on the bedroom doorjamb, holding her panties. "I didn't want to wake you. I have to be in the kitchens soon," she said warily as she approached him.

"You're making excuses," he said as she reached for what he held in his hand. He frowned. "Why are you trembling?" He dropped his arms to her waist. "What's wrong?"

The red of embarrassment flooded her face. "I'm...I'm not on any birth control."

He stared at her, then pulled her to his chest and tightened his arms around her, smiling. The thought of his child growing within her warmed him, despite their current circumstances, despite what his life had been, despite his sorrow. "Don't worry about that," he answered reassuringly, while the image of her pregnant aroused him.

"It may have been my first time, but I'm not that ignorant." Pushing slightly away from him she looked straight into his eyes.

What should he tell her, that he would welcome a child from her? She'd think him crazy. Maybe he was, he thought smiling to himself. Having a child with a woman he barely knew? He knew it was dangerously irresponsible yet, the idea didn't scare him as it would under normal circumstances. But Galen decided he'd analyze what it meant later. For now, all he felt was his desire growing for the little French chef. "I didn't imply that you were. It's just that your chances of getting pregnant the first time you have sex are very slim. I'll pull out early the next time. We'll be safer."

As if on cue, she felt his sex jutting against her and backed away. He knew what she was wondering and he answered her unasked question. "Oh, yes, I'm hard." He placed a hand on the back of her neck, forcing her to come even closer. "Indulge me, siren," he added. As was his nature, he gave her no choice. He kissed her hungrily, erotically, as if it were the first time.

Lorelei knew then that she would never be able to control her response to Galen, never be able to refuse him. Somehow she thought he knew that too—and didn't care if that was the only way to have her. Why her, though? She was nothing like Vivian or the kind of women he was doubtless used to, the ones with perfect bodies, powerful families and lavish bank accounts. She was far from appealing in any conventional way and before last night she'd had precious little sexual experience. She was a struggling businesswoman from a middle-class family, dependent on herself to survive.

Galen carried Lorelei back to bed like a child who had wandered off, as if it was the most natural thing to do. She had truly bewitched him. He couldn't bring himself to let go of her even for a few hours. Once more he wanted to taste her, to take possession of her body. Once again his obsession with her was taking control of him.

An hour later Lorelei was sleeping soundly when Galen awoke to a light tapping on the bedroom door. He got up like a shot, silently opened the door on Justin, then closed it softly behind him to join his brother in the living room.

Justin frowned at Galen's nakedness. "Who's in there? Vivian?" he whispered.

"No," Galen stated flatly.

"No? Then who?" Justin asked, not bothering to hide his irritation.

Galen had never lied to Justin before and wouldn't start now, even if he didn't think his brother would react well to the news. "Lorelei Duplessis."

His brother paused for a moment, taking that in. "I see," he said and he advanced toward his brother like a tiger ready to pounce.

Galen met him with a hooded stare, his eyes dark, narrow slits. He knew his brother—better to take him on than try to make him back down.

"You never could resist an easy ride, could you?" Justin snarled, stopping less than a breath away from him. "Not even when you know how close we are to reaching our goal."

Justin turned away, raking a hand through his loose black hair. "For Christ's sake, she's in the competition! I bet you didn't even think about that!" Furious, he turned to face him again. "Was she worth the lay, at least?"

With unfamiliar hostility Galen grabbed his brother by the shoulders and slammed him into a wall. "Don't you ever talk about her that way!"

Clearly shocked, Justin didn't attempt to retaliate. "How should I talk about her? You barely know the woman and she certainly doesn't look like your type. She looks—" He cut himself off, then paused, his gaze assessing his brother. "It's because of Brenna, isn't it?"

"That she reminds me of her has nothing to do with it," Galen replied, although his tone was uncertain.

"Are you telling me that—or trying to convince yourself?"

He let go of Justin, frustrated. "She's nothing like Brenna, except—" Galen started to pace the room, picking up a bracelet Lorelei had left on the windowsill, turning it in his hand, then closing it in his fist, trying to contain it the way he wanted to contain her.

"Except what?" Justin asked, concerned.

Galen stopped to stare out the window, looking to answer his brother the same way he had been trying to answer the question for himself. "Except that she gives me a sense of peace. As if Brenna never happened, as if the past didn't matter. She reminds me of the way I lived before everything fell apart. The way I was before I killed Bryan. Before I lost Brenna," he added in a murmur.

Justin closed the distance between them and laid a hand on his brother's shoulder. "Galen, listen to me. She's not Brenna and she can't bring Brenna or your old life back. What's more, she can't give you the forgiveness you seek. You must see her for herself. She's a woman from Canada who's going to leave here in a few days to go back to her own life and probably to her own man."

"She doesn't have a man. I was her first."

Justin snorted. "Come on, no woman her age with those looks is still a virgin. Doesn't she wear a ring on her left hand? She's probably married, damn it!"

Galen looked at Justin, incredulous. "Are you listening? Until last night she was a virgin." He turned away again, this time heading for the liquor cabinet, remembering the pressure he'd felt when he penetrated her the first time, the blood trickling down his leg. "And furthermore, I'm aware of who she is and what she's doing here. But it doesn't matter. I'm through denying myself the pleasure of being with someone who turns me on and makes me glad to be alive. So spare me the lecture and be happy I found someone worth hanging on to."

Justin looked at him with understanding and compassion, neither of which Galen wanted at that moment.

After a brief silence Galen offered his brother a glass of Glennfiddich, hoping to steer the conversation away from Brenna and the past. "Did you find out anything new about my little Canadian chef?"

Justin hesitated. "She has a house in the Montreal suburbs, which she appears to own with a guy by the name of Marc Delage."

Uneasy, Galen struggled to remain calm. "Maybe he's a relative. He can't be her lover."

"Couldn't you have been mistaken about her? In the heat of the moment? Let's face it, you don't have much experience with virgins." He paused, meeting his brother's glacial stare. "Okay, so you weren't mistaken. Delage could be a relative or a creditor, maybe the man who sold the house to her. All the papers are in French, Galen. Sam didn't understand much, so the guy could be almost anyone."

"He could also be none of your goddamned business, gentlemen."

Neither one of them had heard or seen Lorelei emerge from the bedroom, clutching a sheet around her. Both men turned to stare at her.

Galen was the first to speak. "I'll see you later, Justin."

His brother could not take his eyes off Lorelei, however. "I said later, Justin," Galen repeated dryly.

Justin swore in Gaelic, slowly tearing his gaze away from Lorelei. "Good luck, brother," he muttered and he left the room.

Galen looked at Lorelei, feeling her anger and seeing it in the way she gripped the sheet covering her. With only a nightlight shining behind her, her face was but a shadow, with the exception of her silver eyes.

He moved to stand in front of her, wrapping his fingers over hers where she held the sheet that was barely covering her breasts. "Are you always so beautiful when you're angry?"

"Don't patronize me, Kennedy."

Her use of his last name lashed him like a whip. "Then who the hell is Marc Delage?" he asked, tightening his hold on her hand.

"None of your business."

"As of last night, any man close to you is my business — my goddamned business," he specified.

"What happened last night gives you no rights over me, so drop the attitude." She tried to push past him but his body blocked her like a brick wall. "Move. I have to get dressed."

"Are you married to him?"

"Since when did a woman's marital status make any difference to you?"

Furious, he yanked her toward him. "I explained to you that Vivian doesn't mean a thing to me."

"Changing the subject won't help. How dare you pry into my personal life? How dare you discuss me with your brother as if you owned me? Now let me go, or, so help me God, I'll scream!"

"Go ahead. I own this place, remember?" He lowered his voice, trying to calm her down. "Will you hear me out?"

She shook her head, smiling grimly. "You still want information you can blackmail me into silence with?" She poked at his chest with her free hand. "Okay, I'll give you information. I'll give you all the information you want. What's it to me, anyway? One more taker, one more man out to use me — what difference does it make?"

"You still think I want to blackmail you, for Christ's sake?"

"Probably. I was simply a 'means to an end'!" she shouted.

"A means to an end?" he barked angrily.

"Yes! Even after I promised you I wouldn't, you didn't trust me not to publicize your affair with Senator Gallagher's wife. Having sex with me was a pretext to buy my silence!"

"To buy your silence." He frowned, wondering how he could make her understand the enormity of the feelings he had for her. He could never blackmail her—unless it was the only way to keep her. "Actually, in your scenario I'd be blackmailing myself," he said. "I've just compromised my life beyond salvation with you and you think I did this to buy your silence? I let you wrestle from me all that I've fought for years to forget. I let you take over my thoughts, my body. You made me cross lines I swore never to cross again. You reached inside my soul and made me afraid of dying, of not being able to be whole again without you. You have just come between my brother and me. All this in a matter of hours. And you say I'm in it just to blackmail you, to buy your silence?"

With trembling hands he wrenched the sheet from her body and began to kiss her savagely, angry at himself for making her cry, for scaring her. Still, he pushed her backward toward the sofa. He yanked her down to sit, then lowered himself to straddle her, enveloping her legs with his thighs. The Lover's Noose, he recalled just before driving himself inside her like an animal struggling to subdue its prey. Gradually he slowed himself down, becoming once more a man seeking to bond, to join, to be at one with his mate.

She closed her eyes and turned her face away from his gaze. "No, no, you can't. I can take so much but no more," she moaned.

He moved slowly in and out of her. "Yes, you can, Lorelei. Look at me." He stopped and forced her to look at him. "Look at me."

She raised her eyes slowly, hypnotized by his plea.

"There's nothing left in me except you, Lorelei."

His words undid her. Her body surrendered once again, making him climax harder than he ever had.

Some time later, he gently stroked her face. "Do you have any regrets?" he asked quietly. She had given him her virginity and he'd never thought that could mean so much to him. He wanted confirmation that she had given herself to him freely. He needed to know she had truly chosen him.

Lorelei frowned. "Why? Do you?"

He looked down at her, perplexed that she would ask such a question after everything he'd told her and the way he had made love to her. "Answer the question without asking another question," he said.

She stared at him for a moment. "No, I don't. If I had regrets, it would mean I wasn't willing to take responsibility for my actions. And that would mean I was a coward, which I'm not."

He lifted her chin up. "Is it so hard for you to admit that you liked making love with me without making it a philosophical issue?" he teased. Receiving no response, he mused aloud, "I guess so."

"You must have regrets, Kennedy, or you wouldn't have asked the question."

He shook his head. He hated when she used his last name. "Regrets? How could I have any, when I still want you?" He tugged her hand to his groin as evidence. "But I can wait a few minutes. I want to explain some things first."

She remembered Justin's visit. "Such as why you're investigating me and prying into my personal life?" She sat up, getting angrier by the minute. "Don't bother with the explanations. Nothing you can say will change anything anyway."

His hand closed around her wrist like a vise. "Where do you think you're going?"

She looked down at his hand disapprovingly. "Let me go."

"Not before we talk."

She knew trying to leave was useless. "Go ahead. I have nothing to say." She leaned back and crossed her arms.

"Good, although I can't imagine you with nothing to say." He sat up too. "As a rule Justin and I investigate everyone we get involved with on any level, so don't take it personally. It's just something our family has to do." He couldn't speak about the violence and the war that was affecting his company's operations, nor about his recent suspicions of arms traffickers in his midst but the time would come—soon, he hoped—when he could explain it all to her.

"You mean rich families like yours, don't you? Because the ground you walk on is not the same as the rest of the world's?" she retorted sarcastically.

"It's not like that."

"The hell it isn't. *Me prends-tu pour une imbécile?*" she added in French. "You want to make sure my family lineage is politically correct? Well, let me save you the trouble of investigating. There's nothing politically correct about me or my family. My father was born to a middle-class family, was a high school teacher and a member of le Parti Québecois. He staunchly fought for the survival of French culture in Canada. Moreover, he was a separatist and he hated the English."

Galen smiled, amused at the way she defended her family. He liked that. "And you think I care about the fact that your father, although right to fight for his heritage but misguided about how best to protect it, was a politically involved man from a middle-class family?"

She leaned over and pointed a finger at him. "More than he hated the English, my father disliked the rich, especially those born into money who think they're better than anyone else, when in reality they wouldn't survive an hour without their family's money."

"So do you hate me because I'm Irish or because I'm rich? Or maybe both?" He reached for her chin and waited for her answer.

"You figure it out," she answered defiantly.

"What I figure is that you don't hate me at all. You never would have given me your virginity if you did." He put two fingers on her lips, signaling her to remain silent. "No, don't, because there's no way you can deny it, even if you tried. Besides, we're getting off the subject." He got on his knees to face her, straddling her again, taking her hands in his.

"I looked into your background for two reasons. First because you're a contestant in the culinary competition and you know as well as I do that that's a high-profile event. The profits all go to the Feed the World Foundation. There's a lot of money involved and everyone has to be clean. If you read the rules and conditions on your entry form, you'd know that you gave us permission to investigate you."

"What has my house got to do with that?"

"Nothing. It's just information we stumbled on, way back when I was trying to find out if you were a reporter—"

"Who could blackmail you," she finished furiously, remembering that he was having an affair with a married woman. "Pray tell, what was the second reason?"

He gritted his teeth. "That was it."

She turned her anger into a sarcastic smile. "So, to protect a woman you say you don't care for and an affair you say means nothing to you, you pry into my personal life, invade my privacy so that you can have something on me if—"

"Stop it!" he shouted. His mouth bore down on hers, grinding her lips beneath his. "Just stop it," he said more softly as he noticed the sheen in her eyes. "You can't believe I would do that, not after all this."

"It doesn't matter what I believe. All that matters is what is."

He licked a tear that slid down her cheek. "I haven't been with Vivian or any other woman since I met you and I give you my word I won't be."

"I appreciate the effort but it won't be necessary."

He arched his eyebrows. "It won't be necessary?"

"Look, you and I come from different worlds. Everything you do is measured in terms of business and politics. I explained to you where I come from. The two backgrounds, the ones that made us who we are, are irreconcilable. Besides, we shouldn't start something we can't finish."

"We, or just you?" he responded with caution.

She looked away from him. "I also think neither one of us is really prepared to acknowledge just what happened between us."

Although he had the feeling her answer would upset him, he asked just the same. "And what would that be?"

"You're reliving something you lost, while I'm experiencing something I never had. So let's just enjoy the next few days and take them for what they are, with no illusions about the future."

Something in her eyes bothered him. Something she was not saying, something that had nothing to do with her spoken protests. Something that haunted her. "You know what I think? I think you're scared to get involved with me but not for the reasons you say."

Her face went pale. "It doesn't matter why. I told you already. Our lives are going different directions and, yes, I won't start something I can't finish."

There was no fear in her voice when she spoke about the future, no fear at all, as if she knew precisely where and when she was going. It worried him now that he suspected her very life might hang in the balance. "And which direction would your life be taking?"

"A very different one from yours," was all she said.

Damn it! Say it! Why don't you just say what you're planning to do? he fumed inwardly while he tried to remain calm. He had to find a way to convince her to remain with him, because he couldn't, just couldn't, consider letting her walk away from him in a few days' time, perhaps to seek the oblivion she was careful not to mention.

"Right now our lives are going in the same direction, and that's all that counts. We're involved in a way that matters." He touched her cheek. "So let's both take the risk, because we've already taken the first step." He lowered his lips to hers in a gentle kiss.

I can't, she answered silently. How could she tell someone that she needed to be free to choose the moment to end her life? That the freedom to do that gave meaning to her existence, gave her back the sense of control she'd lost in living?

"Hey, where were you?" he interrupted, concerned. "Listen," he said, putting his arms around her, "let's just take it one day at a time, okay?"

"Fine but right now your body thinks I'm her, the one you lost. Believe me, in a few days, when I leave here, you'll wake up from this trance and see me for who I am—not her but Lorelei Duplessis, someone you barely know and who will hardly matter in the grand scheme of things. And even if I'm wrong, I can't ignore your relationship with Vivian Gallagher, no matter how much you try to justify it and no matter how much I try to forget it."

"She has nothing to do with you and you know that. You saw me with her. Did I behave remotely the same way with her as I do with you?"

She gently pulled away from him. "There are too many obstacles between us, Galen and what I do know is that between a troubling past and a difficult present, there is no future." She smiled, kissed his cheek and got up to leave.

He looked at her, ignoring what she had just said, knowing that in time she would be able to forget about his affair with Vivian. Time—that's what he needed.

A question gnawed at him, one she had cleverly avoided answering. "Who is Marc Delage and why does he co-own your house?"

"I have to shower and get dressed. I really do. My reputation is riding on the reception I have to prepare in less than twenty-four hours and the kitchens will only be ours for part of the day. Maurice is liable to show up here if I don't go down soon." She put a hand on her forehead as she looked for her clothes. "God, I'm not ready to face anyone just yet."

He stood up and stopped her from leaving the room by placing both his hands on her shoulders. "You haven't answered my question."

When she looked up at him, she appeared so vulnerable and so sad, he wanted to take her in his arms and hold her. She might as well tell him. His detectives would find out anyway. "He doesn't co-own my house. He's the creditor for a loan I guaranteed. A business venture that went bad—that was devised to go bad. My associate took the money meant for the business and left with it. I'm just frustrated I was taken in. And the subject is now closed, Kennedy."

His last name again. That's what she did when she wanted to put distance between them. But the thought of someone's taking advantage of her made him even angrier. He would find out the rest of the information on his own. If what she was saying was true, it would be a pleasure to track down the bastard who'd deliberately done this to her.

He was still thinking about exacting retribution when she switched topics on him.

"By the way, I want your word that you won't vote for me in the competition."

"What? What are you talking about?"

"The competition. I don't want you to vote for me."

"Why not? Are you afraid I'd vote for you just because we slept together?"

"I'd like to think you'd do it because of my superior skills. But that's not the reason." She turned away from him, suddenly shy. "If anyone finds out we slept together before the competition, as I'm sure someone will, I don't want people to have any reason to think I bought your vote. More important, I don't want any bad light shed on this competition or the foundation." She turned back to him, holding out her hand. "I mean it, Kennedy. Give me your word and let's shake on it."

He didn't like her risking first place because of what they had done but she was right about not wanting the foundation to suffer the consequences. She was, indeed, an honorable woman. However, he still wanted her to have the best chance to win, even though he was sure his little chef would easily surpass the other contestants with or without his vote, if what he'd tasted the other night was any indication of her talents. He knew there was a lot of prejudice against Canadians in this field and she would be judged more severely than the others.

A terrific idea struck him, one she'd have a hard time refusing.

"Okay, I'll give you my word but on one condition — well, actually, two conditions."

"Which are…?"

"First of all, you'll have the reception at the gallery. You can use the kitchens in the house and we can set up a tent outside if you need more room."

"Your art gallery? Under normal circumstances that would be fantastic but I doubt the space would hold seventy tables of ten."

"Maybe not but to save floor space we can use fewer long rectangular tables instead of smaller round ones and arrange them on either side of the sculptures, which can serve as the centerpiece of the room. And that way you can have use of the kitchens whenever and for as long as you like."

"But our plans are based on the reception hall. I don't have time to completely revise them in one day!"

He gave a casual shrug. "We'll switch your dinner to the end, make it third instead of second."

"That's hardly fair to the other contestants," she accused.

His eyebrows shot upward. "Fair? Was giving them more time than you 'fair' to begin with? Besides, you want to be 'fair' with those who laugh behind your back and who protested to the panel about having your Canadian team included in the competition in the first place?"

"What are you talking about?"

"Never mind. I've said too much already. That was privileged information. Anyway, we've solved the problems of time and space, so no more excuses. As I said, my conditions are not negotiable."

Scowling, she asked, "What's the second condition?"

He smiled as he ran his palms down both sides of her neck and across her shoulders. "I'll want you to thank me properly for setting the first condition."

She smiled in return, noting his gaze scanning her breasts.

"If it's just proper thanks you want, then I'll oblige you." She curtsied naked, pretending to lift her skirts. "Why, thank you, milord."

He latched on to her hair and drew her head to within an inch of his face. "I want it more proper than that, lass, and I want to feel ye thankin' me. I'd be talking about The Bud, if you catch my meanin'." He switched off the Gaelic to explain further. "I want you on your back, your knees clasped to your breasts, offering your bud to me and only me. Think you could do that for this hungry man?"

"Do I have a choice?"

"Actually...no."

His smile was so captivating, she forgot about his mammoth ego. Then he kissed her, marking her as his. Breathless, she pulled away from him. "Hey, Irishman, I thought I explained to you that you don't own me."

"Ah but possession is nine-tenths of the law, is it not?"

With that he picked her up and brought her to bed, content for the time being to savor their lovemaking and ignore the future, the one she was trying to convince him they couldn't have.

Chapter Twelve

The needs of many are sometimes created by the greed of one.

༨

Lorelei left the Siren's presidential suite dazed, confused, and worried. Back in her old room with the power back on, after she showered and before she dressed, she spent several minutes looking at herself nude in the mirror. The last time she did so, she had just returned from a hospital and the traces of needles and tubes were still evident on her pale, skinny limbs. Today she was glowing. That persistent image of herself as unattractive and virtually asexual had finally been replaced and it awed her.

She was confused about what it would all mean in the end, whether her affair with Galen Kennedy had to continue a certain length of time for it to amount to anything. But those were considerations to be dealt with later. For now she would focus her attention on what lay immediately ahead. The soreness she felt was the first reminder that there could be the possibility of a pregnancy, although remote, if her cycle dates were accurate. The competition was her second worry, more particularly the fact that nobody, especially Maurice, would have to find out about the night she had spent with Galen Kennedy.

Which left Lorelei with just two things to concentrate on. One, her culinary preparations for DesCheneaux's "night of nights", now postponed a day and, two, how to face Maurice. Under the circumstances, she opted for evading her mentor. Best to avoid getting into an inevitable argument with Maurice so close to their performance night and best to prevent making him worry. She did enough of that as it was. Her only alternative, therefore, short of lying, was to restrict as much as possible confronting him, at least for the day. Tomorrow they'd be too busy preparing for the dinner to argue.

Once she was dressed, she went to speak to one of the cooks and informed him that she would be driving into Boston that morning to pick up the rest of their supplies for the dinner. She would use one of the hotel's minivans to collect the special shipment of Italian spices, oils and wines she had ordered months ahead from the assistant chef, Augusto, at the Torgiano Scuola di Cucina. Wexford International, with its fleet of cargo ships, had arranged to make pickups of special items that couldn't be found locally for all the contest participants.

An hour or so later, map in hand, she arrived at the Boston harbor and parked the van near the cargo terminal where the *Irish Siren* was docked. Had she been driving her *bolide*, as Maurice called it, she would have been there in under thirty minutes. She'd better get used to not driving the Porsche, she reminded herself, for soon she would no longer own it.

It was a cloudy, muggy day and the water smelled a bit rank. It didn't matter, though. It seemed that Galen Kennedy's scent had seeped into her skin and clothes, or maybe it was merely a sensory memory that had been following her since she left the hotel.

"Can I help you, ma'am?" a friendly uniformed guard asked, interrupting her thoughts.

"Yes, thank you. I have papers here for some cargo I need to pick up. This is the bill of lading and a customs clearance certificate from our brokers."

He examined the papers and punched a few inquiries into his computer terminal. "Your cargo is still on board, ma'am, for identification purposes. I'll radio in that you've arrived for it. Someone will be down with your merchandise in a few minutes."

While they both waited several minutes, another call came to the guard, informing him that there was a problem. "Ma'am? Apparently some crates located near yours lost their bill of lading pouches and can't be identified. You'll have to go up and take a look. An officer will direct you to the hold where your merchandise is. Once you identify it, we'll have someone bring it down for you. Follow the walkway to the ship and go up the yellow ramp. Good day to you, ma'am."

"Thank you."

She walked up the narrow yellow footbridge to the main deck and waited for someone to take her to the cargo hold. Fifteen minutes later, however, with no one in sight, Lorelei began walking around in the hope of finding someone to give her directions. A sailor finally passed and explained the way to the cargo holds. It seemed no one was going to meet her after all.

She opened the only door she found and went down a steep stairwell that led into a narrow corridor. She was about to turn back, convinced she had gone the wrong way, when she spotted rows of crates at the end of the hallway. She continued walking, looking for a clerk but again to no avail.

Frustrated and pressed for time, she unfolded her bill of lading and started looking for the crate numbers herself, hoping that eventually someone would show up. As she was reading the markings on the crates, she heard heavy footsteps descending another stairwell some twenty feet away from her, followed by a loud banging. Before she could turn toward the noise, someone cried out in pain.

"What did ye do with the crates? Where are the guns for the motherland, boy?" a deep male voice demanded. "If ye be true Irish, ye wouldn't let the bastards annihilate our religion and the blood that runs through our countrymen's veins. This is the last time I ask ye before I kill ye. What have ye done with our shipment? Answer me, boy, or wonder whether I'll shoot ye in the head and make it quick and painless or gut-shoot ye, let ye bleed yerself dry, make ye drink yer own blood and then make ye beg me to kill ye."

A young-sounding man, who had apparently been injured, protested. "There are no rifles here. Your weapons will not ship out on the *Irish Siren* again. You can take my life but for every one of me, there'll be ten others. You and those like you who feed a war that slaughters countless innocents are no countrymen of mine. You're a disgrace—a scourge!—to our religion and homeland and I—"

A muffled pistol shot cut off the speech and Lorelei slapped a hand to her mouth to suppress the scream that welled in her throat. She knew a silencer when she heard one. The shooter didn't want anyone to hear. Nor did she want to alert the shooter to her presence. Tears burned behind her eyelids, threatening to spill. She bit her lip. She had to remain calm, quiet.

A few interminable seconds passed. Then a third man's voice broke the eerie silence.

"Ye're a crazy man, that's what ye be. How'll we find the bloody rifles now? How'll we find out what the kid did with 'em?"

"Shut up, ye whinin' old goat and let's look fer 'em before I twist yer neck with me bare hands. We'll come back and get rid of him later."

The footsteps were advancing toward her. Lorelei wanted to retreat but knew she would be discovered anyway. She decided to try to bluff her way out of the situation.

Stepping into view as if she'd just descended the steps, she forced a look of pleased surprise to her face. "Oh, hello! Finally I've found someone to help me. A guard on the dock told me to come down here to identify my cargo but no one came along to show me where it is." Waving her papers in the air, she took a step forward. "Can one of you help me find it, so I can have it brought outside?"

A man with a huge scar on the left side of his face exchanged looks with his cohort, who moved with barely feigned casualness to block her view of the passageway.

"You're in the wrong hold, lady," the big man said.

"Really?" she exclaimed. "Well, can you tell me where I should go?"

"Let me see your papers."

Lorelei calmly handed them to the man with the scar, betraying none of her fear.

"Follow me," he commanded, this time in perfect English.

* * * * *

A short while later, still trembling inside and heedless that a heavy rain had begun falling, Lorelei watched two of the men loading her supplies into the borrowed minivan.

She felt no rain, saw no lightning, nor heard any of the thunder. She was too numb from shock. She stood there like a coward, pretending nothing had happened, while two murderers carefully handled her boxes.

She stared at the bulges in their jackets, wishing she could get the weapons, turn them on the men and hold them while she called the authorities. But she'd never be able to overpower the pair. She'd have to get away from them, then call for help.

She didn't remember getting into the minivan, much less turning the key in the ignition. She drove away from the dock, then onto the highway, as mechanically as a robot. Her mind was a haze of fury and sorrow. She tried to visualize what the victim had looked like, tried to attach a face to the voice that would be forever imprinted in her mind, a voice that had revealed none of the terror many a man would feel when facing imminent death.

She tried to feel the blinding heat and the blaze of pain the bullet must have caused when it tunneled into him, as if even now she could save him from some of it, ease his suffering and make him feel that he had not died alone.

Images of her parents flashed before her. She prayed their death had been quick, that they hadn't suffered. But even now their fear and pain echoed in the far recesses of her mind.

"*Arrête!*" she sobbed. "Stop it, stop it, stop it!" she cried out, banging her hands on the steering wheel. The car skidded in the rain, making her lose control of it. She braked, then veered into the emergency lane, bringing the minivan to a full stop. Her whole body shook. She took a deep breath, then another, trying to swallow her terror and grief. But she couldn't. So she cried until her throat was parched and her eyes were stinging with pain. Exhausted, she rested her head on the steering wheel and waited until her cheeks were dry, until she regained some self-control.

It had always been there, she reflected. The lack of actual knowledge, the lack of closure, the overcrowded imaginings and conjecturing and the endless abyss her continued ignorance of her parents' end had created in her life. Her pleas to every god she'd ever heard of to tell her why and how her mother and father had died had gone unanswered.

But the young man whose death she had overheard could be avenged and she could tell those left behind what had happened to him — if she could discover his identity.

She slowly got back onto the highway, focusing her thoughts on the young man whose face she hadn't seen.

Should she find a police station right now? But what if the murderers were following her? She glanced into the rearview mirror but saw only anonymous sets of headlights. Should she drive back to Hyannis Port, seek help there? But from whom? Whom could she trust? It wasn't a simple mugging she'd witnessed. And the murder obviously involved illegal weapons aboard a ship owned by a well-known business tycoon.

"Oh! Oh my God!" she gasped. "And I slept with him!"

Her mind raced to the previous night, to Galen Kennedy. She remembered his relationship with Vivian Gallagher. Was the Wexford empire supplying arms to Ireland on their fleet of ships? Did the senator's wife know and had she threatened to tell her husband? Could Vivian be blackmailing Galen into having an affair with her? Was that what he'd meant when he'd said a lot of lives were at stake?

Distraught and no closer to a decision about how she should proceed, she sped blindly to Hyannis Port, ignoring the rain, ignoring the traffic, focused only on reaching the hotel, Maurice and her staff and getting them out of there as soon as was humanly possible. Once in Montreal she would speak to Amanda. Yes, Amanda would know the best way for her to disclose what she had heard and seen. She hated to delay bringing in the authorities to apprehend the man's murderers but it was simply too dangerous to risk trusting anyone. She might tip off the wrong people and wind up dead herself.

Ultimately though, she swore she would help bring the murderers to justice. And she would make sure the victim's family knew how he had died — proud and brave and, with his last breath, bearing witness to the truth.

She couldn't tolerate the idea that the young man's parents might never know what had happened to their son. What if they were told he had disappeared, that no one could find him or explain what had happened to him? What if his body never turned up? They would likely mount a search of their own, spend countless dollars trying to find him and endless sleepless nights imagining what horrifying fate had befallen him. They would pray until exhaustion for his safe return, waiting and waiting. The wait alone would slowly kill them inside. Then would come resignation, acceptance of the inevitable, with only the simple hope remaining that someone would find his remains so that they could get his soul blessed and absolved by the priest, give him a proper burial and bring closure to their grief.

No, she couldn't let it happen that way. The poor people might never recover.

As she herself never had.

Chapter Thirteen

We often pay for the deeds of others.

♋

When she arrived back at the Siren hotel, Lorelei headed straight for the inn's kitchens, where she knew she would find Maurice. The prospect of facing him as a fallen woman paled in comparison to the horrific morning she'd had and the fear that some harm might come to him or her team because of it.

To her relief, everything appeared normal.

"There you are, Lorelei," Maurice called out as he bustled toward her. "Why didn't you consult me before deciding to have the reception in Mr. Kennedy's art gallery? We'll never be ready on time, despite the extra day we've been given."

He leaned on a counter and wiped his sweaty brow with a napkin. "And why, mademoiselle, did you decide to drive to Boston alone? Do you do these things just to torment me?"

Lorelei's face remained expressionless.

"What's the matter, *petite*?" Maurice's voice softened with concern when he noticed her pallor.

Lorelei straightened her shoulders and mustered the semblance of a teasing smile. "You've battled European traffic, worked for dozens of French restaurants, you're a published chef...and a little change of venue scares you?"

Pushing her painful thoughts aside, Lorelei picked up some menu binders and headed toward the counter, where she would try to review the schedule. She found herself almost not caring about the competition anymore.

Maurice laughed. "*Maurice et la peur sont des antonyms, petite, et tu le sais bien,*" he boasted.

"You and fear are antonyms? You must be getting old, then, to be this agitated," Lorelei tossed at him from behind the counter.

"That's a cruel thing to say to a man who is supposed to be your hero."

She gave him a tender smile. "You are my hero. And you know we can do this. I promise we shall be laughing at our anxieties all the way home when we win the competition."

"I would prefer to laugh at the pompous people here instead, especially that blond Irish brute who I know will break your heart, *ma petite*. Already I can see he has done damage."

Lorelei stopped reading. Without looking up, she clutched her pen.

Maurice continued talking. "I may be getting old, *ma chérie* but my mind and my eyes are still sharp. You cannot hide from me. Remember that I consider you my daughter, and, as such, any man who comes around you will have to deal with me first. And don't give me that look—like an outraged young feminist. If you were forty-seven instead of twenty-seven, I would not speak differently. That man, he likes all women. He is *exactement* what I was before I found my Annabelle—*un gigolo*! I can understand why he is crazy about you but I am afraid for you." He sighed heavily. "Also, he is worse than English—he is Irish!"

Lorelei felt a ridiculous argument coming on. Just as well, she thought. That way she could probably avoid having to tell him the truth. "And that means?"

"They can't cook."

It would take a Frenchman to make that kind of remark.

"Well, Maurice, I've heard that in romance, it isn't the cooking that's important but the eating."

He huffed and puffed and sent two very French expletives her way. "You're an insolent young woman, *et je ne trouves pas ça drôle.*"

She smiled, barely. "But I find it funny, old man and now, if you'll excuse me, I have to look over the menu and see what adjustments we'll need to make for the new venue and the extra day. I don't think we'll have a problem with spoilage but let's be doubly careful about refrigeration."

"Hmph. I'm talking about your life and you want to talk about spoilage." With a disgusted snort, Maurice bustled off.

Relieved to be out from under his watchful eye, Lorelei sat on a stool at the counter, reviewing her plans. As she looked at the menu, she conjured an image of the delectable foods being served in Galen's beautiful art gallery.

First, the appetizers. They were to be served at room temperature and could therefore be prepared in advance.

Her menu included wild asparagus slightly cooked in red wine vinegar and served with mint leaves, fava beans and Swiss chard, Umbrian style. She would also be serving a zucchini and tomato salad with basil and quail eggs, along with a carpaccio of paper-thin, lean, raw veal fillets sprinkled with capers, fresh parmigiano flakes, salt, pepper and extra virgin olive oil. Last but not least were the grilled porcini mushroom caps in a blend of special spices.

For the wines, her guests would have a Castel del Monte, an exquisite Apulian varietal with a limpid strawberry-red color and a subtle bouquet reminiscent of hawthorn blossoms. This wine was one of her favorites, combining a slightly fruity flavor with a sense of both youth and finesse.

Next would come the risotto with arugula and pecorino cheese, potato gnocchi with lamb ragù, tagliatelle with marjoram and diced fresh tomatoes and finally shrimp and spinach dumplings in a light lemon sauce. A Bombino Bianco Dauno and a rare Copertino would be the accompanying wines.

For the pièce de résistance her guests would be served a beef filet in balsamic grape sauce, sautéed quails in rosemary and fortified wine and a filet of royal perch with butter on a bed of prickly lettuce. Two wines would accompany these plates, a white Superiore di Cartizze and a deep red Squinzano.

The bread served throughout the meal would be home-baked and come in three varieties — herb, dried tomato and black olive.

For dessert, aside from a plate of assorted Italian cheeses and nuts, she would include strawberries in balsamic grape sauce, a peach flan and a tiramisù, made of ricotta cheese, mascarpone and chocolate cream, none of the three requiring any baking.

Last would come a fine Grappa from her own wine cellar. Produced exclusively from the pomace of Moscato grapes, her Grappa was transparent and crystalline with a rich fruit bouquet, clean and enveloping, to warm any heart and soothe any ailment.

But before they would serve any of this lavishly prepared food, Lorelei was going to surprise — probably shock — her guests, Duplessis-style. It could very well jeopardize her team's chance of winning. However, the purpose of the competition was to raise funds for Wexford International's Feed the World Foundation and, to that end, to raise awareness of the dire need for famine relief measures. Without making a statement on the matter during the competition, Lorelei would not feel she had fulfilled her moral duty. Nor would she feel she had fulfilled her moral duty if she kept quiet about that morning's murder.

Keeping her thoughts focused on the competition, she tried again to put aside the rest. She needed to buy time.

She was massaging the back of her neck when she felt someone remove her hand from her nape and replace it with his own. Lorelei jumped, stiff with panic.

"Ah, the trials and tribulations of a master chef," Galen said. "Where were you all morning, my love?"

When she did not reply, Galen frowned but then seemed to remember they were in a public place. "Hello there, Miss Duplessis," he said in a genial tone.

"Hi," she managed to say, her voice not quite steady.

"I'm the man you slept with last night, remember?" he whispered. "Or are we going to pretend it never happened?"

She looked up at him, her mind racing over what she should reveal or not reveal and the possibilities of his involvement in matters illegal.

"I had to go to Boston and get some last-minute things. What about you?"

Galen saw the worried look in Lorelei's eyes and mistook it for embarrassment, which he understood, given the circumstances but which bothered him nonetheless. "I spent most of the morning remembering last night with you." He walked around to face her and moved aside her menu binders.

"Do you have a problem with that? Because if you do, you'll have a greater one tonight and in the near future."

She wanted to cry but knew she couldn't. She wanted to tell him that making love with him all night had been beautiful and that she would cherish the memories forever. But even that she couldn't say. Instead she shook her head and whispered, "No. No problem."

"What's wrong, then? Did you catch heat about moving your dinner?" Concerned, he caressed her cheek. "When I told your team, that big man with the cleaver almost cut off a vital piece of me."

Her back arched in defense. "The man you're referring to is Maurice Leblanc and he is very dear to me. He taught me everything I know of the business and he had good reason to be angry." She threw a fond look at Maurice as he was chastising the cook handling the dessert trays. "A change like this at the last minute can be very tricky."

"If you need help, I'll be glad to send some of my people down. Why don't I go and speak to M. Leblanc?" he offered.

"Wait," she said, putting a hand on his wrist. "That won't be necessary. Maurice is mainly bluster. He worries, that's all." She looked up at him. "I love him, you know. He and his wife are like family to me—the only family I have left. I would do anything for either one of them."

"For those we love, it goes without saying," he agreed. "But why—"

"I would kill if anybody harmed them," she interrupted him.

Galen noted her solemn, steady gaze and knew she was trying to convey some message. "Has anybody said or done something that—"

"Lorelei, *petite*, Annabelle and Cécile have a few questions to ask about the centerpieces and they are making me *fou de rage!*" Maurice suddenly appeared with the ubiquitous cleaver in hand and the look of a vigilante in his eyes. "Please go and see them, *avant que je commette un crime,*" he added, staring at the man who was hovering near his *petite*.

Galen placed a hand over hers, to make his claim on her clear. "Go and see them, sweet," he said, "before a sharp object pierces my belly." Galen then looked up at Maurice, still addressing his words to her, however. "After you resolve that problem, can you come by my office? I have some papers for you to sign for the leasing of the gallery."

Lorelei reluctantly got up and shot a stern glance at Galen. "What papers?"

"The gallery's not licensed for serving liquor. We'll have to apply for a temporary permit so that your staff may serve alcohol."

Lorelei hesitated. "All right. I'll be there as soon as I can."

* * * * *

Later that day, just before opening the door to Galen's outer office, Lorelei took a deep breath. Should she tell him what she'd witnessed on his ship? Was he involved in the nefarious activity? She was no closer to knowing what she should do than she'd been earlier.

Seeing no receptionist or secretary on duty, she took a seat in the waiting room. After a few moments she heard Galen's voice through his closed office door.

"What do you mean, she knows? I told you, I don't want any complications, or I'll have your hides."

Lorelei sat up in alarm. Had he been referring to her?

Galen emerged from his office moments later. His eyes locked on her legs as she sat demurely in one of the *bergères* chairs in the waiting room. His golden hair was tied back, his white shirt loose and partly opened in the front. The black of his eyes matched those of his perfectly tailored pants. He had rolled up his sleeves to reveal a simple, utilitarian watch. Lorelei knew, however, that there was nothing simple or utilitarian about the man.

They were alone, Galen noted, finally alone. He had dismissed his secretary early, wanting his meeting with Lorelei to be private. For hours his mind had overflowed with thoughts of her, while his body kept giving him dangerous signals of losing control.

"You're here," he said simply. His efforts to tamp down his craving for this woman were fruitless. He was falling in love with her, as inconvenient as that surely was. He should try to make himself fall out of love, he realized but he had no intention even of trying. For as uncertain as the future was, he was looking forward to it simply because Lorelei would be in it — he was determined she would be, despite her stubborn efforts to push their future aside.

He gestured toward his office. "Won't you come in?"

She hesitated, then decided she had no choice but to face him. Galen locked the door behind them and before she had time to react, he grabbed her by the arms, turned her around and gently backed her against the door, bracing his hands on either side of her face. "What am I going to do with you?" His eyes didn't leave hers. "Because what I want to do and what I should do are diametrically opposed."

Lorelei's heart stopped beating. He knows, she told herself.

"What... What are you talking about?"

His mind was buzzing so loudly with desire that he almost didn't hear her speak. "Duty can wait. For once it'll bloody well have to wait." He bent his head to look at the swell of her breasts. "What are you wearing to tonight's dinner? I don't think I can wait to find out." As the last words of his sentence faded away, he leaned forward and kissed her hard and voraciously, afraid she would vanish, scarcely believing she was more than a mere figment of his imagination. His mouth continued its journey downward, licking her behind an ear, kissing her neck, biting the pulse there, inhaling that scent that summoned his body and his soul.

Lorelei felt shivers throughout her body. Protesting was out of the question, leaving just as impossible, when her physical needs were greater than her fear. "Galen we have to... I have to get back," she pleaded, struggling to remove herself from his embrace.

He ignored her pleas, noting that her breathing was fast and hard. He pulled her toward him, bringing her lips back to his, leaning into her yielding body. He felt her nipples grow taut, throbbing with the need to feel his hands and tongue on them.

He understood that need, it matched his own. Without a word he unbuttoned her blouse and tugged her lacy camisole from her skirt. He all but started biting her nipples, his primal instincts uncontrollable. He cupped her bottom with his hands and lifted her so that he could slide his tongue between her breasts, pressing his erection between her legs.

Lorelei could do nothing but cling to him. She fought not to climax, not to let it end so soon, since coming back to the real world would mean having to quell this obsessive need she had to be with him, the urge to give him everything and to take everything from him.

He set her on a chair beside the door, spreading her legs on either side of it and settling himself directly in front of her. He slid his hands under her skirt and began tugging away her panties. Lorelei's head fell back, her breathing harsher as she anticipated his thrusts into her body.

He briskly undid his belt, tearing at his pants to release his sex. "Open for me," he said brusquely, almost crudely.

"No, Galen, please," she implored. "I won't say any—"

"It's too late for that. You're mine Lorelei. Mine."

His hands were still between their bodies, stroking her, knowing just where to touch her. Unable to wait any longer, and taking precautions this time although he thought it was too late already, he guided himself inside her and began thrusting. Lorelei went still, his enormous shaft surging to the hilt into the most intimate recess of her body, impaling her.

He groaned. She was his glove, hot and tight. Galen knew then that there was no other place in the world for him to be than with her.

She moaned, quivering in his arms, clenching fistfuls of his shirt as he drove himself into her. But she was still hesitating, still holding back and he realized it was because she was afraid. That bothered him.

His tone was urgent yet soothing as he whispered hoarsely, "I won't let anything happen to you, Lorelei. I give you my word, as I did the first time I touched you."

His words had the intended effect. She let herself open completely to him, surrendering, feeling her very soul bond with his. He continued thrusting into her, his right hand stroking her to climax. Lightning struck as they peaked together, her cry of pleasure starting at the very instant he threw his head back and growled her name.

Stunned by the intensity and sheer joy he felt in making love with her, Galen slowly became aware that his hands were shaking. His forehead was wet with sweat that dripped onto her breasts. His hair had come loose, his shirt was hanging from his shoulders and his loins ached. Still he wanted her with a violence that tore at him. It worried him. For he did not know to what lengths he would have to go to keep her.

Chapter Fourteen
ಸಿ

Distraught and thoroughly confused, Lorelei deliberately avoided Galen the rest of that day and all of the next. When he would have seated her at his table for her two competitors' dinners, she reminded him that it would not do for him to be seen as giving her special treatment.

The nights were harder. She wanted badly to spend them with him but she was simply too afraid. She was in a strange city with strange people all around her and she'd witnessed a murder. She didn't know whom she could trust. She managed to circumvent Galen's assumption that she would spend the nights with him by pleading that she was exhausted from her day's work in the kitchens. Besides, she told him, she needed to focus all her attention on the competition and on preparing the most complex and demanding meal she'd ever prepared in her career. His company's reputation was at stake, as well, was it not? Did he want her to embarrass herself and him? Grudgingly — and fuming, she could tell — he'd agreed she needed her rest and had left her alone.

Still, two days later, when she returned to her own room to get ready for the dinner on which she'd staked her reputation, she remained as torn and upset as she'd been after her encounter with Galen in his office. She simply could not accept that he was a gun smuggler, much less that he would order or condone murder.

She shuddered at the thought of what was to come. Her lust for him had only grown in their two days apart and that made it much more difficult to face the dangerous situation she had fallen into. She had contemplated ending her own life but never had she wished to be murdered.

Worse, she truly feared for the safety of her loved ones.

Would it be best if she said nothing and forever kept her silence? She had played the part pretty well with the two murderers, maybe they hadn't suspected anything. Silence might be the best way to keep everyone safe. But could she go on living with what she had witnessed, unable to say anything about it to the police, to the victim's family? To Galen? Would she remain forever in doubt as to his involvement?

She watched the sun go down from her balcony window, watched the waves splash against the sand. And all at once, as if the passage of time had indeed served its intended purpose, a sense of normalcy overcame her. With sudden clarity she was able to view her dilemma and weigh the pros and cons with more objectivity.

She did not fear death. She had been steering herself toward it since the age of nineteen. Dying was, therefore, not her major fear.

Neither was ending her relationship with Galen Kennedy. That had been stamped with an expiration date from the beginning. She knew it and so did he.

And so all she really needed to figure out was how to make only the guilty pay for the young man's murder. Once that was done, she would resume her life and continue with her plans.

Although she had no basis for it, her gut-level belief that Galen was not a weapons smuggler remained strong. He obviously had the means and the opportunity to do so, maybe even a reason, since he was Irish but deep down she knew he was caring and honest and maybe even noble. Those qualities had surfaced the first time he made love to her. Beneath all his power and possessions, he was still a man who had suffered, who had cried, who had trusted her to see his vulnerability.

She pulled the light cotton drapes over the balcony window so that they flowed gaily in the early-evening breeze.

Someone was using Wexford ships to traffic arms, she was sure and she suspected the Kennedy brothers were aware of it even if they weren't involved in it. Galen's words came to mind as she prepared to shower. "Look, Lorelei. Vivian Gallagher is using me as much as I am her. I do it because there are a lot of lives at stake. I wish I could explain but I can't. All I can say is that I've never had to go to these lengths before but I have no choice."

She replayed his speech several times while she gathered her toiletries. Vivian was somehow involved, then, though she had not appeared the least bit capable of enlarging her interests beyond what new man she could sleep with next.

Lorelei stared at the shower and opted for drawing a bath instead. She would have to broach the subject with Galen and hope that whatever information he gave her would indicate what his involvement was or wasn't, after which she would decide what to tell him. Somehow she trusted him, even if she despised the fact that he had slept with Senator Gallagher's wife with no other purpose than to use her.

Thus, in a few hours, win or lose, she would be taking the two biggest gambles of her life.

With that thought in mind, she stepped into the bath.

She was wearing an evening gown in a baby blue *peau de soie*. It was long and straight and molded itself to her contours a little more snugly than she was comfortable with. If that wasn't enough, it was also low-cut and strapless. When Annabelle had had it designed and made for her by one of Montreal's most exclusive couturiers, Lorelei hadn't been able to find it in her heart to refuse. They did compromise, however, on adding a bolero jacket that complemented the design and color of the gown.

When Galen saw her approaching the podium, he thought she looked divine. He glanced at his brother and noticed that Justin couldn't contain his admiration either.

The gallery, seating seven hundred people, suddenly became a silent, echoless chamber as the shy, beautiful woman he had held in his arms a few days before became the center of everyone's attention.

"I'll bet you all the married women at this party are reaching for their husbands right about now, big brother," Justin murmured. "Look at Andrew Steinman—he's positively salivating. Look, look, I think he's getting up to give her one of the roses from the centerpieces."

Galen remained outwardly impassive at Justin's remarks, even though he was burning inside. "If he makes any other move toward her, I swear, blood will be shed."

"Then I think I'd better stick close to you, so we don't make the front page of the *Boston Herald*."

For once Lorelei didn't feel the usual apprehension that preceded a competition dinner, she was too busy scanning the audience for a scar-faced man and his cohort. As she made her way to the podium, aware that seven hundred pairs of eyes followed her, she kept reviewing her preparations for the trip home. Maybe she wouldn't even stay to participate in the awards ceremony the next day. She had to get her people safely out of Hyannis Port and back to Montreal as quickly as possible.

She climbed the narrow steps that led onstage and calmly looked at Galen, who smiled and winked and at his brother, Justin, by his side. A man from the audience she had met earlier that night offered her a white rose, which she accepted along with everyone's applause.

Seconds later Lorelei faced her audience and began her speech. "Ladies and gentlemen, before we of DesCheneaux have the honor and privilege of serving you the lavish dinner we've prepared, we would like to share with you quite another meal. The plates our staffers are presenting you hold dried cornflower bread baked with raisins, referred to in Italy as *pizza di grandinio*, accompanied by boiled chicory, which grows in the fields in the springtime. For dessert you will see wet bread with sugar and wild berries, for your beverage, water.

"In Italy this is called a poor man's feast. In Third World countries it would be considered a gift from the gods. By offering you this humble fare, we don't mean to insult anyone, for we all are very proud to be able to share with you our love for our work. However, we believe that, whether simply or lavishly prepared, food is indeed a gift from the gods, a gift we must always learn to share. Thank you."

As soon as the deafening applause began, something Lorelei had not counted on, she stepped aside to leave. But Galen quickly appeared by her side, taking her hand and guiding her back to center stage. He then leaned down to the microphone and cleared his throat. "I'm ashamed to think of how many times I have thrown out perfectly edible food because it was too much for me to eat. On behalf of Wexford International's Feed the World Foundation, I wish to thank Miss Duplessis for preparing this humble meal taking away the shame in being needy, poor and most of all, in being hungry." Galen brought her hand to his lips. "Thank you, Miss Duplessis, for spurring us and the foundation to do all we can to help feed the world's hungry."

As the guests surveyed and sampled their "pre-dinner" meal, everyone got the message and Galen Kennedy's endorsement drove it home.

Justin approached the microphone and put an arm around his brother's shoulders, addressing all their guests.

"My brother and I plan to personally match your every donation to the foundation this evening, so whoever can't stand us, now's the time to get your revenge!"

The crowd's laughter and applause echoed throughout the gallery.

As the three left the stage, Lorelei turned to glare at Galen. "You are truly something, Kennedy. I didn't need that!"

"My father always reminded us to give credit where credit is due." He stopped to look at her. "Besides, don't you want these rich people to dig deeply into their pockets and give?"

"Yes, I do. But don't you realize how close you came to compromising both our reputations?"

He smiled and leaned down to whisper in her ear. "I believe I've already done that—and I can't wait to do it again. Besides, didn't you say you were worried about becoming a mommy?"

Lorelei's step faltered.

He grinned. "I think you'd better run along now and get this show on the road, *ma petite française.*"

Lorelei made her way to the kitchens, utterly bemused.

Carrying his child? That thought had actually crossed Galen's mind and he wasn't upset about it? Well, she fumed, why would he be? It was her problem after all. And she was upset about it. And what about the murder and those two dangerous men? She closed her eyes and shook her head. What should she hope for first? Not getting pregnant? Or getting pregnant but not getting herself or anyone else killed?

"*Quelles problèmes, petite! Qu'est-ce qu'on va faire?*" Maurice shouted, bustling toward her.

For a moment she was so absorbed by her thoughts that she didn't react. But then she recognized the look on Maurice's face, the one that said a catastrophe had occurred.

"*Qu'est ce qu'il y a*? What happened?"

"Lorelei, *un vrai désastre* this time! All our breads have disappeared and someone turned the refrigerators up so high that the white wine is ruined. What are we going to do?"

"What do you mean, the breads are gone and the wine's ruined?"

"Someone stole our breads and spoiled the white wine! It has crystallized! Quelle catastrophe! We will lose the competition. Worse, we will lose face!"

Dismayed but determined not to show it, Lorelei placed reassuring hands on Maurice's shoulders. "Don't worry. We'll replace the breads and, as for the wine, you know a few water crystals won't spoil it as long as we serve it quickly. It will just taste a little more potent. And once our guests start drinking the wine, they won't even notice that the bread is slightly different from what we planned to serve."

"'Slightly different'? *Petite*, we have no bread!"

Lorelei's mind was racing. "I know what to do. While our guests are eating their first 'meal' of the evening, we'll make flat bread. The dough doesn't require much kneading, and we'll just use fast-rising yeast—or did that vanish too?"

She looked around and saw several cooks scrambling to assemble the ingredients. "Antoine," she called out, "the first meal is still being served and then it will need to be cleared. That gives you enough time to make polenta fritters. Fry them with bread crumbs and herbs—use anise and some of the dried myrtles I brought from the ship."

As soon as she issued the orders, Antoine signaled two of his fastest cooks to start working.

"Maurice, will you go to my room and get me my white sundress? It's in my black suitcase. I'll change into it to help make the bread."

"You didn't deserve this, *petite*," Maurice complained as he hurried off. He added a few solemn oaths in his native language, describing in vivid detail what he would do the person responsible for the mess.

Lorelei waited for him to leave before speaking to François, the staff coordinator. "How in hell do hundreds of loaves of bread disappear? Did giant eagles fly in and snatch them? And who fiddled with the fridges?"

A horrified François put his palms out in self-defense.

"Lorelei, the breads were all here this afternoon. You know we baked all night and all morning to have them ready for tonight. They were in the storage area near the back door. Early this afternoon a man came in to check the refrigerators. He said he worked for the hotel and had instructions to make sure everything was in good working order. When we looked half an hour ago, the bread was gone and the wine was— Well! I'm sorry! I did not think anything like this would happen, truly!"

Lorelei realized she could not blame the man. After all, François and the others were gourmet cooks, not security guards. "No, I'm sorry. I didn't mean to blame you. It's not your fault. Clearly we were sabotaged. Now we must remedy the situation and learn from this experience. Lesson one, we must always come prepared for anything. This time we were lucky, because the saboteurs were amateurs. Stealing bread and freezing wine—I mean, really! But next time we might not be so fortunate. So let's get to work."

* * * * *

An hour later Galen was wondering where his little mermaid had disappeared to. As hostess of the evening, she was expected to join his table with the guests of honor, including Senator and Mrs. Gallagher.

"Well, this is certainly typical of an amateur—the hostess absent from the table. Do you think she just has bad manners, or is she so socially awkward that she's hiding from her guests? Maybe she's afraid she'll break another wineglass."

The senator sat stiffly in his chair, clearly uncomfortable with his wife's comments. "Vivian, that was uncalled for."

The woman glared at her husband. "Really, Tom? I think poor people's food is uncalled for. Clearly this classless Canadian didn't belong in this competition to begin with. I think she's making a mockery of it and at Galen's expense."

Diplomacy prevented the senator from making a scene with his wife. "I think what Miss Duplessis did was a good exercise for all of us who have never faced dire poverty. Not everyone was born—or married—into money," he pointed out. "Now, why don't you try these fritters—they're excellent."

"I want the herb bread that's on the menu. Do you suppose she ruined it or something? Doubtless she had no idea how to plan for a group of this size and distinction. Please call the waiter, Galen and ask him for our bread and white wine."

"Since when do you drink white wine?" Tom asked her. "You've always preferred red."

"Well, tonight I want white. It's on the menu, so how can I fully experience this Canadian's version of fine dining without it?"

Galen shot her a weary glance and decided to go see for himself if anything was amiss with Lorelei. Maybe she had taken exception to being seated at the table with Vivian, in which case he would drag her to it by the hair if he had to, because she was definitely going to be by his side that night.

"Where are you going?" Justin asked when he saw Galen get up.

"Since no waiter seems to be nearby, I'll get some bread and white wine for Vivian." He bent to whisper into his brother's ear, "Keep an eye on Viv and make sure she doesn't follow me. I'm going to see how the little chef is doing."

When he entered the kitchens, he wasn't prepared to be see a stern-faced sous-chef guarding the door, holding a rolling pin like a club. Nor was he prepared to see countless cooks kneading dough on every inch of available counter space, his beautiful siren among them, wearing a white sundress, flour dusting her nose, hands and bare arms.

"What the hell are you doing? Get your staff to do whatever it is! Everybody's wondering where you are."

Lorelei sprinkled some flour on the countertop and turned to him. "Our four hundred and fifty loaves of bread were stolen and someone tried to freeze my wines. I didn't realize I had to hire security guards to protect my supplies, but my cooks are now split between guarding the food and preparing a ton of fresh bread."

"Are you serious?"

"Do I look like I'm joking?"

"Who did this?"

"If I knew, he'd be skewered on a stick, grilled over hot coals and served for supper as shish-kebab."

"All right, you'll explain all this to me later. For now I'll get some guards and then I'll make an announcement. I'll be damned if any of the other competitors win because of this."

Lorelei slammed the dough on the counter and wiped her hands on her dress. "You will do no such thing. I don't want anyone to know. If we at DesCheneaux cannot overcome such small obstacles, then we shouldn't even be chefs. Besides, I don't think this was the work of one of our competitors."

Galen tapped her on the nose. "I think you're being a little naïve, sweet and I won't let anyone take advantage of your trusting nature. The competition is off until I find the culprit."

Lorelei shot him an angry glance and fastened her fingers around his arm to stop him from leaving the kitchens. "The culprit is not a competitor but an outsider—an amateur. Bread can be easily replaced and some wines taste even better crystallized than they do chilled. The competitors all know that, Galen. It had to have been someone else—an imbecile—who did this."

Galen suddenly remembered Vivian's words. "Do you suppose she ruined it or something? Please call the waiter, Galen and ask him for our bread and white wine." The bitch! Vivian had arranged this disaster, he concluded, no doubt to humiliate Lorelei.

"Now go and get those guards, so my cooks can do the work they were meant to do."

"I'll do better than that. I'll get you guards and I will personally help you with the bread." He smiled and whispered in her ear, "I've been told I have very good hands."

Shivers ran down Lorelei's arm. In a whisper she asked, "Are you mad? You're a judge. You can't help me. If you really want to help, get me some of those burly men with the walkie-talkies and stay out of my kitchens."

"Then I'll make another deal with you. I'll stay outside my kitchens, which I am leasing out to you, on the condition that, one, I send Justin back here to oversee security and, two, you get back into your gown and come to the table. People are already speculating about your absence and I'm sure you don't want to give the culprit the satisfaction of knowing you're up to your ears in baking powder."

Lorelei put her hands on her hips. "Mr. Kennedy, for one thing, we don't use baking powder for bread and, besides, I hardly think the idiot's walking around waiting to be apprehended. One of the cooks knows what he looks like."

"Ah, he might know who performed the deed but not for whom it was performed. I am sure the author is at this very moment smiling to her—himself," he corrected, "thinking what a wondrous feat he accomplished. Now go and get dressed. By the time Justin arrives, I want you at the table, cool, calm and collected."

Resigned, Lorelei placed the dough in a tray and left the kitchens to change.

An instant later Maurice bustled into the room and addressed the wealthy Irishman without hesitation. "Mr. Kennedy, I am sure you have guests to attend to. As you can see, we have everything under control here."

Galen noted the older man's dismissive tone. "As a matter of fact," he replied, "Miss Duplessis also has guests to attend to and they're starting to think she has bad manners. I will have men posted to guard your kitchen doors and my brother will stay here with your team. I suggest that your protégée quickly grace us with her presence at the table of honor."

"I don't wish to be—how shall we say?—*cynique* but, like her family, Lorelei has never craved the company of the rich and famous," Maurice said, removing his chef's hat and placing it on the counter. "Cooking for them, yes, because they can appreciate her creative artistry. But hobnobbing with them? *Non*. Although she is cultured, speaks three languages and knows the difference between mere fish eggs and fine Russian caviar, she comes from humble roots. All her ancestors were *paysans*, as we say in French but her lack of an aristocratic lineage should not be the object of ridicule, as I am sure it could be tonight."

Galen did not take exception to the man's words because he understood that Maurice cared deeply for Lorelei. "Sir, I know that you love Lorelei and seek to protect her. But perhaps it is this 'protection', however well-intentioned, that has made her feel less than comfortable among those with greater financial means than hers."

Maurice was clearly taken aback. "Monsieur, my wife and I have always had Lorelei's best interests at heart. Lorelei's upbringing is none of your business and I am offended by your—how do you say in English? Ah, *oui*—at your effrontery."

Galen stiffened. "And I am offended that you would consider all wealthy people to be alike and possibly obnoxious. While it is true that those seven hundred guests in the gallery are all wealthy, there are decided differences among them. Some are wise, some are clever and some are fools. Besides, remember that it is the wealth out there that helps fund the Wexford Foundation's efforts to fight world hunger, including this culinary competition. If I were you, sir, I would encourage Lorelei to make the attempt to mix with the rich."

Maurice stepped closer and lowered his voice. "Monsieur, I respect your dedication to helping the less fortunate through your foundation. We are not talking about that, however. We are talking about a young woman who has been subjected to the most severe scrutiny, by both your male and female guests, at each soirée here since our arrival."

"Lorelei is beautiful, talented and smart and she should go freely wherever she chooses to, accepting the admiration she so richly deserves and ignoring any cynics who are foolish enough to think otherwise." With that, Galen turned to make his way back to the reception.

Lorelei was giving instructions to François, who was preparing the second course, when Justin came looking for her.

"Hmm, if you ever want to turn in my brother for a younger, suaver version, I'd be glad to fill in."

She answered him by handing him a lump of dough.

"Here, 'fill in' by kneading. I'm sure you'll be good at it."

She couldn't help but smile at Justin's dismay.

"Why, thank you. I'm good at many things, especially with my hands," he said suggestively. "Or so the American women tell me."

"No doubt." She rolled her eyes and turned to Antoine.

"Please have Mr. Kennedy fitted with a smock and instructed how to knead the dough."

Antoine returned almost immediately with a smock for Justin and Lorelei laughed at the younger Kennedy's disappointed expression as she left the kitchen.

When she arrived at the head table, she couldn't help but notice how close Vivian Gallagher was sitting to Galen. The blonde whispered something in his ear that made him laugh. Her hand rested on his thigh, while her husband remained engrossed in a conversation with the mayor of Boston, oblivious to the intimacy.

Though irritated by Vivian's blatantly possessive attitude, Lorelei sat down demurely on Galen's other side.

"Miss Duplessis!" The senator looked up to greet her.

"How lovely to have you join us at long last. I was just telling Mayor DiGiacomo here that, living in Quebec, you're probably fluent in at least two languages. Isn't that right?" Tom Gallagher asked.

"Three," she replied simply, unfolding her linen napkin.

She slid her chair in as a waiter poured wine into her glass.

"If you were a politician, you'd probably get elected just for being able speak the language of the voter—which doesn't say much about us, does it, DiGiacomo?" the senator said. The two men chuckled and continued eating.

The waiter presented a bottle of white wine to them.

Vivian reached to peel back the linen napkin around the bottle and pretended to examine the label. "My, my, I think this wine is spoiled. It has particles at the bottom. See?"

"Those are ice crystals, Mrs. Gallagher," Lorelei offered. "When you're serving a not-too-dry Alsatian wine, which is the case with this Ste-Odile, it's sometimes preferable to chill it to just below its freezing point. It acquires a potency similar to that of a Grappa and makes you feel as if you're sipping frozen fire. I like the effect, so I proposed it for tonight."

"It still looks spoiled," Vivian replied cattily.

"Then I suggest you stick with the mineral water," Lorelei said as blandly as possible. Suddenly though, it occurred to her to wonder if the woman was responsible for sabotaging her kitchen. Eyeing Vivian closely, she said, "Unfortunately, the technician who came to regulate our refrigerators' thermostat today evidently received no such instructions from his employer to do the same for the soft drinks fridge. So you'll find the bottled water rather tepid, I'm afraid." She tipped her glass at Vivian.

"You know, gentlemen, Miss Duplessis is expert in oenology," Galen interjected. "So I'm sure we'll be pleasantly surprised by her choice of wines for tonight. I, for one, can't wait to taste her 'frozen fire'." He picked up his glass and took a sip.

Lorelei almost choked on her wine.

Vivian stood to go to the ladies' room. "If you'll excuse me, Galen," she said, effectively ignoring everyone else at the table, "I'm going to make a quick trip to the powder room."

"Why don't I escort you there, Vivian. I have to make a call," Galen replied to everyone's surprise.

Watching them leave together, Lorelei felt like a fool.

"Miss Duplessis, won't you do me the honor of this dance?" Senator Gallagher asked from behind her chair, his hands on her shoulders.

She looked up and smiled as serenely as she could. He stood aside to allow her to get up. "It would be my privilege, Senator."

On the dance floor, he stood dangerously close to her.

She began to feel uncomfortable.

"You must excuse my wife, Lorelei. She's envious of you and I can't say I blame her."

Lorelei frowned. "But your wife is a beautiful woman. Why would she be—"

"Jealous?" he finished for her. "She can't stand the way Kennedy looks at you and acts around you."

Lorelei stepped back to look at him, shocked that he would make such an admission and afraid that he knew about her own involvement with Galen. "There's nothing improper about his behavior toward me, I assure you. He's been nothing but cordial to me and my team since we've been here."

"I'm sure he has but any woman who sparks his attention, as you so obviously do, puts Vivian into a frenzy. She thinks I don't know they're having an affair but I do."

He paused when he saw Lorelei's stunned expression. "Don't worry, dear, this isn't the first time. Normally I make sure she conducts herself discreetly but I'm making an exception here, because I believe in a few more days it won't matter much. Galen Kennedy will be behind bars and she'll get over her infatuation soon enough."

"Behind bars?" Lorelei stared at him, aghast. Why was he telling her this and on what grounds did he expect Galen to be arrested? Her mind flashed to the gun smugglers aboard the *Irish Siren* and she shivered. Was Galen involved in criminal activity after all?

Gallagher leaned closer to whisper in her ear. "This is strictly confidential but the government is monitoring his shipping operations. Since you were seen boarding his ship, they asked me to find out if you saw any proof there that he's smuggling weapons to Northern Ireland."

Or if I witnessed the murder, she thought in horror.

"Weapons to Ireland?" she repeated, feigning surprise. "Senator, this is a shock. Are you sure about Mr. Kennedy?"

"Of course we are. That's why we need your help, dear," Gallagher whispered as he tightened his hold on her. "Did you see anything?"

Lorelei resisted the impulse to jerk away and run but she couldn't help the shudder of fear that raced up her spine. No way would the United States Government collude with a senator to tell a near-stranger, who was not even a citizen, about a suspected weapons smuggler, much less a planned sting operation. It was simply absurd. Besides, on a purely personal level, she didn't like the man. If he condoned his wife's having affairs right in front of him, was he any more trustworthy than she?

Lorelei didn't know why Gallagher was telling her what should amount to classified information but she reasoned that the more he told her, the more danger she was in.

As he moved her around the dance floor, she scanned the crowd, looking for help. But Galen was still absent, Justin—obviously having escaped the kitchen—was talking to the mayor and the waiters she saw were hotel staffers, not hers.

She mustn't panic, she told herself sternly. Gallagher would immediately suspect that something was wrong.

"You haven't answered my question," he almost snapped.

She flinched. "Well, aside from picking up my merchandise, nothing much happened while I was there, so I'm afraid I can't help you, Senator."

His sigh of relief was so well-rehearsed, she didn't buy it for a minute. "Well, thank God for that. Because if you had seen something and weren't telling me, you could be in serious trouble, my dear. Remember," he said as his lips almost touched her ear, "some Irishmen have no scruples."

"Is that so?" she replied, his thinly veiled threat making anger rise inside her and almost overcome her fear. "Then I'll make it a point not to get involved with any of them."

"Funny but someone mentioned that your relationship with one Irishman might already be more than platonic."

She paused. "Senator, at the risk of sounding redundant, I can't help you. I'm here in Hyannis Port to win a competition, not wage someone else's war." She managed to disengage herself from his hold, suddenly repulsed by the touch of his hands. "And another thing—don't ever try to blackmail me again. I'm at a point in my life where I have nothing to lose." With that, she headed for the kitchens.

Galen returned to the table to find Lorelei gone. His attempt to have a private talk with Vivian had failed—the reception coordinator had repeatedly interrupted them.

"What did I miss?" he asked Justin.

"I don't know. One minute Lorelei was dancing with Gallagher, the next she was practically running to the kitchens. I called out to her but she didn't even look back."

"Something's gone wrong, Justin."

"Aye but what?" his brother asked.

"*Petite*, what are you doing?"

"I'm packing up my cookbooks and utensils."

"*Pourquoi?*"

"Why? Because we're leaving first thing tomorrow and I want to be ready."

"But you promised the staff they could have a day off at the beach. Surely you haven't forgotten."

"No, I haven't but I heard it's going to rain for the next few days." It was a lie but she had to find a way to convince everyone to leave. "So we might as well go back and relax at home. We'll give them the rest of the week off once we get to Montreal. I'm sure they'll appreciate that more."

"Fine but must you be here in the kitchens in that beautiful gown while your guests expect you to be at the table?"

"Maurice, please, you know I hate socializing. I don't want to go back there. I said my good nights to everyone already. Aren't you serving the Irish coffee soon?"

He smiled but seemed to know she was keeping something from him. "*Oui. C'est bien.* Sit down and relax here while Maurice makes you a nice double espresso. I have seldom seen you so upset. *Qu'est-il arrivé d'autre?*"

"Nothing else happened, Maurice." She just wasn't ready to invent more explanations. "Come to think of it, I'm so tired, I think I'll head upstairs and start packing my clothes. Thank you for the offer but I feel too wired right now to drink coffee." She kissed his cheek. "You'll say good night for me to the team, won't you?" she added.

Maurice grumbled his assent. "Maybe it is a good idea to leave as early as possible. This place has given you nothing but problems since you arrived."

Chapter Fifteen

Each relationship prepares us for the next.

☙

Later that night Lorelei stared at the ceiling of her bedroom, rigid with dread. Until the day before, her only wish in life had been to discover how her parents died. Now another death plagued her. This time, though, she had been there. She might not have seen it happen but she'd heard it. Oh yes, she'd heard it and the sound of that silenced gun, the sound of a life being ended, had been echoing in her mind ever since.

As she lay in the dark, trying at least to doze, trying futilely to block out the memory, an explosion in her head nearly blinded her with pain. She felt incredible heat, yet shivers ran down her arms. She tried to get up, all at once frantic to get help but she couldn't. Her legs, her arms, her entire body felt paralyzed. She struggled to breathe and slowly the pain in her head began to subside.

She was dying, she realized. Yet how could she be?

A cry of despair rang out—her cry?—and a name flashed into her mind—Michael Logan. It was as if it was her own name, as if she was the person to whom it belonged. She looked down at herself. Except it was a man's body she saw and blood was running down the front of her shirt. A face appeared within the night shadows, a smiling, peaceful face and she somehow knew that it belonged to the man who was bleeding. Not her but the man she'd heard executed.

Now she knew what the victim looked like. She knew his name. Somehow she had gone inside his body—had, in fact, been him—as he'd been shot and killed. She had taken from him some of his agony.

It was happening again, and again she would have to learn to live with the nightmare of knowing someone else's pain, of seeing it, of living it, without being able to change the outcome. Was this to be her punishment for not having been able to stop the murder just as she had not been able to stop the one of her parents?

"Michael Logan. God speed," she whispered seconds before blackness claimed her.

* * * * *

In the morning Lorelei awakened to a gloomy day, her last in Hyannis Port. Perhaps her prediction of rain, at least, would prove true and the team would not regret leaving. Even if DesCheneaux did not win the competition, she realized, she would still have something to be grateful for. Now that she had learned the identity of the man who'd been murdered aboard the *Irish Siren* she could give the name to the authorities. Surely this time her dream would help someone.

She would also say goodbye to Galen Kennedy. Or had he said it already by leaving the table last night with Vivian Gallagher on his arm? Maybe she should thank him, then, for making it easier. Nothing would stop her now from closing this, perhaps the last, chapter of her life.

Had Galen had sex with the blonde last night? Had he slowly undressed her, letting his hands roam all over her body? Had his gaze and hands and mouth lingered on every part of her until she felt she would melt from the fire?

Lorelei tried to banish the thoughts and images crowding her mind. She had neither time nor space for them.

She dressed mechanically, preparing for the awards brunch by donning the clothes she would wear for her journey home—a pair of soft leather pants, a matching vest and boots.

Before stepping out, she closed and locked her luggage, determined to leave as soon as the reception was over.

Galen waited among the crowd of contestants, guests and press almost twenty minutes before he saw Lorelei enter the Siren's reception hall. He had hoped to have a few minutes of privacy with her before the awards ceremony but the impenetrable look she tossed him as she walked past him gave him pause. Something clenched in his gut, something like fear. What had changed within her since she retired alone to her room last night, unwilling to accept his calls or a visit?

Determined to find out, he started toward her.

"Stay where you are," Justin said, recognizing his brother's intentions. "There'll be time soon enough to have your *tête-à-tête*."

Galen watched Lorelei kiss the head chef. Then the burly Frenchman touched her cheek and spoke to her. "There's something wrong, Justin."

"We already determined that last night. After the ceremony we're going to find out what."

"It's different today. She's different," he reiterated. He recognized that look of distance, of separation from others, especially those you were going to part from. Doubtless he had worn that same look after he killed Bryan, just before he lost Brenna…

"We're on, brother." Justin gestured toward the stage, interrupting his thoughts.

He and Justin were joined by the town's mayor, who was going to award the medals and the winning prize, a purse of one million dollars. Galen began his speech, explaining that following the DesCheneaux dinner, with its introductory symbolic poor man's supper, a record ten million dollars had been pledged to the Wexford Foundation's hunger-relief efforts. He congratulated all the participants and on behalf of the six judges, whose identities were finally revealed, he announced that DesCheneaux had won the revered Gold Medal of International Gastronomy.

While her colleagues cheered raucously on their way to the podium, Lorelei walked quietly. She looked stunned, distant, removed from her victory, even as she smiled at the mayor, who shook her hand heartily.

Maurice Leblanc looked positively ecstatic. He kissed his wife and hung his medal around her neck.

Although Lorelei was happy for DesCheneaux, especially for Maurice, who deserved such a victory, in a way she was sorry to have won. She wondered if Galen had voted for her after all, or exercised his influence to aid DesCheneaux, thus giving her an unfair advantage over the other teams.

Once her medal hung around her neck, she stepped to the microphone and made a very short speech. "I feel honored to have participated in this extraordinary event and I am especially proud that so many contributed so generously to the Feed the World Foundation. Likewise, our purse money will be donated back to the foundation. As for this medal, I can only say that your praise means a great deal to us. I hope, however, that the other participants realize just what formidable competitors they were." She put her hands together to applaud the other groups.

Soon everyone followed her example. "Thank you all and have a safe journey home," she concluded.

For the next hour Galen watched Lorelei accept congratulations. Everyone on her team was misty-eyed, especially Maurice Leblanc, who seemed to be holding on to her for dear life. His pride in her could not have been more obvious. Galen marveled at her generosity to her colleagues and her modest demeanor even when she was asked to pose for pictures for the press. He didn't think he would ever grow tired of looking at her.

But could their relationship last? Would his love be enough to stop her from withdrawing from him, from life, from crossing that dangerous line between life and death? Because he knew, the way a con man recognized his own kind, that that was where she was heading. And it scared the hell out of him.

He wanted her alive, whole and forever with him.

"Ms. Duplessis? Hi, I'm Gary Burns, freelance photographer."

"Nice to meet you, Mr. Burns. What can we do for you?" Lorelei responded.

"Well, I was sent by the American Culinary Association to shoot a photo spread of the winners." He showed her his letter of introduction. "I was wondering, however, if instead of doing the usual thing, we could take some pictures at the beach with your staff, a representative of Wexford's Foundation and the 959 Special Edition Porsche I hear you own and drove here."

Lorelei hesitated. The car was practically sold and no longer hers. She didn't want to mislead anyone. Yet posing with it would be a nice tribute to her most cherished possession.

"So is it the winners or the car you want, Mr. Burns?" she replied with a twinkle in her eye.

"Come now, Ms. Duplessis, it's you and your team, of course. But I'll admit that I am a car fanatic. So why not combine pleasure with more pleasure?"

"I'm not sure about driving the Porsche onto a beach, though..."

"Oh, not to worry. I found just the right spot." The hope in his voice was too obvious to miss. "I promise, the terrain is smooth. I tested it with my own car."

Given his assurances, she agreed. "Very well. I'll round up my gang and I take it you'll ask Mr. Kennedy to join us?" She wanted to avoid direct contact with Galen.

"No need for him to ask. I'll be happy to join you." Galen, who had been standing behind Lorelei while the photographer made his pitch, put his hands on her shoulders, just in case the man had any ideas beyond the photo shoot. A look of understanding flashed over Burns' face.

Although Lorelei's back stiffened, she pretended nothing was amiss. "I'll advise my team and we'll meet you in the front of the hotel."

"Would you mind very much having a passenger with you?" Burns asked her.

Lorelei smiled. "No, of course not."

"Thank you. I'll get the rest of my gear and meet you outside, ma'am. Mr. Kennedy," he said, saluting before he sauntered out.

"I need to speak to you, Lorelei."

She shrugged but didn't turn around. "I'm sorry but I've got to round everybody up. It'll have to wait."

"It can't wait. Look at me, damn it!"

She turned and raised her gaze, her eyes burning into his.

"Sorry, I didn't mean to shout. It's just that one of our freighter ships is still docked at Boston harbor and I have a meeting there right after this."

"We don't leave until this afternoon," she stalled, knowing that almost everything was loaded into the trucks already. "We can talk then."

He sighed, not totally relieved but glad he had at least broken the icy silence of the night before.

One hour later they were all in position on the beach, the DesCheneaux staff in their white uniforms and Lorelei in her leather outfit with the Médaille d'Honneur around her neck. Gary Burns was totally enthralled by the setting and pose.

Maurice, Antoine, François and the other members of the staff were standing around the Porsche. Asking them to smile was superfluous, with all the champagne they had ingested at the awards brunch, it looked as if the party had never stopped.

The car was parked parallel to the ocean and Lorelei lay on her side on its hood, her chin propped on her left hand.

Galen stood in front of the 959, facing the camera, his arms crossed. He thought that, at that moment, Lorelei Duplessis was the most seductive woman ever to have walked the Earth.

Behind her, Antoine and François were laughing and making jokes rich with innuendo in French, saying that the rear view of the Porsche was as good as the front.

Galen was not amused. "I warn you, Lorelei," he muttered to her, "I understand French and if they don't stop making remarks about your butt, I'll go back there and smack them."

"Who says they're talking about my butt?" she said with an arch smile.

Galen's look of astonishment was priceless. But when she winked at him, his smile undid her. At that precise moment Gary Burns snapped his first picture, freezing the happy moment in time, preserving a few precious seconds Lorelei knew she would one day soon be cherishing alone.

Galen continued staring at her. "You don't know how hard I'm restraining myself from ripping off your clothes and making love to you right on the hood of this car—hard being the operative word," he said to her softly, privately.

"People, could you please look straight at the camera, or we'll never get this done!" Gary Burns shouted.

Galen looked at the camera but he continued murmuring to Lorelei, "One day, sweet, you'll pose for me on that car and in that leather outfit. And I promise you that afterward you'll never look at your car the same way again. You'll remember us. You'll remember the sensation of cool metal under your back and the heat of my naked body on yours every time you go near your precious Porsche."

Little did he know that soon her car would no longer be hers—just as he had never been. Since she had drunk a little champagne at the brunch with the others, her mood, however, was spunky rather than morose. What the hell—what did she have to lose? "In your dreams, Kennedy," she shot back at him.

"Oh, I can afford to do more than dream," he retorted, encouraged by her playfulness.

"But you can't afford me," she teased.

"Name your price," he challenged.

"You can't afford it."

"Try me."

"Exclusivity."

He cocked an eyebrow at her. "You've had that since the beginning, love."

"I wasn't referring to other women," she explained.

"Okay, thank you, everyone, for your time!" Gary called out happily. "You were all great!"

Lorelei slid off the car and immediately faced the interview she'd promised Gary to go with the pictures. It would take place a few minutes later. Maurice approached her as well, then agreed to ride back to the hotel with the rest of the staff to complete their departure preparations.

Before she began the interview, however, Galen took her aside. "What were you referring to, then?" he asked.

She smiled at his obvious confusion. "By exclusivity I was referring to one person's exclusive choice as to when and how to end things between us. The choice has to be mine." If he was somehow involved with the murder she'd witnessed aboard one of his ships, she'd have to get away from him quickly.

He pursed his lips and shook his head. "No way, lady. This is not a bloody business contract." He grabbed her by the shoulders and yanked her closer to him. "This is about you and me. I know you care about me and I know you want me. And I care about and want you too."

"You don't underst—"

"Don't I? You think I don't recognize the signs—the thing that's written on your face every time you think nobody's looking?"

She stared at him in disbelief.

"Right. If you think I can't stop you, think again." Galen knew he was risking everything by confronting her but there came a time when a man had to play his hand, even if he had to play dirty. "All I have to do is speak to Maurice."

Her eyes opened wide with surprise. "I don't know what you're talking about!"

"Don't you?" Releasing her, he took a few steps back. "You'd better wait for me this afternoon and finally tell me why you want to do it, so I can understand. Who knows? Maybe I'll even agree to your condition." He never would, of course. Not in a million years.

She shook her head.

"Hey, we've made love," he said more quietly. "And it was lovemaking, not just sex. Surely that entitles me to at least an explanation."

"There's nothing to explain but we'll discuss it later," she conceded. Then she turned toward the eager reporter waiting for her. She saw Galen give her a final exasperated look, then get into his Jaguar and leave.

The interview lasted longer than she'd expected and was certainly more thorough than what she thought she had agreed to. Her conversation with Galen kept clouding her mind and making it difficult to concentrate on the journalist's questions.

Although certain subjects were off-limits, such as her personal life and the death of her parents, Lorelei was able to discuss freely what she loved the most, her work and the people involved in it.

Once they were finished and getting ready to leave, before getting into the DesCheneaux van, Gary, too, they said goodbye to her and to the 959. Gary congratulated her on her victory and noted her address in Montreal to send her a copy of his photo spread.

Once on the highway, with the asphalt humming beneath the Porsche's tires, she finally attempted to put things into perspective. She had witnessed a murder, one that could possibly mean the Kennedys' downfall if it was discovered that, in fact, Galen and his brother were involved. Maybe the Kennedys were trying to discover whether Senator Gallagher was on to them.

After all, staying close to your enemies was the best way to know what they were up to.

On the other hand, Galen had implied that he'd been sleeping with Vivian to obtain information about something that involved the lives of many people. In that case, the Kennedys could be trying to stop the smuggling and Senator Gallagher.

After all, what high-profile political figure would knowingly let his wife have affairs and close his eyes to the matter? Why would he have divulged secret, privileged information to a Canadian chef, asked questions about her visit to the *Irish Siren*, made veiled threats, if he wasn't involved in illegalities, if he didn't have something to gain or something greater to lose?

She figured it was time to trust someone and her instincts told her to speak to Galen and reveal what she had witnessed.

She was sure the vision in her dream was accurate. The victim's name was Michael Logan and she would do what she could to avenge his death before Senator Gallagher realized what she knew. If it was the last meaningful thing she could do in her life, she would do it.

Chapter Sixteen

Often the more we seek to understand, the less clearly we see.

છા

When Galen arrived at the docks, he parked his Jaguar and headed for the *Irish Siren*. He hated the delay in getting back to the hotel, to Lorelei but Donald O'Hara had insisted he come, saying he couldn't discuss the matter over the phone.

Galen couldn't imagine what the hell would prevent Donald from coming to the hotel to speak with him but he figured it wasn't good news.

Once on board he went straight to the cargo hold where Donald had said he'd be waiting. Galen thought it strange that Donald had locked the door but when he opened it with his key, he instantly understood the need to keep others out. *Jesus.*

Donald was sitting at a desk some ten feet away from the steps, staring up at him. Next to him was Vivian Gallagher's lifeless body, slumped in a wooden chair, gagged and bound, a small blood-smudged hole between her open eyes. A note was pinned to her chest.

Paralyzed with shock, Galen read the bold black letters:

BACK OFF OR YOUR CANADIAN WHORE IS NEXT.

Aside from the wave of fear crashing over him at the crude threat to Lorelei, he felt overwhelming remorse. For all Vivian's vanity and selfishness, she hadn't deserved this.

With two fingers he shut her eyes, which had been left staring into a future she no longer had. He murmured a few expletives, then turned to Donald, who hadn't said a word.

"What do you know about this?"

"I found her while I was checking the freight. Nobody saw or heard anything as far as I know."

Galen didn't need any witnesses to know who'd ordered the killing, if not who'd executed the order. Gallagher had probably discovered his wife's affair with the man who was trying to nail him. But how had he found out about Lorelei?

He looked at Donald with curiosity. "Who did this, do you think?"

Donald shrugged as he stood from the desk. "Could've been anyone with keys to the cargo holds."

Yes, Galen thought, it could've been anyone. He stared at the other man, assessing. Donald O'Hara had been with him many years. It simply didn't make sense that he suddenly would have turned traitor.

Galen sighed. His priority now was getting Lorelei to safety.

"I'll call Jack Doherty. He can use his government contacts to handle all this as discreetly as possible, override the local police force and keep the media circus to a minimum. Once he gets here, you and I head for the hotel to put extra security in place."

Galen left the ship with Donald after Doherty and three other men in black suits arrived in a dark blue van.

Jack Doherty was an old friend of the Kennedys and one of the few who was aware of their suspicions of gun smuggling aboard Wexford ships. He was in charge of a special task force set up by the Bureau of Alcohol, Tobacco and Firearms to investigate and stop the illegal trade of arms from the US to Northern Ireland. Galen had readily agreed to keep Doherty informed of anything irregular he and Justin uncovered and in turn Doherty would allow the Wexford ships to run their scheduled routes without unnecessary inspections or interference. He'd keep his men off Kennedy properties unless he got a call from either Galen or Justin, which would preserve the secrecy of the investigation with the appearance of business as usual.

As he and Donald got into the Jaguar, Galen remembered the note he had found on Vivian. It struck him suddenly, like a fist in the gut, that whoever killed Vivian might not wait to strike again. They might, at that very moment, be murdering Lorelei. He had to get to her before they did. Whoever they were. He was almost positive about the identity of at least one of them and he couldn't wait to see the senator finally get what was coming to him. "You bastard," he muttered, sliding his key into the ignition.

Once underway, he headed for the highway instead of Harbor Road, avoiding the delay of traffic lights. He was in the right lane of the highway when the black Bronco in front of him moved into the left lane to pass the car ahead of him.

Seconds later Lorelei's Porsche came into view. Aside from its distinctive color and design, it had a vanity plate reading Nemesis.

Relief swept through him. She was safe and sound and as soon as they arrived at the hotel, he would convince her to let him take her away, somewhere he'd be sure no one could harm her.

A few minutes later Galen noticed that the Bronco was still driving alongside Lorelei, dangerously crowding her lane.

Seconds later the SUV swerved toward the Porsche, missing it by a hair.

"Christ, he's gonna hit her!" Galen shouted, accelerating toward the two vehicles. Lorelei abruptly sped up as well. "Call the cops!" he ordered when he realized the Bronco was staying on her tail. "Hurry, damn it!" He threw his cell phone at Donald.

Lorelei was swearing by the time she realized the driver beside her had purposely tried to run her off the road. That's when she came eye to eye with a machine gun barrel pointed out the passenger's window. She floored the gas pedal, shifting seconds later into sixth gear and leaving the black Bronco in her dust. "Catch me if you can, bastard," she snarled, ignoring the gunshots she heard in her wake.

She flew past an electronic sign signaling heavy traffic less than a quarter of a mile ahead. She aimed for an exit.

Unfortunately, as she geared down and sped toward the right lane, she noticed a small pickup truck piled with furniture slowly puttering toward the same exit. The lane was made for only one car. She would risk killing the pickup driver and herself if she tried squeezing past him.

Determined to ditch her pursuers, who were now coming back into view, she eyed the oncoming traffic on the opposite side of the highway and decided to make her move. She glanced into her side mirror for a second, veered left across the two other lanes, then downshifted to fourth gear, turning sharply to the left again to cut across the grass median dividing the highway.

She had calculated for everything except an eight-foot wide ditch in the middle of the median. The gap was too wide to jump, especially since she had reduced her speed. Her front end plunged and, at high speed, the car naturally flipped, flying into the air and across the three lanes of oncoming traffic before dropping back onto all four wheels at the far side of the highway.

When Galen saw Lorelei's Porsche narrowly evade the bullets coming from the gun sticking out the passenger window of the Bronco, he knew he had to do something to stop the SUV so she could get away.

"Hang on, Donald," he warned as he sped toward the Bronco, then passed it on the right and cut in front of it, forcing the driver to veer straight onto the median and into a ditch there.

Simultaneously he saw Lorelei's silver car sail through the air and crash-land on the opposite side of the highway. "No!" he shouted as he slammed on the brakes and brought the Jag to a screeching, skidding halt. He jumped out, blinded by fear, the stench of burned rubber in his nostrils. He ran across the median, leaping to avoid the ditch but falling, his hands grasping grass and mud, his feet dangling in murky water. He scrambled up and ran ahead, dodging through three lanes of traffic, dimly hearing a police siren already approaching. He had been driving so fast, he had come to a stop quite a distance from the Porsche, and it seemed to take forever to reach it.

The officers were getting out of their cruiser when he neared the wreckage. "Call an ambulance!" he shouted. Motioning them toward the disabled Bronco, he added, "And if that bastard is still alive, arrest him!" Running, he headed for Lorelei's car.

Holy Mother of God, please let her be alive.

When he saw her emerge from the Porsche seemingly unscathed, he thought he was seeing her ghost.

She just stood there, tears streaming down her face. "Did you see what happened to my car?" she said. "What am I going to do now?"

Galen reached for her with trembling arms, frowning first at her remark, then smiling. She was safe and sound and that was all that mattered. "We'll have it fixed, baby. It will be as good as new."

She took a step back. "You don't understand. I won't get the price I need for it. I'm going to lose my home. I'm going to lose my home to that bastard!"

"Lorelei, you're in shock. What are you talking about?"

"Marc Delage will take my home and…and…"

He stepped closer. "Baby, come here and let me hold you."

When he finally had her in his arms, he closed his eyes and silently thanked the saints above. He managed to shepherd her through the patrolmen's questions, then walk her toward his car. He had to get his miracle woman to a hospital to have her checked out and make sure she was all right.

Before they reached the Jaguar, they saw one of the officers arresting the driver of the Bronco. He and his passenger had also been spared serious injury. Tomorrow Galen would pay the men a visit at the local police precinct, after which the bastards would wish they had died in the crash. Once Lorelei was safe, he would get a confession about whom the men were working for.

It appeared Lorelei wanted to know, as well. She pushed his arm off her shoulders and strode toward the policeman handcuffing the culprits.

Before Galen could stop her, she pulled the gun from the cop's holster and pressed the muzzle to the head of the man who had damaged her car. "Can you afford to pay for the repairs?" she asked him in no uncertain terms. "They're going to cost the Earth, you know."

The man groggily tried to turn his head to look at her.

"Answer me, you bastard! Can you pay for the repairs?"

The man simply stared at her.

"Fine, then give me your boss's name—the guy who's going to pay for this!"

"Drop the gun, lady!" The other cop had approached them and was now pointing his weapon at her.

Galen's blood boiled with fury. Couldn't they see she was in shock?

"So help me God, I want the name, or you'll die choking on your blood with a bullet in your larynx!" She looked quite ready to do what she threatened.

The cop holding the gun looked at Galen, then back at Lorelei. He spoke with less force this time, clearly beginning to grasp her mental state. "Ma'am, please drop the weapon. The suspect might have a head injury and he's clearly on drugs. He doesn't even understand what you're asking him."

"He's right, Lorelei," Galen said softly. "We can wait. Trust me, I have a few questions for him as well." He stepped toward her. "Come on, baby, give the policeman back his gun before his partner is forced to shoot you. Because if he does, then I'll have to kill him and then I'll end up in jail."

Strangely enough, his voice had a soothing effect on her.

She lowered her hand slowly, clearly disappointed that she wouldn't get any satisfaction from the man who'd ruined her car. She let the gun fall to the ground and without another glance walked away.

Galen reached her in a few steps, mouthing a thank-you to the cops, then saying to Lorelei, "Since the ambulance isn't here yet, I'm going to take you to the hospital."

She looked back at the Porsche. "My car. I have to call a transport truck or something. I have to get it fixed."

"Forget the damn car for a minute!" He immediately regretted shouting at her. He lowered his voice and looked at her tenderly. "If I promise your Nemesis will be waiting for you at the hotel when we get back, will you come to the hospital with me?"

She looked at him absently then started walking back to the car. "Fine. I need a phone. My purse. I need my purse. I have to call Gillen."

"Who the hell is Gillen?" he shouted again as he stepped beside her.

"Douglas Gillen. He's my car dealer," she answered, stomping away from him her mind in disarray and irritated she had to answer so many questions. "He has to know, because he sold my car. Now he'll have to fix it before the end of next week."

"Sold it? You're selling the Porsche?"

When Lorelei reached her car, she bit back more tears. She hoped it had sustained the fall well. Her purse had landed somewhere between the back and front seats near the stick shift with all of its contents strewn around. The driver's door was still open and carefully she bent down to collect everything and the purse.

"Damn it, let me do it!" Galen reached for her shoulders trying to gently have her step aside. "Why are you selling this car?"

"I have to pay Delage back. Oh Galen, just take me back to the hotel. Maurice will be waiting and worrying about me." She was terrified that whoever was after her might have hired more thugs to go after her mentor, as well, figuring she'd told him what she'd seen on the ship.

Galen decided to question her later about this business of losing her home. "I'll take you to the hospital first. Then I'll take you home and you can explain everything to me."

Donald was leaning on the Jaguar, waiting. He straightened quickly as they approached.

Galen began, "Lorelei, this is Donald O'Hara. Donald, this is…" He heard Lorelei gasp, then noted that her face had gone even whiter. "Baby, are you all right?"

No, she wasn't. For an instant her gaze remained riveted to Donald O'Hara's scarred face—the face of Michael Logan's murderer. Then, with a tiny whimper, she fainted.

Lorelei woke up with a jolt, disoriented at first, then slowly gaining her bearings. She was in a hospital, on a gurney, in a cubicle—the emergency room. She remembered the accident. The car pursuing her. Someone shooting at her. Then she recalled Galen's look of disbelief when she emerged from the Porsche alive. Or had it been disappointment? Had he known that someone would try to kill her on her way back to the hotel? Had he followed her to make sure it happened? That could be why the man named Donald O'Hara was with him. He'd told Galen she was in the hold of the ship that day and perhaps had seen him kill Michael Logan.

She started to tremble. "I have to get out of here," she mumbled. She scrambled off the gurney, and sat back on it, because her head was spinning and she felt dizzy. She looked around and spotted her clothes folded on a chair, then slowly this time, slid down and reached for them. When she zipped her pants, she noticed her purse was nowhere to be seen. She took a last look around then remembered she always carried extra cash in her pants pocket no matter where she was. After checking her right back pocket, relieved, she found several hundred-dollar bills she had planned to carry while making the six-hour trip back to Montreal. That's all she needed. She peeked around the cubicle's curtain and recognized Galen's voice. He was speaking on his cell phone. When she slowly looked out, she saw him standing further away with his back toward her. She waited a minute then darted out and headed for the nearest exit her head pounding like a jackhammer. Once outside, she cut through the parking lot and crossed the street to a taxi stand.

Out of breath and slightly dizzy, she instructed the driver to take her to the hotel, hoping the American money she had left would cover the fare.

She asked the driver to let her out around the corner from the Siren. She wanted to go in through the kitchens and make her way upstairs without anyone noticing. She would find Maurice, explain the situation to him—omitting the murder, of course—then she would call Douglas Gillen, provided her car was at the inn as promised.

When Lorelei found Maurice, she didn't have much to explain. Her car had already been brought on a flatbed to the hotel.

While they were loading the trucks for their trip home, she called Gillen and arranged to have the Porsche transported to his dealership via a Mercedes-Benz dealer in Boston, who had a shipment of cars leaving for Montreal the next day. Then she called the transport company the Mercedes dealer recommended to have her car picked up in Hyannis Port and dropped off in Boston. Finally she asked the front desk to check for flights from Hyannis to Boston then to Montreal. Luckily she could make the late afternoon flight.

Although pale and in total disarray, Lorelei managed to convince Maurice that she was fine but too edgy to sit through an eight-hour drive home with the rest of them. She told him that she was going to fly back instead. Amid her protests and his shouting, they compromised. She agreed to take Annabelle with her provided she found a seat on her flight. He added that she'd put him through enough torment for one trip.

Lorelei wished she could explain to him the reasons for her hasty departure but she feared that if she did, she would further endanger their lives, not just her own.

A few minutes later she and Annabelle were on their way to Hyannis Airport to catch a flight to Boston and a connecting one to Montreal. If all went well, they'd be home before the end of the day.

* * * * *

When Galen finished filling out all the hospital forms, he waited impatiently for Lorelei's ER doctor to reappear. Finally he decided to go see Lorelei for himself.

When he reached her cubicle, however, he found another patient there. Thinking he had made a mistake or somehow missed her being moved to a regular room, he went to the nurses' station to inquire.

"Let me see, Lorelei Duplessis, Lorelei Dupl— Oh, she left, sir."

"What do you mean, she left?" he growled. "You must be mistaken."

The nurse looked at him over her reading glasses. "That's what it says here."

"But I assumed she would be admitted for observation. She was brought in unconscious after a car accident! You just let her go? She probably didn't even know I was here, for God's sake!"

The nurse checked her register again. "I'm afraid she left on her own sir. AMA."

Against medical advice. Galen pursed his lips and muttered an oath in frustration.

"Can you tell me when?"

The nurse shrugged apologetically. "I'm sorry, no. Apparently she simply took off and, as you can see, this is a pretty busy place."

"Look, lady, that woman was brought here because an attempt was made on her life!" he bellowed. "I have to know now if she walked out of here on her own or if someone took her away!"

An orderly overhearing the shouting approached the counter. "Sir, I might have seen your friend leave. Is she about medium height, long brown hair and wearing a leather outfit?"

Galen sighed in relief. "Yes, that's her."

He smiled reassuringly. "I saw her leave about half an hour ago. She was alone and she seemed fine to me. I assumed she was a visitor."

"Thank you. You've been a great help."

Christ Almighty. Furious he had let her out of his sight, he called Justin, explained the situation to him and told him to grab the little miscreant by the hair or the seat of her pants if he had to, but to keep her at the hotel until his return. She had to be there, where else could she have gone?

"What do you mean she left?" Galen shouted at his brother, who had met him in the Siren's lobby.

"Apparently she took a flight home," Justin explained. "She had already left by the time I went to look for her. The front desk booked the flight for her and another person. Her aunt I think."

Galen headed for the kitchens. Maybe Maurice was still there. "What about the car?" he asked over his shoulder as Justin hurried to keep up with him. "Did it get here?" He knew she would never leave without the Porsche.

"Yes and a flatbed truck from a Mercedes dealer is coming to take it to Boston. When I—"

"Boston? I thought you said she'd taken a flight home," Galen interrupted, stopping in his tracks.

"Damn, would you let me finish? I'm pretty sure she did. When I called the Mercedes place, they said she'd phoned with instructions to ship the Porsche to Montreal. So that's where she must be headed."

Galen's relief was brief. Then he and his brother stared at each other, aware of what could happen.

"I know," Justin said. "If we tracked her movements so easily, so could they. We'll just have to be faster." He patted Galen on the shoulder. "We've got her address in Montreal. It will be easy to find her, if not at home, then at the hotel where she works."

Galen shook his head. "She's been acting strangely since the day before yesterday. She was fine that morning but when I saw her in the kitchen that afternoon, she behaved very oddly. I thought she was miffed because I'd tried to talk to Vivian alone and left her to dance with the randy Senator Gallagher."

An unwelcome thought suddenly came to mind. "Gallagher must have said something."

"Like what? She already knew you were having an affair with Viv—"Justin stopped short. "Wait a minute. You just said she was acting strangely in the afternoon? Let's get to the office. I want to check something."

"What is it?" Galen asked, frustrated with his brother's silence while he led them to the office and opened a file cabinet behind his desk.

"I filed a bill of lading after a pickup from the *Irish Siren* for DesCheneaux—for some stuff we brought in from Italy. Let me check it out."

"What are you getting at?"

"I don't know, Galen but... Yes. Look. She signed for the merchandise, which means she went to pick it up."

"So?"

"So maybe something happened on the ship that upset her."

"Christ, you could be right." Galen began pacing the room, trying to piece together the puzzle, as Justin continued.

"Consider this—she goes to the *Irish Siren* to pick up some stuff. Later, Vivian gets killed on the ship, with a message to you that Lorelei's next. You told me that Lorelei collapsed right after she met Donald, when you two were about to take her to the ER. And then she took off from the hospital on her own. Don't you find it all a bit 'coincidental', shall we say?" He frowned as he offered the papers he was holding to his brother. "Take a look at this."

Galen gave the top sheet a cursory glance. "It's a bill of lading. What about it?"

"Look who signed it."

He saw Donald O'Hara's signature and for the second time that day wondered if it was possible that Donald had turned traitor to Justin and him. It seemed as incredible now as it had earlier. Donald had proved his loyalty too many times over too many years. Still...

"I don't know." Justin sighed, stroking his chin. "Something just doesn't fit. Maybe Gallagher hired Lorelei to spy on us. Then you slept with her and the senator found out and didn't like it."

"If he'd hired her to spy on me, he'd be thrilled that I slept with her." Galen shook his head. "Lorelei didn't come here to spy. I'd bet my life on it."

"Well, then, come up with a better scenario but for God's sake, do it fast. Michael's disappeared. Vivian's dead. Someone threatened Lorelei, then tried to kill her. What's next?"

Galen met and held his brother's worried gaze. "I don't know any better than you what's next. But you can bet it won't be good. And if it has anything to do with hurting Lorelei…"

He clenched his jaw. "We have to find her, Justin. Before it's too late."

* * * * *

Once they'd boarded the plane and were waiting to take off, Lorelei assured Annabelle for the tenth time that everything was going to be fine.

Annabelle finally stopped worrying about Lorelei's condition after the accident but when she spoke up next, Lorelei wasn't convinced that that was such a good thing.

"The first time you are with a man is always the hardest," she said in her lilting French accent. "Yet it can also be the most beautiful experience, especially if you have felt love, even for just a moment."

Lorelei was stunned at Annabelle's words. Had her brief affair with Galen been so apparent? She looked at the older woman, surprised, yet did not acknowledge anything.

Annabelle touched Lorelei's hand and smiled tenderly. "I am sure that the Kennedy fellow was more than adequate and I know he must be thinking about you now, just as you are thinking about him."

"I'll be fine, Annabelle," Lorelei reassured her, declining to talk further of Galen Kennedy. Her mind was racing to the decisions that lay ahead. She had to get the 959 repaired. With luck, the frame wasn't bent, and the car could be restored quickly and sold as planned. She would then pay off Delage. If she had any money left, she could disappear for a while until her best friend, Amanda, could help her figure out what to do.

The flight to Montreal was only an hour long and they landed in Dorval Airport without a hitch. Amanda Fairchild was there to meet them with her son, Evan, Lorelei's godchild.

It wasn't hard to spot Amanda. She had the blondest hair and most beautiful blue eyes any woman had ever possessed. Graceful and incredibly fit, she was known to dazzle criminals into making confessions. Yet she seemed totally unaware of her good looks.

Lorelei understood. Amanda had suffered through a terrible marriage to a cruel man who had abused her both physically and mentally and that had left her insecure as a woman, no matter how good an attorney she was.

"God, Lorelei, come here!" Amanda exclaimed.

As Amanda wrapped her in a hug, Lorelei felt everything that had happened in the past few days hit her. Her whole body began to tremble and uncontrollable sobs escaped her. Annabelle quickly whisked Evan away to an airport coffee shop while Amanda took Lorelei aside so they could speak privately.

"What, exactly, happened down there in Massachusetts?" Amanda asked, worried.

"Other than hearing a guy being shot dead a few yards away from me? Other than being nearly run off the road, getting shot at myself and crashing Nemesis?" Lorelei blew her nose on a tissue her friend handed her, then heard herself laugh weakly. "Well, I also had sex, finally—with a man who might be involved in both the murder and the attack on me. Oh and in smuggling guns to Northern Ireland."

"Good grief, Lorelei, is that all?" Amanda scoffed. "Well, aside from that stuff, how did the competition go?"

Lorelei laughed at Amanda's outrageous response. Then she started crying again. "We won. What a mess!"

"I can see how winning would be tragic. You felt sorry for the losers, right?" she gently teased.

"Well, I don't know. I just don't feel as if we should have won. I slept with one of the judges, after all."

"Well, never mind that for now. First things first. Do you know who's after you?"

"Not really. Irish terrorists, I think," Lorelei answered as if she were commenting about the food service on the plane.

"Christ, I was married to a maniac and I thought I had it bad. I think I'll get Evan to my dad's and you into hiding as soon as possible."

Lorelei put a hand on Amanda's arm. "No one knows any of this, not even Annabelle or Maurice. They just think I'm shaken up after the accident and sad about my affair with Galen. We can't tell them, or they'll worry themselves to death."

"Okay, okay. Come on, let's go find Annabelle and my son and get out of here, so you can give me all the details. Such as, was the possibly murderous, gun-smuggling, culinary competition judge any good in bed?"

Amanda always knew how to make her laugh. And laugh she did, even though she also turned red. Somehow she felt a little unburdened already. Everything was going to be all right now that she was home.

*****

A few days later, Galen was with Justin in their offices, reviewing the report from the Canadian investigator they had hired to find Lorelei. He had not been successful either.

"Galen, not only have I called DesCheneaux repeatedly, but I had Denise make inquiries there too and call Lorelei's house every hour on the hour," Justin said. "The hotel staff told us both that she's on a leave of absence from work—for the next two months. And neither of us got any answer or even an answering machine at her home."

Galen cursed again. "I should have gone myself."

"Right, so you could lead the bastards directly to her." Justin cracked his knuckles nervously.

"Well, I guess if they'd caught her, we would have heard one way or the other," Galen added grimly. "So maybe no news is good news."

"Absolutely. So let's be thankful she hides so well. Jeffrey Heinz is an excellent investigator. If he can't find her, then neither could they."

"Right," he muttered, surging out of his chair to begin his usual pacing. It didn't help. His gut was tied in knots of anxiety, and his brain was in turmoil. He needed to find some other way to track Lorelei, some route they hadn't thought of, some...

He came to an abrupt halt, his gaze riveted to a magazine lying open on the coffee table. As he leaned over to pick it up, a slow smile spread across his lips. "We've been going about this all wrong," he said.

"What do you mean?" Justin asked.

"We haven't been following the right trail."

"Which trail would that be?"

Galen handed Justin the magazine.

Justin looked at it for a moment, clearly perplexed. Then, as comprehension dawned, he too, began to smile.

The magazine was opened to a photo of Galen standing next to a 959 Twin Turbo Porsche parked on a beach, smiling at its beautiful owner, who was stretched out on its shiny silver hood, a crowd of happy DesCheneaux employees cheering in the background under the heading "A Cloud with Silver Lightning".

"The car," Justin said.

"Exactly," Galen replied. "We follow the car."

Chapter Seventeen

Early Monday morning Lorelei listened to the phone ring at the car dealership and then recognized Douglas Gillen's voice and British accent when he picked up. "This is Lorelei Duplessis. How are you, Mr. Gillen?"

"Miss Duplessis, I'm so glad you called. We've been trying to reach you for days."

"I'm sorry for not having contacted you sooner. You see, while I was in Hyannis Port, I had some renovations done on my house. They aren't completed, so I'm staying elsewhere," Lorelei lied. She was not merely staying but hiding at Amanda's. "In the meantime you can reach me on my cell phone."

"First of all, I think congratulations are in order," Gillen said. "You did us all proud by winning the competition. I must thank you personally for the publicity as well. I've been inundated with calls. And if I may say so, you look superb in the pictures."

"Which pictures, Mr. Gillen?"

"Why, you made *People* magazine, Miss D. Haven't you seen it yet?"

"No. I thought the pictures would only show up in some American cooking magazine, like *Gourmet*."

"I'll keep some copies for you. Heaven knows, we purchased a few hundred. Superbly done, Miss D. I wish I could have been there to witness the defeat of those arrogant Frenchmen who think they're God's gift to cooking. Why, I—"

"Well, thank you," she interrupted, amused that he seemed to have forgotten her own French heritage and name.

"I must say, I was surprised to win. The other participants truly outdid themselves, even if they were—well, you know—a bit pretentious."

"I don't know why but there isn't a pretentious bone in your body, Miss D. It must be the English part of your heritage that gives you all that class," he added.

"I don't have any English blood, Mr. Gillen."

"You don't say. I could have sworn… Well, no matter. It's where the heart lies, I suppose. Again, our warmest congratulations to you. Now then, I assume what you really called about was your car, I have some good news and some bad news. Can you come by the showroom sometime today?"

"Yes, I can. But weren't you able to repair it?"

"Yes, we were. That's not the problem. Your gem is as good as new. Even an expert couldn't tell anything was amiss. But you see, the buyer we had lined up, well, he called to tell us he's changed his mind, which is rather unusual, since he hadn't even heard about the accident yet. We've known this fellow a long time and he's never changed his mind about anything—except about his four wives, that is. Quite shameful that, I must say. But he's never changed his mind about a car he was bidding on. However, not ten minutes after Mr. Trent called, another interested party inquired about the car via an agent in England who does some work for us. Naturally, I told him that the car had been involved in an accident but was now completely restored. He said he'd have to think about it, then he called back and made us a rather unusual offer. I think you'll be quite satisfied nonetheless. However, we do have to give him an answer today, so you must come by to sign some papers if you agree to the sale."

As if I have a choice, Lorelei thought. "Well, then, I'll be by, say, in about an hour?"

"That will be fine, Miss D. I'll have several pens on hand—you may have a few autographs to sign, as well, you know."

She laughed. "I'll be there. It's always a pleasure to see you, even if I have no autographs to sign and even if it is to part with my Porsche."

"See you soon then, Miss D. Good day."

"Goodbye for now."

"Well, what's wrong?" Amanda asked from her kitchen table once Lorelei hung up.

"Damned if I know. The first buyer backed out. Gillen said he found me another one but I suspect the new offer is lower."

"How much lower?" Amanda asked.

Lorelei frowned. "I don't know. Gillen said it was an unusual offer. I wonder what he meant. Well, I'll find out soon enough." She placed the portable phone back in place and joined Amanda at the table. "Hey, guess what? I'm in *People* magazine. Can you believe it?"

Her friend brought a hand to her mouth. "Does it include the pictures taken on the beach that you told me about? With your Galen guy in them?"

Lorelei nodded.

Amanda got up and started clearing the table. "Come on, then. Let's go buy a copy. I can't wait to see what the sex god looks like!"

"The sex god?" Lorelei repeated.

"Well, he must be. How else could he have gotten perpetually virginal you into bed?"

"I'm glad someone can joke about this, because I sure can't."

"What else did Gillen say?" Amanda asked while she loaded the dishwasher.

"He said he had some copies of the magazine at the shop and that he'd give me a few." Lorelei stood up. "Why don't you come with me, Amanda? I told him I'd be there in an hour. Can you spare the time?"

"Of course I can. I don't have any court appearances today. I'll call the office. Maybe later we can go spend the day at Ideal Beauté. I think a good massage and facial are in order. Besides, it'll give you a chance to tell me more details about your sex god while I have his picture right in front of me."

"Amanda!" Lorelei turned red.

"Oh come on, don't you think it was time you put out some?" she teased. "You've been too sensible for far too long. What's more, you always think too much. You complicate things that are basically simple."

Lorelei's blush faded. "What am I going to do? What if I'm pregnant?"

"You're twenty-seven years old and you're smart and loving. A child might be just what you need. And Evan could use a little brother, anyway. I'll—"

"You'll what? Be there to cut the umbilical cord?" Lorelei interrupted ironically. How could she plan to give birth when she had other plans…she thought grimly.

"Sure. Why not?" Amanda replied. She cupped her friend's worried face. "You're not alone in the world, you know."

Lorelei placed her hands on Amanda's trying to gather the courage to tell her the truth. "But—"

"No buts. You have a lot of love inside you to give, which is the best reason to have a baby and you won't love your child any less because of who its father was. You won't. Look at Evan. You know, if it weren't for you, we'd both be—"

"Never mind, Amanda. We swore never to speak of it again," Lorelei reminded her while she turned to place her empty coffee mug beside the others. Maybe now was not the time to say anything, she thought. Amanda would try to stop her for sure.

"The way I see it, your most pressing problem is financial. We've got to pay off that bastard Delage and get you the hell out of the country for a little while, until I can find you a way out of the other mess."

"Come to think of it, I probably shouldn't be staying here with you. I might be putting you and Evan in danger."

"Nonsense. By the end of the week the car will be sold, that bastard paid off, you'll get your period and you'll be on your way to France to stay with Annabelle's relatives for a while."

Lorelei smiled. "You know, you're the best sister I never had."

"Same here," Amanda responded with a hug.

When they arrived at the car dealership, Nemesis was parked in the front of the showroom, surrounded by giant posters of the picture from *People* magazine. Lorelei couldn't have felt more honored—or more regretful that she had to part with the legacy Uncle Roche had left her.

"Ah, Miss D., welcome back." Gillen's smile was as gracious as his personality.

"Mr. Gillen, I'd like you to meet my best friend and attorney, Amanda Fairchild. Amanda, this is Douglas Gillen."

"Pleased to meet you, Mr. Gillen. I hope you have good news for Lorelei," Amanda added as she shook his hand.

Aware that several customers were staring at her, Lorelei began to feel uncomfortable. She didn't want to attract attention to herself or Amanda. As far as she knew, there might be a contract out on her life. "Mr. Gillen, could we go into your office?"

"Well, of course. Follow me."

Once behind closed doors, Lorelei felt better. Gillen offered them coffee and poured some tea for himself.

"I hope we haven't made you too uncomfortable with the posters and all. But we're so very honored to have you as our client and we thought that—"

"It's all right, Mr. Gillen. It's just that it's very difficult for me to have to part with my car," she explained, even if it was not her real reason for wanting to keep a low profile.

"Now, now Miss D., have more faith in yourself. In no time I'm sure you'll be coming to see me to buy the next automobile of your dreams. Why, I'm positive! The article said that you were responsible for helping the Feed the World Foundation raise more money than it has in years. We've even received calls here from some of our clients wishing to make donations. Surely this success has enhanced your reputation immeasurably and you'll be up to your ears in disposable income in a trice! And of course I will be at your service to help you select a vehicle that befits your status and fulfills — nay, surpasses — your automotive expectations and desires."

Lorelei smiled and took a sip of coffee. "So, what's the new offer on the car? Please, break it to me gently. Is it much less than what Mr. Trent was willing to pay?"

"My English contact assured me that you will receive the same amount, less a small allowance for the exchange rate of the pound, upon your transfer of ownership and your fulfillment of the second portion of the agreement."

"I don't understand. What second portion of the agreement?"

Gillen smiled and crossed his hands on his desk. "It appears that your car will be purchased by the president of the dealership. He's been looking for a 959 for quite a few years, seeing that there are roughly only two hundred in the entire world. You understand that we had to disclose the matter of the accident to him. Still, he agreed to pay our full asking price on condition that you fulfill a catering contract for one of his best clients, who lives in Scotland and is planning a small reception for the royal family. Your travel and boarding expenses will also be paid. Oh and his agent added that you could, if you so requested, bring along any members of your own staff."

A Scent in the Night

Lorelei looked at Amanda, undecided. Scotland? Being out of the country and across the ocean might be a great way to hide while Amanda sorted things out. But Scotland? She knew not a soul there and it sounded way too close to Ireland for comfort.

Sensing Lorelei's hesitation, Amanda intervened. "Who is this client and when would Lorelei have to leave?"

"Lady Constance McBain. Her son is laird of his clan, one of the few left in the Highlands." After checking his agenda, Gillen added, "Let's see, the car would be on a ship tomorrow. Miss Duplessis would have to be in London a week from now to pick it up at the port and sign the sale agreement. She would then be on her way to Scotland to fulfill her catering contract. In the meantime, however, Mr. Langford would forward you half of the price until the transfer of ownership is complete."

Amanda looked at Lorelei, then at Gillen. "This is a great deal. You can tell Mr. Langford to wire the advance to my bank in my name." At Lorelei's gasp she added, "Mr. Gillen, could you give us a moment alone?

"Of course, Ms Fairchild. I'll be just out in the showroom."

"Lorelei," Amanda said, "we've got to pay off Delage immediately before he seizes your home."

"Now wait a minute, Amanda. You know I was planning to go to France to—"

"What's the difference whether you go to France or Scotland? You'll be out of the country and—"

"But—"

"No buts. You know I can't hold off Delage much longer. If you don't go to Scotland, we can't pay him off."

"What am I going to tell Maurice?"

"Invite him. His expenses will be paid. He'll be as happy as a pig in swill if he knows you and he will be serving royalty!"

Lorelei smiled. "I can just picture him, all hot and bothered but bursting with pride. You're right. It would be wonderful to give him the opportunity."

"There you go."

Lorelei called Douglas Gillen back into his office.

"Where do I sign?" she asked him.

* * * * *

The following days passed so quickly and were so busy that Lorelei barely had time to feel the chaos her life had become. Since winning the award and appearing in *People* magazine, she was attracting far too much attention. The general manager at DesCheneaux wanted her to commit to enough catering contracts to fill her calendar for the next three years and only after agreeing to most of them had she been able to negotiate the two-month leave of absence Amanda had recommended she take while they tried to sort out matters.

In order to keep her true destination confidential, she informed everyone that she was going to Normandy to visit Annabelle's sister. Maurice and Annabelle were the only ones who knew she was going to Scotland, because Maurice would join her as soon as he could get away from DesCheneaux.

In the meantime Lorelei remained alert for any signs of danger, careful at all times not to be followed. Amanda had suggested that they wait until they could determine whether Galen Kennedy had been involved before reporting the murder to the authorities. Lorelei knew her friend was worried that, if Galen was behind the smuggling operation, even if he'd had nothing to do with Michael Logan's death, he might use his considerable resources and power to track her down and silence her. Lorelei didn't want to believe he was capable of either smuggling guns or murder but she saw some sense in her friend's advice.

For the remainder of the week she stayed quietly at Amanda's and went back to her town house only briefly and under cover of night to pack for her trip—her escape. During that week, her period arrived. It was late, which was rare, and the flow was unusually light but she had no symptoms that might suggest pregnancy, which was reassuring.

As quickly as the days flew by, the nights passed slowly. They were the hardest and the longest Lorelei had ever endured. She kept remembering Galen, the frantic way they had made love, the touching and the tenderness that had often followed the storm. She yearned for him and worried that he was involved in something bigger and more dangerous than anything she had ever experienced—and something that would ultimately keep them apart.

She kept repeating to herself that it was better that they remain apart. For if things had progressed between them, it would have impeded her ultimate plans.

Michael Logan's murder continued interrupting her sleep, she would hear again the angry words, the muffled shot, the sound of his body thumping to the floor. Then she would wake up sweating, picturing her parents, seeing their murderers without being able to discern their faces. She would hear her mother's pleas, her father's groans...and she would wish for the millionth time that she had warned them, wished she had stopped them from leaving. Most of all, she wished she had died with them. For living without them—and with the guilty knowledge that she could have prevented their deaths—was still utterly unbearable.

* * * * *

Lorelei's arrival in London was smooth and uneventful. Amanda had arranged to have a driver meet her at Heathrow to take her to the port customs office to sign the release papers for her car and, afterward, to Mr. Langford's dealership to sign over the Porsche. Lorelei managed well enough before saying her final goodbye to the 959. She had its plates removed and handed over the keys, relieved that Langford was not there to look at his most recent acquisition, so she could quickly flee and let her tears flow in private.

She landed at Dalcross Airport, some twelve miles east of Inverness, with a heavy heart but her mood soon lightened with her first breathtaking view of the Scottish Highlands.

For a moment she forgot her worries. It was four o'clock in the afternoon and the autumn sun blazed on the horizon.

A rotund man in a blue chauffeur's uniform startled her at the luggage claim area by exclaiming, "Ye'd be Miss Duplessis, correct? Stuart Moore, chauffeur to the McBains, at yer service, ma'am. Ye're a bonny lass, ye are." He stopped abruptly, then blushed scarlet. "What I meant to say was, welcome, ma'am."

Lorelei smiled. "Thank you, Mr. Moore. Shall we go?"

Bending, he picked up her luggage. "Let me get that, lass and ye just follow me."

Lorelei followed the Scotsman to a blue Bentley. Not bad for a first car ride in Scotland.

"As this is yer first time in the Highlands, I'll be explainin' the road to ye. We'll be travelin' for two hours, approximately, so it'll be sundown when we get to the castle. Mary, our housekeeper, had Cook prepare some refreshments for ye in case ye're thirsty or hungry. They're in the basket next to the other door."

Grateful for the nicely prepared food, Lorelei nibbled as she marveled at the endless mountains and trees.

An hour into the drive Stuart Moore pointed ahead, saying, "Now, I think ye'd be wantin' to take a picture of this, although I don't think any photograph could actually do the view justice." He slowed the car to a stop by the side of the road, got out and opened Lorelei's door, so she could stretch her legs and have a better look.

As soon as her feet touched the ground, she smelled the pine trees on the mountain ridges before her. The sky was the color of fire, the mountains rich shades of green and brown. Far away on the horizon was a lake of copper and gold, peacefully reflecting the fading sunlight.

"What is this place called, Mr. Moore?"

"Close to ye, ye're lookin' at the Five Sisters of Kintail. To your left ye'll find the Red Cuillins and to the right the island of Scalpay. In the middle there," he pointed a finger, "are the Macleod Tables. Now, if ye want to know where we are, why, we're almost touching what ye might call paradise."

Lorelei smiled at the pride with which he described his homeland. "It's very beautiful."

He turned to look at her with his faded amber eyes. Although his curly hair was mostly dark brown, his whiskers betrayed the first signs of aging. "Are ye sure there's not some Highlander blood in ye, lass? Yer hair is the color of this rich earth here."

She crossed her arms, shivering from the chill of the northern winds. "Not a drop, sir. I'm of French ancestry through and through."

"Our own King Robert the Bruce's ancestors were French. 'Tis a fact that the man who defeated a mounted English knight in full armor was riding a pony with merely an axe in his hand. Aye, 'tis said that the color of his hair matched this paradise, the same color ye wear on yer shoulders," he finished.

"Never will I forget this place," she replied, meaning it with all her heart.

"I'm glad ye like it. Now let's go, or me boss will have me hide for keepin' ye out so late after yer long trip."

Half an hour later Stuart once again stopped the Bentley.

Lorelei got out, curious about the spectacle ahead of her. Dusk was settling but here at the water's edge the sky was still blue with white specks of clouds. The lake perfectly reflected the imposing example of ancient European architecture that stood on a tiny islet before them, a fairy tale castle right out of some young girl's imagination, a kingdom lost in time. A bridge with wide stone arches dipped into the water, connecting the kingdom to the rest of the world.

Lorelei blinked, almost afraid she would wake up and find she'd been dreaming. In perspective, the castle stood almost as high as the mountains behind it, majestically beautiful.

"There it is lass—home."

Lorelei frowned. "Here?" She pointed. She couldn't believe this magnificent castle was the McBains' home.

Stuart nodded.

Gazing up at the fortress, Lorelei actually began to feel safe for the first time in what seemed like forever.

She and the chauffeur got back into the car and drove across the cobblestone bridge. The road to the castle was long, winding and narrow, just wide enough for the Bentley to pass. Lorelei craned her neck to look up at the high turrets and ramparts that enclosed so many thatched roof buildings.

Stuart translated the Gaelic inscription carved in stone over the portcullis for her, an arcane reference to two clans, the McBains and McAllisters. "The inscription says as long as there is a McBain inside, there will never be a McAllister outside."

"Were the families related?" she asked, curious to understand the peculiar legend.

Stuart chuckled. "They were related all right—related in hate and in war. The feud is still on, ye know, except that after the old laird died, well, the grandsons decided to be more civilized about it. So today they just ignore each other, except in the games, of course."

"Which games?"

"Well, now, lass, ye have the North of Scotland Highland Games for instance, where the McBains have regularly beaten the bloody pulp out of all the other clans, includin' the McAllisters."

"What sport do they practice?" she asked, curious.

"They don't practice anythin', lass. They compete. Athletics, pipin', dancin' and the like."

Lorelei found the medieval style of living intriguing and amusing. And she looked forward to spending a little time in it.

Chapter Eighteen

What man does, destiny often undoes...

ঞ

The fairy tale-like turrets of the picturesque castle, the gargoyles of fantastic design and the superbly painted ceilings depicting scenes of battles in the time of Robert the Bruce were but a few of the wonderful attributes of the castle that Lorelei had the chance to admire.

Oddly, an English, not Scots butler by the name of Edward had greeted her at the low door when she arrived, offering to take her luggage upstairs and to serve her tea in the study, where she would meet the laird in the absence of Lady McBain, who had traveled to Aberdeen to visit her sister.

Contrary to the stiff disposition English serving staffs were notorious for, Edward smiled at her broadly, welcoming her and congratulating her on her recent culinary award. He was courteous and at times almost familiar with her, rather than impossibly formal, which instantly made her feel more comfortable in such unusual surroundings.

Before they reached the study, Lorelei had to climb a few stone steps to enter the main building. With walls over four yards thick and barrel vaulted ceilings, the room contained numerous paintings. She stopped to look at one, which depicted men and women dancing on the lead roof of the castle. Edward explained that the painting had been made to commemorate a battle against a rival clan by the name of McAllister, a battle that had been preceded by a dance, as was the custom of the times. During this battle, however, many McBains had been killed by the McAllisters, hence, the peculiar inscription over the portcullis.

Edward left her in the study to wait for Laird Alex McBain. She noticed the mahogany furniture, the stone walls, and the carved, solid oak doors. The huge windows consisted of multicolored stained glass, beautifully worked, depicting scenes of war and glory.

She examined the antique weapons that adorned one wall, identifying a classical Scottish bow widely used until the fifteenth century. Next to it was an axe commonly used by Highlanders. She admired three beautifully wrought, basket-hilted broadswords, as well as several different dirks, known as long knives and the black knives often also used for eating.

In the center of the display she recognized a huge claymore with a golden hilt heavily encrusted with rubies and emeralds. The blade, many feet long and paper-thin at the tip, appeared in some places slightly jagged. It was likely that it was a family heirloom used by a McBain ancestor many centuries before. Strange that it was displayed as the central piece of the collection, since it was mainly associated with sixteenth century Scottish mercenaries, not necessarily something to be proud of.

Lorelei was also surprised that such a valuable piece of history and workmanship would be hanging in the open, unprotected from theft. Then she remembered that the claymore was a two-handed weapon because of its size and weight. It would probably take three modern-day men to lift it from its perch and carry it off.

Considering the design, décor, size and impregnability of the castle, the McBain family had obviously been a powerful one in the past, presumably as far back as Robert the Bruce and Mary Queen of Scots. Judging from the style of weaponry displayed and from what Stuart Moore had told her, the clan still had considerable influence in the Highlands.

As she turned from the sword display, she spotted a collection of pistols in a glass cabinet behind an elegant sixteenth century desk. From a distance they looked easier to handle than the claymore but no less magnificent. She suddenly shuddered at the memory of a gun barrel pointing at her during her high-speed chase in Cape Cod, even though at the time she had been more afraid of crashing the 959 than of dying from a bullet wound.

She would never forget the look on Galen's face when she had emerged from her car uninjured. He'd looked as if he had seen a ghost—and indeed, she should have been dead. Yet somewhere in her heart she couldn't believe he would actually want her killed.

She was glad she had accepted Lady McBain's contract, since no one would ever think of looking for her in Scotland. France would have been a mistake, she realized, Annabelle's relatives too easy to trace.

She crossed the room to take a closer look at the pistols behind the desk. She inadvertently bumped an open drawer when she walked past and caught sight of a modern gun. She'd better warn Maurice not to be too uppity with this McBain laird, Lorelei thought.

"Beautiful weapons, aren't they?"

Lorelei jumped, bumping into the desk chair as she whirled to face the owner of the deep and familiar male voice.

"You!" She took a step back. "Wh-What are you doing here?"

Galen Kennedy stood before her, transformed by a belted plaid clan kilt and an ample white shirt that made him look like a master and commander about to exact his due. With his long hair tied back, his shirt opened midway, revealing a patch of chest hair, his arms crossed and his legs braced apart, he eyed her from head to toe with a sardonic smile.

Stunned both by the mere sight of him and by the strength of her response to his physical presence, Lorelei reacted instinctively to the danger he presented. She reached into the open drawer before her, snatched the gun, cocked it and leveled it at him.

"Who the hell are you?" she said, trying to keeping her voice steady.

"Put the gun down, you little fool," he said. "It's me, for God's sake."

"Exactly! It's you, not Alex McBain!"

He sighed. "I'm Galen Alexander McBain Kennedy."

"You lie!"

"My mother is Scottish. My father was Irish. And I would never lie to you."

"What do you want from me?"

"Right now, I want you to put the gun down, Lorelei. It's liable to explode in your face if you pull the trigger. It's very old and needs a proper cleaning."

"I'm not a moron, Kennedy. It wouldn't be loaded if it needed cleaning."

"Put it down," he insisted.

"Why did you make me come here?"

He took a few steps toward her, trying to understand her reaction. Her eyes showed terror, her free hand was in a fist and her gun-wielding arm was so rigid, she could easily pull the trigger by mistake. "I promise I'll answer all your questions as soon as you put that pistol down." He cautiously advanced a few more steps.

"Answer me first!"

"I refuse to answer questions at gunpoint—and in my own house, with my own goddamned gun!" He came to a halt. "I guess you'll just have to shoot me."

"And you think I can't do it, right?" Lorelei was furious that she had allowed herself to be so easily manipulated into playing right into this man's hands.

"Listen to me, Lorelei. You don't have to be afraid of me."

"Shut up!" She waved the gun at him from sheer anger as the pieces of the puzzle began fitting together. "You orchestrated everything right from the beginning, didn't you—including that so-called electrical problem in my suite in Hyannis Port?"

"What's that got to do—"

"You wanted me on your turf, in your suite, in your bed. What a good laugh you must have had when I offered myself to you. A virgin, to boot! At least have enough guts to admit it, you bastard!"

He could and probably should deny everything, Galen thought but his instincts told him that she needed the truth.

"You're right—there was no power failure. And, yes, I did make sure you'd be moved into my suite. But you know I never would have forced you to have sex, even though I wanted you as badly then as I do now."

Lorelei desperately wanted to believe him but she couldn't afford to. "The only reason you wanted me was to shut me up. To make sure I wouldn't tell anyone about your affair with the senator's wife. What better way was there than to compromise the person who could compromise you?"

"That is completely ridiculous!" Galen barked, raking a hand through his hair.

At that moment Edward came into the room with a laden tea tray. Clearing his throat loudly, he put down the tray and held up a small gun he retrieved from a drawer of the serving table. "Miss Duplessis," he said, "I think this gun will be more useful to you. You see, I'm afraid that one is not fully loaded. Here." Quite impassively he placed the gun on the desk. "I always prefer a small-caliber Beretta. You know, less cumbersome and it won't make a mess when fired at close range."

"What the hell—" Galen exclaimed.

"Sir, I'm afraid the lady is right," Edward stated, shaking his head. "You have ruined her. If I were her father, I would have to call you out. Since he's not here, I have no choice but to give her the means to do it herself. You have been far more a rogue than a gentleman to her, sir, from the sound of it. And since you obviously have not offered her marriage, then her honor must be vindicated. Your mother would, no doubt, agree with me. It is the English and Scottish way, sir."

With an exasperated sound, Galen ignored his servant and turned to Lorelei, who was trying hard to suppress a grin. "With that intelligent mind of yours, why can't you see that it's you I want, you I care for?" Bracing both his hands on the desk, he leaned over it, bringing himself face to face with the pistol. "Why can't you believe me when I tell you I'm falling in love with you?"

Lorelei's expression turned grim. "Because you left with Vivian Gallagher the night of my reception. Because you can have sex with someone you don't even like. Because you use women."

Galen felt the sting of her words like a slap in the face. She was putting him on trial for the past and no one could change the past. His voice went low with anger and hurt.

"Nothing happened with Vivian after I met you. It's true I didn't like her but at one time I was at least physically attracted to her. And as I told you, lives were at stake." His voice shook with conviction. "And I never used you. Never."

"I wouldn't have let you."

"Regardless. I never did."

Edward took a step back. "Now then, Miss Duplessis, will you be having your tea before or after you, um…do the deed?"

With the butler's outrageous behavior, she was suddenly less sure of her anger. It burned her, though, that she had been maneuvered so easily—and twice, at that—by Galen Kennedy. The man needed to be taught a lesson. She smiled at Edward and grabbed the Beretta with her free hand.

Galen's face registered outrage.

Edward remained cool, with that stiff upper lip Englishmen were famous for. "I suppose tea can wait, then.

Very well, I shall remove one china setting from the tray, since Sir Galen won't be joining us," he concluded, returning to the serving table with the same calm demeanor. "Perhaps you should at least back up a bit, sir," he whispered to his employer.

Lorelei had to forcibly swallow a laugh.

Galen didn't seem to share her amusement, however.

"Remind me, Edward, did the McBains of old simply hang subjects for treason, or did they have them tortured first? I know you're good at our history."

"It is clear you are speaking under duress, sir, since this young lady has two pistols pointed at you. For that reason I will excuse your insulting threat." He put away one of the teacups in a small credenza by the window. "And I'll have you know that I have been your loyal servant since you were a wee lad. I shall, of course, remain so until your death, should it come before mine, which in all frankness, sir, I think will be the case."

Galen almost smiled. This was getting completely ridiculous. "Edward, would you excuse us for a moment—say, as a last request before my execution?"

"He stays," Lorelei ordered. "I want a witness."

"I'm glad you can joke about this, because I sure can't."

Galen took a chance, knowing she cared for him more than she hated him and closed his hands on one of hers, the one with the loaded pistol. The Beretta, he figured, was empty.

"Vivian's dead, Lorelei," he said.

The words robbed her of her breath. Her lips trembled, but otherwise she remained silent and unflinching.

"She was found on the *Irish Siren* with a bullet in her head. Her killer left a note at the scene for me, implying that you would be the next to die."

Lorelei's eyes blazed with fury. The bastards had killed again. The same ones who'd murdered Michael Logan.

And now they intended to kill her.

"I don't want anything to happen to you," Galen told her. "It's one of the reasons I had to get you here. The other reason," he paused, throwing Edward a hard look, "I'll tell you in private."

She took a deep breath, trying to focus her thoughts and remain calm. "Is the man with the scar on his face—the one who was with you when I had my...accident—still in Hyannis Port? Or is he here with you?"

"What man?" Edward asked.

Galen's brow furrowed. "O'Hara. He's here in Scotland. Why do you ask?"

"You'll find out soon enough. Can you get in touch with him?"

Galen studied her closely for a moment, then said to Edward, "Call the stables. I think Donald went down there. Tell him I want to see him."

His gaze never leaving hers, he said, "It's your call now, Lorelei. Still want to shoot me?"

A few minutes later Donald O'Hara knocked and stepped into the room, looking just as Lorelei remembered him.

"*Bonjour*, Mr. O'Hara. How lovely to see you again," she greeted him, the two guns in her hands still aimed to shoot.

He came to a dead stop. "Is this a joke?"

He looked at Galen and Edward but got no response from either man.

In fact, Lorelei noted, Galen was rigid with fury, though he showed no signs of interfering. That frankly surprised her but this wasn't the moment to contemplate his reasons.

"You must be crazy," O'Hara said to her, laughing weakly.

"No, I'm quite sane. But I'm on the verge of becoming so utterly bored with this charade that I might just start shooting for sport. Who put out a contract on my life, Mr. O'Hara? Are you the ringleader of this little game of gun-running and murder, or are you working for someone else?"

"I work for him," he said, nodding toward Galen.

She heard Galen suck in a swift breath but her gaze remained fixed on O'Hara. She smiled faintly at his answer.

"Maybe I should have been more specific. I know you work for Mr. Kennedy but did he hire you to kill people?"

"I don't know what you're talking about," he protested.

She cocked the Beretta. The small click echoed in the room.

"You bitch! Do you think I'm afraid of you?" O'Hara's face turned red with rage.

"Edward, please hand me my purse." When the butler complied, she said softly, "Thank you. Please open it and step away."

He pulled the zipper back and Lorelei reached inside, drew out her own weapon, then laid the Berretta on the desk.

"This, Mr. O'Hara, is a Glock version of a Smith and Wesson. It's a forty caliber, with a hybrid compensator and a laser-sight titanium-guide tube. And now it's cocked and aimed right at you. I suggest that you answer my question quickly before I test this sweet little gun on Scottish soil. Understand that I have little personal interest in you if what you do is at someone else's bidding. In which case, it's that boss I want. Since I feel generous today, I propose a trade — one of my confessions for one of yours."

When the man simply stared at her, clearly dumbfounded, she sighed. "All right. I'll begin. Although I have here one of the finest handguns my uncle ever could have left me, I confess I'm an eccentric shot. You see, I always miss my target by about two feet, height-wise. See now, if I were to aim, say, at your toes, guess where the bullet would hit you?"

Donald's face turned white.

"If you don't believe me, then I'll demonstrate for you. I will aim for that insignia in the carpet in front of the sofa." She turned slightly took aim at the rug and fired a shot clean through the sofa. "It doesn't matter which gun I use, really." She took aim at the carpet again, this time with the Beretta and fired another shot through the sofa. Galen all but glared at Edward for having given her a loaded gun after all.

"Now, perhaps you would like to answer me—truthfully this time." She aimed her Glock at his shoes and repeated her question. "Who is in charge of your smuggling and murder operations?"

"Liam," he grunted.

"Liam?" she quizzed. "He has no last name?"

"Liam...Torrens."

"Liam Torrens. Does that name mean anything to you two gentlemen?" she asked, glancing at Galen, who, with a black scowl in place, gave a quick shake of his head.

So O'Hara was still playing games, she thought. "Who was the man you killed in the cargo hold of the *Irish Siren*, the day I picked up my merchandise?"

Galen uttered a low, animal-like snarl but another quick glance told her that he was willing to allow her interrogation to continue, at least for now. She could see him trembling, though, and realized that he was close to exploding with rage.

O'Hara answered her question with an arrogant drawl. "I don't know what you're talking about."

She aimed her gun higher this time, at his midsection, which would put a hole right between his eyes. "Maybe if I shoot you in the same place you shot him..."

"Lorelei...don't," Galen said in a deceptively soft voice.

"It would be too easy a death for him."

She thought about what it would do to her if she ended a life, if she hated enough to kill. "Fine but if I don't do it, then neither will you. We'll hand him over to the proper authorities. Give me your word, Galen."

"Lorelei…"

"Your word," she demanded.

He sighed and nodded. "You have it."

But there was one more thing she intended to get out of O'Hara before she released him. He had to admit to the murder, in front of witnesses.

She addressed him directly. "The man you killed likely has a family and they have a right to know how and when he died. They have a right to grieve him properly, you bastard!" She took quick aim and fired the Glock, hitting his left shoulder.

O'Hara staggered and fell backward.

"If you don't say his name out loud," she continued, "I will watch you bleed until your veins run dry and I'll make you drink your own blood. Sound familiar, you sniveling, traitorous coward?" Spreading her legs, she put a two-handed grip on the Glock and took aim at his head. "His name! Now!" she shouted.

"M-M…Mi…chael…Log—" O'Hara's voice disintegrated in a coughing spasm.

"Michael Logan," Galen finished, glaring at the man who was clutching his bleeding shoulder. "Our cousin. He disappeared. Justin and I have been frantic, trying to find him." He grabbed O'Hara's hair and yanked his head backward. "And you knew it, you son of bitch!" he snarled, landing a punch in O'Hara's face. "You fucking son of a bitch! They paid you for killing Michael, didn't they? How much will they pay you for dying? How much?" he demanded, slugging the injured man again.

"Stop it!" Lorelei shouted. "Edward, call the police before Galen kills him!"

But Edward had already phoned for assistance. Soon a few burly men arrived, including Galen's chauffeur and quickly separated Galen from O'Hara, who now lay sprawled on the carpet, half-conscious.

Galen wiped his brow and stared at the man he hadn't been able to believe would betray him. "Let's get him outside. I have a few questions to ask him before the police get what's going to be left of him." He pointed at Lorelei, fuming. "Don't even say it! I'll keep my word, even if you haven't kept yours!"

"I never gave you my word. Besides, I didn't shoot to kill."

"Don't push it, Lorelei! I need that bastard alive. He's the only one who can give me the proof I need!"

She lashed out at him this time. "I was there when he killed Michael Logan. I had to hear it—his voice when he knew he was going to die, the shot, the…the awful silence afterward. Those sounds replay in my head day and night—and I had the right to make them stop!"

Galen tried to remain angry but her words gave him pause. What other terrible violence haunted this woman so much that she sought death to escape it? But he couldn't think of that now. He had to concentrate on nailing Gallagher and getting the proof he needed from Donald.

The tall Highlanders dragged Donald away. Galen's last words to Lorelei before he left matched his implacable glare.

"Don't you dare leave."

She looked down at her left hand just before she put her gun away. What was the matter with her? What was she becoming? A cold-blooded monster? She felt a sudden cramp in her lower abdomen, radiating into her back. The pain was so sharp, she had to clutch the desk and hold her breath.

"*Merde!*"

It took a few seconds for the pain to subside.

"Miss Duplessis, is everything all right?" Edward asked, his tone soft but concerned.

She breathed slowly, nodding.

"A spot of tea will be just the thing, I'm sure. Let's hope it's still warm," Edward said. He hurried to the tray, filled a fine bone china cup and saucer and brought it to her.

She sputtered at her first gulp and glared at him.

"It's fortified tea, Miss Duplessis. I thought you looked a tad pale."

"Fortified with what, rubbing alcohol?" Another cramp hit her, this time viciously. Tea spilled onto the carpet.

"I say, Miss Duplessis, something is quite wrong. May I call a physician?" He took the cup from her.

Breathless, Lorelei concentrated on letting the pain pass through her. "I-I need to lie down, that's all. No need for a doctor, Edward. Just some peace and quiet." She took a deep breath and slowly the pain subsided. "Today was...eventful."

"Why, yes, of course," he replied. "Should I call Mr. Kennedy? I'm sure he would be happy to help you up to your quarters."

"No! I mean, I can make it but thank you for the suggestion." No way would she be carried upstairs like some damsel in distress, especially by Galen Kennedy. He was so mad at her, he was liable to throw her out a window. "Just lead the way, Edward. I feel much better already."

"Please follow me, then. I had your luggage taken up already."

They made their way up a narrow, winding stone staircase. The sleeping quarters were located on the third floor, Edward explained. A long arched passageway divided the bedroom suites. What appeared to be original torches hung on the walls. "Your chambers, Miss Duplessis," Edward announced, opening a heavy Gothic door.

A Scent in the Night

Lorelei stepped inside, awed by the beautiful, intricate tapestries covering two of the walls. A canopied bed sat in the center of the cozy chamber between two stained glass windows draped with brocade. A huge stone fireplace opposite the bed was flanked by two *bergère* chairs and a *dormeuse*.

"It's wonderful," Lorelei whispered as she sank down onto one of the chairs, drained from climbing three flights of stairs. After a few moments she looked at the butler. "Edward, you never believed I would shoot Galen, did you? That's why you pretended to defy him, right?"

"My dear lady, I never pretend!" he scoffed. "The Beretta was loaded, you might recall," he reminded her.

She grinned, picturing Galen's reaction to that little fact.

Edward was an excellent judge of character.

"I believe Mr. Kennedy will...ultimately...repair the damage he has done you, Miss Duplessis. His judgment of late, I have noticed, has been sorely lacking. I can attest to his character, however and say with no qualms that it is neither superficial nor selfish, much less cruel."

"I know that too, Edward." She motioned to the other chair. "Please, sit."

He smiled, taking the chair facing her. "I'm sure he had his reasons for acting the way he did. You see, Mr. Kennedy has suffered much in the past and perhaps does not express his emotions adequately. As for you, I am in awe of what just transpired. You've earned my utmost and undying respect and I'm sure the McBain clan's, as well. I have yet to see any man—save Galen Kennedy, of course—behave with as much nerve and audacity as you displayed." He stood up with a smile. "This is a splendid turn of events. I understand now why Mr. Kennedy wanted you here with all haste."

He plumped a pillow on the love seat and walked out of the room. Before closing the door, he paused. "Would you like me to send Mary to unpack for you?"

"Thank you, Edward but I won't be staying long enough for that. I just need a little rest."

Looking disappointed, he nodded. "As you wish. I'll tell Cook to add warm broth to the menu. You look as if you could use some, young lady." With that, he left.

Alone, Lorelei felt the horror of what she had almost done wash over her. She could have killed Donald O'Hara. She'd certainly wanted to. She was no better than the murderer himself.

Another sharp pain came and went. *Merde*, what was wrong with her?

But then, considering she hadn't slept in over twenty-four hours and, less than thirty minutes ago, had held two men at gunpoint, she supposed it was a miracle she hadn't yet collapsed.

On that thought, she kicked off her shoes, peeled off her pants and climbed into bed. After a short nap she would be as good as new.

As she pulled the beautiful Egyptian cotton bedspread to her waist, she was overcome by another cramp. To subdue the pain, she pulled her knees up to her chest and hummed a lullaby, putting herself to sleep the way she used to do during the horrible weeks after her parents died.

Chapter Nineteen

What you don't know can't hurt you, can it?

༄

So, his little avenger was sleeping, Galen mused. He didn't really want to wake her after her ordeal but he wanted her to eat the light snack Cook had prepared. She had looked so pale and distraught when he left her with Edward.

Their time apart had been hard for him. He had barely slept, not knowing if she was safe, not knowing if he would ever see her again or if he was destined to lose that part of him she was unknowingly carrying in her heart. But she was home now and whatever it took, he'd keep her there. She was his.

She had fallen asleep with the lights on. He placed the tray on the bureau and nearly stumbled on the pants she had dropped on the floor. She was partly covered by the bedspread but she was still wearing her sweater. Her luggage sat at the foot of the bed, unopened. Doubtless she was planning to leave as soon as she awoke. Hell, she probably wanted to get away from him as quickly as possible.

Well, he wasn't going to be the only one who came to terms with their relationship. She would have to as well, even if he had to knock her over the head, caveman-style, to accomplish the task.

Was she pregnant? He'd wondered at least a hundred times. If she wasn't, it would be a pleasure to remedy the situation. She would look splendid swollen with his baby, a baby with her gray eyes, her strength and intelligence, her courage and, most of all, her heart. He could easily picture his leather-clad temptress with her forty-caliber Glock transformed by love into a gentle, devoted mother.

Since she was sleeping, this might be a good time to take that gun away from her without a big argument. What the hell had her uncle been thinking, giving it to her? And how the hell had she managed to get it past customs? She could have been arrested had they caught her with it. He couldn't believe her audacity.

On second thought, he could believe it. She had been terrorized in Hyannis Port and carrying a gun was probably the only way she felt secure.

He took the weapon from her purse and went downstairs to put it away in his safe. Then, climbing the stairs two at a time, he made a quick trip to his room to change into jeans and a T-shirt before returning to wake her. Quietly opening her door, he entered, crossed to the bed and leaned over to whisper her name.

She was sleeping very deeply and didn't respond.

Overwhelmed by the need to hold her in his arms again, he took off his shoes, lifted the cover and slipped under it with her. He curled himself around her and rested his face against the back of her neck. A minute later he felt the front of his jeans growing wet from waist to thighs where she was pressed against him.

Lifting the bedspread, he was appalled to see blood everywhere.

"Lorelei! Wake up, baby!" He bolted upright and shook her gently but she showed no sign of rousing.

He checked her pulse to reassure himself she was still alive. Then, leaping from the bed, he ran to open the door and shout for Edward.

Moments later his trusted friend appeared, his horrified gaze taking in his master's blood-stained clothes. "Sir, what happened? Are you hurt?"

"No, it's Lorelei!" Galen replied, racing back to the bed.

"She's bleeding. Jesus, I can't even tell where it's coming from! There's blood everywhere! We have to get her to the hospital."

"Shouldn't I call for an ambulance?"

"No. It'll take too long." He raked his hands through his hair. "God, she's lost so much blood!"

"Where is she injured? Perhaps we can stop the bleeding."

"She's not injured—at least, not as far as I can tell. I think... Christ Almighty, Edward, I think she's hemorrhaging internally. Let's go—fast!"

Seconds later Galen had Lorelei wrapped up in blankets and was carrying her out of the room, Edward on his heels.

"It's my fault, sir. She was in pain after you went outside with Mr. O'Hara and the others. I should have insisted she see a doctor. How could I be so daft? She didn't want me to call the physician, so I thought perhaps it was simply an attack of nerves after all the drama of the evening."

"Edward, stop blaming yourself," Galen growled. "It wasn't your fault. If it's anyone's fault, it's mine. I started this, remember?"

Edward drove the Jaguar around to the front and stepped out to open the passenger door. "We'll have her there in no time, sir."

"Just hurry," Galen implored him, gazing down at the woman in his arms. "Lorelei, can you hear me? Open your eyes, baby. Please."

The drive to the hospital tested Galen's nerves in more than one way. Besides being half-crazed with worry, he saw a side of his butler he hadn't known existed. The man drove like a demon, skillfully passing drivers in tight arcs, missing oncoming cars by mere seconds. He glided through every red light and narrowly avoided several catastrophic crashes.

A couple of blocks before they reached the hospital, Galen's cell phone vibrated in his shirt pocket. He wrestled it out and answered it. Two minutes later he shut the phone with an oath.

"Trouble, sir?" Edward asked.

It took a moment for Galen to control his rage enough to speak. "Someone just walked into Donald O'Hara's jail cell and shot him in the head. No one saw anybody go in or out." He banged his fist on the armrest. "Christ! How many people does that whoreson Gallagher have on his payroll? I swear, before this is over, I'm going to strangle the breath out of him with my bare hands."

And still that won't be enough, he thought. Not nearly enough to pay for all the grief and suffering the bastard had caused.

"Laird McBain?"

A doctor in a green scrub suit approached Galen, who halted his frantic pacing of the hospital waiting area upon hearing his name. Edward, perched on the edge of one of the plastic chairs, stood to listen.

"I'm Ian McPherson," the doctor said, offering his hand.

Galen shook it absently, impatient for news. "What's wrong with Miss Duplessis?"

"My father and yours were friends for a very long time. I'd been hoping to meet you one day but I never thought it would be under such circumstances." He looked down at his chart. "Is Miss Duplessis a…close friend?"

"Close enough," Galen said.

The doctor cleared his throat. "Has she any family here?"

Irritated, Galen shook his head. "No, she hasn't. What the hell's the matter with her?"

"Well, sir, it's rather a personal matter." The doctor put down his chart. "She should pull through but she lost a good deal of blood. You brought her in just in time."

Galen grabbed the doctor's shoulders and leveled a look on him. "One more time—what is wrong with her, man? Tell me and tell me now!"

The doctor hesitated, still clinging to his ethical code. Then with a sigh he relented. "We can't be certain yet but it's most likely that she had a miscarriage in the very early stages of gestation. We'll know more when all the test results come back. Meanwhile we're replacing the blood she lost."

Despite his earlier imaginings, Galen was shocked. "If it helps your diagnosis," he said more calmly, "it's quite possible she was pregnant. The time of our relations would fit with early pregnancy."

If the doctor was surprised that the McBain laird had admitted his involvement with the patient, he didn't show it. He did, however, seem to feel more at ease discussing her condition with him. "Fortunately, I doubt any permanent damage was done. I'm confident she'll be able to conceive again."

Lorelei had been pregnant—Galen didn't need any further test results to confirm what his gut told him. Although he had just a few hours ago imagined her carrying his child, he was still struck by the reality. And she'd suffered a miscarriage. Had she known and made the decision not to tell him?

"What caused the miscarriage?" he asked.

"It's hard to tell. A pregnancy is always fragile in the first few weeks. And we don't know what the patient's physical or emotional condition was before she got to this point."

Galen could very well imagine what it was. And most of her stress was his fault. "Has she said anything?"

"No, she was unconscious through most of our examination. Whatever she did manage to mumble was in French."

"May I see her?" he asked, realizing his tone was hostile. He was angry at himself and angry at her for not trusting him enough to tell him.

"You may but she's still sleeping."

Telling Edward to go on home, that he would call when he needed to be picked up, Galen followed the doctor down the hall.

Obviously aware of his irritation, the doctor touched Galen's arm as they walked toward Lorelei's room.

"Remember, she may not have even known about her condition, sir."

When Galen gazed at Lorelei's pale, slender form engulfed by hospital sheets, he forgot why he was mad. "I'm sorry if I was rude to you, Doctor. I'm just concerned."

Actually he was deeply saddened that she'd lost their child and damned close to panic at seeing her suffer so.

The dim room was quiet save for the machine that monitored Lorelei's vital signs. She was so still, she looked like a broken angel. He sat in the plastic high-backed chair next to her bed and held her hand, gently tracing each finger.

For the next two days and nights Lorelei mumbled in French, turned over and occasionally opened her eyes, only to close them again before gaining any real consciousness. It was as if she were trying to stay asleep, incapable of—or unwilling to—face life.

Galen remembered the cryptic words she had spoken in Hyannis Port, when they first made love, when she sensed that he had been tormented by guilt and plagued by thoughts of ending his life. "Sometimes when you're sad enough and troubled enough that you almost want to die, it's not necessarily because you're looking for the easy way out. Sometimes you're just impossibly weary from fighting the pain, from worrying that you're bringing everyone around down with you and dying seems like the only thing left to do to save your soul and avoid slipping into madness."

Galen's heart skipped a beat. Then, as now, he felt in his gut that she had spoken from her own experience—and that, to her, fulfilling her death wish was only a question of time.

On the third day of his vigil, shortly after dawn, Galen was pacing Lorelei's room when he heard a hoarse whisper.

"Uncle Roche?"

He whirled to see her eyes closing.

"Baby, it's me—Galen," he said, quickly going to her side. "Open your eyes." His voice was hoarse from all the one-sided conversations he'd had with her, trying to reach her subconscious and coax her awake. "Come on, sweetheart, do it for me."

"I…can't," she murmured. "I…don't want to…anymore."

"Damn it!" He'd known the despair she was fighting was deep, but it seemed to be even deeper than he'd imagined. Why hadn't he realized it? Was he so self-absorbed that he'd completely ignored her needs?

He sat on the edge of her bed, brought her face to his chest and cradled her like a baby. "You have to come back to me, Lorelei," he murmured. "Now that I've found you, you have to come back. I simply could not bear to lose you."

Later that day she was hooked to two more intravenous units. Galen consulted regularly with Dr. McPherson but none of the man's ministrations had brought any change in Lorelei's condition. Galen could see that McPherson was both puzzled and concerned that his patient remained unconscious since, as he kept saying, there was no medical reason for it.

Galen knew the reason, though and it wasn't medical. She simply did not want to wake up and he was becoming more frightened by the hour that she never would.

*****

What do they want? I can't give up now. I have to find them.

Lorelei was waging a war with her memories, with her losses, remembering the particular spot where the police had found her parents' abandoned car. How many times had she gone to that lonely back road to investigate, to look for clues, even crawling around the grassy shoulder?

Pas de nouvelles, bonnes nouvelles—no news was good news, the police kept telling her. But she had recognized the truth in one detective's eyes, the resignation, the compassion for a teenaged girl who had camped out in the countryside for days, hoping she would find a trace of her parents, something to tell what had happened, where their remains lay, so she would know. So she could mourn and move on.

She could still see the Lexus in the impound lot, a few pieces of yellow police tape clinging pathetically to the exterior, her mother's empty purse inside but no sign of her loving, vibrant parents. Had their assailants even recognized them as human beings, or were they only a means to an end?

She wanted so badly to join them. She had tried once to do exactly that. She had run herself into the ground until she was nearly twenty pounds underweight and her immune system was seriously compromised. Then she'd become ill. Very ill. Double pneumonia, coupled with severe anemia, would have kept her in the hospital for a few weeks even under normal circumstances. But her circumstances hadn't been normal and the weeks had stretched to months. Oh how she'd tried then to let go, to give up the pain and struggle it had become to remain in her body. To die.

But Uncle Roche hadn't let her. He'd appeared in the fog in which she drifted, badgering and nagging at times, soothing and gentle at others, one way or another engaging her barely conscious mind until, finally, she'd rallied. Then he'd given her his love and understanding and reason enough to go on living—at least for a time.

But somehow she was back in the fog again and Uncle Roche wasn't there. He was dead, she remembered. And she was tired—so tired she couldn't even move her limbs or lift her eyelids.

Maybe now was the time. Now that she was so close...

The steady beep of the machine monitoring Lorelei's heart rate, pulse and blood pressure suddenly became a shrill whine. The electronic graph line stuttered, then went flat, and the green numbers indicating blood pressure began falling.

"Nurse!" Galen shouted. "Someone, help!"

Before he could run to the doorway to repeat his distress call, two doctors and a nurse bustled into the room with a defibrillator, pushing him out of their way.

Dr. McPherson quickly rubbed the electrical pads. "On my count, one, two, three—clear!"

Lorelei's body jerked but the line on the monitor remained flat.

"Lorelei!" Galen cried, his own heart banging inside his chest so hard that he could barely catch his breath.

"Raise it by sixty," the doctor ordered.

The nurse turned up the voltage, McPherson applied the paddles again and suddenly the shrill whine emanating from the monitor became a steady beep once more.

"Pulse sixty, blood pressure one-twenty over seventy," the nurse said.

Everyone sighed in relief.

"What the hell happened?" McPherson asked his staff.

"I don't know," the nurse answered. "Her pressure just suddenly dropped."

"I want someone watching this monitor from the station at all times," McPherson ordered. "We nearly lost her." He grabbed her chart and started jotting notes. "I want another blood count and electrolytes and keep the crash cart here."

Galen winced as the doctor turned and raked his gaze over him. He was sure he must look like hell.

"Mr. Kennedy," McPherson said, "why don't you go get some fresh air and maybe some food? We'll be keeping a close watch."

"I'll stay." He was determined to wait until Lorelei awoke, until he could be sure she wouldn't try dying again.

"Sir, she's out of danger now."

"Is she?" Galen murmured, staring at Lorelei's pale face.

Then, turning his gaze to the doctor, he said, "Thank you, but I'll stay."

The doctor sighed and left.

Galen gently cupped Lorelei's face. "I know you can hear me, baby. I know you can open your eyes if you want to. I'm begging you. Please…please, come back to me."

Her eyelids felt like lead. Still, she struggled toward the voice that kept calling her name, begging her to come back. After what seemed like hours of trying, she finally broke through the fog. Slowly her eyelids fluttered open. She blinked, squinting as she tried to focus.

"*Où suis-je?*" she asked, her voice sounding rough and unfamiliar to her ears.

Galen's eyes burned and he had to swallow against the tightness in his throat to answer. "You're in a hospital, sweetheart." He gave her a light kiss on the lips. "Do you remember what happened?"

"Yes. No," she answered groggily. She tried to sit up, but he gently held her down.

"Just stay put for now, okay? Don't spend all your strength."

"Why am I here?" She dimly remembered arriving at his castle.

Galen lightly caressed her belly over the sheet. "Do you remember being at the castle and feeling bad, like you wanted to lie down?"

Frowning, she nodded.

"Edward took you upstairs to your room — remember?"

"Yes..."

"You fell asleep. I tried to wake you but I couldn't. You were bleeding." He paused, then, as gently as he could, said, "You had a miscarriage, sweetheart."

Lorelei looked at him with disbelief. "A miscarriage?"

She closed her eyes briefly and shook her head. "Impossible."

He frowned. "Why? We had unprotected sex."

She remembered the pain then. It had radiated into her back, like exceedingly bad menstrual cramps. "I...had my period. I couldn't have been pregnant," she said.

A knock came at the door and Ian McPherson walked in. "Well, hello, Miss Duplessis. I'm happy to see you're finally awake. How are you feeling?"

Galen spoke up. "She says she had her period recently and couldn't have been pregnant."

McPherson opened her chart and started writing. "I see. And when was this period, Miss Duplessis?"

She shifted uncomfortably in the bed. "I don't remember exactly. But I do remember it was a week late."

"And how long did it last?"

"A day."

"Was that normal for you?"

Blushing, she admitted, "No, it usually lasts three or four days. But I had no symptoms of being pregnant," she insisted.

"No nausea, sleepiness, general fatigue?"

"Yes but—"

"Do you remember being in any kind of pain before they brought you to the hospital?"

"Yes. I had cramps just before I went to bed yesterday."

"Um…" Galen shot the doctor a quick look. "You've been here over three days, sweetheart."

"Three days?" She looked incredulous.

"Don't worry, Miss Duplessis, we've been taking good care of you," McPherson tried to reassure her. "Now, can you describe the pains you experienced?"

"Well…like menstrual cramps but much worse. I could hardly breathe when they happened."

The doctor put his pen into his breast pocket, then spoke in a matter-of-fact but gentle tone. "Miss Duplessis, your blood test results show us that you were, indeed, pregnant. Your hormone levels when you first arrived were indicative of early pregnancy and they've been dropping steadily back toward normal levels since then. I'm afraid it's true, you did have a miscarriage."

His brow furrowed with concern, Galen watched Lorelei's expression change from stunned disbelief to foggy bewilderment.

"But what about the period I had?" she asked.

The doctor shook his head. "About twenty-five percent of newly pregnant women have some spotting or light bleeding they can mistake for a period."

Lorelei did her best to assimilate what the doctor was saying but her brain simply wasn't functioning yet. She had been pregnant?

Unable to cope with the implications, she turned to easier, more practical matters. "Why do I have all these tubes hooked onto me?" she asked.

"You lost a great deal of blood. We've replaced it but you need to rest for a few more days. We must also give the uterus a chance to return to its normal position. Otherwise you might compromise your ability to bring another pregnancy to full term."

Suddenly realizing that he meant to keep her in the hospital, she came fully awake in a flash. "I appreciate your concern, doctor," she said quickly, "but I feel fine now. I'll be careful once I'm home but I'd like to leave as soon as possible."

Galen put a hand on her arm. "She'll stay," he told McPherson.

"I won't," she countered.

"Lorelei—"

"I'm an adult. You can't force me!"

"Baby, listen to me—not three hours ago you went into cardiac arrest. You nearly died, for God's sake!"

"Miss Duplessis—"

Lorelei wasn't listening to either of them. She had to get out of there. She had to be alone. And, oh, God help her, she had yet another death to grieve. "I'll be fine. I've survived worse."

Galen stared at her, realizing she wasn't thinking rationally. He wasn't even sure she'd heard him say that she nearly died. Enough was enough.

"Doctor, would you excuse us for a moment?" he asked.

McPherson looked uncomfortably at both of them, then nodded. "Certainly. I'll be back in a few minutes."

When the door closed behind him, Lorelei started to get up. "I'm not staying here!"

Restraining her, Galen took a deep breath. "Why not? Do you have some pressing engagement? Have you no regard for your health at all?"

Even as she struggled against the arm he'd placed across her chest, Lorelei knew he was right and that she was behaving absurdly. She simply couldn't help it. "I am not staying in this hospital," she said vehemently. Then, as her strength deserted her, she sank back against the pillows. "If I'd wanted to die, neither the doctor nor you nor God himself could have stopped me."

Galen wanted to demand an explanation for that one, but her pallor and exhaustion were scaring the hell out of him. This was not the time to confront her about her insane death wish.

"Fine," he said agreeably. "But you have a contract to fulfill and Maurice is on his way here. And you're clearly in no condition to deal with either."

No, she wasn't. More than that, however, Lorelei suddenly realized that dying in Scotland without having settled matters and saying goodbye to Maurice, Annabelle, and Amanda would never do.

Her eyes filled with tears. "Please, Galen, I can't stay here. It's so…sterile…so impersonal. And it reminds me of…unhappy times."

"I understand. So let's compromise, shall we?" He took hold of her hands. "Stay here one more night and I'll stay with you. I promise I'll make it worth your while," he teased, smiling.

She gave him a wary look. "Meaning what?"

"I'll tuck you in and tell you a bedtime story."

Her gaze searched his. Clearly, she thought, this was important to him. And deep down she knew she was too weak to lift a finger, much less walk out of there to fend for herself.

"Fine," she muttered. "One more night."

* * * * *

Lorelei awakened to the scent of spice and the sound of someone else's heartbeat beneath her ear. Her face was nestled in the crook of Galen's neck, his long blond hair draped over one cheek. A smile curved her lips. He had kept his promise. He had stayed with her.

"Galen?"

"Hmm?" he answered, his eyes closed.

"Good morning."

"Hmm."

"Galen? It's time to get up."

He opened his eyes and stared down into hers. "Have I ever told you that you have the most beautiful eyes and mouth I've ever seen?" His voice was a soft drawl.

"Flattery will get you nowhere."

"Will this?" He cupped her cheek and kissed her so softly and tenderly, she almost forgot where she was.

"You said I could leave today," she murmured, breathless.

He looked into her eyes. "I've missed you." He kissed her again, this time more intimately.

Her hand curled into his hair as her senses began to respond to his touch. He ran a hand over her hospital gown, cuddling her to him, then sliding upward to cover one breast.

He caressed it gently for a moment or two, long enough to make the blood pool thick and hot in his loins.

"Christ..." He let her go and raked a hand through his hair. "I can't believe what I become with you."

Her breathing was as labored as his and she opened her mouth to speak, then cut herself short when the door burst open. An elderly nurse bustled into the room, her smile quickly fading to a scowl. She glared at Galen as he got out of Lorelei's bed. "Good morning, Miss Duplessis. Laird McBain. May I take your pulse and temperature, miss?"

Lorelei's voice came out as a ragged whisper. "Yes, of course."

"I'll be back in a few minutes, love," Galen told her.

"Before you return, sir, you might want to consult with the doctor," she suggested. "He'll tell you when it's safe to resume relations."

Galen made her wait a good long hour, long enough for her to get dressed and count all the different patterns of plants on the wall-to-wall paper of the private room she was in. He was lucky, Lorelei thought, that she had no purse on her, no money in any of her clothes this time and thus no means to go anywhere. Not that she could walk fast or run for that matter. Her belly was still sore, and she was told not to exert herself for at least a week.

"The hell with this!" she muttered while she ripped off her hospital bracelet and opened the door—only to collide with Galen's chest.

"Are you ready to leave?" he asked.

"I was ready an hour ago! Where have you been?"

"Settling your account." As she opened her mouth to protest, he added, "And I don't want to hear a word about it. You miscarried my baby and the very least I can do is pay the hospital bill."

Frowning, she thought about that for a moment, then conceded the point with a short nod.

"And," he added, "I also spent some time convincing Dr. McPherson that you wouldn't collapse on the way to the elevator. He's extremely distressed that you aren't staying longer. I had to guarantee that I'd see to it you got plenty of rest."

"I'm perfectly fine," she insisted.

"You're not and we both know it—and so does McPherson. But I do agree with him that what you need most is rest. In my experience, however, hospitals aren't very conducive to it and McPherson finally agreed you'd probably rest better at the castle than you would here."

"Humph."

He smiled at her. "Now don't get all hot and bothered. Well, hot is okay, as long as it's for me and as long as you can wait until we can do something about it."

"You are an infuriating man, Galen Kennedy."

He laughed. "Good. Now you understand how I feel."

"What's so funny?" she asked, frowning.

"You are. You're funny when you're mad. In fact, you're so delightfully funny that I think I'm going to kiss you."

Before she had time to protest, he was kissing her thoroughly. When he released her, Lorelei realized that they were standing in the hallway and to the right and left of them a half dozen nurses and a few ambulatory patients had all stopped what they were doing to stare at them.

"Kennedy!" she protested.

He ignored her outburst. "Come, I have a surprise." He took her hand and showed her to a wheelchair.

"I'm not getting into that."

Galen frowned. He was expecting her refusal. "Humor me. Just up to the exit and I promise it will be worth your while."

She hesitated before refusing again because he was looking at her with a strange gleam in his eyes. There was concern but also something else. "All right, but just to the door," she finally agreed and sank into the wheelchair.

Once they stepped out of the elevator, an orderly helped her out of the chair and she slowly made her way to the front entrance, her hand in Galen's.

Her breath faltered when he opened the door for her to step outside.

There it gleamed, a silver 959 Twin Turbo Porsche.

Lorelei was too stunned to speak. What a cruel joke it was to see one again at close range. "Looks just like mine," she finally said in a whisper.

"*It is* yours, sweetheart." He was smiling as he handed her the keys. She had just enough time to notice the golden medallion on the key chain with the engraving Nemesis on it before tears blurred her vision. She continued staring at the medallion, unsure what to do.

Galen cleared his throat. He hadn't realized returning her car to her would move him so deeply. "This car brought you back to me. It could never belong to anyone but you."

Her lips trembling, she tried to hand him the keys. "But I can't acc—"

"Yes, you can. I bought it back for you and not even God himself could make me return it."

"But the money has to pay—"

"The loan shark. Yes, I know. It's been taken care of. Your house is safe."

"But—"

He stopped her protest with a fingertip to her lips.

"Lorelei, what good is having money if one gets no pleasure from it? It gave me enormous pleasure to be able to secure your home for you. And the look on your face a second ago, when I handed you those keys, was worth my entire fortune. Please, don't spoil it."

With wet cheeks and shaking hands, she hugged him and cried.

He caressed her temples with his thumbs. He knew she shouldn't be driving. But when he watched the light come back into her eyes, he understood her survival depended on letting her take back the controls of her life. "I hope I'm not going to regret this…"

She looked at him without answering , knowing what he was referring himself to. "Thank you," she whispered.

"Well, what are we waiting for? Didn't you tell me you wanted to leave?"

Still she clung to him, trembling and quietly crying. His eyes were becoming misty too. "Lorelei, please, you're turning me to mush."

She wiped her tears with her fingers and offered him a shaky smile.

A Scent in the Night

"I shouldn't let you drive," he said. "McPherson would have a fit if he knew. But I figure you'll waste more energy fighting with me about it then you will driving, so..." He heaved an exaggerated sigh and shrugged.

Her smile widened. "You're right about that."

"By the way, may I hitch a ride home with you?"

She took a deep breath. "It would be my pleasure. I do hope you have a strong heart, however."

Galen laughed as he got into the passenger seat. Her happiness was all that mattered. He had indeed fallen in love with her and for once in his life he didn't give a damn about the rest.

When they slid into the car on their respective sides, he reminded her, "Don't forget to drive on the left."

She glanced at him, her gaze making a quick sweep of his legs, then she pressed a button and he felt his seat move back.

"Thank you," he said, stretching his legs and giving her what he feared was a totally besotted grin.

Lorelei felt the warmth of that grin clear down to her bones. Mesmerized by him and by the surreal events of the past few days, she had to tear her gaze away from his face.

She started the car and easily slipped it into second gear under Galen's watchful eye.

He wanted to tell her he was sorry she had lost their child but he would have to wait. The fact remained that he and Lorelei knew very little about each other beyond what they had learned through physical intimacy. Yet that intimacy had forged an unbreakable link between them, even if the fruit of that link had not come to be.

He wanted to assure her of the depth of his feelings, to break down the barriers she attempted to erect between them, but he also knew she needed to cry, to mourn what could have been theirs.

As he watched her drive, he noted her confidence behind the wheel of the powerful car, the same kind of confidence she had displayed in Hyannis Port when making her presentation. Gone were her fears and insecurities. She seemed to enjoy bringing dangerous power under her control.

He thought back to her unblinking, unerring coolness when she'd fired her forty-caliber Glock at Donald's shoulder, aiming to wound, not kill. At times like those she seemed to separate herself from everything and everyone around her, remaining utterly focused on her goal, fearless and unaffected by any outside force.

He felt her putting that distance between them now. The chasm he feared he could not cross.

At the gates of the hospital parking lot, he directed her to turn left and head for the mountains. It was a glorious sunny day.

"I had a difficult time shifting when I drove over here," he commented. "Either the transmission is not what it should be, or the technical merits of this car are overrated," he teased.

"Thank you for bringing her back to me," she answered simply, ignoring his banter.

Her polite reply confirmed his fears. He put a hand over hers while she shifted gears once more. "What's wrong?"

She turned to face him briefly. "Nothing."

No hesitation, no faltering — and no truth. He focused his attention on the road as it twisted and turned, gaining altitude.

She switched lanes to pass a slower driver, suddenly facing oncoming traffic. With scarcely an inch to spare, she completed the maneuver, undisturbed by the close call. How he wanted to challenge her numbness to the usual boundaries of life. He pursed his lips in frustration. The wait was killing him.

Lorelei was an expert at masking her thoughts and emotions but still, she wished Galen wasn't sitting beside her.

She wanted to be alone on the open road. She needed full-throttle speed to drive away her private demons. But she couldn't risk the life of anyone other than herself. She was well aware of Galen's skeptical gaze, of his mounting frustration. He had discovered the truth about her. She didn't know how but she was certain he knew her secret—her wish to meet death at a time and place of her own choosing, to put her pain and guilt behind her once and for all. She suspected it was only a question of time before he tried to change her mind. And she was dreading the confrontation, didn't know if she'd be able to maintain her façade, which had grown awfully brittle of late.

"I never thought such beauty existed," she said, softly disturbing the silence. "These mountains are breathtaking, and the trees are so intensely green."

"Tell me about your childhood," Galen quietly suggested, placing a hand on her thigh. He felt her stiffen, and, sure enough, she shifted into a higher gear, accelerating through the countryside she'd admired with blinding speed.

Yet from her expressionless profile, one might not think she had even reacted to his question.

"Why?" she blurted out, immediately sorry she had answered in such a telling way.

"Stop the car," he calmly ordered.

She hesitated a moment, then, with a sigh, downshifted and drove the Porsche into a small clearing. As soon as the car halted, he lifted her chin with an index finger, forcing her to look at him. "Because there's going to be more to this relationship than sex. There's going to be trust." He leaned over and kissed her lightly on the lips while he turned off the ignition.

Aye, there's going to be more than sex, he repeated to himself, knowing his need for her had long since crossed mere physical bounds. "This seems like an appropriate place for a picnic, don't you think?"

She looked surprised, then worried. She clearly did not want to continue the conversation.

"Open the trunk," he said, getting out of the car.

She flicked the lever to release the trunk latch and once outside even Lorelei couldn't object to the idea of a picnic. The smell of the pine trees permeated the welcoming breeze. The sun was comfortably warm and the color of the sky as heavenly as it could be.

She watched Galen retrieve a huge basket from the trunk of the 959. He looked at her, his lips twitching into a tender smile.

Oh God, how could this have happened? How could she have allowed herself to fall in love with him?

Once he spotted the perfect tree under which to sit, he pulled a blanket from the picnic basket and spread it on the ground.

"What a pretty pattern," Lorelei noted, the green and blue squares blending nicely with amber and red.

Kneeling, he handed her two plates and some utensils. "Actually, this is the McBain plaid. In the past Scotsmen flew banners of these colors as a sign of allegiance or, often enough, of war—depending on the time of year," he said, chuckling.

"I think Scotsmen were always looking for an excuse to do battle. If you weren't fighting among yourselves, you were fighting England," she pointed out.

"When the survival of your family and clan depends on it, you don't need excuses."

Sensing he had taken offense at her comment, she said, "I'm sorry. I was only teasing."

"I'm sorry too. I guess I'm a bit sensitive on the subject."

He handed her some napkins, thinking of his own conflict with Brenna's family, an unresolved hostility that had escalated after Bryan's death.

Lorelei opened one of the containers filled with chicken drumsticks and laid it beside the plates. "I noticed the antique weapons in your study. Am I mistaken, or were some of the McBains mercenaries as well?"

He smiled as he uncorked a bottle of rosé wine. "Where did you learn about dirks and claymores?"

"I studied art history," she answered, handing him a glass for the wine.

He eyed her with interest and poured. "You never cease to amaze me." He filled a second glass and raised it to hers to make a toast. "To a mind as exhilarating as the body that comes with it."

"Cheers...I think," she responded dryly. She spun her glass gently by the stem to release the fragrance of the wine. "You didn't answer my question," she reminded him.

He brought his knees up and rested an arm over them. "The McBains were rebels, not mercenaries. They had honor and were kin to Robert the Bruce. They fought beside him, not against him."

She mulled over his statement, her curiosity ignited. "Tell me, have conflicts ever arisen within your family because of your Scottish and Irish origins?"

He gently rocked his glass to let the wine breathe. "Not really. My parents loved each other very much and my brother and I were taught to respect both cultures, cultures that are not all that different from each other, when you think about it. Now, enough about my ancestry. Tell me about yours."

She took a sip of wine and shifted her gaze away from him. "There isn't much to tell."

Galen put his glass down and took hers from her hand, as well. He gently clasped her fingers and gazed into her eyes. "We've been intimate with each other. We almost became parents together. Surely that deserves more than 'There's not much to tell'."

She fought the urge to mask her feelings and hide from him. Lowering her head to stare at his hands holding hers, she closed her eyes briefly to regain her self-control.

"I had an extremely happy childhood, even if I was an only child. My parents were loving, understanding..." Her voice trailed off and she sighed. "They were perfect parents. But I lost both of them at nineteen."

He traced her knuckles with one finger and pried open her hands, which she had folded into fists. "How did they die?"

She looked away. "They were on their way to Niagara Falls for their twentieth wedding anniversary. They never made it there."

He tipped her face and forced her to look at him. "How did it happen?" he asked quietly, instantly sensing that much of what he wanted to know about her revolved around that event.

She stared at him for a few seconds but he knew she wasn't seeing him. He knew her mind had gone to something grim but he didn't know how grim until she spoke again, her voice quavering.

"They were presumably carjacked, then later murdered. All that was left was the car and my mother's empty purse. Their bodies were never found."

Her pain was starkly reflected in her beautiful gray eyes.

He saw her tears and brought her head to his chest, holding her tightly. He felt her tremble, so slight and delicate in his arms and he wanted to hold her forever. "Lorelei, you must put your grief to rest."

She lifted her head, her expression suddenly hostile.

"How can I, when I don't even have a grave to visit? How can I properly mourn them when I don't even know how they died?" She tried to get up but he held her down.

"You don't need a grave to grieve."

She snorted. "And how would you know what it takes to grieve?"

"You think I've never lost anyone? I have and I do know — plenty."

Clearly chagrined, she cast him a sidelong glance.

Before she could speak again, he continued. "I also know that suicide isn't the answer. You just pass on your grief to those you leave behind, because they'll feel responsible for not having given you enough love to make you want to live."

"You know nothing!" she shouted, refusing even to consider his words. Refusing to acknowledge the truth her heart recognized in them.

He arched his eyebrows. "So you don't plan to end your own life?"

"That has...had nothing to do with it," she corrected in a last-ditch attempt to hide her intent. "When my parents disappeared, I became obsessed with finding them or finding out exactly how they died, so I could stop picturing the hundreds of ways it might have happened, reliving their deaths over and over again. I wanted closure but instead I was tortured by my imagination. Had they been strangled, stabbed, shot? Was my mother raped, my father forced to watch? Had they suffered long, or was it quick? And where were their bodies? Had they been buried in shallow graves or simply dumped in the woods, mangled and dragged off by animals? Or were they — " She broke off, the nightmarish questions to which she would never have answers suddenly suffocating her.

Struggling to her feet, she turned away from Galen and began stumbling blindly into the forest, completely forgetting the doctor's warnings about exerting herself.

Galen jumped up and went after her, quickly catching her by the waist and pulling her into his arms. She was panting not from exertion but from the pain she had kept inside her for so long.

"You will run no more from this, do you hear me?" he said. "What is important is not how your parents died but how you remember them when they were alive. If you carry their love in your heart, that's all you need. Aye, it's all that matters."

She braced her hands on the trunk of a tree, trying to catch her breath. "I-I wasn't really running. It's just that sometimes I can't bear the pain. Sometimes I feel like I'm losing my mind and I can't stop it. For years I kept hoping and praying for something to free me from this obsession. I...I tried tracking down clues, day and night, seldom eating or sleeping. I was exhausted, run down, anemic, and...well, I got pneumonia. A bad case. I had to stay in the hospital for what seemed like forever and I was so sick, and there was just...too much pain. I couldn't...I couldn't fight anymore. I couldn't even lift an arm. All I could do was lie there and...and hurt, inside and out. So I made the only decision I could still make."

Her admission disturbed him. "What stopped you from doing it—from simply dying?"

She turned around, leaning back on the trunk. "Nicholas Rochefort arrived."

"Who?"

"My uncle—my mother's brother. He was the black sheep of the family, the only one in three generations who hadn't become a teacher. He was an artist. He'd made some money on investments—not a huge fortune by your standards but far more than anyone in our family had ever made. He traveled, so I didn't get to see him often. But I adored him. When my parents...died, he'd been out of touch with the family for quite awhile and I didn't know how to find him. I must have been in the hospital at least a month, maybe longer, when he showed up. I was...well, pretty out of it most of the time. But I finally realized he was there. He...he told me to give him the thousand deaths I'd imagined for my parents. He wanted to take my pain onto his own shoulders."

Remembering how she had offered to take his pain from him, Galen imagined she'd spoken much the same words her uncle had spoken to her. Good words. Clearly, her uncle had been a good man.

"Uncle Roche didn't once try to change my mind," she continued, "but by taking on the responsibility of finding out how my parents died, he slowly gave me back the strength I needed to fight my other battle, the medical one."

She pushed herself away from the tree, heading for their picnic blanket.

He put an arm around her while they walked back. "So why do I get the feeling you deliberately court death?" he asked. "Especially when you drive that...that—"

"Be careful how you speak about my car," she interrupted. "It's Uncle Roche's legacy to me. I think he knew he was dying when he bought it for me."

"Don't evade the question, Lorelei. Why still court death if you opted for life?"

She looked away, trying to formulate an answer.

"Arrogance? The fact that my uncle was no more successful than I at getting at the truth?" She crossed her arms defensively. "I guess I wanted to know I could still do it if I wanted to, if the time was right." She noticed his worried expression. "Also, I developed a taste for speed and for fine machines. Men aren't the only ones who like racing, you know."

Mildly relieved, he rubbed her arms. "That kind of arrogance can get you killed, you know."

"So can crossing the street."

"True but you're not a professional driver."

They were straying from the subject and he knew it.

She took a step back, arching her eyebrows as she placed her hands on her hips. "Kennedy, are you implying I'm not a competent driver or, worse, that I'm reckless?" She took a step closer to him and looked at him straight in the eye. "Because I'm neither. The way I handle my car might seem arrogant but I know its limits and mine. I only ask it what it's capable of. The rest is judgment and instinct. Arrogance—confidence, if you will, helps you overcome fear, that's all."

"You don't fear your car or its power or speed," he muttered. "All you fear is living—that's what I think." He could see that his words had had the desired effect on her. Recognition.

"You don't—"

"Don't what? Don't understand?" He clenched his fists. "I'm fucking tired of hearing you say I don't understand when what you really mean is you don't want to have any sort of meaningful, adult conversation about a subject. Let's see if I've got this right. Your parents die mysteriously. You go crazy trying to find them and when you can't, the fact that you can't put any closure on their deaths makes you almost lose your mind. So then you get sick and—feel free to correct me on this—you decide to let go, to let yourself die, like you did yesterday in that hospital room. How am I doing so far?"

"Fine," she bit out angrily.

"So then your uncle appears, takes the load off your shoulders, gives you other goals to focus on and you get over your illness and start concentrating on dealing with your life rather than your parents' deaths. You study. You work. You succeed. You learn to race and shoot. In short, you begin to live and even enjoy doing it. However," he cocked one eyebrow at her, "with that enjoyment comes guilt. You ask yourself, why should you enjoy life when they couldn't? Then your uncle passes away and no one's left to shoulder the 'responsibility' he took on for you. So your last act of love becomes to sacrifice yourself, to give up your life as your parents were forced to give up theirs."

"I'm not a coward—"

"No, you're not. A martyr maybe but not a coward."

Anger flared in her eyes. "A martyr?" she repeated.

"You love so much and so well, Lorelei, that you suffer severe survivor guilt. And you're afraid you'll be somehow disloyal to your parents if you continue to enjoy life when they can't. To justify the little joys, you formulate plans to end your life. Death becomes your choice."

She tried to break away from him but he held her fast.

"Think of who your parents really were when they were alive," he insisted. "Wouldn't they want their beloved daughter to have a good life, a joyful life? Just as you'd want them to do if it was you who died? Do you honestly think they'd want you to put a death sentence on yourself day after day?" His hands on her shoulders, he shook her gently. "Tell me, do you truly think that?"

"No! No!" she cried out and once more she ran from him.

He caught up with her quickly but did not touch her.

She doubled over, her breathing labored, sobbing. He stepped around her and tried to embrace her. She staggered a few paces farther away, wanting to keep running, unaccustomed to having anyone witness her pain.

"I don't know what to do!" she finally sobbed, no longer fighting him as he gathered her close.

He smiled slightly as he said, "We have our whole lives ahead of us and the power to make things happen—good things. It's normal to be a little bit afraid of that." He traced her quivering lips with one thumb, watching the play of emotions in her gray eyes. "And think of what you'd be missing if you gave up now." He licked a tear from her cheek, brushed his lips across hers and hugged her close to his heart, saddened that she had carried such a heavy burden of guilt by herself all those years, aware he had been doing much the same thing, if in a different way...

They resumed their lunch in the quiet forest, commenting only on the beauty of the day and their surroundings. When they finished and Galen was folding the blanket, he looked at Lorelei standing a few feet away, staring at the trees.

He placed the blanket and picnic basket in the car trunk, then walked toward her. Coming up behind her, he drew her back against his chest, his hands resting lightly on her shoulders. "Penny for your thoughts," he said.

She was silent for a moment, leaning against him. "I wonder if it would have been a boy or a girl," she said.

Her voice sounded remote but at least she was acknowledging her miscarriage, he thought. "We must try to believe it was for the best," he said quietly. "Maybe it was nature's way of telling us this baby wasn't meant to be."

She sighed and put a hand in her pocket, searching for her car keys. "Its getting late. Let's go to that castle of yours, Kennedy. I'm dying to see the kitchens."

Lorelei headed for the car, aware of Galen walking behind her, aware of his frustration that she'd put an abrupt stop to his efforts to get her to reveal any more of herself. She didn't want to discuss the miscarriage. Yet she couldn't help wondering, if she were still pregnant, would he expect her to have an abortion...or to have his child? Now she would never know. And maybe she didn't really want to know. As he'd said, maybe it was all for the best.

Chapter Twenty

Self identity we have,

Respect we earn,

Belonging we are given.

෩

When Lorelei and Galen arrived at the castle, Edward and the rest of the staff were waiting for them. After having driven at hair-raising speed through the mountainous countryside of the Highlands, scarcely believing that the Porsche was hers again, Lorelei felt rejuvenated. Despite her inner turmoil, she was glad to be at Galen's castle.

Strangely enough, she felt safe and at home there. He had made it so. More than that, he had forced her to face her obsession with death. She still felt a vague sense of guilt that she might have prevented her parents' ill-fated journey but she realized that somehow it no longer overwhelmed her. Galen was right. Her parents had given her life and would want her to enjoy—really enjoy—it. They never would have held it against her that she hadn't told them of her dream. Quite the opposite. They would have been astonished that she felt in any way responsible for their deaths. Most of all, she knew they would want her to be happy.

She wondered if she ever would have realized those simple truths if not for Galen. She doubted it. She'd been so focused on what was inside her, with all windows closed and curtains drawn, that she'd had no view of the outside reality. It had taken a big, determined, arrogant Scots-Irishman to shove his way in and drag her out into the sunshine.

And oh, it did feel good. Frightening yes, but good. For the first time in what seemed like forever, she felt almost carefree. Because of Galen.

Would he—could he—ever truly love her as she had discovered she loved him? She knew he wanted her and she believed he cared about her. But did he truly love her? If he didn't and if his attraction to her faded...dear God, how would she ever survive that loss?

* * * * *

Once they finished the lavish dinner Edward had ordered prepared in her honor, Galen insisted on carrying Lorelei upstairs to her room. When he closed the door, however, she realized they were in his suite, not hers. It was huge, complete with a living room and a library, books piled on every available surface.

"Dr. McPherson informed me that it would be dangerous for you to engage in any kind of strenuous activity for the next two weeks or so. He kept stressing 'any kind of activity', and I couldn't resist asking him exactly what he meant. Do you know, the man actually blushed?"

Lorelei was shocked to hear herself giggle. She never giggled. "The nurse who warned you about 'resuming relations' prematurely, then kicked you out of my room, came right out and said to me, 'Now, young lady, you tell that big, strapping man of yours to keep his pants zipped and leave you be until the doctor says otherwise.' I was never so embarrassed in my life."

Galen chuckled but his tone was serious as he put his hands gently on her shoulders and said, "In any case, they're both right. So it's just as well that I have to take care of some things at Wexford House. I'll be leaving for Ireland tonight." Pleased to see the flash of disappointment in her eyes, he added, "I should be back in two weeks—just about the time McPherson said he'd be able to give you a clean bill of health."

Stepping closer, he lowered his head until his lips were but a few inches from her own. "I want you so badly, I hardly trust myself to be near you." He kissed her lightly on the mouth, feeling her lips part beneath his, making him ache for more. Two weeks was going to feel like two years.

"I want you to promise me that you'll rest until I return. And I mean really rest, because when I come back, I'll want you whole and sound and…"

His words trailed off into another kiss. When he felt her shiver of arousal, he forced himself to stop.

She took a deep breath. "What about your reception? When will your guests be arriving? What should I do?"

"The guests won't be coming here. They'll be at Wexford House six weeks from now. Plenty of time for you to recuperate."

"But I can still supervise a reception here, even if I don't do the lion's share of the cooking. Maurice will be here in a few days and you've got enough staff here to—"

"There will be no reception here. It was never meant for Scotland."

She frowned, puzzled. "It was all a lie, then."

"No," he said, shaking his head. "There will be a reception but later and at Wexford House. I didn't want to raise your suspicions, so I simply failed to have my agent tell your Mr. Gillen the party was to be in Ireland."

Lorelei was uneasy, knowing that the ruse had worked.

"I see."

"No, you don't. You're looking at me as if I betrayed you." He placed a hand on her cheek. "I let you assume the reception was here—and soon—because I wanted you where you'd be safe—and because I wanted you back. If I had to do it again, I would."

"I understand that, which is why I'm still here."

But why did she have the feeling that he still wasn't telling her everything, that he would only tell her what he wanted her to know? "I'm also incredibly grateful to you — more than I'll ever be able to say — for saving my car and my house. But that doesn't negate the fact that you manipulated me. This time you pulled my strings successfully but don't think that will always work. I'm used to making my own decisions and taking my own risks. I wouldn't be happy otherwise."

Galen stopped smiling. "Is that a warning?"

"You're rich. You're powerful. We come from radically different worlds." She shrugged away from him to pace the room. "If you try to buy or manipulate me again, I'll be gone in a heartbeat."

"So it's a threat, not a warning."

She ignored his unnaturally subdued voice. "You're an intelligent man and by now you must have figured out some things about me. I'm just saying I won't always let you have the upper hand."

"Let me have the upper hand? Did I hear right?"

Challenge was stamped all over his face. "Lorelei, have you forgotten that there's a contract out on your life?" he exclaimed. "And you knew it — having been chased down a highway and shot at. Yet you foolishly left Hyannis Port, exposing yourself to more danger. Then you smuggled a gun into this country, which could have gotten you arrested and imprisoned and you held that gun on me and shot Donald O'Hara. And you're warning me about having the upper hand?"

"Yes," she answered cautiously, "but — "

"But nothing! Let me warn you of something — I'll compromise on many things but not your safety and my peace of mind about it. And it would be best for you accept that immediately."

"Then I fear you'll be suffering some sleepless nights, Kennedy, because I don't respond well to bullying."

Exasperated, he said, "The only sleepless nights I intend to have, Duplessis, will result from our sexual activity. You've already generated enough worry to last me a lifetime. So I suggest you restrict your arrogance, your pride and all those barriers you erect to protect yourself from feeling anything to your work. In our relationship, there's no room for them."

She pursed her lips. "But I'll bet there's plenty of room for sex — when you want it, how you want it and where you want it!"

Irritated at her deliberately rebellious attitude, he stalked to the window and pulled the curtains closed. "That's not what this is about and you know it."

Aware that she wasn't being either entirely fair or rational — aware too, of being afraid of how vulnerable she felt with him — she said, "So far, that seems to be the main thing."

"Don't be childish."

"Childish?" Now who wasn't being fair? Her voice rose as she said, "I seem to remember a little investigation you asked your brother to conduct on my private life and the questions you wanted answered afterward, questions you had no business asking." She stomped toward him. "You may say that you care for me and that it troubles you if I keep secrets from you but you've kept your past under lock and key too. What slips out is in bits and pieces and I have to guess at the rest. So what's left besides sex? And don't you dare say I'm being childish."

She was calling his bluff, Galen realized and he deserved it. It was too soon, however, to reveal some of the key points about his insanely complicated life. One point in particular would have her turning on her heels and stalking out faster than he could blink. Christ, he was going to have to tell her. He knew that. But before he did, he wanted desperately to make her as crazy in love with him as he was with her. Surely then she'd at least give him a chance to explain and once he did, she'd understand.

A voice in the back of his mind whispered "coward", and he couldn't entirely ignore it. But he also couldn't risk losing her.

"Sex is one of many things I want from you," he said as calmly as he could. "It's also one way of expressing how I feel about you." And with measured strides he closed the distance between them. There was no gentleness in his kiss. He devoured her mouth, a thrill shooting through him as she moaned with pleasure.

Separating himself from her with difficulty, he drew a ragged breath. "That's how I feel. And since I believe you're an intelligent woman, I'll let you figure it all out during the next two weeks until I come back."

Still trembling from his kiss—from the pleasure it gave her and the fear it instilled in her at how dependent she was becoming on him—Lorelei crossed her arms. "All right," she said. "You don't mind, then, if I call Maurice and tell him to meet me later at Wexford House? Or would that damage your male ego?"

He spoke sternly. "If I didn't know better, I'd say you're trying to goad me into an argument. Would that make you feel more independent, parting after a fight? Because this time I might just oblige you."

She arched her eyebrows at his tone.

He sighed. "Look, I don't want to leave after we've argued."

Surprised at his honesty, she added her own. "I don't want to argue either."

"Good," he acknowledged, turning away to stoke the logs in the fireplace. "Let Maurice come here as scheduled. At least you'll have some company."

Maybe so, she thought. But then she would have to tell her mentor about the miscarriage and her relationship with Galen and she hadn't sorted any of that out for herself yet.

"No use making him come here and then travel again. Besides, the fewer explanations I have to give him, the safer it will be for you."

This time Galen arched his eyebrows. "Safer for me?"

"Can you imagine his reaction if he finds out that you lured me here under false pretenses, that I was pregnant from our encounter in Hyannis Port while it was known you had a thing going with a married woman and, finally, that I had a miscarriage? Knowing him, he'd probably think you brought me here to force me to have an abortion."

Galen frowned. Were those Maurice Leblanc's likely worries, or were they hers? Galen wondered if she really had pegged him as just some rich, selfish bastard. "Tell me something, Lorelei," he began. "How did you think I'd react if you hadn't miscarried?"

That very question had been gnawing at her and now, since she was no longer pregnant, she would never know the answer. "I don't know," she replied honestly.

Her answer angered him further. "You don't know, or my reaction wouldn't have mattered to you?"

Her eyes widened. "What do you mean? Of course, your reaction would have mattered to me if..."

"If I'd known you were pregnant?" he finished. It was time to hear the answer to the question he had been asking himself since she was hospitalized. "Would you even have told me if I hadn't dragged you here to Scotland?"

Her answer remained the same. "I don't know."

"I guess that's honest enough," he muttered and he briskly marched to the door, barely holding on to his temper.

He faced her just before leaving the room. "Tell me, what gives women the goddamned right to make these decisions?

How dare you decide whether or not a man should know if he's conceived a child with you?"

She lashed out. "We dare because for years and years men have continued to make women the sole responsible party in a pregnancy. We dare because men have always given themselves the choice to reject their own flesh and blood, to deny their responsibility to their offspring."

It came down to a question of trust, Galen realized, and she still didn't trust him. "Is that why you ran away from me? You thought I would reject the child you were carrying?" he asked.

Lorelei heard the hurt in his voice. In a conciliatory gesture she approached him and touched his arm. "Galen, I swear to you, I didn't know I was pregnant. But even if I had, we knew so little of each other, I…I'm just not sure what I would have done. For instance, how would I have protected myself and my child if you decided you wanted full custody? With all your money, I wouldn't have stood a chance against you in court. You were a stranger to me…and in many ways, you still are."

Wrapping her arms around herself, she turned away from him, unable to bear his accusing look. "But I didn't know I was pregnant. I left Hyannis Port because I was afraid. Afraid for myself and for those around me. I wasn't sure who, exactly, wanted me dead."

"You mean you weren't sure if I wanted you dead?" he asked in a dull voice.

She turned to look at him pleadingly. "I couldn't believe you'd be involved in any way with the attack on me. I thought about it—for pity's sake, it was logical, given that Michael Logan was murdered on your ship. But in the end, logic had little to do with it. In my heart I knew you'd had nothing to do with the murder or with the attack on me. But, please, Galen," she gave her head a quick shake, "try to understand that I was scared and confused and I knew I was in danger. I believed utterly that if I didn't get away from there, I'd be killed."

She had certainly turned the tables on him. And in the end Galen knew she was right. In her place he might have done the same thing—run like hell, as fast as he could.

He took her hands in his. "Thank you for that—for your faith in me," he said. "As long as we're being honest here, I want you to know how disappointed I was when McPherson told me you'd lost our baby. I believe you were, too."

She dropped her gaze from his, staring at his chest as she gave a little nod. "In a strange way I was."

He wanted to tell her that they'd make other babies, beautiful babies, together but he feared she was a long way from being ready to hear that. Instead he said, "Sweetheart, it's important to me that we learn to share what we feel and to trust each other. I don't want to constantly wonder about the pain you keep bottled up inside or worry to death over how it's going to affect you. I care for you, Lorelei and I want you to feel safe and not alone anymore. And as for me, I want to feel at peace when we have to be apart."

He watched her closely, saw her considering his words. He could only hope she'd heard his sincerity, as well.

When she raised her eyes to meet his once more, he saw a mixture of cautious acceptance and, he thought, hope in her clear gaze.

"Then I'll wait for you, Galen," she said. "And I promise to rest. Despite what you think, I don't want to cost you your peace of mind. I'm not good at trusting people but I'll-I'll try. And I hope you'll understand that lately my survival has meant doing just the opposite."

He did understand that. And with a sinking feeling he wondered what would happen to the fragile bridge of trust they were building when she discovered his most damning secret.

* * * * *

During the following days, despite Edward's apprehensive looks, Lorelei made her way into the castle's kitchens, convincing the housekeeper and Cook to let her sit and watch. Two days later she was showing one of the cooks how to make a French-Canadian Tourtière du Lac St. Jean, a renowned Quebecois meat pie. By the end of the week she was cooking a few dishes herself under the pretext of practicing her menu for next month's reception in Wexford.

Now that the twenty-five pounds of mince meat she had basted was placed in the fridge to soak in the herbs, spices and oil she had chosen, she could sit for a few minutes by the oak table in the enormous kitchen to review the menu she had prepared for the reception, a menu that would feature all the beers brewed by Wexford International. As appetizers she would serve bread made with tiny chunks of lard, marinated black olives and various savory toppings sure to satisfy the pickiest of guests.

The main course would include a variety of homemade sausages, fried in onions and simmered in a dark beer labeled The Red Head. She had instructed Mary the housekeeper to buy the ingredients, including beef and cherries, pork and apples, bacon, spinach, Gorgonzola cheese, three-pepper veal, and finally lamb, port wine and rosemary. She would serve the sausages with spicy homemade fries and crispy artichoke hearts.

For dessert she would make a famous Italian lemon sorbet called *granita* floating on Wexford's black currant ale labeled Blue Beard.

In a way she was happy Galen wasn't there. She was hoping to pleasantly surprise him next month with this special, Wexford-inspired dinner. At that thought she glanced at the kitchen clock, noting it was nearly time for his usual second call of the day. She always made sure she was resting someplace in the huge medieval castle when he rang, so that she wouldn't be forced to lie to him. She folded her notes on the menu and recipes then hurried upstairs to bathe and await the call.

However, while she was putting away her clothes so Mary wouldn't have to, she saw his reflection in her armoire's mirror. He was standing in the doorway of her bedroom.

As delighted as she was, she also knew she'd been caught.

She turned around to face him. "You're back?"

He advanced toward her. "I am. And from what I saw and smelled in the kitchens, you've been busy as a bee. What happened to your solemn promise to rest?" His tone was stern but Lorelei could tell he wasn't really angry.

For each step he took, she backed up one. "I wanted to surprise you. I cooked some—"

"You wanted to surprise me into issuing you further advice?"

"You mean commands, don't you? You told me to restrict my ego and my pride to my work, which is exactly what I did."

He sighed, exasperated. "You know, winning an argument with you is damn near impossible."

"How astute of you to notice." In her retreat she bumped into the dresser.

He came to a halt a scant foot away from her. "It would seem that a week is the most I can survive without you. For that reason I'll just have to forgive and forget." Closing the distance between them, he cupped her face and gently kissed her, his lips lingering, his tongue finding hers and making it his.

He slowly pulled back and took her by the hand, heading for his room through a communicating door. "I spoke to the doctor, by the way."

Lorelei was happy Galen had come back. Lately his presence had started to give meaning to everything she did.

"You did? When? He came to see me just this morning."

When she saw the gleam in Galen's eyes, she suddenly understood why Dr. McPherson had made his surprise visit that morning. Seconds later Galen began to unbutton her blouse, enough to slide his hand inside and caress one of her breasts. She meant to ask if he'd brought protection but his ministrations were already making her breathless. Besides, surely he'd thought of that and she'd be spared the awkwardness of bringing up the subject. "Let...Let me shower first, Galen," she said. "I've spent the whole day in the kitchens and I—" She gasped as he reached to caress her other breast. His touch was like a brand, as hot as the sun. "Please..."

"I've missed your scent," he murmured, "that fragrance only you have. I've missed feeling you under me. I've missed your warmth and I've missed your eyes, those eyes that could light a thousand skies." He removed his hands from her blouse and tipped up her chin. "Go and take your shower, if you must."

She hurried away.

Galen was at a loss to explain how he had fallen in love with her so deeply and so quickly. Would she accept that love as it was, or would she need a pledge, a commitment, a vow he couldn't give her?

* * * * *

She returned half an hour later in a white lace nightgown that highlighted her olive-toned skin, making her look exotic and beautiful. That's how it had always been with her. He set out to seduce her and she turned the tables, seducing him. But tonight would be different, he vowed. Tonight he wanted to love her until she belonged to him body and soul.

He walked toward her, admiring her in the light of the fire he'd lit moments before. When he touched her arms, he felt shivers run down his spine. He marveled at how the simplest touch could move him to the depths of his soul.

Scarcely believing he was finally going to make love to her again, he slid the silky straps of her nightgown down her arms and bent his head to suckle one of her breasts.

Lorelei's eyes closed as her body awakened to the tender caress of Galen's lips and tongue. He let the gown slip completely from her and she felt a thrill race through her as his hot gaze raked over her body. Then he picked her up and carried her to the bed.

Galen was breathing hard by the time he set her gently on the bed, not from exertion but from the sight of her soft curves glistening in the firelight. He wanted to taste and savor every inch of her. He suckled her nipples until they were as hard as pebbles, his loins aching as his free hand roamed her belly and buttocks, tracing circles around her navel, exploring her every secret.

She clutched the sheets, then tangled her fingers in his hair as his mouth finally moved from her breasts to her belly. When he reached the juncture of her thighs, when his tongue probed her folds, delving deeper and deeper until she was the only thing he tasted and breathed, she climaxed in a slow writhe, his name flowing from her lips to his soul.

She was still tight when he carefully entered her, still wet from his loving. His strokes were slow and measured at first, then quick and powerful, bringing her another shuddering climax.

He cried out as they came together, becoming one, more powerful than life or death.

"You belong here, Lorelei, with me."

Tears slipped from her eyes. Galen was making a place for her in his life. He was giving her a sense of belonging, something she hadn't had in a very long time.

Fleetingly, the thought passed through her mind—He hadn't used any protection after all. What if she became pregnant again? — but for some reason the thought didn't alarm her. Even if she did conceive again and it turned out that Galen didn't want a permanent relationship, at least she'd no longer be alone. At least she'd have someone to love.

Seeing the quiet tears of surrender sliding down Lorelei's cheeks moved Galen to the core. "Remember," he said as he slipped inside her again, "you belong with no one but me. Only me."

* * * * *

They remained in Scotland a few more days. Mary and Edward were very solicitous, seeing to her every need, treating her as a permanent member of the household.

During the day she was shown the castle grounds and environs and at night she shared with Galen moments of intimacy so beautiful, she never would have dreamed they could actually exist. She'd nervously broached the subject of birth control and, looking grim but without saying a word, he had complied — as often as their passion allowed.

"May I come in?" Lorelei asked one afternoon as she peeked into Galen's study, where he was reading over some business reports he had received earlier in the day. He was wearing a dark green sweater with a pair of gray linen pants, but whether in a plaid kilt or jeans and a T-shirt, he had such a commanding presence, it often took her breath away.

He looked up and smiled. "You don't have to ask permission to come in anywhere here — ever."

She walked toward him. "Speaking of permission," she said, "I have a favor to ask."

He crooked one finger to beckon her closer.

She obliged him and he put his hands around her waist and brought her down onto his lap. "If you kiss me nicely, I'll probably say yes to your favor before you even ask it."

She smiled, then brought her lips to his in a scorching kiss that left him breathless and hopelessly aroused. He tightened his hold on her, trying to bring her even closer. She slid her hands to the nape of his neck and undid the leather thong that held back his hair. When her fingers slowly began playing with the long strands, gently massaging his scalp, he groaned with pleasure. When she edged away from him, caressing his lower lip with one thumb and gazing into his eyes with enormous tenderness, he felt an unfamiliar sense of vulnerability, something he had never experienced with a woman.

Then it dawned on him. She had utterly beguiled him, made him forget where he was and what he'd been doing, had made him surrender his will to hers. She had made him feel every bit as dependent on her attentions as he made her feel. She had taken total control, even if only for a few minutes, of their relationship. Vivian had often sought to manipulate him with sex but to no avail. With Lorelei it was different, because she gave everything even while taking everything.

"Why?" he asked, not sure she would even understand what he was talking about.

"Because...because I want to give you back some of the pleasure you give me," she said. "Because I want you to feel what I feel when you touch me and...and because it was beyond my control," she candidly answered while continuing to play with his hair. "Does it bother you?"

He grabbed both her hands and brought them to his lips.

"I guess it does," she observed. "So your manly pride is more important than your pleasure?"

"For a man, pride and pleasure usually go hand in hand."

"You know, you're getting a little too arrogant for my liking. Maybe I should practice my wiles on someone humbler." Although he knew she was teasing, her saucy smile gave him pause, for he knew few men would be able to resist her.

"You'll do no such thing," he retorted like the besotted lover he was. "It's just that…you make me feel very vulnerable at times," he explained, his tone more serious.

"And you're afraid of that," she said.

"I'm not afraid of it. I'm just not sure I like the feeling."

He smiled, staring at her delicate hands. "It probably amounts to the same thing, doesn't it," he admitted, his eyes gleaming when he looked up at her.

"It also means you don't trust me," she whispered, disappointed at her own conclusion.

"Oh but I do," he corrected her, bringing her head down for another searing kiss to shatter any doubts she might have about his lack of trust in her. He took possession of her mouth as she had done his, rendering her as vulnerable as she had him, stripping away her self-control.

"Can't you guys at least close the door?" Justin complained from the doorway.

Lorelei nearly fell off Galen's lap.

Galen's eyes narrowed. "Welcome home, Justin," he growled.

By the time a blushing Lorelei recovered and stood to greet Justin, the brothers were locked in a glaring match.

"Justin, it's good to see you again," she said.

Justin turned his attention to her. Smiling, he came into the room and kissed her on both cheeks. "And you. You look wonderful," he said, holding her face in his hands for a few seconds.

Annoyed, Galen got up to stand behind Lorelei, placing his hands possessively on her shoulders. "What did you want to ask me, sweet, before we were so rudely interrupted?"

She turned to look at Galen, silently chastising him for his unkind words. "Oh, I'd almost forgotten. I thought it would be nice to give Mary and Edward and Cook the night off. I heard the Bridge Society is meeting tonight. Besides, I've been dying to prepare a supper unsupervised for the longest while." She looked at Justin and smiled, hoping to ease the tension in the room. "It would be nice if you joined us, Justin."

"Thank you but I've business in Wexford that can't wait. I'll be leaving as soon as I speak to Galen," he said.

Lorelei wondered whether her presence was the real reason he was leaving so soon after arriving. Disappointed, she moved toward the door, then belatedly remembered that Galen had not responded to her suggestion. "Galen?"

"I'd be delighted to be your dinner guest tonight," he said. "But only on one condition."

"What condition?" she inquired, frowning.

"You give the staff the night off only if you promise not to exert yourself too much."

"I promise," she replied. Then, looking at Justin, she added, "Have a safe trip to Wexford."

"Goodbye, Lorelei," he answered, sounding a little downhearted.

Once she left the room, Galen closed the door and faced his brother. "What the fuck is the matter with you, barging in on us that way? Lorelei nearly died of embarrassment."

Justin approached his brother, pointing a finger at him.

"What's the matter with me? With me, you say? You must be kidding."

"Are you jealous—is that your problem?" Galen nearly shouted.

Justin uttered a frustrated sound. "We've already discussed this, Galen. I'm not going to try to compete with you. But, yes, I like Lorelei very much, which is why I can't stand to see her blindly getting more involved with you by the hour when you haven't yet managed to tell her the truth. Have you?" he challenged.

Galen could offer his brother no argument. Still...

"The time's not right, Justin," he said. "She's just recovering from a miscarriage. I want our relationship to be on solid ground before I tell her."

Justin stared at him for a long moment, his mouth a grim line. Then he shook his head. "You must be out of your fucking mind. You let her get pregnant? You bastard! If you wait any longer to tell her what she has to know... Galen, she'll never forgive you. Never. And then where will you be?"

* * * * *

That evening Lorelei presented Cornish hens basted with smoked bacon fat, dry mustard, maple syrup and raspberry vinegar and surrounded with small red potatoes and fresh rosemary. She loved the dish. Its aroma could tempt even the most devout dieter. She had also steamed some fresh spinach with nutmeg, garlic and olive oil and made a raspberry coulis sauce to enhance the sweetness of the poultry.

Dessert was an elaborate but delicious affair. Layers of paper-thin phyllo dough shaped into tulips, basted with butter, baked, cooled and then filled with *crème patissière* topped with fresh raspberries, a mint leaf and sprinkles of icing sugar.

"Should I have my orgasm now or wait until we're in bed?" Galen asked when she presented the pastries.

"Shame on you, Galen!" Lorelei replied.

Lorelei had served the meal in the castle's rustic kitchen, with candles and a roaring fire Edward had laid in the centuries-old hearth. The fire and the candlelight, along with the music of Loreena McKennitt on a CD playing softly in the background, lent a warm, cozy, yet sensual atmosphere to the room.

Galen sipped the Alsatian wine Lorelei had served, acknowledging that, despite their differences and problems, the only peace he'd ever found was with Lorelei.

As she went back to the counter for dessert plates, he suddenly pictured her seven or eight centuries before, wearing a long dress, a gold chain around her waist and her hair in braids and ribbons. Entranced, he followed her and whispered from behind her, "I want you. Now."

He grasped her hands and raised her arms to take off her sweater, then her camisole. He slid his thumbs up her naked spine, watching her shiver at his touch. She braced her hands on the counter in front of her, as if suddenly her legs weren't steady enough to hold her. He lifted her long hair and languidly kissed the nape of her neck, his tongue following the rhythm of the music.

He finished undressing her, then himself, then caressed her belly and breasts until she was panting. His arms went around her waist and he lifted her slightly to stroke his hardness against her, to build the frenzy in both of them, the one that would take them spinning together into a vortex of light.

They never made it to the bedroom. The laird did with his lover what his ancestors had doubtless done countless times before. In an act of pure possession, he scooped her into his arms, laid her back on the big oak table, spread her legs wide and buried himself inside her in both lust and love, to the accompaniment of her moans of pleasure.

* * * * *

Their trip to Ireland began with a ferry crossing from Kyle Lochalsh to the Isle of Skye, where one of the Wexford fleet, the *Blue Siren*, had docked. At Lorelei's first glimpse of Ireland, Galen handed her a pair of binoculars, through which she could view its imposing cliffs and the angry waves slapping their jagged edges. She was captivated by the lighthouses perched on gigantic rocks overlooking the crashing surf.

The ocean spray was a balm to her senses. She spent most of the trip in Galen's arms, content and safe and, temporarily at least, at peace.

They docked in Cork and, after Lorelei personally supervised the unloading of the Porsche, drove the rest of the way in the 959 followed by Edward and Mary in Galen's Jaguar.

When Lorelei saw the Wexford fortress, with four towers flanking its castle and a magnificent rose garden stretching at least a hundred meters across the front, she gasped. It was every bit as impressive as McBain Castle. She turned off the car's engine, stepped out and looked around. She noted the castle's strategic location, facing the river and the superbly kept battlements above the third floor. Although Wexford House didn't have the fairy tale quality of the McBain castle, the Irish château bespoke history, tradition, and power.

She glanced at Galen's profile while he silently admired his home, his muted pride revealing his love for the land of his ancestors. Alas, Lorelei thought, many here had hearts filled with anger and hatred and seemed to think they had been born only to fight.

Chapter Twenty-One

Lorelei ran down the stairs with a selection of fabric swatches, intent on asking Galen his preference. His guests would be arriving in two weeks and he had asked her to redecorate the rather neglected ballroom for the occasion.

She headed for his study and, seeing that the door was open, walked right in.

"Galen, would you look at these patterns I chose and tell me which one you like best?" she began. Then she looked up and came to a dead stop. An attractive woman about her own age was in Galen's arms, staring at her with what looked like faint amusement. Galen's expression was unreadable.

Was the woman a relative? Lorelei wondered. "I-I'm sorry, I thought you were alone. I'll-I'll come back later," she stammered.

"No, wait," the woman said, glancing at Galen. "I guess we forgot to close the door," she added coquettishly. She let go of Galen and introduced herself. "I'm Brenna Kennedy, Galen's wife. And you would be...?"

Galen looked sick.

A wave of heat coursed through Lorelei and ended in her face. Her legs nearly buckled. She shook the woman's hand, numb from shock. "Lorelei Duplessis."

"Are you the woman who appeared in *People* magazine with my husband?"

"Yes, she is," Galen said, "and you have no idea what it took me to get her here," he answered in her place, disengaging himself completely from Brenna.

Blood drummed in Lorelei's temples and a weight on her chest slowly crushed the breath right out of her. The room became smaller and smaller, with no air left to breathe.

"These can wait," she mumbled, whirling away to leave the study. If she stayed any longer, she would suffocate.

Galen followed her out, grabbing her forearm. "May I see you in a few minutes, love, after I get Brenna settled? I won't be long."

She didn't look at him. She couldn't. She wanted to flee, to escape, to suffer her humiliation alone. She tugged her arm free and began climbing the narrow staircase leading to the upper floors before he had time to blink.

Frustrated as hell, Galen watched her rigid back as she went upstairs. "Lorelei, I must speak to you. Just wait a damn minute!" He climbed the stairs two by two.

Lorelei slammed the door to her room and leaned against it, breathing hard.

"Lorelei!" He banged on the door, nearly dislodging her.

The pulse at her neck was beating so rapidly, she feared she might pass out. While Galen continued pounding, she slowly went totally blank. She had learned in the past how to numb herself to emotion, to put distance between her and pain, not to feel.

She pushed herself off the door took a deep breath, and turned the knob. "There's no need to shout. My hearing's fine."

He frowned at her controlled reaction. There were no tears in her eyes, no urgency in her voice. She just stood there with her hand resting casually on the doorknob, not even demanding an explanation.

"We need to talk," he said in a rush. "It's...not what you think. God, I hate that line but it's the truth." He hoped she would let him in but she didn't.

"I'm sure you have a good explanation but at the moment—"

"It's just a piece of paper," he interrupted. "Our marriage is just a piece of paper. It ended a long time ago. I haven't seen or heard from Brenna in five years."

He hadn't denied the woman's shocking words. She could not bear this again, this betrayal, losing someone she loved, losing a part of herself she had given away, only to see it discarded by the person who received it.

"Whatever. If you don't mind, I want to be alone now."

Her voice was so firm, he suspected she was about to explode. She needed time to calm down. And he needed to get Brenna out of the way. "Okay but I'll be back in five minutes." He placed a hand on the door, stopping her from closing it. "This changes nothing between us."

"You're right," she said flatly. "I couldn't trust you then, and I certainly can't now. So nothing's changed."

He ignored her sarcasm as he tried to ignore the panic rising in his gut. "I'm going to find out what she wants and if it's a divorce, I'll be more than happy to oblige."

Footsteps echoed up the staircase. Alarm registered in Lorelei's eyes.

"Stay here and wait for me," he said in a reassuring tone.

She nodded but only because she wanted him to leave her alone.

When he left, her gaze landed on the bathroom door. How easy it would be just to end it, right here and now. She had almost done it for her parents, hadn't she? Was Galen Kennedy worth it? She looked away, afraid to cry, afraid to care. She needed respite from all the emotions he generated in her, a chance to find her balance and to face this outlandish situation without melodrama.

Lorelei grabbed her car keys and left her room, taking the back staircase. In the kitchens she found Edward quietly sipping a cup of tea.

He looked up, startled. "Miss Duplessis, may I help you with something?"

"No, thank you, Edward. I'm just going out for a while."

"At what time may we expect you for supper?" he asked.

"I'll be dining out. Don't make any plans for me."

Edward was clearly perplexed at her curt answer. "I say, Miss Duplessis, are you all right?"

Lorelei sighed and opened the kitchen door. "I really must leave, Edward. Goodbye."

* * * * *

After speaking with Brenna, Galen was distraught. The woman didn't want a divorce, she wanted to rekindle the home fires. And Lorelei was nowhere to be found. She had not, as he'd asked, waited in her room for him. He slammed open the door to the kitchens with disgust. Lorelei wasn't there either.

"Edward, have you seen Lorelei?" he asked.

"Why, yes. She left a while ago and informed me she would not be having supper here tonight."

"Where did she say she was going?"

"I wondered that myself but she didn't volunteer the information, sir. She appeared to be in a hurry."

"But where could she have gone on foot?"

"On foot? I believe she took her car. She had keys in her hand when she left." Edward became concerned. "Mr. Kennedy, is something amiss?"

"That would be an understatement, Edward. Brenna is back and—"

"She's back? From Londonderry? When did this happen?"

"Just this morning, as I was going out, I found her on our doorstep. Obviously I couldn't turn her away. I let her in and we were in my study when Lorelei came downstairs.

"I take it Miss Duplessis knew nothing of your…marriage to Miss Coyle?"

"No, she didn't. I was waiting for the right moment… I guess I fucked up royally, didn't I?"

Edward stood and placed his teacup in the sink. "I'm sure Miss Duplessis will be back. After all, she wouldn't miss a chance to give you a good setdown, would she? Perhaps it's best to give her some time to cool the urge to use a gun on you again, sir."

"As supportive as ever, hey, Edward?"

"It bore good results last time, sir, if I do say so myself."

"You'll be happy to know I took the gun away from our little avenger."

Edward smiled. "Mr. Kennedy, nothing can stop a woman scorned, not even the lack of a pistol."

Galen smiled ruefully back. "And I'm sure you'll be there to supply her with one if need be, old man."

An hour later an unsmiling Galen was pacing his study like a caged animal. Soon it would be dark. Where the hell had she gone? The grounds were relatively secure—he'd made sure of that when he arranged for Lorelei to come to Wexford House. He had private guards everywhere on the property. But outside its perimeter, out in the neighboring countryside, he couldn't guarantee anything.

Growing closer to panic by the minute, he called for Edward, who appeared a few moments later.

"Sir, has she returned?"

"No and soon she won't be able to find her way back. Without her purse, which was still in her room, she has no money on her and no identification. Even with a full tank of petrol she couldn't have gotten farther than the abbey. Send Conrad to take a drive toward town and Colin to take the road to the mills. Tell them if they spot her to call me immediately and continue following her until I reach them."

"Right away, sir."

At ten o'clock at night Galen was with Edward in the study, pretending to review the guest list for the upcoming reception. The phone rang and he leapt to pick up the receiver.

"Kennedy here. Where? Did you search the car? I'll try to find the other set of keys. Stay by the road and call Colin. He's in the Land Rover. Both of you wait for me there."

Concerned, Edward waited for Galen to relay the news.

"They found the Porsche?"

"It's by the road on Muldoon's Point. It appears she ran out of gas. There's no sign of her, though. She might have gone for help or gotten lost trying to walk back." Galen took a deep breath. "Pack up some flashlights, flares and the first-aid kit. Also, siphon some petrol from one of the limos. We'll bring the car back if we can. I'm going to change and join the search."

Before leaving the room, Edward had an idea. "Sir, why don't you bring one of the hounds with you? They're bloody good trackers. I'll have Mary bring down an item of Miss Duplessis' clothing. Perhaps if they smell her scent, they can guide you to her."

"That's an excellent idea, Edward. I'll get Thor and you gather the stuff we need. If Thor reacts to her scent the way I do, we'll find her in no time."

Edward simply arched his eyebrows at the remark and hurried to his duties.

Five minutes later Galen was running down the main staircase clad in jeans, hiking boots, a sweater and a suede jacket. Mary had given him one of Lorelei's camisoles for the dog to sniff. He inhaled her scent one last time before stuffing the filmy garment into a duffel bag.

Chapter Twenty-Two

Are you doing it for me,

Or to me?

ಶಿ

"Going to look for your errant cook? No—that's right—she's also your mistress, isn't she? Tell me, Galen, is her *duck à l'orange* as good as what's between her legs?"

Galen stopped at the foot of the stairs and looked up at Brenna, who stood at the top. The urge to reply in equally vulgar terms was so compelling, he had to bite his lip. His estranged wife was wearing a black negligée and cradling a glass of wine in her hand.

"I must say, she has excellent taste in wine, although I'll never learn to pronounce the name of what I'm drinking. You think she'll mind that I opened the bottle she left in our room?"

"That is no longer our room, Brenna but mine. And 'tis I who minds you drinking the wine." Where was the simple, innocent-seeming girl he had once upon a time fallen in love with? Now she reminded him of Vivian Gallagher, cool, sleek and deadly.

"My darling husband, that woman is nothing but a tramp scheming for your money."

"Stay out of this, Brenna," he warned, turning to leave.

"I'm your wife and she's not. You owe me the respect that goes with that title."

Galen turned around and gripped the banister. "You ceased being my wife when you walked out on me and never came back. You can't expect us to pick up where we left off.

Too much has happened since then. What's more, a lot hasn't happened. We have shared nothing for five years—not a word, not a call. Nothing. And you expect—what?—that I'll welcome you with open arms and forget the past five years? You say you've come back because you've forgiven me? Maybe I don't want to be forgiven, Brenna, because maybe there's nothing to forgive."

He hesitated, then went on. "At this moment I'm sure of very little where we're concerned but I do know that we've both changed. You're very different from the Brenna I knew and I've changed too, probably for the worse. However, we have to acknowledge those changes and move on with our lives—separately, as before."

Everything about him had changed, Galen acknowledged to himself. Not even Brenna's reappearance would persuade him to let Lorelei go.

"In the eyes of the Church and the law, we are married!"

"Not in any real sense of the word, Brenna. Our marriage certificate meant nothing to you five years ago, so I don't see how it could mean anything now."

She threw her wineglass to the floor and stomped her foot. "But you won't even give us a chance! I love you, Galen, and I want you back."

She came down the steps, clearly hoping to bridge the gap five years apart had left between them. "Give yourself the chance to rekindle what we had. This new girl—she reminds you of me, that's all. Try to remember that when you go looking for her tonight. She doesn't love you the way I did—do." She reached him and placed a hand on his arm.

"Come back to me tonight, Galen. I'll be waiting for you," she said softly and she motioned upstairs toward his bedroom.

Then she turned around and, holding her head high as if she had every right to make demands of him, Brenna went back up the stairs.

He shook his head as he watched her. If she actually believed he was even slightly tempted, she had another think coming. But how in God's name was he going to get rid of her without risking any more lives, including his own?

As Galen loaded the Jeep with supplies for the search, Justin pulled up the driveway in his black Viper. He had been back in Scotland on family business and had just returned.

Edward joined them with Thor, who was nervously pulling at his leash.

Justin got out of his car and looked questioningly at Galen. "What's going on? You're not going hunting this late at night, are you?"

"We're going on a search, not a hunt. Lorelei's missing, and they found her car up at Muldoon's Point. She's been gone since six this evening. If you're up to it, you can drive the Jeep there and I'll take our horses and ride cross-country."

He gestured toward the horses standing saddled and ready.

"I can meet you there and you and I can look for her on horseback. We're bringing Thor to track her." He was about to haul himself onto his horse when he remembered his unexpected guest. "Oh and Brenna's back."

"What?" Justin yelped.

Galen signaled the dog to get into the Jeep. "You heard me. She's back. Did I mention that this has not exactly been a good day?"

Justin shook his head. "Christ, I hate to say it but it's your own fucking fault that—"

Galen put up a hand. "Don't go there, Justin. I'm in no shape to argue with you."

Justin patted his brother on the back. "Looks like I arrived just in time, then. By the way, now that you have your wife back, may I have Lorelei? I mean, now you have two gorgeous women, while I have none. Besides, I'm thinking the Canadian must be pretty pissed at you right about now and, you know, this way we could keep it all in the family."

Galen glared at him so hard, his eyes fairly glowed.

"I didn't think so," Justin sighed. "Okay, let's go. I'm sure we'll find her—unless she takes one look at your ugly puss and decides to run for cover." Justin walked to the Jeep. "Relax, man. Lorelei knows how to take care of herself. And the woman is nuts about her car. She wouldn't go far without it."

"That's what I'm worried about, Justin—why she didn't stay near the Porsche."

Before the two brothers each went their way, Mary shouted Galen's name as she hastily ran down the front steps of the castle.

"Wait, Mr. Kennedy, wait!"

Wondering if the housekeeper had received word from Lorelei, Galen started toward her, Justin and Edward following. "What is it, Mary?"

"Well, sir," she gasped, breathing heavily, "there's a man on the phone—said his name is Maurice Leblanc. Claims he's kin to Miss Lorelei and he's demanding to speak to her. When I told him she was out, he insisted on speaking with you, sir."

Galen shook his head. "I need this like a hole in the head," he muttered. "I'd better take this call," he told the others. "I'll be right back."

Heading into the house, Galen turned to Mary, who was on his heels. "What did you tell Mr. Leblanc about Lorelei?"

"Nothing really but—"

"But what?"

"Miss Brenna, she—uh—she's the one who answered the phone first."

Mary's distress was so evident Galen knew she had overheard Brenna speaking to Maurice. "Damn! When it rains, it pours."

He stepped inside, practically running. "I'll take it in my study but please stand by on the other line," he barked.

When it dawned on him that Maurice was due to arrive that same night from Montreal, he swore under his breath.

"Hello."

"To whom am I speaking?" Maurice asked in a very abrupt tone.

"Galen Kennedy, M. Leblanc."

"Where is Lorelei? Why isn't she at the airport to meet me?"

"I'm sorry, sir but Lorelei had some car trouble. Our driver had to go and fetch her. Where, exactly, are you?" he asked as politely as he could, although he knew the Frenchman would not easily be appeased.

"Where do you think I am, in China? I'm in Waterford Airport and have been for the past two hours! What has happened to Lorelei?" he shouted into the receiver, clearly not satisfied with Galen's explanation.

"I meant to ask, where in the terminal are you?" Galen replied, ignoring the man's tone, his patience at an end, even if the Frenchman had every right to be angry.

Maurice seemed to sense his irritation and answered more calmly. "I am waiting just outside the exit gates."

"I will send someone to pick you up, sir," Galen immediately offered, though he hoped to stall Maurice's arrival. "However, since we're located almost two hours away, and it's quite late already, perhaps you should wait until morning. You must be very tired. Why don't you check into the Diamond Hill in Waterford? We have an account there. I'll send one of my drivers to pick you up in the mor—"

"Do you take me for *un imbécile*, Mr. Kennedy? You don't want me to come there tonight because something has happened to *ma petite, non*?" He paused just long enough to catch his breath. "And unless you want me to alert *les forces de l'ordre*—I mean, the police—you will tell me the truth!"

"M. Leblanc," Galen said in a clipped voice, "I don't have time to listen to your threats, nor do I care if you call in the army. Every minute I spend talking to you is a minute I lose trying to retrieve Lorelei. So you can do whatever the hell you want. Just tell my housekeeper here where we should pick you up tomorrow." Galen passed the call to Mary, then marched out of the house, intent on finding Lorelei ASAP.

*****

"*Le fils de pute vas savoir comment je m'appelle!*" Maurice muttered under his breath. "The son of a bitch doesn't know whom he is dealing with!" he shouted again in English, eyeing a janitor who had conspicuously eavesdropped on his telephone conversation.

Incensed that he hadn't received a credible explanation for Lorelei's absence, Maurice Leblanc, great-grandson of Gaspar Le-Blanc-de-Seine, himself descended from a long line of French feudal lords reaching as far back as the eleventh century, would not be deterred by a mere Irishman, no matter his noble ancestry, political affiliations, or vast financial means. Therefore, with an almost regal bearing, he approached a clerk at the taxi counter, determined to get to Wexford House posthaste.

Chapter Twenty-Three

Justin was leaving a small clearing when a voice called out to him from up in the tree Thor had started to sniff.

"Justin, up here!"

Justin looked up from his horse. "Lorelei? My God, don't move! You'll kill yourself if you fall!"

"I couldn't move if you paid me to, Justin. I have vertigo. Heights make me dizzy and I lose my bal—" Suddenly the branch she was sitting on started to crack, giving way under her weight. "*Merde! Je vais tomber!*"

"Hold on!" Justin shouted as he tried to steady his mount. He looked back up at Lorelei. "Reach for the branch to your left."

Lorelei clung to the trunk for dear life.

"Come on, Lorelei, you can do it."

Her head started spinning and she closed her eyes until the sensation stopped. She tried to picture herself on the beach in Hyannis Port, the sand beneath her feet. Her left side hurt fiercely when she attempted to reach down. "This is crazy. I might as well jump, Justin! Can't you come get me?"

"I wish I could but the branches wouldn't hold me."

Justin dialed Galen's cell number while he continued talking with her. "Why in hell are you up there in the first place?"

He swore out loud when the branch cracked again. It wasn't going to hold her much longer.

"I had no choice. A big dog was chasing me. And that was after I lost the men who'd been trailing me."

Men trailing her? Here? And a big dog this deep in the woods? More like a wolf, Justin concluded. They were common to these forests. Lord, she could have been mauled or, worse, killed. "Now listen carefully. You have to move to the branch on your left, then lower yourself to hang down by your hands."

"How am I going to do that?" Lorelei had sat motionless in the cold for hours. "I can't even feel my hands, let alone my legs."

"Well, rub your hands together to warm them up and try to imagine the nice hot bath you can take when we get home."

While Lorelei muttered about her predicament and tried to follow his instructions, Justin described their location to Galen. When they'd finished speaking, he almost wished he hadn't called his brother. Galen was going to have a conniption when he saw Lorelei's situation. Justin sighed and put the phone back into his jacket. "Galen's on his way, but that branch won't hold you much longer. So let's get you down now, shall we?"

"Why did you call him? I don't want to see him, much less talk to him!" She rubbed her hands furiously. "I got pregnant because of him, miscarried because of him, got shot at because of him—and he didn't think it was necessary to tell me he was married? I don't want to speak to him again for as long as I live, which might not be that long anyway."

She took a chance and looked down. "Just help me get out of this tree before he comes."

Justin scanned the trunk again. "Lorelei, you have to reach for that thick branch on your left. As soon as you're hanging down by your hands, I'll catch you by the waist."

"All right. But I warn you, I'm ticklish."

Justin grinned. "Well, don't go too wild, or we'll both tumble off this horse." He scratched his chin at the thought. "Hmm, a tumble with Lorelei—maybe that's not such a bad idea."

"You Kennedys are all the same, always thinking about sex," she commented.

"How can a man think of anything else when they look at you?" he teased.

Lorelei was grateful Justin was trying to relieve the tension by making jokes. She was still terrified, however, of having to rely on her fingers, stiff from cold, to hold her weight such a distance from the ground. Fear, exhaustion, and the nagging pain in her side prevailed and she nervously began her maneuvers.

Justin watched her silently as she took a deep breath for courage, slid off her perch, made it to the thicker branch, and dangled there. As he'd promised, he grabbed her by the waist, slowly lowering her to the ground. Her legs buckled beneath her and she fell into a pile of leaves.

Justin quickly dismounted and helped her up. "God, you scared me. Are you all right? Anything broken, bruised?"

Still dazed, Lorelei took a few seconds to answer. "Can you hold on to me while I try to walk? I need to feel solid ground under my feet." When Lorelei looked up, she saw Galen sitting immobile astride a horse some fifteen feet away.

Justin gave him a stern look as he held Lorelei by the waist. "Don't mind his scowl, Lorelei. He was born looking like that. In fact, he scared the doctor who delivered him. But if you ask me, his bark's worse than his bite and all that."

Galen's expression didn't change. In fact, it hardened as he advanced on his horse. "I'll take her home now, Justin."

The inflection of his voice betrayed his tightly leashed temper.

"I'm not mounting that beast." Lorelei looked up at Galen with the most insolent look he had ever been given.

Justin intervened. "Do you mean the horse or the man sitting on it?" He smirked at his brother.

"Is there a huge difference?" Lorelei responded.

"Well, not really, now that you mention it. Both are bad-tempered, pigheaded and have huge...uh...egos."

"Enough, Justin. Please leave us alone," Galen growled.

Before getting back onto his horse, Justin touched Lorelei's arm and whispered in her ear. "He's angry because you made him worry. No matter what he says, just remember that he truly cares for you."

Lorelei watched Justin leave, then turned to face the blond giant on his equally gigantic horse. He had no reason to be upset with her. Hell, if someone should be upset, it was she. "Just point the way out of here, Galen. I'm tired, hungry and cold and I haven't the strength to argue with you."

He dismounted and strode toward her with the intention of giving her a piece of his mind. When he was a foot away, he spoke quietly but dangerously. "Do you realize the turmoil and worry you have caused in my household? Do you not care that your precious Maurice is frantic about your disappearance? Does it faze you in the least that you've made fools of us both by running away? I thought we could settle this like adults. So you were angry, shocked, all of which you were entitled to be. But couldn't you have waited for us to talk, to—"

"Well, excuse me," she interrupted, poking his shoulder. "Excuse me for feeling hurt, humiliated and furious. Excuse me for needing to take a drive to keep from doing something more drastic while waiting for your lordship to arrive with his explanation of how he conveniently forgot to tell me he was married. Excuse me for getting followed by two shady characters and successfully losing them. Excuse me for running out of gas and having to abandon my car in the middle of these godforsaken woods. Excuse me for not being able to rely on the gun you removed from my possession to defend myself against a huge dog that mistook me for his supper. And excuse me for having to climb a tree and sit there for hours in the cold and rain waiting for someone to realize I was missing!"

She paused only to catch her breath and then continued ranting. "If you think I'm going to stand here and let you berate me into believing I behaved irresponsibly just so you can hide the guilt you feel for having caused all of this, then think again, babe, because I hold you personally responsible for everything that happened. What's more, I'm sick to death of you, your past, your secrets and most of all your arrogance in trying to dictate to me how I should react to something beyond shocking. Ha! Instead of chastising me, you should be damn grateful that I can take care of myself and that I have enough strength to pick up the pieces of my life you shattered without so much as a second glance!"

Breathless, she finished off with, "Now, either you show me how the hell to get back to civilization, or I'll find my own way there, as I always eventually manage to do—alone!"

As she turned to leave, Galen grabbed her by the waist and without a second thought lifted her across his shoulder, placing a hand firmly on her bottom. "If you don't cease talking, woman, I will strap you down on my horse and give you the thrashing you so rightly deserve."

With her head down and her hair dangling, Lorelei began to feel dizzy again. Plus, her left side hurt like the dickens.

"You conceited, over-indulged, narcissistic Neanderthal, put me down!"

He mounted the horse, still carrying her on his shoulder as if she weighed no more than a feather. His strength would never cease to amaze her. Then he set her on the saddle facing him.

His angry eyes had suddenly become concerned. "Now, let's start at the beginning. Who followed you? Did you get a good look at them?"

She arched her eyebrows and sighed. "Yes, I did. I even got their phone numbers. Now let me see, where's that notebook I was using to write everything down while my car was driving itself?"

"Lorelei, I swear to God, if you weren't a woman, I'd smack you right in the—"

"And if I had my gun, I'd make you a woman!"

Galen took her hands and gently brought them to his lips. "Okay, I'm sorry. I apologize. Can we please be adults about this? Can you understand that your life was in danger and that we were all worried about you?"

"You evade the issue, Kennedy."

"Which issue would that be, the one of your foolhardiness?"

"Actually, it would be the one of your wife," she spat.

He flinched. "We'll discuss that later, at home and in private."

"We'll discuss it now, Kennedy, or I'm getting off this horse!"

Galen sighed. "Right. Fine. What would you like to know?"

"Don't be obtuse. It's unbecoming."

He placed his hands on her waist, pausing a moment before speaking. "Look, I've been separated from Brenna for five years and I've never heard a peep from her since the day we broke up. Today she returned—God only knows why. It shocked me as much as it did you, because up until twelve hours ago she was part of my distant past and there was no reason for me to think she was ever coming back."

He tilted her chin up with one finger. "I didn't mean to lie to you, to hurt you, or to humiliate you. I was going to tell you about it soon, when I explained why I couldn't marry you."

"Do go on. This sounds intriguing."

Her sarcasm was not lost on him. "Our families go back a long way together, Lorelei. I committed to her and them, and unless she wants a divorce, I can't ask for one. It's just not feasible politically."

"So you still love her?" Lorelei stared blankly at the trees surrounding them, suddenly feeling very cold and alone.

"That's not what I said."

"It's what you didn't say, Galen. It's the truth you keep inside that counts."

"I know you're angry because I didn't tell you I was married but as God is my witness, it wouldn't have made a difference if I had. You would still be here with me, in my arms and in my life."

She arched her eyebrows. "Mister, you've got one hell of an ego. And it's clearly warped your thinking—because I can guarantee you I wouldn't be here of my own volition had I known you were a married man!"

"Look, I know you're angry with me but I didn't want to lose you over a mere piece of paper—and that's all my marriage is."

She looked down, shaking her head. "Even if I could overlook such a betrayal of trust, which I can't, I can't overlook the reality." Her eyes were grave when they met his. "I don't know which makes me sadder for you—that you still love your wife and seduced me because I reminded you of her, or that even so intimate a part of your life can be dictated by politics."

She looked away to the trees again, trying to summon the strength to face the truth. "Your life is a lie Galen and I can't live that lie with you. Your wife didn't come back for a divorce. She's here for you and her rightful place in your life."

Galen's shoulders stiffened. "My marriage changes nothing between you and me. I will not let you go."

"I'm not yours to let go. She, however, is and what you've told me is that you won't let her go." She shook her head at him. "I will not be your whore, Galen."

He grabbed her and gently shook her shoulders. "You were never that—never!—and you know it. You will wait until I sort this out."

"Sort what out? You already explained that you won't ask for a divorce. I'm the one who has a decision to make."

He shook his head. Parting with her was unthinkable.

She placed her hands on his arms. "Galen, it would be futile for me to compete with so momentous a past and I don't have the will to accept living on the sidelines. I told you before that we come from different worlds and irreconcilable realities and now I need to go back to mine."

"Your place is here."

Lorelei let out a sigh and started to raise her voice.

"Galen, I'm trying to make this easy for you. Can't you understand that I'm making the choice you can't bring yourself to make?"

"Easy? You're going to make things easy? You, of all people, should know that, to the contrary, you always make things hard." He grabbed her hand and placed it on his crotch, where she could feel the bulge in his pants. "This happens with you all the time, no matter the place, the time, or the circumstances. I'm thirty-nine years old, Lorelei, yet I have no control over myself when it comes to you." To demonstrate the depth of his obsession, he wrapped her fingers around his hardness. "Easy, you say? Your very existence is a hardship and one I can't do without." He gave her a quick, fierce kiss. "I don't know what will happen with Brenna but until I do, you will not leave."

His hand went to her back and pulled her to him. She had no choice but to lean on his chest and put her arms around him. With his free hand he held the reins and motioned the horse to start the journey homeward. With her head nuzzled in his neck, his body shielding her from the cold, an exhausted Lorelei closed her eyes and fell asleep.

She needed to withdraw from the complicated reality surrounding her, the one she felt so helpless to change and yet so unwilling to walk away from.

* * * * *

The doorbell rang ominously through the castle's stately rooms. Edward was about to sip Mary's special brew of tea, laced with what he hoped to be a fair amount of spirits.

Instead he rose to answer the door, Mary at his elbow. He prayed it was not the police with grim news about Miss Lorelei.

Straightening his tie and jacket, he opened the heavy oak portal, only to find a huge man clad in a beige doeskin coat and a felt hat shielding an obviously balding head. The unexpected visitor toted luggage in both gloved hands and wore a most unsmiling expression behind his red mustache.

"I am Maurice Leblanc. I have come to—"

"Mr. Leblanc, we were expecting you." Edward welcomed him, clearing his throat as a signal to Mary to remain calm. From the corner of his eye, however, he could already see her making the sign of the cross. "Please come in."

Appearing unimpressed by the size and grandeur of his surroundings, Maurice quickly entered, letting his luggage fall to the floor with two loud thuds.

"I gather that arrogant Irishman has not found Lorelei yet?" With his hands on his hips, he spoke menacingly to Edward. But the English man-at-arms of the Kennedy family was known for his unflappable countenance before even the most hostile of parties.

"Come in, monsieur. Let us converse within," Edward suggested, hoping his employer's estranged wife was out of earshot.

With Mary scurrying behind them, they made their way into one of the smaller dining rooms, where Edward had left his tea. "I'm guessing you haven't eaten in quite a while, sir," he calmly noted, instructing Mary to prepare something for their guest.

"I don't need food, monsieur," Maurice said in a near shout.

"Perhaps a stiff drink, then." Not waiting for a response, Edward handed Leblanc a glass from the credenza and poured him a generous amount of amber liquid from a decanter.

The Frenchman gulped down the liquor as if it were water. Once he handed back the glass, he stared at Edward intently. "I need to know what happened to Lorelei."

"Why don't you remove your coat and sit down? It's a rather long story."

When they were both seated comfortably, Edward said, "Now then, as you must know, Miss Duplessis was first summoned to Scotland, the McBain castle being Mr. Kennedy's Scottish residence. It was Mr. Kennedy's most fervent wish to be reconciled with Miss Lorelei after having had some disagreement with her in Hyannis Port."

Although Edward was keenly aware of the impatient tapping of Maurice's fingers on the table, he placidly continued his explanation of events. "Now then, where was I?"

"You had reached the part where your employer had persuaded Lorelei, through an elaborate and deceitful scheme, to come to Scotland," Maurice answered in an impatient tone.

"Yes, well, it was all for a good reason, you see. I believe Mr. Kennedy is in love with Miss Lorelei."

"Really?" Maurice replied sarcastically.

Edward frowned, remembering how stricken Galen had been when he found Lorelei hemorrhaging in her bed. "I give you my word that he is."

"Forgive my sarcasm but since the 'disagreement' in Hyannis Port involved his liaison with a senator's wife, I do not consider his being in love with Lorelei even remotely possible. So why was Lorelei brought to Scotland and then Ireland, only to go missing at this hour of the night?"

Edward sighed, trying to formulate a reasonable explanation that would appease Leblanc. "Miss Lorelei apparently experienced mechanical problems on her way to Waterford to pick you up and was, therefore, delayed."

"Admit it. You don't know where she is!"

"Honestly, Mr. Leblanc, Miss Lorelei and Mr. Galen had a disagreement earlier today because she insisted on driving to the airport alone," Edward further lied without so much as a twitch. "She later left the house surreptitiously. No one knew where she had gone. I am sure she will soon be home, since her Porsche was found near the Abbey, not too far from here."

"Her Porsche?" Maurice asked, surprised at Edward's mention of Lorelei's former car.

"Yes, sir. I believe it bears the plate Nemesis?"

Maurice waved his hands in the air. "What is going on here? Lorelei sold her car!"

"She did but Mr. Kennedy purchased it back for her. You see, as I told you, he cares for her very much."

"In my country, sir, when a man is in love with a woman, he buys her a ring and proposes marriage. Cars are purchased for mistresses, not for—"

"Edward, may I have some tea?" Entering the room unannounced, in a revealing black negligée, Brenna imperiously addressed the butler while she stared, openly curious, at Maurice. "I was not aware we had a guest," Brenna said as she approached the two men. "Introduce us, Edward," she said.

"Ms. Brenna Coyle, M. Maurice Leblanc," Edward announced, evenly meeting the glaring eyes of his employer's wife.

"It's Mrs. Kennedy, Edward, or have you conveniently forgotten that Galen and I are married?"

"Perhaps the fact that you have been away and out of contact for more than five years, madam, has led me to believe otherwise," he responded levelly.

Maurice stood up abruptly, obviously shocked.

"You must excuse Edward, Mr. Leblanc. Ever since that little Canadian tramp arrived here, he has forgotten to accord me due respect—behavior he should endeavor to change if he wants to remain employed in this household," she added with a pointed glance at the butler.

Maurice's thin thread of control snapped when he heard the word tramp connected to his beloved Lorelei. "Where I come from, madame, respect is accorded only where earned. And at the cost of being brutally frank, I would find it difficult to give someone like you..." He paused to take a measured look at her scant attire. "Any form of consideration, except for that reserved for...I believe the correct term in English would be—"

"Whore?" Edward promptly suggested.

"How dare you both!" Brenna shouted as Mary made her way into the room with a tray of food. When the housekeeper saw that Brenna had joined the two men, she hastily made another sign of the cross with one hand and fled the room.

"I think Ms. Coyle frightened the maid, Maurice," Edward said in a familiar tone, knowing the man wouldn't mind the liberty now that they had found a common enemy.

"If so, you may never get to eat." Putting an arm over the Frenchman's shoulders, he motioned Maurice toward the door leading to the buttery. "Let's go to the kitchen, where we can eat and speak more freely."

Seeing she was being ignored, Brenna marched out of the room, muttering that she hoped they'd never find the Canadian bitch.

When Maurice and Edward sat at the wooden kitchen table, the Frenchman lifted his full wineglass in silent contemplation. "Edward, that woman is at the core of the disagreement between Lorelei and M. Kennedy, *oui*?"

"I believe so, Maurice," Edward admitted, bringing his teacup to his lips.

"It seems your employer has a serious problem on his hands but I will not let him hurt my Lorelei any more gravely than he already has," Maurice vowed. Once Lorelei was found safe, he would take her away from this Wexford bordello.

Chapter Twenty-Four

At Wexford House Galen saw Justin, Edward, Mary and Maurice Leblanc, who was still wearing his travel clothes, waiting for him. Tight-fisted and silent, the Frenchman lit up when he recognized Lorelei, then looked angry when his gaze swiveled to Galen.

"Everything all right, sir?" Edward asked.

"Yes but Mary should prepare Miss Lorelei a warm bath. She's wet from the rain and very cold. Oh and she needs food, preferably something hot, like soup." He gently nudged Lorelei to wake up. "Lorelei, sweet, we're home."

As Lorelei roused and looked around, she felt a stabbing pain in her side. "Please let me down. I don't feel well."

"Of course. You're exhausted, baby."

Maurice hugged her so fiercely, she thought she'd never be able to breathe again.

"*Ma petite fille*, what happened to you? *Tu nous a fait peur!*"

In a raspy voice she answered him. "You worry too much, old man. What's that stubble on your face? Haven't you slept at all?"

"How can I sleep, eat, or see to my *toilette* when *ma petite* is lost in the woods of this pagan countryside?"

Lorelei smiled weakly. She didn't want to add to his worries. Tomorrow she would tell him everything. "You sweet man, you know I can take care of myself. Now, tell me all about your trip. Did you bring those books I asked for?"

While Maurice gently led Lorelei up to her room, Galen silently vowed that tomorrow he would take away her car keys. He couldn't survive another ordeal like this evening's, wondering if he'd ever see her alive again.

He noticed Edward, his face suddenly white, staring at his jacket.

"Sir, are you hurt?" the butler asked.

Galen looked down and saw blood on his jacket sleeve, his sweater, his pants. "No, I'm not. Christ, this must be Lorelei's!"

He blindly ran toward the stairs with Justin and Edward in tow. He climbed the steps two at a time, overtaken by panic. Was she hurt? Was she hemorrhaging again? He practically slammed open her bedroom door. When he looked around and did not see her, he rushed to the bathroom. "Lorelei, where the hell are you?" Then he turned and saw her sitting on the small love seat near the bay window. She had taken off her jacket and was cradling her sweater, which was soaked with blood. She looked up at him, dismayed. "This was my uncle's sweater. Now what am I going to do? I'll never be able to get the stains out."

Galen knelt down beside her and took her hands in his.

She looked as if she was in shock. "Sweetheart, look at me. May I see your side?" He unclasped the sweater from her fingers and lifted it to look at her wound. "Justin, get the Jaguar. We have to get her to hospital."

"How did she get hurt? Where is she bleeding?"

"I don't know. It's her left side. Come on, Lorelei. I'll carry you, sweetheart."

When the word hospital registered with Lorelei, her physical shock was replaced by horror. "No! I'm not going to the hospital!" She wanted to go back to Montreal with Maurice, where she could hide from the men who were trying to kill her.

"Lorelei, you're injured. We must go. I'll be there with you."

"Do you have a hearing problem ? I said no. *Non, non je n'irai pas. Non pas celà*!"

"Damn it, Lorelei—"

"I'll be fine as soon as I get these damp, dirty clothes off and take a nice long shower. I was fine before you arrived and yanked me onto your shoulder like a saddlebag and made me sit on that beast of yours."

She was distraught, Galen knew and making no sense. Still, he felt his control slipping. "Lorelei, I have no patience for this."

Justin patted his brother on the back. "If she can tell you off like that, then she's not as badly off as she looks. Maybe we should just call the doctor."

Lorelei, who seemed to have regained her composure, gave him a beseeching look. "Please, Galen, not the hospital. Call a doctor if you must but don't make me go. Please!"

Galen frowned, undecided.

Edward stepped in front of Justin and smiled at Lorelei.

"Sir, I already sent for Dr. Scallan. I asked Conrad to pick him up ten minutes ago. He should be here soon."

Galen turned to look at Lorelei again. "Why are you so afraid of going back to the hospital?"

She signaled Maurice's presence with her eyes. Galen understood she didn't want to speak in front of him.

"All right, sweet. You get your wish—for now. But if the doctor says you have to go to St. Mary's, then you'll go. I want your word on this."

She sighed in relief. "Fine. Now, if you would all please leave, I'm filthy and damp and I'd like to shower before the doctor arrives," Lorelei announced.

Galen shook his head disapprovingly. "Edward, call Mary. She'll help her wash."

Lorelei slowly got up from the loveseat and told Edward not to bother. "I can wash myself. No need to call Mary."

"Lorelei, it's either Mary or me. You choose." Galen's tone was stern.

Maurice advanced toward Galen. "I forbid any of you barbarians to touch her! Haven't you done enough? Everybody, *dehors*!"

Even Mary, who had just arrived, understood Maurice's bellow to get out and made to obey.

Maurice turned to her. "Madame, when everybody leaves, you will help *ma petite* wash the Irish filth off her body. Then you will call me, so that I can sit with her and make sure she eats."

Justin smiled at the older man's threats and fulminations.

Galen took them more personally. He crossed his arms and remained rooted to the spot where he was standing.

Dr. Scallan arrived in the nick of time. "Good day, everyone. Galen." As he brushed past him, he smiled at Lorelei. "You must be the injured woman. Now let's see what this nonsense is all about."

"I'd like to wash first, if you don't mind."

"Let me look at the wound and then you can wash." While he prodded her side, he said nothing but he smiled. "How did this happen?" he finally asked.

Unsure whether he should know about the men following her, she recounted only falling while running away from a large dog that was chasing her. "When I tripped and fell, something sharp jabbed into my side—probably a broken branch or something. I bled a little but then it stopped. It started again when Mr. Kennedy here threw me over his shoulder and forced me to ride his horse."

Edward, Maurice and Mary all turned to Galen, giving him reproachful looks. Justin covered his smile with one hand.

"I'll have to clean and disinfect this wound right away. When did you say this happened?" Before applying alcohol, he warned her. "This will hurt a little."

"It happ— *Merde*! That burns like hell!" She winced from the pain while trying to focus on the doctor's question. "I guess it happened about five hours ago."

"Hmm, I'm afraid we'll have to stitch this."

Galen approached the doctor, concerned. "Shouldn't you do that at the hospital?"

Lorelei sat up. "*Non*!"

Her pleading eyes made the doctor smile. He turned to Galen to reassure him. "I can give her a local anesthetic and do it here. It will only take a few minutes."

When the doctor finished stitching her wound and giving her an antibiotic injection and something for the pain, Lorelei was finally allowed to wash herself, accompanied by Mary, who was openly distressed about Lorelei's injury.

Maurice returned to his room to wash and unpack.

While the rest were the sipping tea Edward had served, the doctor asked more questions about Lorelei's accident.

Justin became suspicious. "Why are you so interested in the incident?"

"Because her wound wasn't caused by any broken branch. It was a bullet that grazed her. It's a flesh wound, mind you—nothing to be overly concerned about—but from a gun nonetheless. I would say a forty caliber."

Galen's hands began shaking. So two men had been following her again. He'd half hoped she made up the car chase to excuse her impulsive decision to wander into unfamiliar woods. He looked at Justin, trusting that his brother would know better than to say anything. The fewer people outside the family who knew, the better.

"Dr. Scallan, I'm sure there's another explanation. Perhaps the wolf she affectionately referred to as a large dog…?"

"Galen, you think I don't know what a gunshot…"

The doctor trailed off when Galen gave him a pointed look.

"Well..."

"Maybe it was a large dog—with forty caliber canine teeth," Justin quipped.

"Or simply hunters," Galen suggested. Scallan was a trusted friend but less reliable people might hear about it if the doctor reported a gunshot wound to the authorities.

As he held the doctor's gaze, a silent message passed between them. Finally Scallan nodded.

"Thank you," Galen said.

After escorting the doctor to the door, Galen returned to Lorelei's room to obtain the whole story on her escapade. When he arrived, however, she was fast asleep, the painkiller and exhaustion having taken their toll on her. Maurice had just left with the food tray and Justin put a finger to his lips, motioning his brother to be quiet.

"Did she eat anything?" Galen whispered.

"Barely. Once the doctor left, she was out like a light."

Galen approached the bed and stared at Lorelei's pale face.

"Maybe the men she saw were farmers. Don't the Whelans keep livestock around there? Paul Griffin, that boy who use to work for us, is their nephew or something. Maybe we should speak to him tomorrow when he comes in," Justin suggested optimistically.

"The Griffins' halfway house is at least one mile south of there. Besides, only if Scallan was wrong about the bullet, they would have used shotguns, not forty caliber pistols." He placed a hand on her forehead, frowning. Did she have a fever?

"Anyway, don't you have to be somewhere—" Justin began.

"Yes, he does," Brenna said from the doorway. "It's almost eleven." Approaching the two men, she stopped at Lorelei's bedside and continued in a sarcastic tone, "Well, if it isn't the forest rangers back from their rescue mission. I see that the damsel in distress was brought back safe and sound."

"Yes, she was and we'd appreciate it if you'd lower your voice so she can sleep," Justin said.

Brenna wrapped her hands around Galen's right arm and looked up at him. "Well, excuse me for sounding a little annoyed. With all the commotion she caused, I couldn't sleep all night, I couldn't spend any time with my newly reacquainted husband, and," she paused, glancing at his watch, "we're going to be late for church if you don't go get ready, love."

Galen clenched his jaw. He'd been up all night and wanted only to sleep. The last thing he needed was to spend the morning with Brenna. But he had no choice—and she knew it, damn her. They had to attend the Mass for her brother, Bryan, who had died exactly five years ago today.

"Keep me informed on her progress, Justin," he said. "I'll have my cell phone on."

"Don't worry. I'll take good care of her—just as if I were you."

Galen leveled a look on him that said clearly he hadn't appreciated the remark.

Justin smiled wolfishly.

* * * * *

Lorelei slept all day and through the following night. She woke up shortly after dawn when her fever broke. She was drenched in sweat and badly needed to splash cool water on her face. She carefully got out of bed, her side still tender from the stitches. On her way back from the washroom, she grabbed the local newspaper, which had been left on the coffee table.

When she turned on her bedside lamp and unfolded the paper, her face paled.

Donald O'Hara, a local man whose photo she recognized, had been found shot to death in his cell the day after he was apprehended for the murder in the United States of another Wexford International employee, Michael Logan, whose body remained missing. Farther down the article said that yet another man, by the name of Gerald McRae, had also recently been found dead, left in the city dump in Aberdeen. The authorities were presuming that the three homicides were connected but they were saying precious little else.

"So I'm the only witness left," she whispered. The door suddenly opened and Justin stepped into the room.

"You're up," he observed cheerily.

She clutched her heart. "You startled me."

"Sorry, I didn't mean to. I thought you'd still be sleeping, or I would have knocked." He sat next to her on the bed. "How are you feeling?"

"Stiff, as if I've slept for a week. Where's Galen? Or should I ask, where's the newly reunited couple? Out on the town?"

He glanced at his watch. "They must still be sleeping."

Only when he saw Lorelei's expression did he realize what he'd just said. "Galen slept in the guest—"

"Je m'en fou de tout celà! I don't care Justin, I don't care anymore. Kennedy's private life is no longer part of mine. He can do what the hell he wants." *As long as he doesn't make me part of it*, she added to herself while she was already making mental plans to leave Ireland. "Did you know that Donald O'Hara and his friend were killed before they could stand trial?"

His silence spoke loudly enough.

"You patronizing snobs! Both of you!" She stood up, incensed, clutching her side because she did so abruptly. "No wonder I was shot at yesterday! I'm the only other witness to Michael Logan's murder." She stood in front of him and pointed her finger at him. "You should have told me. You should have said so before making Maurice come here! You don't care, do you, about the people whose lives you risk?"

"We won't let anything happen to you or—"

"Really?" She snorted. "Oh and you're doing a fine job of not letting anything happen, aren't you?"

"Hey, you went out on your own the other day without telling anyone," he pointed out.

"And why is that, you think? For yet another secret, another humiliating secret I had to discover on my own!"

"Galen was waiting for the right moment to tell you. I swear! He—he has feelings for you. He was afraid you would leave. He cares, Lorelei, we all do."

"Then why didn't you tell me, Justin? Why didn't you have the heart to tell me? I've gone though so much already. So much." She shook her head remembering that she had made plans to end her life. To end her suffering without having to take on more.

Justin gently clutched her arms. "My brother's life is complicated. *Aye*, and he complicates it even more by feeling responsible for everyone. But he's done nothing but pay for it. Believe me Lorelei, he keeps paying for other people's deeds."

"Whatever convoluted life you guys lead, is beyond me. And I've stopped caring as of two days ago. God! I feel like I'm in some TV soap opera—"

"His marriage is all but over."

"Really? Then why didn't he divorce her? Anyway, it doesn't matter really. I'm sure he can't because politically, he can't, maybe economically, he can't. You know what, Justin? I don't care. The only plan I have now is to get out of this situation and more importantly get my family out of it. If I had known Donald O'Hara had been murdered, I wouldn't have gone out alone and I certainly wouldn't have let Maurice set foot here." She shoved the newspaper at him and prepared to dress.

"Where do you think you're going?"

"I want to see my car." She sighed, trying to figure where Mary would have put her jeans.

"Oh, no, you don't. You're getting right back into bed and resting. Doctor's orders."

"I want to see my car."

"No, Lorelei. I have strict instructions—"

Lorelei pushed him aside when he got in her way.

"Jesus!" he swore, following her to the bathroom.

When she reached the door, she clung to the knob for a few seconds, dizzy from her sudden exertion. "Don't tell me I can't go to the bathroom alone?"

"Let me at least call Mary."

"No." She took a shallow breath. "I can manage."

"Fine, then. I'll be waiting right here. And don't lock the door. I promised Galen I'd be looking in on you," he said only half-jokingly.

Lorelei realized he wasn't going to let her leave the room.

"Look—all I want to do is check out my car. I promise, as soon as I do that, I'll return to bed."

"Lorelei—"

"Justin, I was pursued and shot at and, strangely enough, my gas tank emptied out within minutes. I want to know if someone sabotaged my car and if so, who the hell it was. I think I'm entitled."

"All right, all right," he reluctantly agreed.

Chapter Twenty-Five
ೞ

They left the house twenty minutes later to walk to the garage where all the cars were parked.

"Lorelei, have you met Conrad Monroe? He's our resident mechanic, driver and *homme à tout faire*."

"Pleased to meet you, Conrad. I'm impressed, Justin. I didn't know you spoke French."

"Neither did I, ma'am," Conrad offered. "I hope he didn't call me somethin' inappropriate, or I'll have to whup the boy, seein' as he's young enough to be me son and I've known him near as long as if he were."

Lorelei smiled at the burly man who looked as if he could knock anyone down with a single swing of one of his meaty hands.

"No, he didn't, Conrad. He complimented you on your many skills. Tell me, did you have a chance to look at my car? I'd like to know what caused the gas leak."

They walked to her Porsche while Conrad wiped his hands. "I put some fuel in it this mornin' and it hasn't seeped anywhere. The carton I put under it is as clean as can be, lass." He threw his rag into a plastic bin. "I don't think there's a leak. It could be that one of the fuel pumps needs changin', though. That would account for the engine stallin'. I have no such pump here, though."

"But the car didn't stall. I turned off the engine when I smelled gasoline."

Conrad raised his hands in disagreement. "I checked the tank, miss and it's not leakin'."

"I'd be surprised if it was. I just had the tank replaced after a recent accident."

"What the hell are you doing out of bed?" Galen shouted from the garage door, with a highly irritated look on his face.

"Good morning to you too, Kennedy. Thank you for asking how I'm feeling. My fever broke last night and I seem to be none the worse for wear." She paused as he approached. She noticed he hadn't shaved. "What's the matter? Have your husbandly duties proved too much for you? That would explain your disheveled look but not your surly tongue."

"Lorelei..." Justin began.

Ignoring him, she continued indifferently. "If you must know, I came to inquire about my car. Despite your orders to keep me in bed and out of the way, I decided a breath of fresh air would do me good, especially if I got to see her."

She patted the hood of the Porsche.

In response to her barbed remarks Galen said, "Your blessed car failed you, as I recall."

"If so, I want to know why, because I have to make sure as hell it won't happen a second time." She turned to Galen's mechanic. "Conrad, can you start her?"

"Sure but I don't know why you—"

"Just do it, please!" she fairly shouted.

Galen was about to yell at her for yelling at his mechanic when Justin hauled him aside.

"Look," his brother said, "she knows about Donald and the fact that we didn't tell her. She's pissed off that the Porsche let her down. She's hurt that you lied to her and she's humiliated to be living in the same house with Brenna. She's also worried about putting Maurice's life in danger by having him here while someone's still after her. Let her be, Galen."

Galen gritted his teeth. He knew he wasn't being rational—a part of him knew it, anyway. He simply couldn't quell the panic that rose in him when he thought she might have disappeared and put herself into harm's way again.

Grimly he stood beside Justin and watched the proceedings with the Porsche.

As soon as the engine was on, fuel began leaking from under the car. Lorelei signaled Conrad to turn it off.

"Hey, Conrad," Justin called out, "maybe you should hire her as your assistant."

Conrad gave the three of them an apologetic look.

Lorelei was relieved to know she hadn't been wrong.

"Check the gas line and the big pump. The leak must be coming from one of the two."

"I know that, miss," Conrad grumbled as he went back under the car.

"Why don't you check the valve first before you remove the pump? That could also be the problem."

"There's no valve that I could see, lass."

"What do you mean, no valve?" She bent down to Conrad's feet. "There has to be. It's a small safety valve that controls the fuel flux to the pump."

"I know what it's supposed to do." While Conrad was tinkering, no one spoke. "Move over, lass. I'm comin' out."

The heavyset mechanic pushed himself out from under the car and stood. "Now that's the problem, you see. The valve is missin'."

"That's impossible, Conrad. Let me look."

"Not a chance, Lorelei. You'll tear your stitches," Galen said, grabbing her arm.

"Galen, I've got to see. The valve can't be missing. It could be out of order but not missing."

"Maybe it fell off?" Justin suggested.

Lorelei rolled her eyes. "Shows how much you know about cars. If I didn't think you had other redeeming qualities,

I'd say you're an insult to that Viper you drive. Conrad, explain to him about valves."

Conrad straightened up his shoulders. "It can't be missin' unless it's been removed."

"Removed by whom?" Galen asked sternly.

"Gee, I wonder." She pursed her lips. "Maybe it was those two men who were following me? You know—the ones who shot at me?"

Galen scowled.

Ignoring him, Lorelei continued. "From what I know, if the valve is damaged or missing, as in this case, fuel will leak only when the car is running. And because you'd leak gas pretty quickly while you drove, some of it could hit the muffler and ignite, or, if you were to stop, say, at a light, someone could set a match to your leak and you'd go up in flames with practically no trace of tampering."

Galen was astounded at what she had just said. He could feel the hair on his nape stand up. "Who taught you all this?"

"Maurice. He loved fast cars when he was young."

"Can you check again, Conrad, just to be sure?" Galen asked.

The mechanic was already under the car. "I'm afraid she's right, sir. I can see now the scratches of the wrench someone used to remove it."

"Please order another valve, then and install it right away," Lorelei told Conrad.

Galen shook his head. Did she think he was going to let her out of his sight again after this latest attempt on her life?

When Conrad got back up, Galen caught his eye and gave a quick, small shake of his head.

The man got the message. "Lass, this is an unusual car," Conrad said. "I don't know if any valves would be available on such short notice. We'll probably have to order one in from Dublin."

"Try to get a Volkswagen valve, or an Audi. Even a BMW's should fit."

"That I could get quicker—uh, if it's in stock, that is."

Galen put a protective arm around her shoulders, steering her away from the car. His tone was brisk. "What's the rush? You aren't taking it anywhere until I find out who those men were. Which reminds me, you have some explaining to do about your little escapade with them."

Lorelei ignored him. "Oh and, Conrad, aside from you, the next person who touches my car loses his fingers."

"Did you hear what I said?" Galen persisted.

She spun around to face him, her eyes flashing. "Why didn't you tell me that Donald O'Hara and his friend were killed?"

"You were in the hospital."

"I'm not now, nor was I a week ago!"

"I didn't want to worry you further. I—"

"Don't patronize me, Kennedy! You didn't tell me because you don't want anyone but you to be in control. You did the same thing by not telling me you were married."

"My marriage is only on paper. And we'll discuss this privately in a few minutes."

She tapped her foot, shaking her head. "It's too late for *that*. As for Micheal Logan's murder, there's obviously a contract out on me and it looks as if the only way to catch the assailants is to pose as bait." Her eyes rose to his. "I want my gun back."

"Bait," he echoed, gazing out the open garage doors, meditating on his own plan. Then, angry and resolved, he turned to Justin. "If it's war they want, then war is what they'll get—on our terms and with people we know we can trust. Call Duncan and tell him to get the clan to the airfield. Arrange for the choppers to pick them up and schedule a meeting as soon as they get here. I'm going to pick up some men at the docks, the usual ones. I want them armed and posted everywhere on the grounds. No one is to enter or leave the premises without my permission or yours, Justin. I want traffic kept to a bare minimum."

Lorelei pursed her lips. They were completely ignoring her.

He put one hand on Lorelei's arm and the other on her cheek. "Sweetheart, can you have Maurice make as much as possible from what we already have? I don't want any food shopping or deliveries unless absolutely necessary."

"Are you still considering having the reception?" Justin inquired incredulously.

Galen's tone was stern. "Absolutely. You see, I'm betting one of Lorelei's pursuers might be sipping champagne with us. This will be a good chance for us to find out who."

Lorelei cleared her throat. "Reception or no, didn't you hear what I said, Kennedy? I want my gun back."

Galen smiled. "You won't need a gun. Nor do you need to live and sleep by your car day and night, so don't even think about it. As I told you, you're not going to drive it or any other vehicle anywhere until we resolve this matter."

She nearly screamed with frustration. "Drive? You think this is only about my car? Listen! Someone came in here and worked on that thing without anyone realizing it. I may love this car I may be obsessive about it but what worries me is by getting to it they could just as easily get to me, or Maurice for that matter. So the only way I'll get any sleep even in bed is if I know I can defend myself and my family should the need arise—which it damned well might, since whoever's after me seems to have access to this property."

Conrad was beside himself. "I didn't give the keys to anyone, sir. 'Course, I'm not here day and night. We've never had need before to guard the cars 'round the clock. Mark me words, though, I'll be findin' out the bastard, or me name ain't Conrad Monroe."

Lorelei apologized. "Conrad, I wasn't accusing you."

"No one is accusing you, Conrad. We're just trying to figure out who tampered with the car," Galen explained.

"You have no right to keep my gun!" Lorelei persisted.

"But you can't even shoot. You said so yourself in Scotland."

"You fool. Do you consider knowing how to damage a man's genitals without killing him a poor shot? I purposely shot Donald O'Hara in the shoulder to get him to confess and I did it with my left hand. If you want, I'll show you what I can do with my right." She eyed his crotch.

Justin scratched his chin. "Tell me something—do you French Canadians have some historical animosity toward men's private parts, or is it just a feeling my brother brings out in you and that fellow Maurice who stalks us regularly with his kitchen knives?"

Galen's face lit up. "You know, maybe having you practice shooting wouldn't be a bad idea after all. You can aim at my brother. You never know when you might have to defend yourself against his idiotic remarks. You could even shoot him in the mouth if you can't locate his, uh, 'private parts'."

Conrad gave a hearty laugh. "Now that's tellin' him, boy!"

Lorelei put on her best smile, intent on getting back her gun. "Please, Galen, give me back my Glock. I won't even carry it around with me. It will stay in my room."

His eyes met hers. "When you smile that smile, woman, you completely disarm me and I think you know it. If I give you your gun, will you promise to stay in bed today?"

"Can't I sit in the kitchens instead? I promise I won't work and I'll have Maurice make you something nice for dinner. Deal?" She offered her hand for him to shake. Instead he grabbed it and pulled her close.

"I don't make deals with beautiful women on handshakes." He lowered his head and kissed her on the lips. She tried to pull back but he didn't let her.

Justin turned around, muttering and left.

Conrad laughed.

Lorelei felt thrilled but saddened at the renewed contact with Galen, a contact she desperately needed to avoid.

* * * * *

Two hours later, when Galen returned from his trip to the docks, he went straight to his study to see to the arrangements for extra security. He was not surprised to find Maurice Leblanc viewing the pistol collection he'd brought from Scotland for a private viewing the Historical Society had requested. He knew he owed the man some explanations and at least a few apologies but he was not particularly inclined to offer them at the moment.

"I want a word with you, Mr. Kennedy," Maurice said in a quietly commanding tone.

"Let's sit somewhere more comfortable." Galen showed him to the small sitting room off the library. "Should I ring for coffee or tea, M. Leblanc?"

Leblanc sat down in one of the wing chairs. "Thank you, no."

"As you wish," Galen said, taking a seat on a leather sofa and casually crossing his legs.

"For someone who has a wife and lover under the same roof, you appear to be taking matters very calmly," the Frenchman drawled.

Galen was about to explain in no uncertain terms that his personal life wasn't open for discussion but Maurice imperiously waved a hand in the air, signaling he did not wish to be interrupted.

"You realize that it is Lorelei's desire to leave Wexford *immédiatement*," he said. "Her recent escapade was only one example of how strongly she feels about being as far away as possible from you. But since I believe there is more to this story than the sudden reappearance of your estranged wife, I will wait for your explanation before I take Lorelei away from here."

Although Galen wished to counter the older man's scorn, he was sure it was attributable to his desire to protect Lorelei.

"Let me inform you, M. Leblanc, that this is the second attempt that has been made on Lorelei's life. So I'm sure you'll agree with me that leaving the safety of Wexford House just now would be highly dangerous for her and for you, as well and therefore out of the question."

"What are you talking about?" Maurice asked, his expression concerned.

"Didn't she tell you how she came to have the accident in Hyannis Port?"

Maurice stared at him for a few seconds, then gestured him to continue.

Galen recalled that moment when he thought she had died, feeling again the pain tearing him apart. "On the day of your formal dinner, Lorelei overheard a murder aboard one of my ships. Believing she had gone unseen, she decided not to tell anyone, including me, who might have been involved, until she could safely contact the authorities."

He hesitated briefly before continuing. "You see, our family has been worried for the past several years about gunrunners who might somehow be managing to use our ships to traffic arms into Northern Ireland. The boy who was killed, Michael Logan, was attempting to obtain information about the smugglers for us."

Pausing, Galen stood and walked to a bookcase, running his fingers distractedly along one of the shelves.

"Unfortunately Lorelei was seen and recognized and when she was driving back from the photo shoot the day after, she was run off the road and shot at. I know, because I was driving right behind her and her pursuers, who also crashed, and to this day I still wonder how she made it out alive."

Maurice murmured a few curses under his breath, his hands clutching the wooden armrests of his chair. "Surely her assailants were arrested and jailed, *non*?"

"Yes but there's more. Shortly before the accident," Galen continued, "I was summoned to the *Irish Siren*, where I saw Vivian Gallagher dead from a bullet to the head. She had a note pinned to her saying that Lorelei would be next in line for the honor if I didn't back off from our investigations." Galen looked straight at Maurice. "In answer to your question, yes, I was having an affair with Vivian. I suspected then, as I do now, that her husband is behind all this. But I needed evidence, more information, proof if I could get it."

Galen read the unspoken question in Maurice's eyes. "It was no more than sex and it took place before I met Lorelei."

"You used Mrs. Gallagher. That you did so before meeting Lorelei doesn't change that fact."

Galen matched Maurice's glacial stare. "You would have done the same if it meant cutting out a cancer eating at the homeland your father and forefathers broke their backs to build."

Maurice stood up and faced Galen eye to eye. "*Je m'en fou de tout ça!*"

"Meaning what?"

"Meaning, I don't care for your explanations. I care about Lorelei, that is all. The rest is irrelevant, because neither you nor I will solve this Irish war."

"So what do you expect me to do?"

"You say her assailants were captured. Let me protect Lorelei now." He paused and looked at Galen. "Let her leave."

"One of the men involved in the criminal activities we've been investigating, the one who murdered Michael Logan, was found executed in his cell—at the order of his employer, no doubt. A second one was assassinated in Aberdeen a day later."

To Galen, the idea of Lorelei's leaving was even more unthinkable now that a second attempt had been made on her life. "But two other men tried to kill Lorelei again here in Ireland."

Maurice was aghast. "What!"

"She was shot at again, not injured running away from a big dog as she told you. Her car had been sabotaged as well." He raked a hand through his hair. "These people are heartless and they will not stop on their own." Taking a step closer to Maurice, Galen pointed a finger at him. "The time has come for all of us to stop them. The less we do, the more lives we put in danger."

"You speak like *un fanatique*!"

"I speak like a man in love with his land and in love with his woman."

"So what do you suggest?" Maurice asked, arching his eyebrows.

"I suggest we all stay put. I have clansmen coming from Scotland to protect this house, as well as a small Irish contingent of my own."

"I did not mean just about the security. I meant about Lorelei. How can she stay here with that—that—person you call your wife continually reminding her she is nothing but your mistress?"

"I'm more in love with Lorelei than I ever was with my wife. Brenna and I have been all but exes for the past five years. It's only out of respect for our families' relations that I did not insist on a formal divorce," he answered, realizing for the first time what little was left of his feelings for his wife.

Maurice shook his head, walking slowly away from him.

"*Je vois*," he answered meditatively. "I see you have no intention of divorcing, Monsieur, and neither has your wife. What you feel for *ma petite* is therefore not relevant. It is cruel for you to expect her to accept it." He had reached the door. "I know that in your own way you care about her but she will lose her self-respect by staying here. Surely you understand how humiliating it is for her."

Hoping the older man would help him keep her at Wexford, Galen softened his tone. "Maurice, I don't like the current situation any more than you do but I can't do anything about it right now. I can't divorce her. I owe her family, not economically, but I owe them. However, I give you my word, what's left of the marriage is only ink and paper."

"Monsieur, she and I don't care. You have made your choice. You must let her make hers."

It was unthinkable for him even to consider being apart from her. "For Lorelei's safety, she must stay."

"You don't understand yet, do you? Lorelei has never depended on anyone to fight her battles nor to protect her from them. And she is not afraid of dying." His voice faltered.

"She will take chances you and I would never have the courage to take."

As Maurice was opening the door to leave, Edward appeared carrying a tray. "You rang for tea, sir?"

Galen looked at Maurice, then back at the butler.

"Actually, I didn't, Edward."

"But I distinctly heard Stuart asking Mary to prepare tea for you," the butler added, his tone assured. Setting the tray down on the small mahogany table in front of the sofa, he sat down and began pouring the tea. "How do you take yours, Maurice?"

"Thank you but I don't drink tea."

"Come now, surely a cup of this fine English brew will do you good." After Edward motioned the Frenchman to his cup, he poured another one for his employer, then finally one for himself. Both men stared at him as he crossed his legs and made himself comfortable on the sofa.

Galen smiled. He understood why Edward had barged in. He wanted to be included in the discussion.

Winking at Maurice, Galen walked to the coffee table and took a cup. "Good brew, Edward?"

"Of course, sir. Please, don't let me interrupt your meeting. Pretend I'm not here. I shan't make a sound unless you ask my opinion, sir."

Galen sipped some tea, then gently put the cup down on the table. "And just what opinion do you have, Edward?" he asked lightly, knowing his butler had eavesdropped on his conversation with Maurice.

"I think Miss Lorelei will do everything in her power to leave this house. Why, this morning she left with Mary to go to the market. Off they went, the two of them, with not a care in the world. Surely, Maurice, you'll have to convince her to—"

"Convince her to do what, Edward?" Lorelei interrupted as she entered the room dressed in suede leggings, a matching tunic and a woolen vest. She stopped right in front of Galen.

"Well, messieurs, has the cat got all your tongues?"

Deceptively calm, Galen asked simply, "How was the market this morning?"

"As you can see, I made it back in one piece," she smugly answered.

"*Petite*, you could have been hurt!" Maurice, dismayed, almost shouted.

"Not to mention killed," Galen added. "Isn't it enough that not three days ago you—"

Nobody heard or saw Justin approaching the room except Lorelei. With her back to the doorway she pulled her gun from inside her vest, then spun and aimed it right between Justin's eyes, all in under three seconds.

The room went silent. Edward continued to sip his tea, clearly enchanted at this display of power his future mistress put on.

"You were saying, Kennedy?" Lorelei said glibly.

Justin spoke instead, crossing his arms in front of him.

"How come you're the one who pisses her off, Galen and I'm the one who gets the gun pointed at him?"

Galen's lips twitched into a smile. "Duplessis, you said you'd leave that thing in your room. Now don't play games. This isn't a James Bond movie."

"Please, *petite*," Maurice added.

Lorelei looked at Maurice and noticed his worried look. Nodding, she put her gun back inside her vest. "If I stay or go, it's because I've decided it's the best course of action to take for everyone involved, not because anyone tells me to."

Turning around, she left the room as abruptly as she had come in.

Lorelei spent the rest of the afternoon in her new room, reviewing her recipes for the upcoming reception. She had requested relocation to a wing of Wexford House other than the one she had shared with Galen.

Mary had made a fuss about the move. "Mr. Galen will be bloody furious! And I'll be temptin' the Devil, is what I'll be doin' by doin' this!" she had exclaimed.

But Lorelei remained adamant. It was imperative she stay as far away as possible from Galen and his wife. Her mental health required it.

When she heard a faint knock on the door, she retrieved her gun from under her pillow. "Come in."

"Put your gun away, sweet. Terrorists don't usually knock."

In the semi-darkness of sundown with no lights on, Lorelei couldn't quite see the expression in Galen's eyes. He was wearing black jeans with a matching T-shirt. His hair was loose and she realized he had not shaved that day.

She was sitting on the bed, her back propped up by pillows and he came to sit beside her.

"Why did you move so far away from me?" he asked. His right hand came to rest on the side of her neck. His voice was full of need. His touch was warm and sensual.

Lorelei tried to ignore all the sensations he elicited. She closed her eyes, attempting to block out his hurt, as well.

"You know why," she whispered.

"But I can't let you go, Lorelei, neither across the ocean nor across the house. Can't you understand that?"

Exhausted from the circumstances surrounding them, unable to give him what he wanted, she closed her eyes again and surrendered for a moment to the warmth of his hand.

He let go of her to retrieve something from his pocket.

He handed her a small velvet pouch. "Happy birthday, sweet."

She stared at the present in surprise. She had lost so much track of days with all that had happened, remembering it was her birthday had been secondary. Perturbed, she loosened the drawstring.

"How did you know?"

"It was on your application for the culinary competition."

The pouch contained a bracelet encrusted with rubies and emeralds in intricate medieval settings. "It's...beautiful. I can't—"

"You can and you will. It belonged to my great-grandmother, who received it from her great-grandmother. Look here."

He turned up his sleeve and showed her that, around his wrist, he wore a nearly identical bracelet, although the design was less intricate, more befitting a man. He plucked the one he'd given her out of her hand and slid it onto her wrist. Smiling, he admired it for a moment, then, cupping her face in his hands, he kissed her.

His lips were gentle yet demanding. His tongue caressed hers until her heart began to race and she thought she would surely die from the grief of living without him.

The sound of people singing "Happy Birthday to You" brought their lips apart. Maurice was first to enter the room, leading the party with a huge Paris-Brest cake on which were twenty-eight candles that warmly illuminated the room.

Edward followed him with Mary, Conrad, Dr. Scallan and Justin. Galen got up to make space for Maurice to place the tray on the bed so Lorelei could blow out the candles. She looked at everyone, especially Maurice, whose eyes had gone misty, then blew. When all the candles went out, Edward uncorked a champagne bottle and Maurice began cutting the cake.

Galen leaned over and kissed her hard on the lips in plain view of everyone. "I wish I could have made this a better birthday for you but there'll be others, I promise."

She wanted to tell him not to promise, not to hope but she couldn't, because deep down she wanted to believe, even if only for a moment, that what he said would come true.

Later, when everyone else had left, Maurice closed the door and sat on the chair beside her bed. Edward had lit a fire and the crackling of the dry logs was the only sound in the room. Maurice's frown, however, spoke more loudly than words.

"Why didn't you tell me you witnessed a murder in Hyannis Port? *Pourquoi?*" he asked impatiently.

Lorelei looked him squarely in the eye as she shifted her legs sideways on the bed. "What would you have done in my place? Would you have told me or Annabelle? Would you have placed anyone else in that kind of danger?"

Maurice looked down and gently squeezed her hand.

"If I had a guarantee that my silence would have prevented it, yes. But no one can give that guarantee. *Regarde,* you kept silent, yet they didn't believe you had. So you protected no one, least of all yourself." He caressed her cheek affectionately. "Families are there to help. Annabelle and I consider you our daughter. You have hurt me by not wanting to share your burden."

"I love you, Maurice," she insisted, almost in tears. "You must believe that that was the only reason I did not tell you!"

He nodded, acknowledging the truth. "*Je sais, je sais.* But now that I know too, we are together in this *bordel* and together we must decide what to do."

"Such as leave?"

"Such as leave," he repeated.

"I can't stand it here much longer, even if I have no choice," she said.

He nodded. "You love him, *non*?"

Lorelei looked away before answering. "Whether or not I love him is irrelevant. He's married and regardless of how he feels about his wife, theirs seems to be a marriage of political convenience and I'm clearly not worth the risk of divorce. Anyway, loving should be easy, not so damn hard and complicated. So, yes, I love him but it won't make any difference in the end. I'm still leaving as soon as I can."

"You know I have always admired your character and your courage to see things through despite the pain it might cause you, Lorelei," Maurice began. "But occasionally you must let time do some of the work for you."

"Maybe it has already," she answered, remembering the child she had been carrying, the child denied to her and Galen, perhaps to signify that theirs was not a love that would last.

Chapter Twenty-Six

The door to the kitchen creaked as Justin strolled in. "There's something to be said about the smell of fresh-baked bread and a terribly attractive woman kneading the dough for it," he said.

Lorelei sprinkled a bit of flour on the counter and smiled at him. "And what would that be?"

"Just that I wouldn't mind it's being me on that counter."

Lorelei ignored his remark, knowing he meant nothing by it. "By the way, it's croissants, not bread, I'm making. Why don't you try them? The ones on the table are still warm."

Justin lifted a flaky crescent to his lips with all the anticipation of a ravenous twelve-year-old and took a bite. "Mmm, your fingers work magic. This croissant melts in my mouth."

As Lorelei continued kneading, she felt Justin come to stand right behind her.

"Sorry but I have to reach over you to get a cup from the cabinet." When she leaned back to avoid the cupboard door, her head ended up on his shoulder.

Instead of retrieving a cup, Justin put his hands on the counter on either side of her and playfully nuzzled her neck.

"Hmm, what Galen says about your scent is true. A man could be tempted to sin against his brother for you."

"Please, Justin, don't tease me."

He stepped back and gently massaged away the tension in her shoulders. "You're with my brother, who is ruminating over his life, so I would never demonstrate anything more than platonic affection. Should my brother decide to remain with Brenna, however, even if I don't know anyone in his right mind who would, I'd like you to give me a chance to court you. We could—"

"Please, Justin, don't."

"Why not?"

"How could I ever be happy if I came between two brothers?"

He stepped back, spinning her around. "I care for you, Lorelei."

"And I you. But not like...like that."

Justin sighed dramatically. "Then I want you to promise you'll find me someone just like you, someone who can make me forget you."

Lorelei chuckled at his antics and started folding her dough again.

"I'm serious, though, Lorelei. As much as I love Galen, if he chooses Brenna, I might just come after you. If he finally breaks with her, then I'll respect his choice—as long as you keep your promise." Justin finally took two cups from the cupboard. "The way I see it, I win either way."

"You Kennedys seem accustomed to making demands, you know."

"Nothing you can't fulfill, honey. Besides, I was asking, not demanding."

"Speaking of which, why didn't Galen ever ask Brenna for a divorce?"

When Justin didn't answer, she looked up at him. "Does he have children with her?"

"No, nothing like that. But I would prefer that he tell you."

"*J'en ai assez de vos secrets*. I'm starting to get really tired of your secrets," she said, slapping the dough and muttering.

Justin changed the subject. "So what is my dinner date wearing for the upcoming gala?"

"Your dinner date?"

"By order of the great laird, I was asked to be your escort in his stead — not that I mind in the least being seen with such a beautiful woman and having permission to flirt with her."

Enraged at Galen's maneuvers, Lorelei pounded the dough more forcefully. "How could he be so cruel as to expect me, under the circumstances, to attend the reception as a guest rather than remain behind the scenes as the caterer, to force me to face him and his wife in public? Hasn't he humiliated me enough? How much hurt does he think I can endure?"

Justin sobered for a moment, then flashed a cheerful, devilish smile. "Then stop making things so easy for him, Lorelei. Use our 'date' to the reception to make him suffer as much as you are. Feel free to flirt shamelessly with me. Many women find me suave, debonair and bloody handsome, you know."

"You don't have to tell me. I'm not blind." She gave him a measured look.

"I could still forget that Galen's my brother," Justin said hopefully.

She laughed and placed the lump of fresh dough in a bowl, covering it with a damp cloth. "Justin, I'm positive you're a marvelous escort but I hate using you as camouflage to deceive his precious wife and his relations and his community."

"You don't know Galen very well, do you? He's not trying to camouflage anything. First of all, he's very proud of you. Secondly, if he didn't want you seen at the reception, you wouldn't be there. Thirdly, Brenna is anything but 'precious' to him these days. It's just that he has yet to resolve the chaos of his past. In the meantime he's playing a balancing act, because for reasons that concern his past, he can't simply dump Brenna and for reasons that concern his future, he can't bear to let you go."

Despite Justin's eloquence on his brother's behalf, Lorelei's patience was wearing thin. "Someone had better give me some details soon, because this mysterious past of his is beginning to sound like a convenient excuse to have his cake and eat it, too."

"Let's forget about Galen for now. Let's focus on our upcoming 'date'. It will be the perfect opportunity for me to show you what you've been missing by choosing my bloody elder brother."

"Justin..."

"Okay, okay. I got the message. So what will you wear?"

She walked to the table and took a croissant. "I don't know," she mumbled with her mouth full.

"Since I'll be gallantly pretending I'm the next best thing to my brother, may I choose your dress?"

Lorelei looked at him, puzzled. "What is it you want me to wear? Maybe the baby blue *peau de soie* gown I wore in Hyannis Port?"

"No. The gold dress you were trying on yesterday," he surprised her by saying.

"You were there?"

"Didn't you notice? I'd transformed myself into a fly on your bedroom wall."

"Justin!"

"Relax. Your door was open and I happened to be going to my room to pick up my jacket. I heard Mary making a commotion and I looked in to see what all the fuss was about."

"The commotion was about the dress being too tight on me." She made a mental note to shop for new bras when she returned to Montreal.

"Not from where I was standing." He held his hands open. "For me?"

Lorelei smiled. "Fine, the gold dress it is. For you."

Justin heard a sound and turned to look at the door. It swung closed, which meant that someone had just entered and left the kitchen unobserved.

Concerned, he returned his gaze to Lorelei. "I was about to suggest you stop working for a few minutes and have a cup of coffee with me but…"

The thought of the beverage she adored the most after wine suddenly made her insides churn. A wave of nausea swept over her. "Thanks anyway. I've already had a cup."

Justin nodded, then went after the silent visitor who had listened in on their conversation.

Chapter Twenty-Seven

Galen was in his study. Justin brought him the coffee he'd meant to drink in the kitchen. "You know, it's rude to eavesdrop." He put the cup down beside the papers scattered on Galen's desk.

Galen looked up, seemingly unaffected by the comment, but Justin knew better. "If you weren't my brother," Galen growled, "I would have killed you."

"And if you weren't such an ass, I wouldn't have to resort to such methods to make you realize that the truth is staring you right in the eye."

"If you're trying to make me believe you were acting for my benefit, you must take me for an imbecile. You want her, Justin. But you feel only infatuation for Lorelei, not love." Galen crossed his arms and leaned back in his chair. "And, by the way, don't mistake my silence for acceptance."

Justin slapped his hands on Galen's desk, looking threateningly at him. "Oh, you call it silence? I call it cowardice." He paced in front of the desk. "You've been sitting on the fence too long, Galen. Look at what our Irish kin are doing to us. They use us, betray us, kill our friends when the whim takes them. And because you hoped you could be friendly with both sides, you made us sitting ducks. You're doing the same thing now with Brenna and Lorelei. Now, maybe you're not even sure when to be Irish or when to be a Highlander but why not fuck it all and just be a man, a man protecting his family and the woman he loves—providing, of course, you know which one it is."

Angry, he headed for the door. "The way I see it, it's not a hard choice to make. In fact, it's probably the easiest one you'll ever have to make." With that, he left the room.

Galen scowled. It was true that his marriage to Brenna had prevented him from overtly taking sides in Northern Ireland's war, since her family belonged to one of the political parties involved. Killing her brother should have placed him squarely in the middle of the warring factions but again his marriage, though defunct for all practical purposes, seemed to sustain a semblance of peace and prevent further bloodshed between the two families. But the situation was different now and there was no help for it.

He had to decide once and for all and live—or die—with the consequences.

* * * * *

The hustle and bustle of the next few days reminded Lorelei of DesCheneaux—food preparation for thirty or so guests with a minimum of three settings per day. But unlike at the hotel, she wasn't allowed to do much, since she was still said to be recovering. She snorted in disgust. When Justin wasn't around, Mary would check on her and when the housekeeper was busy, the duty fell to Edward. Maurice would occasionally shove a recipe at her but she hated being unable to cook or otherwise actively participate in welcoming Lady McBain's guests or preparing for her reception.

The mornings were difficult, given that a gnawing nausea would assail her, forcing her to remain in her room until it subsided. Since she was still taking the iron pills prescribed to help her body recover from the miscarriage, feeling sick didn't surprise her. The iron supplements she'd had to take after having pneumonia had done a number on her stomach, too.

She stayed out of Galen's way as much as possible.

Brenna was always around him and seeing them together was extremely painful. If only she could leave, she often thought.

One afternoon, however, Brenna came into the small parlor that had become Lorelei's retreat from her stressful circumstances. She was reading a book when the door opened and a wisp of pungent perfume made its way to her nostrils.

"I hope I'm not disturbing you but I was wondering what you thought of this fabric. I'm planning to replace the linens and drapes in the master bedroom for our eighth wedding anniversary. Isn't that a splendid idea?" Brenna gushed.

She might as well have stabbed Lorelei in the stomach.

Lorelei decided not to show her distress, however. She gave Brenna the most serene look she could muster. "Well, if you choose that pattern, you'll have to change the furniture as well. Its style is medieval, while this fabric is contemporary rustic."

"I've already looked at the furniture. The bed will definitely go. I'll not sleep there anymore," she said pointedly.

"It's my bedroom and you'll not change a thing," Galen announced as he walked in and looked at Brenna disapprovingly.

"But, darling, you promised."

"I did no such thing. You may redecorate the tower room if you want to. It's been neglected for decades."

He took the fabric out of her hands. "Would you give me a few minutes alone with Lorelei? I have something to discuss with her."

Brenna touched his cheek. "When you ask so nicely, how can I refuse?"

At Galen's stoic expression, Brenna frowned, then left quietly.

He closed the door behind her. When he turned Lorelei looked at his tight jeans. His leg muscles bulged at the seams.

His white T-shirt was sleeveless and with his long blond hair loose and his broad chest and shoulders, he looked like a Viking. He was one of the best-looking men she had ever seen. Somehow, she was still attracted to him. But he had never really been hers nor could ever be. She had to get away from him before it was too late.

He sat down on the armrest of an antique brocade chair, then cursed and stood to lock the door.

"What now? Why did you lock the door?"

He smiled and let his gaze travel over her from head to toe. "I don't want anyone disturbing us."

She noticed the bulge in the front of his pants. "What's the matter, your wife isn't enough for you?"

"She doesn't occupy my bed, Lorelei."

Lorelei's response was skeptical. "So you think I'll…what? Service you?"

He didn't flinch at her crude words. He knew better. He understood she was angry and hurt, and entitled to feel both. But he was in love with her, and was convinced that in time she would change her mind, especially if he got her pregnant again.

He stepped toward her. "Service me? I think you'd like to. I even think it'd be doing both of us a favor."

She looked at him in disbelief. "A favor?"

"Never mind. I didn't come here to argue—or for a quickie. I came to tell you that we know who tampered with your car. Someone's picking him up as we speak."

Her eyes widened. "Who was it? What will you do with him?"

"It's not your concern."

"I hate it when you patronize me. I'm the one he tried to harm. I'd say it most certainly concerns me."

"But I'm the one they're trying to get at, Lorelei."

"Still, don't put a man's life on your conscience. Promise me."

"I can't promise anything. Michael Logan is dead and you were almost killed too. This is war, Lorelei and I mean to do my best to stop it."

"No, this is revenge, Galen and you shouldn't indulge in it. I'd never be able to look you in the eye again if you killed someone when you didn't have to." She remembered his violent response to Donald O'Hara's betrayal—in his rage he easily could have killed the man.

Without another word Galen left the room, awash in turmoil and doubt. How would Lorelei react when she found out he'd already killed a man when he might not have had to?

*****

The following week Dr. Scallan returned to Wexford House to remove Lorelei's stitches and he declared her wound fully healed. But he suggested she come into his office for blood tests to make sure the rest of her was "all in order", he said and he scheduled an appointment at his clinic for the next week.

Chapter Twenty-Eight

Often it's the same hell, just a different day.

◊

Two hours before the reception, after having checked with Maurice on the cocktail preparations, Lorelei headed for her room to dress. On her way up she overheard Brenna talking on the phone behind the staircase. "If I get pregnant, I'll have Galen back, I'm sure. I'll let you know. I've got to go now. The hairdresser just arrived."

Lorelei ran up the rest of the stairs in tears. So they had resumed having sex. Somehow she had hoped Galen wouldn't—that he wouldn't even be able to, at least not while she was there. How naïve of her.

The thought of seeing them together at the reception and pretending she was merely an acquaintance hired to supervise the event made her stomach knot. She dreaded it more than anything else she'd ever had to do. She wiped her tears with the back of one hand, slowly walked to the dresser, and sat down and looked at herself in the mirror. She had to get a hold of herself. She couldn't show her pain. She had to erase it from her mind.

In less than an hour her hair was up. Mary's sister, Karen, a hairdresser, had been hired to style Lorelei and Brenna for the reception. But when Lorelei put on the gold brocade gown and looked at herself in the mirror, all she saw was a shell of herself.

Her legs trembling, she sat on the edge of the bed. Why couldn't she just leave and go home? No attempts had been made on her life in the past few days. Galen said they'd caught the culprit who'd tampered with the Porsche. And not even

Justin or Galen looked as concerned as they had a week before. Why couldn't she just go back to Montreal and see Amanda, who'd be there with her witty humor, cursing all the men in the world and telling Lorelei how silly she was to cry over one?

Someone knocked at the door. "Lorelei, it's Justin." She didn't move. Maybe he'd think she wasn't there. He knocked again. "Lorelei, I know you're in there. I'm going to open the door." Seconds later Justin looked in and smiled. "The beautiful Lorelei, waiting for her handsome escort," he said, offering his arm as he approached her.

"I'm sorry, Justin but I won't be going downstairs after all. I don't feel well."

He looked at her solicitously. "What's wrong? Are you nauseated again?"

"No...well, actually, my stomach is a little unsettled."

He affectionately patted her cheek. "I take it you haven't told Galen you're pregnant yet?"

Lorelei paled. "I'm not pregnant."

He shook his head and smiled. "Lorelei, I heard you throw up two mornings in a row. I realize this isn't the ideal moment for you to tell my brother but he has a right to know."

"Justin, I'm not pregnant!"

He didn't believe her. She wasn't sure she believed it anymore either. What a fool she'd been not to talk to the doctor about birth control after her miscarriage. But then, she'd been in love with a man she'd thought might come to love her, a man who had shown her there might be a future worth having. Being pregnant with his child could easily have seemed a natural part of that future, one she almost would have welcomed. But now...

"I think you should take the test," Justin said.

"And I think it's just nerves and the iron pills I have to take."

"Maybe but if you are pregnant, you'll have to face it sooner or later. No one will let you walk away from here with a child growing inside you." He sat next to her on the bed. "I don't think Galen should be denied the right to be a father, nor I an uncle. And remember, Lorelei, no matter how fond of you I am, my first loyalty must be to my brother," he pointed out.

"Loyalty to your brother?" she echoed. "Heaven forbid you should think of the child, whose father can't decide whose bedroom to sleep in at night. Heaven forbid you should have any compassion for a woman scorned, humiliated and powerless to change anything happening around her. And heaven forbid you should give that woman a chance to come to terms with the consequences of loving a man who is incapable of returning her love. What gives you the goddamned right to judge my actions and not those of your own brother? You Kennedys always find the most convenient excuses to force people to do things your money can't already make them do. You want to know what I think?"

"Hell, there's more?"

"Yes, there is." Incensed, Lorelei started looking for her luggage. Retrieving the first piece, she dropped it onto the bed and started to gather her things from the dresser. With brush in hand, she turned toward Justin, waving it like a weapon. "Now hear this, brother of Galen 'Almighty' Kennedy. I will decide if I want to be a man's mistress. And only I will decide under what conditions I will bear and raise a child. For no matter what compensation you Kennedys might offer to claim an heir, it would never be enough to compensate for living without love!" Tears were streaming down her cheeks but she ignored them and went about throwing things into the open suitcase.

"Stop packing," Justin said gently. "I didn't mean to sound so imperious or threatening. I'm simply concerned for both you and Galen." He placed his hands on her shoulders and gently shook her. "I care for you, Lorelei and I would never ask you to accept less than what you deserve, regardless of my brother. As for him, right now he's in great turmoil but he knows exactly how he feels about you and I hope to God he'll come to terms with it soon. It's the Brenna situation he's confused about. All he's trying to do now is find a way to do what he couldn't five years ago. Now, I agree that if you are indeed pregnant, you shouldn't tell him until he makes it clear where he stands with Brenna, or you'll never trust that he chose you out of love. That is, providing he stays far enough away from you that he doesn't hear you retching in the morning or notice how much more radiant you look day after day."

"I asked you to come and get Lorelei, brother, not seduce her." Galen was standing in the doorway, his hands clenched into fists as he watched his brother hold Lorelei by the shoulders.

Justin winked at Lorelei. "Don't mind him. Only an idiotic, insensitive Highlander would be jealous of his own brother, who is simply trying to support the innocent lady who's being forced to face the brute's wife in public." Justin's tone was openly challenging.

Galen approached the couple. "Don't do me any favors I haven't asked of you, Justin."

"Stop it, both of you," Lorelei interjected. "I'm not an invalid and I know how to get downstairs myself. You two can stay here and punch each other out like adolescents for all I care. But I'll be damned if I'll let either of you treat me like a chattel to be shuffled about. In case you haven't noticed, I don't belong to either of you!"

Justin took her arm. "Because we are gentlemen above all else, we apologize and promise to behave like perfect hosts. Right, brother?"

Galen turned around and left the room, angry at himself for losing control of his emotions once again.

Lorelei turned around towards the dresser mirror and dabbed at the wet tears that marred her cheeks. Justin approached and pulled out his hankie without saying a word. Meanwhile, she quietly repaired her makeup. A minute later he led her out. "Come on, let's go. And don't worry. I'll stay close the whole night—I give you my word."

When Lorelei and Justin descended the great staircase, Galen was flanked by Brenna and his cousin Robert. He couldn't tear his gaze away from Lorelei. Despite her discomfort and insecurity under the despicable circumstances, she looked radiant, self-assured and seemingly unaffected by the scrutiny of the many guests.

The males especially seemed eager to get their first good look at the pretty Canadian chef who had appeared with him in *People* magazine. It unnerved him to have to let everyone eye and assess her without him beside her. It felt as if he had relinquished a piece of himself, when all he wanted to do was tell everyone she was his.

He watched grimly as Justin introduced her to their mother, who had arrived just that day and would be leaving equally hastily for another visit to a friend after the reception, and to the mayor. Justin's hand rested on the small of her back—her bare back, Galen noticed to his chagrin.

"Well, well, what have we here?" Robert piped up. "A siren if ever I've seen one, wouldn't you say, Galen? Not bad at all for a French Canadian, eh?"

Galen remembered why he loathed Robbie. His cousin was both crude and pompous. The expensive education his parents had paid for had done nothing to improve his spoiled child disposition, even though he was now thirty-three.

When Justin and Lorelei turned toward them to speak to the chief of police, Brenna shifted nervously at Galen's side. "If you ask me, I think her breasts are going to fall out of her dress soon. Where did she think she was going, a bordello?"

Robbie smiled. "Jealous, cousin? But why worry? Galen's with you, isn't he?"

Just as Galen was about to reply to both of them, his cousin continued. "You're right, though, Brenna. She is nicely endowed. I wouldn't mind sampling her delicacies. I suppose Justin already has. Shall we ask him for the details, old boy?"

He patted Galen on the back and took a hefty swig of wine.

Galen's blood was boiling. Although he could usually remain cool even when provoked, this was just too much, especially from a parasite like Robbie.

Pretending reciprocation, he laughed and smacked his cousin on the back. Robert, who was nearly a foot shorter and fifty pounds lighter, was not prepared for the attack, and he choked on his wine, spitting the liquid out on Brenna.

"Galen, really!" Brenna exclaimed before rushing off to the powder room to repair the damage to her gown.

"Why don't we go to my study, Robbie," Galen said grimly, taking his cousin by the arm. Robert had no choice but to follow as Galen propelled him forward. Once inside, he closed the door and locked it, then grabbed Robert by his shirt collar, lifting him up from the floor and slamming him against a wall.

"You arrogant, crude, overindulged adolescent! You are no longer welcome in this house or on any property that belongs to me or my family. And if you ever cross my path again, I will rip your balls off and feed them to you."

Robert was gasping for air. A loud rapping on the door was followed by the sound of a key turning in the lock.

Justin walked into the room, followed by Brenna. He glanced at a blue-faced Robert swinging a good twelve inches from the floor. "Let him go, Galen. He's not worth the trouble. Besides, if you killed him, you'd dirty the Aubusson and Edward would be furious. Come on, let him go."

Galen finally, reluctantly released his cousin. "Leave. Now," he said with quiet fury.

"You think you're so mighty, Kennedy? You're not even fit to carry the name. You'll never truly be one of us," Robert spat at him while straightening his tie and jacket. He started toward the door.

Brenna walked up to Galen, enraged. "Why the hell does he have to go? If you must know, Robbie was only trying to defend me. He was embarrassed and outraged that you would let your mistress live in the same house as your wife and parade herself like a cheap slut in front of all our friends. How could you?"

"You, I will deal with later. In the meantime, if I hear you make one more comment about her, I'll expect you to leave as well. Lorelei has done nothing to you. I'm sick to death of your uncalled-for hysterics. Now, if you'll excuse me, I have a reception to host." He calmly walked out of the room, slamming the door behind him.

Justin arched his eyebrows at his brother's reaction. Was he finally beginning to realize Brenna was playing a game with him? He hoped so and he hoped the guilt-inducing bitch would soon leave. Then again, Galen had once thought he loved her deeply—and that he owed her mightily. And, knowing Brenna, she'd use every wile to keep Galen attached to her. After all, like most men, even Galen could be ruled by his gonads.

* * * * *

The mayor returned to speak to Lorelei about the soup kitchen for the needy he was planning to open in a few days with the Women's Auxiliary of St. Patrick's parish.

"I think the idea is wonderful," Lorelei told him. "However, this being such a tight-knit community, might some people in need feel ashamed to come to eat? Maybe you could organize cookouts instead of handouts. Then those in need can feel like part of the community, not a burden on it. I could come and prepare some of the meals and teach others how to cook for large groups. Tell me when and I'll be there."

The mayor's face lit up with a huge smile. "What a splendid idea, Miss Duplessis. We would be honored if you could lend us a hand."

The mayor's wife also looked delighted. "Our opening day will be Saturday," she said. "Can you make it?"

"My wife gets right down to business, as you can see. That's why she's president of the Women's Auxiliary," the mayor said, affectionately draping an arm around his spouse.

"Maybe you could become an honorary member, Miss Duplessis."

"Now, Marge, Miss Duplessis is a career woman. She lives in Canada. She's only here temporarily for this reception."

"What a shame, Miss Duplessis. Such a charming woman should find herself a man here in Wexford and settle down. You know, we have many eligible bachelors, including one of our own nephews."

Lorelei smiled wryly. If only they knew she had already found the man she wanted. She just couldn't have him. She took a sip of mineral water from the delicate crystal glass she had been holding since Justin left her side. The fizzy water was the only thing that wouldn't nauseate her. When she turned to see where Justin had gone, she saw Galen walking right toward her. He looked enraged.

"May I have a word with you, Miss Duplessis? Excuse us for a moment, won't you?" When everyone nodded, she and Galen walked to one of the parlors.

"What's happened? Where's Justin? Is something wrong?"

He made sure they were alone first, then closed the door. He crossed to the sofa and leaned on one of its armrests.

Was Justin the only thing on her mind? "Tell me something. Did you wear that dress just to aggravate me, or was it to make my brother and two dozen other men drool over your breasts all night?"

Lorelei gasped. Quickly setting her glass on the table beside her—lest she decide to throw it at him—she spoke in a voice that vibrated with suppressed fury. "If you think that I live to aggravate you, Kennedy, then you give yourself too much importance. As for this dress, I wore it at your brother's request. He, after all, was gracious enough to play your little game and escort me so that you could prove your husbandly fidelity to your political friends. But I'll tell you this—if any of the men here tonight do fantasize about my breasts, perhaps I can feel some satisfaction for the hurt and humiliation you're making me endure!"

She was hurrying to leave when Galen grabbed her arm.

"Don't play with fire, Lorelei, because you'll get burned."

Lorelei looked into his eyes, refusing to be intimidated.

"Then we'll burn together, Kennedy, because from this day on my sole purpose will be to make you rage with the desire to have me while reminding you that you're not man enough to do so."

Justin suddenly opened the door and looked at his brother disapprovingly. "I'm not sure which one of you I should be rescuing. From the looks of it, it's you, brother."

He looked at Lorelei. "Come on, Lorelei. No offense but I can't wait 'til this evening is over. I'm sick of being a bodyguard. Besides, it's damn irritating that I can't hit anybody no matter how asinine their behavior!" He let her pass ahead of him. "After you."

When they left, Galen took the glass Lorelei had left on the desk and threw it at the fireplace.

Chapter Twenty-Nine

Exhausted from an evening of conflicting emotions, Lorelei stepped out of the shower. At least she had begun packing her suitcases. The idea that she could leave if she wanted to made it easier to endure her stay.

She was forced to admit there was a strong possibility that she was pregnant again. She had been denying it to herself for days, hoping frayed nerves and iron pills were responsible for the symptoms. But when Justin confronted her with his suspicions, she'd been unable to ignore the truth.

The truth, indeed. She was pregnant. Her life was in danger. Galen was with another woman. His wife. In short, she was back to where she had started. *Et oui*, same hell, just a different day.

She padded out of the bathroom to the closet and grabbed her robe, removing the towel she had used to dry herself. She would eventually tell Galen she was expecting — once she was beyond his reach and sure he'd made up his mind about their relationship and Brenna. It was imperative that her pregnancy not influence his decision.

Someone knocked at her door before she had time to prepare for bed. She quickly donned the white terrycloth robe and unlocked the huge medieval door. Stone-faced, Galen put a hand flat on the ancient wood. "I told you never to lock a door against me." He almost collided with her on his way in, shutting the door and locking it behind him.

"This is my room."

"And this is my home."

"You're right. It's your home, not mine," she noted with sarcasm.

"Don't presume for a moment to keep me out of anywhere I want to be."

"I don't presume anything." She gestured toward her open suitcase. "As you can see, my bags are packed, Kennedy. So I won't presume to be your guest any longer either."

He shook his head when he saw her luggage. The thought of her leaving made him ache inside. He would lock her in the castle's tower before he'd let her take one step away from him. He briefly scanned the room to see if anyone else was there with her.

Realizing what he was doing, Lorelei was stunned. "Oh, so you think I have your brother here, hiding? Sorry to disappoint you but he left not ten minutes ago. That gave me just enough time to take a shower and wash him off me."

Anger swept over him like a flash of lightning. If she were a man, he would have struck her. Then again, Galen couldn't believe he had actually suspected her of having a dalliance with his brother. He grabbed her wrist and pressed her palm to his chest. His other hand slid inside her robe and caressed one of her breasts. "You're not going anywhere."

She looked up at him defiantly. "You're drunk!"

"Not as much as I'd like to be," he drawled. He wanted her and was so afraid of losing her, he was ready to do anything, even beg. Aye, he would beg if he had to. "You belong to me."

Whether she belonged to him or not, it wouldn't change their situation, Lorelei realized. She would still have to live in the same house as his wife. She would still be his live-in mistress. How presumptuous of him and how selfish to think she would accept those conditions. "Hmm, a *ménage à trois*," she mused aloud, tapping her chin with one finger.

"Let me sleep on it and I'll give you an answer in the morning."

Instead of giving in to an absurd urge toward violence, he examined her from head to toe, visually stripping her bare.

Infuriated by his insolence, Lorelei tightened the sash around her waist. "I'm not for sale, Kennedy, so stop looking at me as if I were merchandise."

He hated it when she called him Kennedy. "But your services have been purchased and paid for and don't you forget it."

Lorelei took one step forward and slapped him.

"Bastard." While he touched his stinging cheek, she stuck her chin up. "I will have the money you paid for my car returned to you tomorrow before noon. So that settles the transaction by which you think you own me. Now get out!"

"Did you think I was talking about money?" He smiled as his hand dug back into her robe, his fingers touching one velvety nipple. "I purchased you with my soul and my peace of mind. You can't cancel that sale. And don't you ever tell me to get out again." His hand roamed to the other breast.

"I mean to hear you say the words, Lorelei," he said between his teeth.

Lorelei continued staring at him. Frustrated by her silence, he circled her nipple until it became hard between his fingers.

Lorelei bit her lip at the sensation, angry that he could still get a reaction from her despite her hurt, her anger, the urgency she felt to push him back and out of her life.

"Answer me," he said more softly, more desperately.

"Please, I don't want to hurt anymore." He took another step toward her, forcing her to take one backward.

Gone was any trace of a gentle, persuasive lover. His eyes betrayed his inner turmoil, his own frustration and rage.

She bumped into the table behind her. "Haven't you done enough? Stay away from me!" With one hand she tried holding him back, the other she raised to slap him again.

The alcohol he had drunk that night was wreaking havoc with his self-control. "So you want it rough? Good, because I'm tired, angry and sick to death of compromises."

"No, Galen, stop," she protested when he began to strip off her robe.

He smirked. "You're mine—bought and paid for. You have no say in this, sweetheart."

"Don't you dare call me that."

He warred with himself. In his mind he wanted her willing but his body wanted her, period. "Then take off the robe."

"Stay the hell away from me, Kennedy!"

"I can't," he admitted.

The fight suddenly went out of her. She thought of the child she might be carrying. She thought of the one who had never come to be. She thought of what she felt for this man who wanted her so desperately. "What do you want from me?"

He paused and inhaled her scent. "I want you to feel how I've been feeling inside, watching you separate yourself from me, giving everyone else more of yourself than me, as if I never meant anything to you, when I know that I did."

He hoped that he still did.

Her eyes were brimming. "It doesn't have to be like this."

He lifted her by the bottom and placed her on table, saying in his Irish brogue, "Aye, it does, because you're a fever that's slowly killin' me, lass." He swung an arm out behind her, sending a lamp and crystal bowl crashing to the floor. With more space to maneuver, he slid her back until she touched the wall. "Let me love you."

When she realized what he intended to do, she dug her hands into his sleeves. "*Vas-te faire foutre!*"

He smiled faintly, his hands pausing in their attempt to open her legs. "Fuck you?" he deliberately mistranslated. "If you insist."

Lorelei tried with all her strength to hold her legs together but failed. His hands, three times stronger and more powerful than her own, grabbed her calves and draped them over his shoulders, exposing her sex to his gaze. She continued struggling. "You'll get nothing out of this except my body!"

"Right now I don't care—or hadn't you noticed?" He knew she couldn't deny him. He clasped her soft folds in one hand and set her body on fire. He opened her and inserted two fingers. "This is what I want. See how easy it was for me to get it? In no time I'll have you panting."

Then his mouth descended mercilessly on hers. "I love you, Lorelei."

"This isn't love! It's not enough!" she cried.

"I'll make it enough." His outward anger belied his touch, which gentled into ministrations so intimate that Lorelei couldn't think anymore. Then he lowered his head and probed her with his lips, his tongue parting her delicate folds and thrusting itself inside her.

The reasons she had for fighting him were rapidly fading from her mind, or what was left of it. Brenna's presence no longer mattered. Galen's hands and lips and tongue were all that occupied her thoughts.

He gently bit the inside of her thigh, sensing her surrender. He began kissing her slowly and languidly, wanting to give her pleasure. "Your body doesn't care what your mind says, Lorelei. All I have to do is touch you."

With every stroke of his tongue he was showing her how much control he had over her. She tried to fight her own passion but she couldn't. She might be on the edge of a precipice and he was calling her beyond it but still she could not refuse. Yet some remote part of her knew that she couldn't face a future lived in the shadows.

"I don't want to be your mistress. I can't!"

He looked into her eyes, which were clouded with both passion and hurt. Aye, she was fighting not to feel the compulsion they shared but she was losing. He could show no mercy. "You'll be anything it takes to keep on having my hands, my lips all over you, my flesh thrusting into yours, however gentle or however angry I may be." He wanted her to admit it, that she could refuse him nothing, that deep down she craved this with the same ferocity he did and that she would always capitulate, no matter how wrong her mind felt about what her body was doing. It was exactly how he felt and he was desperate to hear her surrender to it too.

"I'm going to make you ask for it, beg for it and compromise everything for it, just as I have," he growled.

No conditions was what he wanted—no conditions for either one of them.

He went back to laving that tiny part of her that controlled her will. He wanted her to lose all sense of time and place. He wanted to reach the essence of her womanhood and the depths of her soul. And he knew he was close.

She climaxed violently, shaking and crying in his arms, and he finally looked up to see her eyes brimming with the truth he had hungered for. "I love you," he repeated, this time with peace in his voice.

"So do I," she sobbed quietly.

He brought his mouth to hers. "Then taste our love."

His tongue offered her own essence mingled with his, the taste of the union of their bodies and souls, the recognition of their undeniable need for each other. They would be mates forever.

Sated with the knowledge that she could refuse him nothing, that she loved him, he finally stripped off his pants, shedding with them the past and the emotional blackmail he had endured. He would be inside her soon. And always.

A Scent in the Night

When they looked at each other, his tears mingling with hers, they joined in body and in spirit. And in those few seconds when they reached the pinnacle of their passion, the world around them ceased to exist. Their love for each other was the only reality that mattered.

Chapter Thirty
ಐ

When Galen finally left Lorelei's room, he had made up his mind about a number of things, Brenna included. The time of reckoning was long overdue.

When he entered his room, intending to change clothes and have a talk with Brenna, he found her lying naked across his bed, propping her head up with one hand and sipping champagne with the other. She had opened a bottle of Veuve Clicot he had been saving for Lorelei.

Watching her slowly sip the bubbly liquid, he realized he had been wrong in ever thinking that these two women were remotely alike. Vain, capricious ego had led his wife during the years they were together. Lorelei was headstrong but she could act with humility and compassion. Brenna was selfish and narcissistic.

He realized that part of the reason he had married her was his Irish blood and the solidarity he felt for his countrymen in need, including Brenna and her family. She was a product of a war-torn Ireland and like many other victims she'd needed a roof over her head and food in her belly and emotional and financial security. The fact that he'd been attracted to her and that meeting all her needs had made him feel powerful had probably compelled him to marry her.

He looked at his wife now the way he would regard a stranger. This was not the Brenna he thought he had known and she was certainly not the woman with whom he wished to share the rest of his life.

"I thought I should apologize for my behavior earlier," she said. She briefly closed her eyes and exhaled. "Make love to me, Galen and I'll make you forget all the pain and hurt of the past. I'll kiss it away one scar at a time and then you'll realize you could never live without me again."

He slowly advanced toward her, indifferent to her perfume, indifferent to her body, indifferent to her entirely. As soon as he sat on the edge of the bed, she pulled his head down and attempted to kiss him. He felt nothing at the assault of her lips. No passion, no affection and no desire to go any further. Lorelei had freed him from the past and the pain. It was time he freed himself from the guilt.

He unlaced her arms from around his neck and abruptly stood, wondering why he had even bothered sitting in the first place. He couldn't stand one more minute with her. "It's finished, Brenna. You're attempting to rekindle something that ended a long time ago. It's just a memory now and I need far more than that."

Brenna slid off the bed, leaving her empty glass on the night table. "How can you stand there and tell me this is only a memory?" She took his hand and placed it between her legs. "Touch me, for God's sake! Can't you see how wet you make me?"

He removed his hand as quickly as she had put it there. She disgusted him.

"This is real, Galen, more real than what you'll ever have with anyone else, because this comes with the commitment we pledged to each other!"

"What's left is only a piece of paper, Brenna. You ended our marriage when you left without a word."

Desperate, she attempted to play on his guilt. "You killed my brother, yet I've forgiven you. But if you leave me now, you'll never forgive yourself."

"I don't want your forgiveness. I don't need it anymore. Your emotional blackmail will not be enough to keep me at your beck and call. I'm sorry but I should have divorced you five years ago."

He headed for the door, his mind already made up.

"It's that slut, isn't it? That little Canadian whore who's turned your head!"

He clenched his fist on the doorknob, resisting the urge to strike her. "I think you'd better leave this house. By tomorrow morning I want you packed and on your way. I'll contact Sam Kavanaugh to draw up the papers. Let him know where he should mail them to you." He closed the door firmly behind him.

Chapter Thirty-One

Lorelei had just finished discussing the next day's menu with Maurice when she got the call from Dr. Scallan's office confirming her appointment for three o'clock that day.

Since she didn't want Galen to suspect she was pregnant until she was sure herself and since he wouldn't allow her to leave the house alone, she asked Justin to keep his brother busy so she could leave without Galen's knowing. Justin was so sure she would come back with good news that he agreed on the condition that she take Colin or Conrad with her.

Justin was as good as his word. At two o'clock that afternoon she saw him and Galen drive out together in the Jeep, heading for the docks where the *Blue Siren* had just anchored.

Half an hour later she headed for the garages. Since the air was a little nippy, she wore leather pants, a sweater, a bomber jacket and a pair of snakeskin boots her uncle had brought back from one of his trips.

She found the garages deserted. Neither Conrad nor Colin were anywhere in sight. She worried about having to break her bargain with Justin and she knew Galen would be angry if he knew the place had been left unguarded. She contemplated returning to the house and calling the clinic to reschedule but she realized she couldn't bear to wait another day. She had to know if she was pregnant with Galen's baby.

Instead of retrieving her keys from the tool room, which was locked, she decided to use her extra set. As she took them out, however, she noticed that the key was already in the ignition. How sweet of Justin to have done that.

Surprised at how easy it was going to be for her to leave on her own, she started the car, listened to its rumble for a second or two and began to shift into gear. Suddenly the passenger door opened and a man with a gun pointed at her got in. "Drive out slowly. Do anything to attract attention, and a bullet goes through your head." Stunned, all Lorelei could do was blindly shift into reverse and slowly back out of the garage.

Once at the gates, she was sure someone would notice that she was leaving with a stranger. To her dismay, the gates were not only deserted but open. Had the guards been hurt or killed? Lorelei took a deep breath in an attempt to remain calm. She would find a way to thwart her captor.

"Turn left, bitch."

She did so. "Where are we going?" she asked.

The man nuzzled her cheek with the gun. "Shut up and drive."

Lorelei pursed her lips. Her assailants had missed killing her twice already. She had a feeling they wouldn't miss on the third try.

A few minutes after being on the road, the man pulled out a cell phone and made a call. "I've got her. Here," he said as he handed her the phone. "Say hello to your boyfriend." He held the receiver to her ear and poked the gun into her side, motioning her to speak.

"Hello?"

"Lorelei? Are you all right?" Justin asked, sounding breathless.

Terrified, Lorelei trembled. "Justin, is that you?"

She heard a gunshot through the phone and jolted. A masculine voice she didn't recognize came on the line. "If you're not here in fifteen minutes, I'll be executing his sidekick as well."

The phone went dead and so did her heart. They had killed Justin, she concluded with horror. Tears began flowing down her cheeks, blurring her vision.

Her captor, unaffected by her anguish, continued pointing his gun at her, signaling what directions to take.

She already knew where they were going. They were heading for the docks, where Justin had taken Galen. If only she had told Galen about her clinic appointment, they never would have gone and Justin would still be alive.

She continued driving like a robot, numb with grief and fear. She regained control of her senses as they approached the port, praying to God that Galen was still alive and that she would be able to see him. They passed a parking lot, where she saw the Jeep.

"Drive to the left, near the pier and up to the *Clover*." As she spotted a big cargo ship in the distance, Lorelei realized they weren't going to the *Siren* after all.

As they approached the rear of the ship, her captor signaled her to stop at the ramp that linked the vessel to the dock.

The gunman used his cell phone to alert someone they had arrived. They waited five or six minutes for the cargo door to open and then drove up the ramp and onto the ship.

Once inside, the man reached over and turned off the ignition, removing the key and taking her purse. "Get out slowly," he ordered.

When she got out of the car, he locked it and walked behind her, poking her back with his gun. As they advanced to the far end of the huge cargo hold, she saw two men on the floor. She recognized Justin on the left, keeled over in a pool of blood and Galen, distraught, on the right. Their wrists were handcuffed to a pipe running from the ceiling to the floor.

She ran to Galen, heedless of the gunman's shouts for her to stay put. Crying, she hugged Galen to her. "Oh Galen, what have they done to you, to Justin?"

Galen feared what the bastards were going to do to her.

"Why did you leave the house, love?" He searched her face for fear but saw none. Would her boundless courage stand them in good stead, or would it be their undoing?

He looked beyond her to the man at her back. "You and your vermin friends killed my brother and if there's a God in heaven, you'll pay for it with your lives," he growled.

Lorelei saw that his wrists were bleeding from his forceful struggling against the cuffs.

"Look at me," she softly commanded him.

What he saw was a woman of determination, with clenched teeth and a grip on his upper arms stronger than he'd thought her capable of. The deadly look in her eyes almost scared him.

The man who had abducted her nudged her shoulder with the barrel of his gun, hoping to scare her. She turned her head slightly to give him a look of utter contempt.

"You'd better say your goodbye quickly, Kennedy," he said. "They're going to come and get her soon." With her keys and purse in his hands, the gunman left the area, using a steel door in one wall.

Galen looked at Lorelei. "I'm sorry, love."

"Don't be. They're the ones who are going to be sorry," she murmured.

Galen arched his eyebrows questioningly.

Tears clouded her vision and they were not exclusively for Justin or Galen or even for herself. She was crying at the realization that the moment had come in her life when she actually wished death upon someone, a wish she had the means to fulfill, a wish that was going to become reality.

When she turned to look at Justin, she saw the gash on his right temple where his blood had started to cake. While she was saying a silent prayer for his soul, she noticed a slight twitch in his brow.

She quickly moved to kneel in front of him and gently raised his head to get a better look at him. She checked for a pulse in his neck and placed an ear on his chest. "He's breathing! Oh my God, he's breathing!" She looked up at Galen with tears of joy. "He's alive, Galen!"

Galen shook his head, not believing her words. "They shot him in the head, Lorelei. Look at all the blood he lost."

"But he's breathing. The bullet only grazed him." She examined the wound more closely. "We've got to wake him up!"

"Lorelei, there's nothing we can do."

Hopeful that Galen was wrong, she held Justin's head in her hands and leaned over him. "Justin, it's Lorelei. Justin, wake up. Please, Justin, open your eyes." Lorelei raised her voice. "You mean to tell me my child will grow up without an uncle? Come on, Justin, I promise if you wake up, I'll let you pick the name!"

Galen gasped. "You're pregnant?"

She smiled, then leaned over and kissed him lightly on the lips. "Now Justin has to wake up, or our child won't have a name."

"Hmm, have I died and gone to heaven?" Justin mumbled.

"Justin, open your eyes," she pleaded.

"What's that wonderful scent I smell?" he mumbled.

Galen's voice trembled. "It's Lorelei, Justin. She just kissed you. And I'd kiss you right now myself if I could, brother."

Justin kept his eyes closed but shifted a little. "No offense but I'd prefer that Lorelei keep kissing me. I'm sure I'd feel much better afterward."

Galen's eyes filled with happy tears. "If you promise to live through this, I might just allow it this once."

Lorelei smiled and leaned down to plant a second chaste kiss on Justin's lips. "Welcome back."

He finally, blearily opened his eyes, which were glazed with pain.

Lorelei retrieved some tissues from her jacket to wipe the blood off his face.

"Jesus, woman, that stings!" he complained. "Leave it be for now."

"So what's the plan? We have to get her out of here," Justin asked Galen in Gaelic.

Galen answered him in kind. He didn't want Lorelei to understand but she knew better. She was already walking away from them to her car.

Justin sat up and arched his eyebrows. "Where is she going?"

"Lorelei, come back here," Galen ordered.

"What's with her?" Justin asked.

"Lorelei, you're going to have to find a way to break into your car and jump-start it."

Justin turned to his brother and shook his head, "Breaking into it'll activate its alarm system."

"Sorry to interrupt your little discussion," Lorelei said, "but just what do you think I could do if I succeeded in getting the car started?"

"You could go for help, of course."

"And, what, leave you two here to have all the fun?"

Before Galen had the chance to protest, he saw her unlock the driver's door with a key. He smiled wryly. He had underestimated her once again.

When she got in, she opened the passenger door, got out, walked around the car and sat in the passenger seat. She reached under the seat for a tiny hidden latch. When she felt it click, she opened a flap under the seat and removed her gun and the bullet clip she had stowed away. She slid the gun into her waistband and walked toward the two gaping brothers.

"Well, gentlemen in distress, be glad that this chef always comes prepared."

The brothers were speechless. Galen finally figured out how she had managed to smuggle her gun into Europe. She'd hidden it in the car. As ever, her audacity was astounding.

Justin was the first to get his voice back. "As much as I'll enjoy being rescued by such a beautiful woman, I'm afraid I'll never live this down. How can we ever again parade through Scotland as men of consequence, brother?"

Galen smiled. "Sweetheart, give me the gun, then get back in the car and hide. If anything should happen to us, press the green button over there to open the hold and activate the ramp, then drive out as fast as you can and go for help."

Lorelei was incensed that he'd think she would actually agree to his plan. She placed her hands on her hips defiantly.

"I'll let you play hero another time, if you don't mind. I want this child to know both his father and his uncle."

She inserted the clip into her gun. "My uncle always said that if you carry a gun, you've got to be prepared to use it. And if you have to use it, you should shoot to kill. Thus, when he left me his collection, he did so knowing I'd be prepared for any eventuality, including this one. He didn't underestimate my capabilities."

She looked at the door her abductor had used, visualizing whether it had swung in or out when he opened it. Then she walked back to the Porsche.

"Where are you going? At least explain yourself, woman!" Galen was so frustrated with her stubbornness, he made a mental note to give her a good setdown once they got out of this predicament—if they ever did, he thought grimly.

"Whatever she does, she'd better do it quickly, before we set sail," Justin said.

When she got to the car, she went to the driver's side, put her right hand on the steering wheel and her left on the door frame and she began pushing forward nine hundred and ninety-five pounds of metal.

When Galen realized what she intended to do, he tried to get up. "Lorelei, you'll hurt yourself. Damn it, you're pregnant!"

Lorelei continued applying herself as if their lives depended on it—which, at the moment, seemed to be the case.

When the wheels finally began to move, Lorelei steered the car on a diagonal until it stopped three feet away from the brothers.

Galen was about to give her a piece of his mind when Justin kicked him, motioning him to stay silent. "She doesn't want us to be sitting ducks. You can't blame her, Galen. She means to protect us and there's not a thing we can do about it, given the fact that we're in handcuffs and she has the one and only gun."

"Are you two finished talking about me as if I'm not here?" Lorelei inquired. "We probably haven't got much time, you know." She stood in front of them, wiping her brow with a sleeve of her jacket. "Now then, gentlemen, I will stand to the left of that door. If whoever comes in is not the one with the keys to your cuffs, let me know."

"How will we get someone to come back in here?" Galen asked, unwillingly to accept a plan that put her at the most risk.

Lorelei slipped inside her car again and turned on the CD player. "I hope you'll like this. It's called 'The War Dance', from a collection of Native-American music I discovered not too long ago. Under the circumstances, I find it appropriate."

When the sound of drums and chants began to echo in the cargo hold, Lorelei plastered herself to the wall beside the door, the Glock in her right hand, her index finger on the trigger.

Not a minute passed before a man opened the steel door.

He swore when he saw the Porsche parked in front of it, blocking his access to the hold. Lorelei took one step and pressed her gun to his neck. With her free hand she reached for the door and closed it behind him, trapping him between the steel of the portal and the steel of her car.

"Drop your weapon slowly and kick it toward me," she ordered.

"You'll never get out of here alive, you bitch."

"Neither will you if you don't shut up."

When he lowered his semiautomatic from his shoulder and kicked it to her, Lorelei bent down and picked it up, ready for any sudden movements he might make. She draped the weapon over her shoulder and told the man, "Now free these two Kennedys."

"I don't have the key."

"Really? That's too bad, because that means I have no use for you. Kneel." Her tone was blunt.

The man hesitated but when she prodded him with her gun, he knelt. She saw sweat bead on his forehead when she pressed the muzzle to it.

"Wait," he said. "I do have the key."

Despite his offer, she remained still. She wanted to shoot him for all the anguish he had caused, for nearly killing Justin, for imprisoning her and Galen for his political ends.

Galen saw the rage in her eyes and intervened. "Revenge is not yours to exercise, remember? Do you want to have a man's blood on your conscience, a man you didn't have to kill? This is not your war, Lorelei. You just got caught in the middle of it."

Her back remained stiff.

"Please, baby, you'll never forgive yourself."

His words rang true and had the desired effect on her. She stepped aside and motioned the man to get up and remove the handcuffs from the brothers.

While he was kneeling before Galen and Justin, she remained behind him, watching the door in case anyone else came in.

Justin took the semiautomatic from Lorelei to guard their captive while Galen hurried to activate the hold's door and ramp. "Get into the car, start it and back it up," Justin told Lorelei. "It'll take five or six minutes until the ramp is down and we can leave. Go on!"

She ignored Justin's order, trying to figure out how the hell she was going to fit two giant men and herself into the Porsche.

She looked behind her for Galen. She noticed that he had not only handcuffed but also gagged his captive. She reached for Justin's arm. "The engine is in the back," she said. "You sit in the luggage compartment in front but on the right so you don't block my view. The open hood will protect you from bullets although you'll have to keep as low as possible, or I'll be driving blind." She went to the car and opened the trunk. "Get in. We'll pick up Galen on our way out."

Justin shook his head at her cleverness.

When she started the car, she hoped they would have enough time to leave before anyone realized what was happening. She turned the car around in a flash and let Justin hop in.

She drove to the open cargo door, noticing outside that the ramp had not yet reached the ground. "Get in, Kennedy," she said to Galen.

Galen got into the car, closed the door and pressed the electric button to slide down the passenger window. He asked Lorelei for her gun and prayed she wouldn't protest. To his surprise, she didn't.

A Scent in the Night

"Hang on, boys," she said. "We're about to jump ship—literally. Oh and, Kennedy, you're going to be paying for any repairs Nemesis might need this time."

Galen smiled. "Consider it done. Now get ready to drive."

Lorelei smiled while pumping fuel to the engine, waiting to hit six thousand RPMs. Praying to God for their safety, she shifted directly into second gear and released the clutch, hoping the car wouldn't stall. The tires spun and smoked as the car jolted to ninety miles per hour and jumped the ramp.

When they hit the ground, Justin swore as he saw men lining up on the ship's deck, aiming guns at them. "Get us out of here—fast!"

Lorelei accelerated away from the dock, not quite sure which way to take. Then the shooting started and all she could do was drive. Miraculously, no one got hit, not even the 959, which felt as though it was about to take flight.

When they were back on the road to Wexford House, Galen signaled Lorelei to make a right turn onto a tree-lined lane. "Turn here and slow down."

The road got very narrow and when it looked as if they couldn't go any farther, she stopped the car and turned off the engine. "What now?" she asked.

Galen reached into his back pocket and removed a cell phone. Justin had gotten out of the luggage compartment and stepped onto the ground beside his brother's window.

He leaned down, curious. "Where did you get the phone?" he asked.

"I took it from Peter after I cuffed him."

"You know that guy?" Lorelei asked.

Galen punched in a number and waited for the ring. He hoped the phone would work from this location. "Of course," he replied abstractedly. "He's a distant cousin of Brenna's." Galen tried the number again but without success.

He cursed the phone.

"Brenna? What does she have to do with this?"

Justin spoke up. "It's time to tell her, Galen."

The time for truth had indeed come. Lorelei must know the one last thing about him that could still cost him their relationship. "Five years ago," he began slowly, "I was looking into what I thought was a major error in a bill of lading and I went to inspect some cargo coming off one of the *Sirens* myself. I surprised Brenna's brother, Bryan, in a hold and he confronted me with a gun. I...I had to kill him...or be killed." He paused, finally realizing it was true. He'd had no choice, as Justin had often tried to tell him. His voice stronger now, surer, he went on. "For obvious reasons Brenna left me but as long as we remained married, even though we separated, her family left my people alone. But now—maybe because I got involved with you—I'm afraid her family decided it was time to retaliate."

Lorelei was both shocked and confused. Galen had killed Brenna's brother? But what had that to do with herself? Someone had put a contract out on her in Hyannis Port and that contract had followed her to Wexford. But wasn't that because of what someone thought she might know about a murder and other criminal activities?

"What about Donald O'Hara and the weapons he and his cohorts were smuggling?"

"That's something we have yet to resolve," Galen said darkly.

Lorelei was too stunned to pursue the matter further at the moment.

Galen noticed she had said nothing about Bryan. "It doesn't bother you that I killed a man?" he asked.

Lorelei saw the anguish in his eyes. So that was the source of the guilt that haunted him. Along with the need to protect his extended family, was that guilt another reason he felt he couldn't divorce Brenna? Knowing Galen, she was almost certain of it.

She looked at him squarely. "Had you planned to kill him?"

"No. But—"

"Were you glad to kill him?"

"No, of course not."

Choosing her words carefully, she said, "I know you to be a principled man and one who would gladly trade his own life for someone else's, particularly a family member or friend's." She placed a hand on his arm and squeezed it. "If you killed a man, it was because you had no choice. You have to forgive yourself, Galen."

At her words Galen realized that some of his heaviness of heart was gone. The burden of guilt he'd carried for so long began to lighten. Though his brother had often tried to tell him much the same thing, hearing it from Lorelei felt like a liberation. She was truly familiar with the darkness of grief and guilt—and had every reason to distrust his motives, yet, coming from her, somehow it eased the anguish he had thought to be his permanent, personal hell on Earth.

"That's what I've been trying to tell him," Justin said. "Welcome to our family, Lorelei. From this day on you belong with us. Now, if you don't mind, Galen, would you get out of the car and let me sit down before I collapse?"

"Are you okay, Justin?" Lorelei asked, alarmed.

"I'm fine. A tad sore but we Kennedys have hard heads, in case you hadn't noticed."

Galen and Lorelei both laughed while Galen opened the door and helped his brother sit down in his place.

"Shouldn't we be calling home?" Justin said.

"That was next on my agenda. But before I do that, I've got something to say to Miss Duplessis. Would you excuse us for a minute?"

"Can't this wait?" Justin complained.

Galen didn't bother answering. He walked to Lorelei's door, opened it and took her hand, leading her to a secluded spot behind a stand of trees. They had to agree to some ground rules, he'd decided. He and Justin were now involved in an all-out war and he wanted her out of the way, first for her safety and, second, because it wasn't her fight. She'd been subjected to enough of it already. When he turned to face her, he knew it wasn't going to be easy for Lorelei to sit back and wait on the sidelines, however.

He cupped her face, gazing into her eyes. "I love you, Lorelei. God knows I probably don't deserve you but I love you. And you've accepted me, what I've done and—"

"Shh." She put her fingers on his lips. "It's over. It's finished and—"

"That's precisely it. It isn't finished." He shook her gently by the shoulders, hoping she would understand the gravity of the matter. "I love you so much that I can't bear it when you put yourself at risk," he continued. "This is not your fight, Lorelei."

She frowned.

"Back on the ship," he said, "I asked you to hide in the car until it was safe for you to go for help. I expected you to let Justin and me deal with armed terrorists who aimed to eliminate you. Do you realize what would have happened if, instead of Peter, three or four men had come through that door? You'd be dead."

Her hands went to her hips. "What are you saying?"

"I'm saying that you take unnecessary risks because you don't trust anyone to take them for you. Because you're prepared to die, no matter who you leave behind."

"That's not true!" How could she explain it to him? She needed to remain in control not because she didn't trust him but because she hated feeling helpless. She had felt helpless to save her parents or even to avenge their deaths but she could never, ever stand idly by again if someone she loved was in danger.

"You cannot and will not decide things for everybody all the time. You push me away each time you do that, Lorelei. It's not good for our relationship if I always have to fight to be included."

She turned and stood motionless, her back to him, staring into the woods. "I love you. I was afraid to lose you. I can't deal with someone dying on me again, Galen. I—I just can't."

She covered her face with trembling hands.

"You have to trust me, Lorelei, trust those you love."

He turned her around and took her in his arms, stroking her hair, sorry he had made her cry. "For now, though, let me say again how much I love you and how much my existence and happiness depend on yours." His lips touched hers, trying to convey the depth of his emotion. Then he backed away and tapped the tip of her nose with one finger. "But don't think you're off the hook." He took her hand and led her back toward the car.

"I finally got a line and called home," Justin informed them. "But no one's answering. I'm thinking the house must have been raided."

The brothers looked at each other grimly.

"When I picked up my car from the garage, Conrad had vanished and so had the guards at the gates," Lorelei informed them, attempting to conceal her worries about the safety of the household, including and especially Maurice.

Sensing her distress, Galen wrapped an arm around her shoulders. "They may just be hiding, love. The men we hired are very good. No one could have disarmed them all."

Justin tried another call but it too, went unanswered.

"What do we do now?"

"Get a hold of Simmons and tell him to meet us at the old cottage with as many constables as he can round up. We'll organize a counterattack from there."

"Where are you going?" Lorelei asked when Galen turned and began to walk away from her.

"We left tire tracks on our way in here. I'll brush them out with some branches."

Half an hour later, while Justin was again talking to the police captain, Lorelei watched Galen sit by a tree, seemingly deep in contemplation.

"A penny for your thoughts," she said softly.

He looked up at her. "When will the violence end? What will it take to make Irishmen realize they're still killing each other for something none of them was responsible for to begin with?"

It was the first time Galen had ever really talked to her about this side of his life, Lorelei realized. And she also realized that what he hated most about the conflict was that it often pitted family against family, apparently for no good reason.

"I don't know much about the war except for what I learned in history classes." She sank down to the ground beside him. "But it seems to me that when a war goes on for years and years like this, it becomes a way of life. The reasons it started fade and the opportunities it provides for the greedy take over. Many are happy to profit from the bloodletting, and some politicians make their careers through it. For those who fight, it gives a sense of purpose to their lives and a sense of honor to their deaths, both of which are often sorely lacking in so-called modern society."

Galen looked at her strangely.

"What?" she asked.

"For a French Canadian living over four thousand miles away, you have an amazing sense of perspective. Perhaps you should be a politician."

She found a small twig and began tracing lines on the ground. "The mountains here are so beautiful you can almost think you're touching heaven." She looked up, still amazed at how beautiful the Irish countryside was. "But it's such a mean and violent part of the world, I'm not sure I'd want to bring a child into it."

Galen looked at her and his heart skipped a beat. Was she still thinking of leaving? "What are you saying?"

"What I'm saying is, I don't know if I can live in a place where I have to watch my back all the time, a place where people hate each other because of their names and where I'm shut out of anything important because I'm not kin."

She got up and began pacing. "I don't want to live in a place where people make their own laws to suit their own code of ethics or their lack thereof. I especially don't want to live in a place that can make me want to kill a man, the way I wanted to kill Peter today. I'd lose whatever humanity and love I have left."

Galen got up and placed his hands on her shoulders.

"Then we'll leave. We'll go live somewhere else. I'm loaded, remember?"

She smiled, knowing what a sacrifice it would be for him to follow her home to Montreal. She touched his face and smiled. "This place, this beautiful heaven, is also etched in your eyes, Galen. Your heart would be empty without it. I can't take it away from you. You would never be the same man." And she kissed him gently on the lips.

Someone snorted in the background. "Oh, come on can't you guys stop pawing each other already?" Justin complained.

His face was pale and Lorelei knew he needed medical attention. She gave him a sympathetic look. "Galen, why don't you call Dr. Scallan and ask him to meet us at the cottage too?

That gash on Justin's head is nasty and should be looked at and cleaned up."

"I'll be fine," Justin answered. "Maybe you can kiss my boo-boo away."

Galen smiled. "Get your own woman, bro," he retorted.

But he motioned Lorelei toward his brother. "While you soothe the big baby, I'll call Scallan. Pass me the phone."

"Come on, I don't need a doctor. A well-endowed nurse maybe…"

* * * * *

Wexford's entire police force must have been called in, Lorelei thought, for twenty-five constables and a contingent of fifteen soldiers were already waiting for them at the cottage when they emerged from the woods on foot. Armed to the teeth, the men looked more like a private militia than government employees.

They entered the little house to decide strategy.

Although Galen included Lorelei in the discussion, something told her he would try to exclude her from the fight to regain control of Wexford House.

Once all the men were outside waiting for Galen, Lorelei braced herself for the confrontation.

Galen took her hands, brought them to his lips and asked her to sit down. "Do you trust me, Lorelei?" he asked quietly.

She understood the silent message behind his words.

"You don't want me to go with you, right?"

"I want you to stay here where it's safer."

"After all I've done, you don't think I can take care of myself?"

He smiled ruefully. "I'm in awe of your capabilities. But this war is not yours to fight. I know you're thinking of Maurice but there's nothing you can do to help him other than let these professionals take over. Besides, as a guest in my home, he's my responsibility."

He paused. "You didn't answer my question."

She looked at his hands and feared for his safety. "I do trust you but I don't see what that has to do with this situation. I want to go with you."

"Lorelei, I can't deal with the added pressure of your being there, expecting our child and maybe getting hurt."

"What makes you think I'll be safe here?"

"I asked Dr. Scallan to stay with you. When he finished patching up Justin, he suggested he go for provisions in case you have to be here for a while. He promised to be back within the hour."

She looked out the door toward the group of men outside and pursed her lips. "I have a bad feeling about this, Kennedy. I promise, I wouldn't get in your way."

"Do you know how exasperating you can be sometimes?" he said.

"Do you see how you're shutting me out?" she countered.

He knew that if he didn't convince her, she'd find a way to follow them. He took a long breath and began again.

"Please, I'm asking you to stay here because I'd like to know that, somewhere along the line, you've developed some degree of faith in me."

Lorelei looked him in the eye. "I do have faith in you, Galen. I always did." She thought a moment longer, then sighed. "All right. I'll stay here. You can have your peace of mind, even if it means I'll be sick with worry. And don't think for a moment that waiting is easier, because it isn't. Waiting for someone you love can be torture—like dying slowly, one piece at a time, until you're but a shell of yourself."

She looked at him pleadingly. "Please, take care of yourself, and come back quickly."

Galen took her in his arms. "Always. I'll always come back to you."

Chapter Thirty-Two
∞

The ride to Wexford House in a police van seemed unbearably long. Tonight Galen did not feel like the wealthy owner of a prestigious brewing company nor the president of a leading relief organization. He felt dispossessed and damn near powerless. His money seemed useless in the face of fanatics who were ready to die for what they believed in.

Perhaps he had lived too comfortably, protected by his wealth, ignoring what was going on in his own backyard.

So tonight, he thought grimly as he gazed out the van's windows, he was just a man fighting for his family and his home, the one his forefathers had built stone by stone. That was all he really wanted, he realized, all he really needed — that and the love of the one person who had somehow brought meaning back into his life.

Eager as he was to safeguard his household, half of him was elsewhere, in a small cottage in the woods east of Wexford, embodied in a woman who had insinuated herself into his heart. He pictured her sitting by the fire and he could almost see the rise and fall of her breasts as she dozed.

He could smell her scent, the one that had kept him awake for nights on end. He could practically taste her delicious lips, feel her legs around his waist, so in tune he felt with her.

"We're just about there." Justin handed him a rifle and ammunition Simmons had brought.

"Aye." Galen sighed and put the ammo into his jacket pocket. His fingers encountered something metal and, puzzled, he pulled it out. Lorelei's Glock. "Christ! Justin, I forgot to leave her the goddamned gun."

Justin pursed his lips. "She'll be fine. Scallan's with her, and God blessed her with a mouth capable of annihilating anyone who crosses her."

"Aye, her words sometimes sting," Galen agreed, "but they can cleanse at the same time. That's how I finally began to heal after all these years of feeling guilty and half-dead inside." He held her gun and admired its sheen. "I should have left her the gun just the same. She said she had a bad feeling about staying behind."

"That's typical of a woman in love who wants to be beside her man in case she has to rescue him again." Justin chuckled and got out of the van. "Come on, let's get this over with. I'm itching to get my hands on the bastards."

They had agreed with Simmons to proceed silently through the gardens to the northeast side of Wexford House, where there was a secret entrance to the sub-basements—once dungeons, now wine cellars but still impenetrable without a key. If Galen knew Edward, that was where he would be hiding with the rest of the household.

As Galen and Justin crept behind the hedges to the east side, they spotted several unfamiliar armed men patrolling the grounds. Someone came outside and approached one of the men.

Justin pointed toward the two people talking and whispered, "Is that who I think it is?"

"Aye," Galen muttered grimly. "It's my darling wife." The woman who had pretended to leave had returned after all. How could he have not known? How could he have not realized what a sham her sudden reappearance had been? How could he have not read the anger still left in her?

Galen felt a moment of sadness that the girl she'd once been had become a devious, deceiving creature. Or had she always been one and he'd simply been too blind to see it? It didn't matter. He'd never be taken in by her again. Lorelei had removed both his blindfold and the chains that had bound him. For the first time in years he was free—free to live as he chose, free to give his heart to the woman he loved.

First, though, there was a small matter of reclaiming what was his family's and delivering justice to those who thought they could threaten his loved ones and get away with it.

"Are you okay?" Justin looked at him, worried.

Galen remained silent for a few moments. Then, his thoughts sharply focused and his voice dangerously soft, he said, "Give the battle cry. Our clansmen will know what to do. Show no mercy, brother. I know none is left in me."

As Galen began to move toward Brenna, Justin gave out the ancient Highlander battle cry. The intruders were taken by surprise as almost thirty McBain clansmen swiftly emerged from the woods, followed by Simmons' men.

Brenna ran inside to take cover. Galen followed her. Once in the hall, he tried to guess where she would hide. The house counted four parlors, eleven bedrooms upstairs and three downstairs, two kitchens, three studies, dining rooms and countless sitting rooms. Something told him, though, that she would be in his bedroom, so he quietly made his way there.

"You always did know me well, Galen. How very husbandly of you to come here first," Brenna greeted him, clad in fatigues and aiming a semiautomatic weapon at him.

"What did you hope to gain by this? Haven't I given you everything you ever wanted, even after you left me?"

She advanced toward him.

"What is it you want, Brenna?"

"Everything you own. With your empire we can get more and better weapons and help those who need it, something you've never had the courage to do. No, you always preferred to help a bunch of starving foreigners, didn't you? You're nothing but a coward, Galen Kennedy and a disgrace to the Irish!" She spat at him, then wiped her mouth with a sleeve of her jacket.

He didn't flinch. He had to maintain his self-control and get her weapon away from her. "They've poisoned your mind, Brenna, these people you've allied yourself with. You may be fighting for a principle but they're not. They want money and power and they're using you to get it."

Her gaze was distant, unaffected. "And you? You're just like every other wealthy bastard who's reneged on his blood to preserve his money."

"Me? Brenna, look at who you work for—look at Gallagher! I know he's the one pulling the strings. Look at how much money he has. Don't you see he's just using you do to his dirty work?"

She waved her gun in the air. "You don't understand the Irish!"

"No, you don't understand. After me, he'll ask you to kill again, because what you get for him will never be enough."

"I don't care about what he wants. It's what I want!"

Pointing at herself, she shifted slightly. "It's what I want, do you hear? And killing just you won't be nearly enough, you fool! Don't you know by now what it is I seek?"

"What?" He crossed his arms.

"I want revenge. Revenge for Bryan's life. An eye for an eye, as they say."

Which meant she might kill Justin first, Galen realized. A brother for a brother. Well, he'd die before he'd allow that to happen. "You'll have to kill me before you get to Justin, Brenna," he said. "And that would defeat your purpose if you want to take revenge on me for killing your brother by killing mine."

"But, darling, it's not Justin's death that will make you suffer the way I did." She approached him and smiled. "It's that Canadian whore's." She licked her upper lip. "I wonder how Robbie's doing with her at the cottage? Hmm, do you think he's screwed her yet?"

Galen was stunned. Shocked and afraid for Lorelei, he felt a wave of nausea mount from his stomach to his throat. Robert the parasite was a terrorist? And he knew Lorelei was at the cottage? He remembered how Lorelei had pleaded not to be left behind and he cursed himself for not listening to her.

Brenna was gloating at his shocked expression. Killing her would not be enough, he thought. With nerves of steel, he asked, "You sent Robbie after Lorelei?"

"Why not? A token of cousinly affection, shall we say? He is my cousin-in-law, after all."

"What in God's name has Lorelei ever done to you?"

"Not a thing, darling. She's just paying for your deeds."

He was not above begging, he thought. Nothing was worth more than Lorelei's life. "I want you to call Robbie right now and tell him not to touch her. I'll hand over whatever you wish."

"Foolish Galen. How, then, would I exact my revenge?"

She poked her gun into his ribs. "You'd do anything for that slut, wouldn't you?"

Galen took a single backward step.

At that precise moment Justin lunged through the communicating door to the dressing room behind Brenna and grabbed her around the neck. He lifted her chin sharply so that she was barely able to breathe.

"Drop your gun," he barked.

Unable to withstand the pressure around her neck, Brenna let go of her weapon.

Galen moved forward to grab it. "If Robbie so much as touches a hair on Lorelei's head, Brenna," he growled, "by God you'll wish Justin had shot you!"

Justin let out a whistle to alert their men that they had a captive. Several clansmen appeared in the doorway and took charge of Galen's wife.

Justin faced Galen with a thunderous expression. "I should have let you kill Robbie that night of the reception."

"Better late than never," Galen replied. "Let's go."

"So be it," Justin said, heading for the door on Galen's heels.

Chapter Thirty-Three

An hour passed and the doctor had not returned. Lorelei's instincts were on alert. She was God knows where in the middle of a forest. The cell phone Galen had taken from Peter and given to her to use was dead. And—*merde!*—Galen still had her Glock.

She could always make her way back to her car and drive into town, she supposed but what if Galen came back looking for her in the meantime? He'd be terrified to find her gone.

With nothing to do but wait, she decided to build a fire and lend the old cottage some warmth. Back home in Montreal, lighting a fire and watching its glow used to give her a sense of security. Tonight it only gave her a sense of longing, a desire that only one man could fulfill. Sitting on the sofa facing the hearth, she closed her eyes and pictured Galen's profile, his majestic body moving in the firelight, the hunger in his eyes. For a moment she thought she could actually touch him. Then, barely able to keep her eyes open, she felt herself drifting off to sleep.

In a dream she sensed that Galen was in danger. Someone—a woman?—was pointing a gun at him, threatening his life. She had to help him! She struggled to reach the woman—was it Galen's wife?—and disarm her, but she couldn't seem to move. Would she have to stand by helplessly and watch him die?

No...No!

She awoke with a start, her heart pounding and she heard the sound of leaves rustling. A glance at her watch told her another hour had passed since Galen left. The door opened but it wasn't Dr. Scallan. The man who came in was younger and looked vaguely familiar, in his thirties, with auburn hair and green eyes. He was wearing a black leather jacket and jeans and carrying two bags of groceries.

"Hi there, my name is Robert. I work with Dr. Scallan, and he asked me to come and stay with you since he was called to the hospital on an emergency. I hope you're hungry. He gave me a lot of food to bring you."

Lorelei pretended not to be alarmed at the presence of this strange man. After he put the bags down on the kitchen counter, he reached to shake her hand and she thought she glimpsed a holster under his partially unzipped jacket.

Despite a disturbing feeling in her gut, she tried to remain calm. After all, if he had wanted to kill her, he could have done so already.

"Would you like a sandwich?" he asked. "I've got—let me see—ham and a variety of other cold cuts. I suppose it's a humble meal for a renowned chef such as yourself but it's nourishment nonetheless."

"Thank you, I'll have some ham. But please let me prepare the sandwiches. I need something to do or I'll likely fall asleep." *I also need to get my hands on a knife*, she thought.

"Please, I insist. Scallan told me you needed to rest."

Not wanting to appear suspicious, she let him prepare her a sandwich while she sat down at the kitchen table. If necessary she could lift the end of the table and push it at him and then flee the cottage. "Who told you I was a chef?"

"You're a celebrity here in Wexford, or didn't you know? I also saw your picture in *People* magazine." He handed her the sandwich and started preparing one for himself.

She felt the need to keep him talking. "What exactly do you do for Dr. Scallan? Are you a medical technician?"

"No. I take care of his estates."

"Does he have many?" she asked, trying to sound interested.

"Enough," he answered noncommittally.

He was obviously lying. "Are they all in Wexford?"

"No, not all."

While his answer was again vague, his gaze had begun roaming over her in a way that gave Lorelei the shivers. She knew then that this man was not here simply to keep her company. He had come to kill her but there was something else he wanted first. Something she'd use to her advantage if need be.

She had to get out of there. Even getting lost in a dark forest would be safer than remaining in the cottage with him.

"Would you excuse me for a minute?" She got up and headed for the washroom, where she assumed there was a window she could climb through.

He dropped his sandwich and put a hand inside his jacket. "Where are you going?"

"To the washroom," she answered innocently.

"There's no running water," he pointed out.

"I know. I'm just going to get some toilet tissue to take outside with me. I'm afraid it can't wait." She couldn't believe her own cleverness. Once she was inside the bathroom, her shoulders sagged. The window was too narrow and too high for her to even attempt climbing out.

She took the roll of toilet paper with her and returned to the living room. "I'll only be a minute." Once outside she slowly walked toward a clump of trees and pretended to unzip her pants, aware that he was watching her from the doorway.

She bent down behind some undergrowth and stayed down until she saw him look away from her and turn to go back inside. She quickly crawled on her hands and knees to the next tree, then got up and ran blindly through the forest.

She must have been running for a few minutes when she bumped squarely into his chest. Her heart almost stopped.

He stuck a gun at the center of her neck and smiled.

"The first time I saw you, I told Galen I wanted to meet you." He put his left hand between her legs and squeezed.

Lorelei was so repulsed, she felt like throwing up.

"I've never fucked either a Canadian or a famous chef before. Do you think it'd be worth my while, or should I just kill you instead?"

Lorelei didn't even blink. She remained silent.

"Well, answer me!"

She continued staring at him defiantly.

With his free hand he slapped her so hard, she nearly fell to the ground.

"So you like it the hard way? I can deal with that. Walk!"

He pushed her and pointed the gun in the direction of the cottage. "When I'm finished with you, Kennedy won't even want to look at you."

Once in the large rustic living room, she turned around to face him, livid. She would let none of her fear surface in front of this opponent. She would transform her fear into fury.

"Are you so small a man that you have to rape a woman to get at another man?" She shoved past him. "Are you so afraid of Galen Kennedy that you had to stalk that woman in a remote cottage in the dead of night when he was nowhere nearby? Do you feel like a hero now? Does threatening to rape a defenseless woman make you hard?" Her face was but inches from his. "Is that what it takes to make you come, boy? You use a gun to hide behind so no one realizes you haven't got any balls?"

He grabbed her by the hair. "You don't understand, bitch. Galen Kennedy killed my best friend, he did. He killed our leader and with him all we had worked to achieve."

She winced with pain as he yanked her hair but she remained still.

He slowly released her, sat down on the sofa and crossed his legs, continuing to point the gun at her. "He thinks he's got it all. He's nothing but a fool. Brenna will see to it that that he loses everything."

"Brenna?"

"Yes, dear Cousin Brenna. She almost lost it when the bastard killed Bryan."

Keeping up a conversation with him would buy her time, Lorelei realized, maybe even enough for someone to come to her rescue. "Surely Galen didn't kill an innocent man."

Robert rested the gun in his lap and retrieved a cigarette from his jacket pocket. He lit it and took a long puff, watching the smoke rise as if he hadn't a care in the world.

"Besides, Galen is family. You have to stop fighting your own family," she pleaded.

"That bastard stopped being family when he killed Brenna's husband."

Lorelei's mouth fell open. "You mean Brenna's brother...don't you?"

Robert smiled and smugly took another puff. "Bryan Gallagher was her husband, not her brother." He tipped the ashes on the floor. "Only Galen never knew it."

Lorelei was too shocked to speak.

Robert laughed, getting up from the sofa. Slowly he stomped on the cigarette butt, then advanced toward her.

"Thomas Gallagher's son," she whispered, all the pieces of the puzzle finally fitting together.

"That's right. Galen's 'marriage' to Brenna was nothing but a sham, a means to Bryan's ends—to give him a foot in the door...or, I should say, a foot aboard Wexford's ships."

"Bryan's father was actually the one pulling the strings but Bryan and Brenna were only too happy to go along—all in the name of the cause, you understand. Galen, trusting fool that he is, fell for the ruse." He stood in front of her and pinched her cheek. "Now we have no choice but to eliminate you and the Kennedy brothers."

"Why?"

"Well, mostly to control the Kennedy fortune and get unimpeded access to the shipping lines. But also to give Brenna her revenge."

She looked at him quizzically. "I don't understand."

"You're not very smart, are you? If Galen divorced Brenna, we'd lose the ships, the trucking routes and the money completely. If only Galen died, his brother would inherit his share and, if you happened to be pregnant, the brat would inherit too. If, on the other hand, all of you die, Brenna will be the sole heir, since she, her father-in-law and I will be the only people — or, I should say, the only living people — who know she was never legally wed to Galen in the first place."

He lowered the gun and put his hands around her neck, propelling her backward until her back hit the wall. The fingers squeezing her neck felt like a vise she couldn't pry open. She tried to kick him but missed. She was beginning to pass out.

"The more you fight me, bitch, the harder I'll squeeze."

When she stopped struggling, he removed one of his hands from her throat and shoved it under her blouse to grab one of her breasts, pinching the nipple until she thought he had ripped it off. She attempted to knee him in the groin with all the strength she could muster but that only aggravated him more. He put both hands around her neck and resumed strangling her. In the last instant before darkness overcame her, she heard someone bellowing her name.

A gentle, pine-scented breeze caressed her face. She heard a sound like that of ocean waves — or was it rustling leaves? The sun god she had first seen on a midsummer night in a pool of light had returned, with hair spun of gold and eyes of black velvet. Not sure if she was still living, she knew she wanted to touch him.

He looked at her lovingly, his eyes misty and his hand trembling against her cheek. "After what he's done to you," he whispered, "killing him won't be nearly enough."

"Please don't." Her voice was so raspy, it was barely intelligible.

"Don't what, love?"

"I know...what you want to do. Don't. He's not worth it."

He gave her a small, crooked smile. "Don't do this, don't do that. Why do I suspect I'm in for a lifetime of capitulating to your decisions?"

"Only when you're not being sensible. I'd expect the same from you."

As they watched one of Simmons' men take Robert from the cottage in handcuffs, Lorelei noticed the lethal glare Galen gave the man who had almost killed her.

She tried getting up, dreading his answer to her next question. "How is everyone?"

Galen replied as he helped her to her feet. "Everyone is fine. Maurice and Edward are actually better than fine. They're sotted."

"They're what?"

"My brother means they're roaring drunk," Justin explained from the cottage doorway.

"Here, drink this. It will help clear your voice." Galen held a glass of water to her lips.

She swallowed a tiny amount to soothe her throat.

"Drunk? Maurice and Edward?"

Galen smiled. "That's right, love. During the siege they hid in the wine cellar and they decided to toast the occasion with my St. Émilion Grand Cru," he added dryly.

"Until they recover and that might take quite a while, that leaves only you to cook for us," Justin announced pitiably.

"Not that we mind, of course."

"But we do mind," Galen answered, "for Miss Duplessis and I have a lot to discuss during the next few days and I'm afraid she won't be available to do any cooking."

Lorelei merely looked at Galen and smiled, for once agreeing with him entirely.

Amid her protests regarding the retrieval of her car, which was going to be Colin's responsibility, Lorelei was commanded to return to Wexford House with Conrad in the Land Rover.

Galen and Justin made a stop at the hospital to see Dr. Scallan, whom Robert had beaten, fortunately not fatally, then went to police headquarters to answer questions.

When Conrad saw the bruise on Lorelei's face, he began cursing everyone and everything under the sun. He disowned the Irish for being brutal, the Scottish blood in Robert and the British of course, on whom he blamed the whole war in Northern Ireland. His vocabulary was so colorful that Lorelei laughed until tears were streaming down her face. In the end, he was laughing too.

When one of the constables dropped Galen off at home, he was praying Lorelei would be in bed, their bed, resting quietly. Otherwise there would be hell to pay. Those had been his exact words to her before they'd left the cottage, but his threat did not appear to have intimidated her in the least. As a matter of fact, she had smiled and told him almost flippantly that he would not be able to complain when he returned home.

He was also thinking about what he'd learned at the police precinct. He had never been married to Brenna Coyle after all. Brenna Gallagher, actually, once she'd married Bryan Gallagher, who had used her maiden name to complete their elaborate ruse. No wonder he and Justin had been able to learn so little about the senator's past—the bastard had gone to great lengths to conceal it. Galen shook his head in wonderment.

He was about to mount the stairs when he heard two men arguing rather loudly in his study. He recognized Maurice's and Edward's voices.

"I am like her father. I will pay for the wedding that will take place after that Scotsman, or whatever he is, gets his divorce. In the meantime she will be staying with Annabelle and me. I will not let that brute seduce *ma petite!*"

"It's a little too late for that, my good man," Galen interjected. "Not only have I already 'seduced' your 'little one', but you're both going to become 'grandfathers' in eight months or so. You can forget the divorce—it turns out I was never legally married. And if I was you, I'd start planning a christening, as well."

Edward beamed at him jubilantly. "You're free to marry Miss Lorelei? And she is with child again? Why, that's wonderful news, sir. I knew you could do it. And this time we'll take much better care of her so she won't have a chance to miscarry again." Edward shook Galen's hand and patted him on the back.

Maurice, however, was outraged. "*Ma petite is enceinte*? You have made her pregnant—twice?" He advanced toward Galen with a menacing stride but stumbled on Edward's foot, which was strategically placed in his path. The butler caught Maurice before he could fall—or strangle Galen.

"Sir, why don't you go find Miss Lorelei? I'll deal with Maurice here. After all, we'll be family soon."

"Thank you, Edward," Galen said while Maurice continued cursing him in very colorful French.

Galen went upstairs and softly opened the door to his bedroom, on the off chance that Lorelei really was resting peacefully as he had instructed her to do. He was not surprised in the least to find the bed empty. The little witch would probably go on provoking him until he had a heart attack. Doubtless, his pregnant, exhausted, beaten-up gourmet chef was, at that very moment, in a cold, damp, greasy garage, examining her beloved Porsche. She was probably convincing poor Conrad to build her a special jack that would lift the car high enough for her to slip under when she was in an advanced state of pregnancy.

Galen fairly stomped down the stairs. No wonder even her uncle had dubbed the car his Nemesis. Well, he would sequester her keys for the duration of her pregnancy, he decided. He'd change the damned ignition if he had to. No more driving a race car until she delivered his baby. And even then, he thought, the risk of losing her would be too much for him to bear. He would never allow her to drive the car alone again, that's all.

Galen shook his head at how ridiculously protective he had become.

Still, when he opened the garage door, he was good and ready to unleash a tirade. But his mouth fell open in shock.

Lorelei's unmistakable scent filled the normally dingy area. Lit candles surrounded the Porsche. And Lorelei herself was lying on the hood of the car, wearing the leather outfit she'd worn for the photo shoot in Hyannis Port and in the exact same pose.

His loins were instantly aching. But he shook his head, took a step forward and crossed his arms, hoping she would think he was extremely displeased.

"It took you long enough to get here, Kennedy."

The use of his last name no longer angered him because he had lately discovered it was just her way of hiding her insecurity. "I am quite disappointed by your continuing rebelliousness, Duplessis. And if you think that by doing this you will avoid—"

"Your lecture?" she finished pleasantly for him. So she considered their discussions lectures?

"Call it what you will."

"Actually, I had something else in mind," she replied in a sensual tone.

He decided it would be better to go on the offensive rather than admit defeat. "Sorry, love but I cannot make love with you here and risk exposing you for anyone to see."

"Well, that's precisely why I've forbidden everyone entrance to the garages until further notice under threat of being shot." She hesitated, then continued more tentatively.

"You once promised — or maybe you threatened — to make me some new memories with this car, so that every time I looked at it, I'd remember the sensation of cool metal under my bare back and the heat of your body on top of mine. I believe you said I'd be wearing this very outfit..." She paused and said softly, "I think we need those new memories now. *Je t'aime*, Galen."

Galen was completely undone. She loved him. Without reservation, without regret. He could see the depth of her love in her silver eyes and he knew what she was offering him — everything. And he would not wait a moment longer to make her completely his.

Epilogue

Thunder rumbled as the priest sprinkled holy water on the casket. Catherine Logan and her husband, Ian, stared grimly at their son's coffin as it was lowered into the centuries-old cemetery of St. Kevin's Church.

Into her ninth month of pregnancy, Lorelei touched her belly. Galen, now her husband, read her thoughts and understood the tears she was shedding for the twenty-three-year-old man whose murder she had witnessed in silence. He took her hand, squeezing it gently.

As friends and family of the deceased took turns dropping white roses onto the casket, bagpipes played an ode to the young Irishman who had given his life to help free Ireland from the war raging in its north.

At Galen's behest, Justin had flown to Hyannis Port to organize a search for the body of Michael Logan, who had been shot by Irish terrorists and thrown overboard from the *Irish Siren*. The body had finally washed up on the shores of Sandwich Beach.

"Mrs. Logan," Lorelei softly addressed the distraught mother after the service. "I'm Lorelei Duplessis. May I have a word with you and your husband?"

The husband looked at her warily, clearly uncomfortable about sharing his grief with a stranger.

Lorelei continued gently. "I was there when Michael was killed. I thought you would want to know he died quickly and surely painlessly." Lorelei touched Mrs. Logan's arm.

"He died honorably, defending something he believed in—peace. He made that clear even to those who killed him. I only wish there was something I could have done." Lorelei looked at Mr. Logan, whose face was streaked with tears. "I am so sorry for your loss. But you should be very proud of your son. He died, after all, for the sake of the country and the people you raised him to love."

The older woman collapsed into Lorelei's arms, sobbing. Both cried for several minutes.

Slowly disengaging herself from the grief-stricken mother, Lorelei brought Catherine Logan's hand to her belly as one of the twins began to kick. She shyly took Ian Logan's hand, as well, explaining to both of them that she was carrying twins and that one was a boy. "My husband and I would like to name the boy Michael Logan in memory of your son and we'd like you to be his godparents." Lorelei caught Justin's glance of approval. As promised he would name the girl and christen her.

Catherine Logan began crying again.

"His spirit lives on, Catherine," her husband said. "This child to be is a gift from God."

Catherine smiled tenderly as she felt one of the infants kick. "It's probably him, lass. Michael never stood still when I carried him."

And Lorelei felt unburdened for the first time in years. Despite enormous odds, life had ultimately prevailed.

*****

"Has Ian asked any more questions about the identity of the murderers?" Justin inquired, lowering his voice so as not to be heard.

Galen quickly cast a glance at the man who held his wife by the shoulders. "He didn't, but he will soon, knowing him."

"What will we say?"

"What we've been saying all along, that they're all dead."

"What about Gallagher?" Justin asked. "Ian's not stupid. He's seen enough of this war and this violence to know someone else was pulling the strings."

"*Aye* he will ask. Let's just hope by the time he does, the bastard will have died once and for all."

"*Aye*, let's hope that what went around, will finally come around."

About the Author

A French Canadian law graduate at the age of 23, Isabella Montwright, after practicing law for 11 years, became head of the legal department of an established alcohol firm and wine bottler. Her secret passion for writing evolved, and thus in 1996 Isabella wrote her first manuscript depicting the enigmatic Lorelei Duplessis, renowned chef and sommelier. Shortly after writing this story, Isabella Montwright, like the character she created, met the man of her life in Italy. Together they created the company which houses an important Italian wine collection named after the fictitious, Lorelei Duplessis.

Isabella's writing and culinary careers continue to evolve in tandem. She was asked to join the brotherhood of "La Chaine Des Rotisseurs" a French culinary association which dates back in 1248, when the king of France first gives recognition to the chefs of the royal household. Her enthronization took place in the picturesque castle of Merano, in Northern Italy where reality meets with dreams.

Today, Isabella writes in her free time and is chef in a wine and food tasting bar she operates in Southern Italy with three friends, built on the ruins of the palace of the Emperor Frederick II, (whom some say is often seen roaming the gardens on which it was built).

Isabella welcomes comments from readers. You can find her website and email address on her author bio page at www.cerridwenpress.com.

Tell Us What You Think

We appreciate hearing reader opinions about our books. You can email us at Comments@EllorasCave.com.

Why an electronic book?

We live in the Information Age—an exciting time in the history of human civilization, in which technology rules supreme and continues to progress in leaps and bounds every minute of every day. For a multitude of reasons, more and more avid literary fans are opting to purchase e-books instead of paper books. The question from those not yet initiated into the world of electronic reading is simply: *Why?*

1. ***Price.*** An electronic title at Ellora's Cave Publishing and Cerridwen Press runs anywhere from 40% to 75% less than the cover price of the exact same title in paperback format. Why? Basic mathematics and cost. It is less expensive to publish an e-book (no paper and printing, no warehousing and shipping) than it is to publish a paperback, so the savings are passed along to the consumer.
2. ***Space.*** Running out of room in your house for your books? That is one worry you will never have with electronic books. For a low one-time cost, you can purchase a handheld device specifically designed for e-reading. Many e-readers have large, convenient screens for viewing. Better yet, hundreds of titles can be stored within your new library—on a single microchip. There are a variety of e-readers from different manufacturers. You can also read e-books on your PC or laptop computer. (Please note that

Ellora's Cave does not endorse any specific brands. You can check our websites at www.ellorascave.com or www.cerridwenpress.com for information we make available to new consumers.)

3. *Mobility.* Because your new e-library consists of only a microchip within a small, easily transportable e-reader, your entire cache of books can be taken with you wherever you go.

4. *Personal Viewing Preferences.* Are the words you are currently reading too small? Too **large**? Too… ANNOYING? Paperback books cannot be modified according to personal preferences, but e-books can.

5. *Instant Gratification.* Is it the middle of the night and all the bookstores near you are closed? Are you tired of waiting days, sometimes weeks, for bookstores to ship the novels you bought? Ellora's Cave Publishing sells instantaneous downloads twenty-four hours a day, seven days a week, every day of the year. Our webstore is never closed. Our e-book delivery system is 100% automated, meaning your order is filled as soon as you pay for it.

Those are a few of the top reasons why electronic books are replacing paperbacks for many avid readers.

As always, Ellora's Cave and Cerridwen Press welcome your questions and comments. We invite you to email us at Comments@ellorascave.com or write to us directly at Ellora's Cave Publishing Inc., 1056 Home Avenue, Akron, OH 44310-3502.

Cerridwen, the Celtic Goddess of wisdom, was the muse who brought inspiration to storytellers and those in the creative arts. Cerridwen Press encompasses the best and most innovative stories in all genres of today's fiction. Visit our site and discover the newest titles by talented authors who still get inspired - much like the ancient storytellers did, once upon a time.

Cerridwen Press
www.cerridwenpress.com

Cerridwen Press

Cerridwen, the Celtic goddess of wisdom, was the muse who brought inspiration to storytellers and those in the creative arts.

Cerridwen Press encompasses the best and most innovative stories in all genres of today's fiction.

Visit our website and discover the newest titles by talented authors who still get inspired—much like the ancient storytellers did...

once upon a time.

www.cerridwenpress.com

Printed in Great Britain by
Amazon.co.uk, Ltd.,
Marston Gate.